EQUALIZER
REQUIEM

EQUALIZER REQUIEM

by MICHAEL SLOAN

BearManor Media

2020

Equalizer: Requiem

© 2020 by Michael Sloan

Published in the United States of America by:

BearManor Media

4700 Millenia Blvd.

Suite 175 PMB 90497

Orlando, FL 32839

bearmanormedia.com

Printed in the United States.

Typesetting and layout by John Teehan

ISBN—978-1-62933-645-9

▶ 1 ◀

ROBERT MCCALL KNEW they were coming for him.

He had just driven through Middleburg, Virginia, a quaint New England town where the country road meandered down to the G.W. Parkway through heavily wooded areas. The trees were like glowing sentinels in the moonlight. A rainstorm lashed the forest and the ribbon of road made it treacherous. McCall had taken a short cut through the trees and to his right was a steep ravine that fell right down to a serene lake. He had just turned a corner on the country road, watching his speed in the driving downpour, keeping it down to forty-five miles an hour.

It had been the flare of a match.

It had caught his attention for just a moment, which meant that the assailants were sitting right at the edge of the woods. They had been no more than eight to ten feet back in the shelter of the oaks. So they had been tracking him on their GPS screen for some time. Certainly through Middleburg and then onto this side road which would eventually lead back onto the main thoroughfare.

They had been waiting for him to make this detour.

McCall had already made the turn in the road, which left him with two choices. He could slam on the brakes which might be even more hazardous in the driving rainstorm. Or he could accelerate to a spot in the woods where the assailants were waiting for him. That would be the best option, but he only had a second to make the decision and he would still be in danger of sliding across the road to the edge of the precipice. Clearly, the intention was to ram his Jaguar head on. There would be no start up time because the other car was already gunning forward. It would clear the densely packed trees in three seconds, allowing for its own acceleration. It would have come out of the forest like a bat of hell, slamming right into the Jaguar, sending McCall careening across the rain-slicked road. He could not tell for sure what kind of vehicle the assailants were driving, but the shape looked to be a Mercedes.

McCall accelerated past the woods where the Mercedes rocketed out to ram him. The occupants in the vehicle had not been anticipating that the Jaguar would *suddenly stop* in the driving rainstorm that was lacerating the woods. Two seconds to get ahead of them. Another second to execute a tight one-hundred-and-thirty degree turn so that the Jaguar was facing back down the country road with the steep incline now on McCall's left.

The Mercedes flashed past where the Jaguar had been a second before, expecting to ram it. The car swerved with its added momentum, finding traction on the road, turning back to find McCall's Jaguar now *facing them*. McCall had already slammed on his brakes. At the same time, he reached into the glove compartment for his Glock 19 pistol and then jumped out, using the door for cover.

Time eclipsed down for him as it always did at moments like this. The slow-motion effect was subliminal. It gave McCall the time to aim and fire the Glock before the Mercedes had even straightened out. He noted the Mercedes was a C280, probably a 1995 model, which meant that the windshield had OEE glass, which was thinner than the new models. McCall put six bullets into the windshield of the car. The assailants swerved violently. He had not been able to see anyone in the back seats, but this felt like an assassination attempt and it would have made more sense for the assailants not to have brought along any witnesses.

At least four of the rounds had hit their targets. The Mercedes careered across the country road, bounced up the curb and then slid down the steep ravine through the trees. McCall slammed the door of the Jaguar and sprinted across to the ditch on the other side. There was still no traffic on the country road. McCall stared down in the deluge and saw where the Mercedes had plunged through some trees and had come to a halt just before the shimmering lake. He slid down the steep slope, finding his way through the copse of trees until he was at the lakeshore. The Mercedes had crashed, the fender crumpled, glass shattered through it.

McCall slowly approached the wrecked car, still holding onto the Glock 19. There was no movement from within the Mercedes. He opened the driver's side door. One of the assassins lay impaled by the steering wheel where it had smashed into his chest. His companion had taken two bullets to the head. Both would-be assassins were dead. Hampered by the torrent of driving rain, McCall climbed into the wrecked Mercedes and searched the assailants. They carried nothing with them. No folding money, no change, no wallets, no passports.

But both of them were wearing *silver rings* on their right hands. One was a *demon-claws silver skull.* Beside it was a slim silver ring. McCall knew what was engraved onto them: *Remember that you must die.*

Memento Mori.

He knew he had not seen the last of the *Memento Mori* mercenaries when he had killed Matthew Goddard in his

4 | Equalizer: Requiem

suite at the Liberty Belle Hotel in New York City. Goddard had said: "There are a hundred of us." McCall had thought after what had happened in San Antonio and at the United Nations building he had not thought they would have regrouped this quickly. Who was organizing them now that Matthew Goddard was out of the picture? Mercenaries like these did not fight for ideologies. They fought for money. So why come back to try to kill McCall now? What was their new purpose?

He was certain that someone else was pulling the strings.

McCall noted that the Mercedes had finished up at a steep angle to the lake, caught between some shrubbery. He leaned forward, put the car into neutral, crawled back out and slammed the car door. He ran around the car and started to push the vehicle forward. It did not take much coaxing. The Mercedes rolled down the gradient, gathering speed. Then McCall stepped away. The car rolled off the bank into the lake. It took a few seconds for the car to sink. Then moonlight covered its surface like a gleaming shroud, lacerated by the unrelenting power of the storm.

McCall climbed through the deluge back up to the road. No cars or trucks were coming in either direction. It was a lonely spot, he thought, far from the nearest houses with the penetrable forest hiding its secrets. He ran back to his Jaguar. He dropped the *Memento Mori* silver rings into the pocket of his leather jacket. Then he turned around and headed back toward Maryland.

McCall felt like the specter of Matthew Goddard was breathing down the back of his neck.

He found Control in Easton, Maryland in an old-world tavern called *Bannings*. The place was packed with a raucous, lunchtime crowd. McCall's boss at The *Compa-*

ny was already seated at a table overlooking the historic main street of the quaint Colonial town. His full name was James Thurgood Cameron. He looked in good condition after being incarcerated in a house deep in the Virginia woods. McCall had rescued him from the two-story, cedar-sided log cabin surrounded by maple trees. Three of the *Memento Mori* mercenaries had been guarding him. McCall had found Control by accessing an old abandoned fairground. He had come across some white marble stairs that were just sitting there in the middle of the forest. That had led him to the cabin. McCall had carried the barely conscious Control through the woods and drove him back to New York City. That had been a month ago. Control was back in his element now, living in a Colonial town near Washington D.C., back at The *Company* on his own terms.

Matthew Goddard had been responsible for kidnapping Control. But he had done more than that. He had *erased* Control's entire identity. Which McCall had thought had been a pretty neat conjuring trick. Once Control had been terminated, there would have been no evidence that he had *ever existed.*

But that was in the past now.

McCall glanced up, perhaps unconsciously, at a stained-glass mural of *Blind Justice* in the décor of the restaurant with the scales holding a sword in her hand. That seemed fitting to McCall. Control had always strived to find justice in the shadowy netherworld that he operated in. A world that McCall knew all too well and which he avoided now at all costs.

Yet he had the feeling that he was about to plunge back *into* that world again.

Control was wearing a Saville Row suit, a pink striped shirt, a red tie with small, chess pieces on it and gold cufflinks with the initials JTC. The cologne he wore was pungent. McCall knew he purchased it from a small shop in Mayfair in London. He held out his hand when McCall joined him at the table.

"Good to see you again, Robert."

McCall shook hands. "You didn't move far from your old place in Virginia."

"I guess I didn't. Easton is a quiet, rustic place far away from Washington D.C. for Jenny to have some peace of mind. We found a house right on the Chesapeake Bay."

He picked up his iPhone 7 cellphone, tapped an icon and turned it around for McCall. It showed a picture of an historic four-bedroom house on half acre of grounds with wide porches at the front and the side where a fenced-in backyard and redwood deck could be seen. It looked lovely, but it was not a home McCall could live in. Too much space, too lonely, too isolated. Too many memories to come to terms with.

"How do your daughters like the new house?" he asked.

"Kerry and Megan are very happy there," Control said. "Good school, surrounded by woods, the Chesapeake Bay a stone's throw away. Jenny has gone back to Georgetown University and she is loving it there. We're settling in nicely."

"What has happened at the *Company*?"

Control put the iPhone 7 on the table. "Jason Mazur is my second-in-command now. My secretary Emma—who insists she be called that and not an *assistant*—says he still has a 'hard on' for you, but you are yesterday's news."

"Not anymore," McCall said.

Control looked at him. He knew that McCall had met him for lunch for a reason. A waiter came over to their table. Control ordered oysters dredged in seasoned flour, dripped in light butter, then fried. He followed it with a stuffed half-chicken with Risotto. McCall ordered fried Chesapeake Bay oysters and the beef and Guinness stew flavored with stout.

While they waited for the oysters, McCall said: "There was talk of a mission in North Korea."

"It wasn't sanctioned by the *Company*," Control said. "A black Ops operation organized by Granny and Mickey Kostmayer, supported by a handful of handpicked mercenaries. They destroyed a North Korean prison camp and liberated over one hundred prisoners. They were flown in four AVIC AC 392 helicopters over the Chinese border. The North Korean troops moved their location and captives to an older prison camp. That was when Kostmayer escaped. He was close to the Yalu River at the Sino-Korean Friendship Bridge and managed to get into Dandong. Kostmayer briefed me back at the *Company* after I had returned there. Granny was killed in the initial prisoner breakout. All the other mercenaries he and Kostmayer had enlisted to their cause were all killed in the ensuring firefight. But you already know this from Mickey."

"I wanted to hear it from you."

Their oysters arrived. Control ate a couple of them before he said: "Why don't you tell me why you want to go to North Korea?"

"Who says I am thinking of doing that?"

"Call it instinct. A gut feeling. Am I wrong?"

"You never are far from the truth," McCall said..

He took his cell phone out of his jacket pocket and turned it around for Control to see the text he had received from Granny.

Odds against me. Still a prisoner in N.K. Come and get me and others. Granny.

McCall tapped an app to return the text back into memory and returned the cell phone to his jacket pocket. He ate his oysters. Control merely nodded. The ambience in the tavern was noisy and raucous, but it did not reach their quiet oasis.

"This communication doesn't mean that Granny is still alive," Control said. "The text could be spurious. Could have been written by one of the North Korean guards."

"Who communicated in English?"

"Unlikely, but not impossible."

"Read it again." McCall handed his one-time boss the cell phone. "It's phrased like Granny. If it *had* been written by the Commandant of the North Korean prison camp, I need to go there myself and find out the truth."

"This mission will not be sanctioned by the *Company*," Control objected.

"It doesn't have to be. I am not asking for permission. I do not work for the *Company* any longer. But I can't do this without your intel."

Control's half-chicken with Risotto and McCall's beef and Guinness stew were served. While they ate, McCall surveyed the boisterous tavern. Unconsciously he was looking for men who might be wearing *silver demon-claws skulls* on their right hands with a slim plain silver band beside them. He did not see any.

Across from him, Control said: "You know Mickey Kostmayer will want to accompany you on this mission."

"He barely made it out of that North Korean prison camp alive," McCall said. "He's been running on adrenalin and nervous energy ever since he got back to New York. Sitting down in that underground parking facility beneath the United Nations building with a homemade bomb of C4 explosives in his hands while the bomb squad was on their way would have taken a toll on anybody. Even Mickey Kostmayer, whose nerves are wound tight at the best of times. He was lucky that Colonel Michael Ralston—*Gunner*—disabled the bomb. Kostmayer sat with it on his lap until the bomb squad made sure there was not a second detonator rigged up to explode. Which there certainly could have been. The wiring on the device was faulty and it did not function. I won't allow Kostmayer to go back into a life-and-death situation."

"Shouldn't you let Kostmayer decide that for himself?" Control said. mildly.

"Not this time," McCall said. "I know Mickey. Too much trauma will put his psyche into overload. I told you on the phone. This is a solo mission. There is one person I can reach out to, but it's a long shot and his help may not be viable."

"Who is this person?

"No one you know."

"But he could get you into North Korea?" Control asked.

"Maybe."

"You'll need help once you get there."

"That's why you're going to give me the intel I need," McCall said. "Unless you're not."

"In which case you'll just go to N.K. anyway."

McCall sat back and smiled. "That's the general idea."

Control shook his head. "I don't like it."

"You don't have to like it," McCall said, evenly. "Just make the arrangements."

Control finished his meal and said: "What aren't you telling me?"

McCall paused for a moment, then reached into his jacket pocket, brought out the *demon-claws silver skull* and the silver band and placed them both on the table.

Control picked up the *demon-claws skull* and turned it over in the light streaming through the picture window from the street.

"This was what you lifted from Matthew Goddard's hand when he tried to kill you at the Liberty Belle Hotel," he said. "The mercenaries at the Valencia Hotel in San Antonio were wearing these same silver demon-claws skulls."

"So was the assassin I took out at the West Texas Reginal Water Plant in Boerne, Texas," McCall said. "Matthew Goddard told me there were a *hundred* mercenaries working for him."

Control looked at his one-time agent in alarm. "But Matthew Goddard is dead. These mercenaries would have disbanded."

"Two men tried to run me off a country road outside D.C last night," McCall said. "It was only a fluke that I saw them coming out of the trees. I put six bullets into their windshield which them sent them down into a ravine."

"What did you do with their bodies?"

"I pushed their Mercedes into one of the lakes. It sank without a trace. There was no one on the road in that monsoon we had last night."

"You left no trace of them?" Control asked.

McCall looked at him. Control nodded and handed the silver rings back to McCall who put them into his jacket pocket. He glanced around to make sure they had not been overhead, but no one in the boisterous room was paying any attention to their quiet oasis.

"So, these mercenaries are regrouping," Control said. "But to what purpose?"

"I don't know," McCall said. "But they're reporting to someone."

"Who?"

McCall shrugged. "That is a very good question."

Control waved off the waitress who wanted to serve them dessert and coffee, paid the bill and stood. "Take a walk with me."

McCall get to his feet and followed Control out of the restaurant.

The elegant Spymaster stopped at McCall's black jaguar that was parked outside the Banning Tavern. "I see you've got your Jaguar back."

"I didn't really need it living in New York City, but it was time to get it back on the road."

Control turned to look at his old friend. "You remember when we walked through the Old Church at Sleepy Hollow to look at Elena Petrov's grave and I asked you to make sure the odds you weren't equalizing weren't too high?"

"I remember."

"Is there anything I can say to talk you out of this mission to North Korea?"

McCall shook his head. "Not a thing."

Control nodded. "I didn't think so. Meet me at the *Company* in the boardroom at 09:00 A.M. tomorrow. I will get you that intel on North Korea. I promised Kerry and Megan I would buy them something here in Banning at the Pottery Barn in Easton Square Place."

"You're a good Dad."

"I try my best. Do you still stop in the churchyard at Sleepy Hollow and put yellow sunflowers on Elena's grave?"

"Not as often as I should," McCall admitted.

Control nodded, as if he understood. "Time goes by."

"Not for me," McCall said, quietly

"See you tomorrow, Robert."

Control strode off down the street. He was clearly unnerved by what McCall had told him and McCall understood why.

This was a suicide mission he was going on in North Korea.

Across from them in a little park, the young woman set down her Nikon Monarch 3 10X43 binoculars on the table and picked up her iced tea. She knew when her two mercenaries had not reported in from Washington D.C. that they had been killed. She did not care how it had happened. She figured that Robert McCall had spotted them and killed them. He would have disposed of their bodies in the woods outside Middleburg, Virginia, somewhere on the road to Washington D.C. The mercenaries were expendable. But she would not tolerate any more failures. She wanted revenge for her lover Matthew Goddard, but she would wait until the right moment to exact it.

McCall pulled his Jaguar away from the Banning Tavern.

Ironically, the young woman toasted him.

▶ 2 ◀

GRANNY KNEW THEY would be coming back for him.

It was pitch black in the corrugated hut where he was incarcerated, which measured eight feet by ten feet. It was stifling hot in the metal coffin. Luckily, the hut was not air-tight and cold air escaped from the edges of the rusting latches. Granny had slowed his breathing down in anticipation of what was coming. His eyes were closed, almost in meditation.

Granny was in the middle of taking apart a motorcycle… *in his mind.*

It was a 150cc Viper Dirt Bike with front and rear hydraulic discs with manual transmission capable of doing 55 MPH. It had a Twin Space Heavy Duty Steel frame. The clutch was a manual with four gears with a Stroke Single Cylinder with a fuel capacity of 1.3 gallons. The lightweight frame measured 65" by 32.2" by 43" with a kick start. It was a shiny green color. Granny had stripped down the dirt bike to the nuts and bolts and was in the process of putting it back together again, piece by piece. It would take him time, but he had a lot of that.

Granny had a photographic memory which he had since the age of six. He could remember putting together a LEGO Star Wars Ultimate Millennium Falcon building kit with 7541 pieces. It had taken him a week and it had been his most precious possession at the time. He could select and choose from memories he had not thought about for a long time. Events and times and places which he could picture with amazing clarity. People and faces he could remember at will, some of them good, some bad, but all of them pieces of a gigantic jigsaw puzzle, no different than the Star Wars Millennium Falcon kit he had put together when he was a boy. Some memories were more prominent than others.

Granny conjured up Mickey Kostmayer's face in his mind. He knew he had escaped from a work party who had been assigned to clear large rocks and massive tree limbs from a forest road near the prison. Granny had heard a couple of the North Korean guards talking about the prisoners' rebellion. They did not know that Granny had overheard them, because no one in the prison camp knew Granny spoke Korean. In fact, he spoke eight languages fluently. Kostmayer had escaped into the woods right on the edge of the Yalu River. One of the Korean guards talked about a man they had lost in those woods when they were chasing the prisoner. Granny nodded and smiled.

Kostmayer.

He must have made it into Dandong in China, just over the Sino-Korean Friendship Bridge. Or maybe he had swum to one of the little islands in the Yalu River and made his way from there to the harbor. Kostmayer would have found a way to get back to the United States. But all this was speculation on Granny's part. For all he knew, Kostmayer was lying dead in those woods or in one of the streams that bordered the work area. But the North Korean guards had not reported him missing. They had returned to the prison camp fearing for their lives. Failure was not an option for them. They had lost a prisoner and

Granny believed that they had been severely beaten. He had been surprised they had not been beheaded.

Granny replaced Kostmayer's face with the face of Robert McCall. He had nurtured a fleeting hope that *The Equalizer*—Granny thought the name suited Mc-Call well—might find a way to rescue him. There were other foreign prisoners in the North Korean prison camp as well. Granny had acquired a cell phone from the Commandant of the prison and had sent a terse text message to McCall. But then the phone had been seized and Granny had been thrown into isolation in this sweltering metal coffin to rot. So, he did not know if his text had ever arrived. Certainly, he had never got a response from McCall's cell phone. It had been worth a shot, but Granny held no real hope that the message had been received.

He heard the hinges squeaking on the corrugated door of the low hut.

Pale sunshine filtered in, replacing the blackness.

Four North Korean guards grabbed Granny from the low wooden stool where he had been sitting, his head almost scraping the top of the corrugated roof. They held him in a vice-like grip. Granny could see the lean, tall Commandant of the prison camp in the doorway. His name was Myang-Sook-Jang. He carried a swagger stick which Granny wanted to tell him had not been used since *Bridge Over the River Kwai*. The Commandant was dressed in a Koran uniform with shiny black boots. His eyes were obsidian, black orbs that were sunk deep in a pockmarked face. When he spoke it was in a toneless, hoarse whisper.

"Who did you send your text message to?"

Granny was being held rigid by the four guards, but he shook his head as best as he could. "*What* text?

You guys took my cell phone away when I first got here, Max."

"Tell me your name," Myang-Sook-Jang said.

"It's Granny."

"Your *real* name."

"Tough to pronounce. Granny suits me well. Even my mother calls me that. Kind of a nickname."

"Who did you send the coordinates of the camp to?" Jang asked him.

"No one. I don't know where we are."

"Who at the CIA do you work for?"

"The CIA wouldn't know me if they fell over me."

"You deny you were sent to North Korea as part of a covert mission of aggression?"

"I am an independent contractor working for South Korea," Granny said. "The plane I was in got shot down. North Korean troops picked me up. Don't know what else to tell you, Max."

Myang-Sook-Jang made a gesture, like he was dismissing Granny. Three of the guards held Granny on the stool. The fourth picked up a canteen cup from a pail of water in a corner and a cloth. He returned and held the cloth tight across Granny's face, covering his mouth and breathing passages. Then he poured the water from the canteen cup over the wet cloth from a height of twelve to twenty-four inches. Granny choked on the water being poured down his throat. The procedure had been performed on him twice in the time since he had been captured and brought to this older prison camp. The military called it waterboarding. Granny had researched it for a mission he had undertaken for the *Company*. It had been developed by the Spaniards called *Tortura del agra*. The Dutch East Indian Company had used it when they had massacred

English prisoners on the Island of Amboyna in 1623. The Japanese military called it *Kempeitai*. The Gestapo used it during World War II. The French had used it in in the Algerian War from 1954 to 1962. Granny had once rescued a husband and wife from the Khmer Rouge at the Toi Sleng prison in Phnom Penh in Cambodia where they had been similarly tortured. The American military had used waterboarding aggressively during in the Vietnam War.

It made Granny feel like he was drowning. He writhed and gagged. The cloth was held about twenty to forty seconds, then removed. Granny gasped for breath. He was unimpeded to allow him to take four full breaths. Then the wet cloth was affixed to his mouth and breathing passages and the procedure was repeated. It caused near asphyxiation. Granny coughed and nearly passed out. Then he was brought back to consciousness and the wet cloth removed from his mouth and nose. He was allowed to breathe for another full breath, then the torture was repeated.

And repeated.

Finally, Myang-Sook-Jang must have been made another impatient gesture because the wet cloth was removed from Granny's mouth and nose. The guard dropped the pail and the canteen cup into the filthy corner where it had been placed before. The three guards let go of Granny, then one of them hit him in the stomach to make him throw up the water he had swallowed. Granny doubled over, spitting out more water, sputtering and gagging.

He looked over at Myang-Sook-Jang who stared at him in the gloom. Then the guards emerged from the corrugated hut and the gate was shut and locked.

Granny was left in utter blackness.

He was traumatized, shaking, forcing the sensation of nearly drowning to subside.

Then he went back to building the dirt bike racing motorcycle in his mind from the ground up.

McCall was not certain if the Asian grocer and his wife were still on the same corner in his old neighborhood. The old Asian woman was stacking Lotto tickets behind the counter of the convenience store. Her husband, maybe a little younger than her, but not by much, was restocking the shelves where the cookies, donuts and cupcakes were kept. A television was playing a soccer match with the sound turned off. The old Asian woman looked up when McCall entered the store and nodded, smiling, as if she had been expecting him any day. The old Asian man looked up from his shelves at the sound of the bell that opened the front door of the store. When he saw that whoever had entered was no threat, he went back to meticulously rearranging the packages of twinkies, donettes, dingdongs and fruit pies.

"We have missed you, Mr. McCall," the old Asian woman said. "Why you never come to see us anymore?"

"I moved out of the neighborhood," McCall said.

"It is our loss," the old Asian man said.

McCall moved over to where the old Asian man was on his hands and knees. He reached into a box of Hostess products, removing more packages of cinnamon rolls, Zingers and Mini Muffins.

"How long have you and your wife been living on this corner in Greenwich Village?"

"Fifty-eight years," the grocer owner said.

"Quite an achievement."

He looked up at McCall with irony and went back to stacking the shelves.

"Which province in North Korea are you from?"

That gave the old Asian a moment's pause. His wife stopped sorting out the Lotto tickets, picked up a Styrofoam Starbucks cup and brought it out to her husband. He did not bother to look up. His wife went back to the long counter and picked up more Mega Millions and Powerball tickets.

"I am from Vietnam," the old Asian man said.

"That's what you want the neighborhood to believe."

He shrugged. "Vietnamese, Korean, no one in this neighborhood would know the difference. I am an old Oriental man who keeps to himself and out of trouble."

"But it wasn't always that way," McCall guessed.

The old man shrugged again. He went back to carefully placing the Hostess products on the two bottom shelves. He said: "I am from the Kwanso Province in North Korea. I was born in the capital city of Kanggye."

"You know my name is Robert McCall. What is your name?"

"Kyung-Jae. But in your country, I am just 'Jerry.' My wife is He-Ran. You won't know what that means."

"'Grace and orchid,'" McCall said

The old Asian man just nodded and smiled.

"How long has it been since you were home?" McCall asked him.

"Fifty-eight years," he said, again with irony.

McCall knelt down beside him. "I need your help."

"I am an old man. You have your own life. What sort of help could I give you?"

"I want to go to North Korea."

"Dangerous place for westerners to travel to," Kyung-Jae said. "Better off you should go to Florida or Las Vegas."

"A friend of mine is being held prisoner in a prison camp on the border before the Yalu River below the Sino-Friendship Bridge. The prison camp was hit by western forces and many of the Korean prisoners were liberated. But the camp was moved to another prison camp not far from the original location. I need to find that second prison camp. Can you help me?"

It was a long moment before the old Asian man straightened, the box of Hostess products empty. He carried it back to the counter, collapsed it and tossed it on top of other boxes ready to be tied up for the trash. McCall straightened. He-Ran had stopped stacking the New York Lotto tickets and was watching her husband. A young man entered the store, grabbed a bottled water and a wrapped croissant and left. The old Asian woman was still looking at her husband, as if fearful.

"I do not remember those times," he said.

"I think you do, Kyu-Jae."

"Please call me 'Jerry'. Everyone else does. You have seen much heartbreak in your life, Mr. McCall."

"That is true."

"You are a dangerous man."

"Only to those who would harm my friends and the people I care about."

"Your quest to North Korea would be perilous."

McCall noted that all pretense of the 'old Asian accent" had disappeared.

"It will be, but it is a journey I must undertake."

Kyung-Jae said: "It has been many years since I was home, but I can make some inquires for you. Come back to see me tomorrow."

McCall nodded and held out his hand. The Asian man's hand was gnarled, but his grip was strong. McCall shook He-Ran's also, which was firm, but shook slightly. The early signs of Parkinson's. McCall tried to let her know her husband was doing the right thing. Years of a wary existence in a small neighborhood community had frayed her nerves. But her eyes were kind and she squeezed his hand.

"*Haeng un eul bin da.*"

McCall knew she had said: "Good luck."

He nodded and walked out of the mom-and-pop grocery store.

Candy Annie and Mickey Kostmayer strolled through Central Park hand-in-hand. Kostmayer wore a leather bomber jacket, faded jeans and loafers. Candy Annie was in her mid-twenties. She wore a beige skirt, a lilac silk shirt and sandals with pink nail polish on the toes. She did not consider them a couple yet. That would be very presumptuous of her. But she had reached down for Kostmayer's hand and he had taken it. It had given Candy Annie a warm feeling inside. She had been living in Kostmayer's apartment on Fifty-Fourth Street and Second Avenue ever since Robert McCall had dropped her off there. Before that, Candy Annie had been living in a niche about seventeen feet long literally below the streets of Manhattan. Over the years she had scrounged an old-fashioned, four-poster bed, a cedar oak dresser and a redwood rocking chair, a sofa and two armchairs, a TV, circa 1990's, mainly provided by Jackson T. Foozelman, the old black man who had befriended her twelve years before when she had been lost and stranded in the big city. The only thing she brought up with her to the *Upworld*, when Mr. McCall and Fooz had rescued her, was a bright quilt that now lay in Kostmayer's bedroom. Candy Annie and Kostmayer veered toward where the chess tables were set up in Central Park. She pictured her wonderful apartment. It was decorated in pale sandalwood, a couch and two armchairs in a Pueblo motif, a coffee table from the Southwest, a Frederic Remington painting prominent on one wall and some exquisite Indian pottery. Candy Annie was fond of a wooden ladder that rose almost to the ceiling like the kind that Kostmayer said the Mexican soldiers had used to scale the ramparts when they stormed the Alamo. Candy Annie had come to think of the apartment as her home now, which seemed to be fine with Mr. Kostmayer. She knew he had been through a terrible ordeal when he was being held as a prisoner in North Korea. But that was all she knew. Kostmayer never talked about it. He had escaped into the forest surrounding the prison camp, she knew that much. He had talked about a friend of his that he had "left behind". Candy Annie did not know who that was, although Mr. Kostmayer had an odd name for him. It sounded to her like "Granny." Once Mr. Kostmayer had been back in the picture, Candy Annie had assumed she would be looking for a new place to live, but Mr. Kostmayer did not seem to want her to do that. He had told her she could stay in the apartment for as long as she wanted. Candy Annie had insisted she give Mr. Kostmayer back his bed, but he said he was fine sleeping on the pull-out couch.

But he had nightmares. They woke Candy Annie up in the middle of the night. She came out a couple of times to try to comfort him, and had held him close, which appeared to have given him some concern, since the t-shirt she wore to bed was about three sizes too small for her and it rode up her legs in an alarming manner. Or so he had told her. After his last nightmare, he had asked her to stay in the bedroom and she had heeded his wishes. But it had bothered Candy Annie a lot that she was an intrusion in Kostmayer's life

She thought she had fallen in love with him, although she did not really know what that meant. She had lived her life beneath the streets of Manhattan and had no way of judging whether a man would be attracted to her or not. She guessed she *did* have a curvaceous figure. Which could be attractive to Mr. Kostmayer, except she did not think he noticed her at all.

Mr. McCall had been wonderful to her. He had found her a job as a waitress at Langan's Pub and Restaurant on Forty-Seventh Street just off Seventh Avenue below Times Square. At the time, Candy Annie had tried to thank him. She had even tried to strip for him right there in Mr. Kostmayer's apartment when he had first brought her there. But Mr. McCall was too much of a gentleman to take her up on her offer of a sexual favor. In truth, except for one brief encounter with a homeless guy who had been living below the New York streets, and who was really very sweet, that had been the total encounters she had with sex. Now she felt a rush whenever Mickey Kostmayer was in the apartment at night, although she had never acted on it. She did not know how he felt about *her*. Mr. Kostmayer was friendly and a little—what was the word Mr. McCall had used—*ironic* at times. Candy Annie was not sure what that meant, but Mr. Kostmayer had always treated her with care and respect. But could he be more to her than that? Candy Annie entertained the fantasy that one of these nights she would pad into the living room, put her arms around Mr. Kostmayer and make love to him, in her own way, which was not very experienced, she had to admit. But that had not happened to her as yet, and it may not ever happen.

But she could dream.

In the meantime, Mr. Kostmayer's guilt about his friend was consuming him. It was eating away at him like a cancer and it just broke Candy Annie's heart. Mr.

McCall had told her that Mr, Kostmayer would have to deal with his guilt, or sorrow, in his own way. But Candy Annie wanted to help him get through this difficult time.

She and Kostmayer moved through the trees to where the chess tables were set up. Kostmayer spotted Mike Gammon playing with a gorgeous set of *Game of Thrones* pieces that he obviously carried with him. Across from him was an intense stockbroker who looked as if he had thrashed Bobby Fischer that day. Kostmayer thought Gammon was four moves away from checkmate. He looked up when he saw Kostmayer and Candy Annie step up to the table.

The ex-homicide detective said: "Nice to see you again, Candy Annie. Mr. McCall told me you got a pretty sweet job."

"I'm working as a waitress at Langan's Pub on Seventh Avenue," she gushed. "It is the best, Mr. Gammon! The people are super-friendly. I have dropped my share of trays piled high with steak-and-kidney pies, but I am getting the hang of it. This is Mr. Kostmayer, a friend of Mr. McCall's."

Mike Gammon nodded. "I've seen you here before. Usually playing chess with Granny."

The stockbroker moved his Queen across the chessboard and hit the timer. There was a look of triumph on his face until Gammon moved his rook without even glancing at it.

"What's happened to Granny? I haven't seen him around lately."

But Kostmayer's attention had been caught by a slim, slight man, maybe in his thirties, wearing a jean jacket, faded jeans and boots. His blond hair was streaked the same way Granny wore his. He was jogging through the trees away from the chess tables.

"Wait me for here, Annie," Kostmayer said, and took off after the figure who was by now almost swallowed up in the trees.

Candy Annie smiled at Mike Gammon. "Mr. Kostmayer always calls me *Annie*, not *Candy Annie*. He is the only one who that does. Makes me feel special."

The stockbroker moved his rook. Gammon moved his other knight. "Checkmate." he said.

The stockbroker looked mortified.

Kostmayer caught up with his quarry just as he had cleared the trees and turned him around. It was *not* Granny. The man was a little taller than Granny with the same white-blond hair and gray eyes. Kostmayer let his arm go.

"Sorry. I thought you were a friend of mine. He has the same build, same clothes and the same Illya Kuryakin hairstyle. Sorry I chased after you."

"No problem," the young man said. "Hope you find your friend."

He moved away. Kostmayer jogged back to the chess tables. Mike Gammon was putting his *Games of Thrones* chess pieces back in a velvet bag.

"Was that Granny?" Candy Annie asked him anxiously.

"No."

"Let me know when you see him again," Mike Gammon said. "We have a long-standing chess match we need to finish."

Kostmayer just nodded curtly and moved away. Candy Annie was embarrassed by his rudeness. "He is worried about his friend Granny."

"We all are," Gammon said.

Candy Annie ran to catch up with Kostmayer who was striding through the trees. She put her arm through his. "Mr. McCall says you're going to find your friend."

Kostmayer stopped and looked at her. "When did McCall tell you that?"

Candy Annie looked flustered. "I don't know. When he came to see you at your apartment a few days ago and you were out. He said he would catch up with you later."

"My friend is dead," Kostmayer said, brusquely. "That's the bottom line. Don't mention his name again, Anne." He moved away from her. "We need to go home."

He strode through the trees toward the 59th Street entrance from the park.

Candy Annie followed him, feeling Kostmayer's tension curling up inside her chest.

▶ 3 ◀

LIZ MONTGOMERY HAD NOT expected to see her sister again.

Her attention was fixed on the fence that separated the compound from the rest of the prison camp. She had seen some movement there and was hoping against hope that it was the guards bringing Granny back. She had lost count of how many days he had been held in what Walter Coburn said was little more than a metal corrugated coffin about eight feet by ten feet. Liz knew that prisoners who were incarcerated in solitary confinement were reduced to husks of their former selves. They were broken men.

But not Granny.

Somehow, Liz knew that he would find a way to mentally rise about the torture that was being inflicted on him. Walter Coburn had said that Commandant Myang-Sook-Jang used waterboarding techniques to break his captives. She knew that Jang would use whatever means he had available to torment his prisoners. But Granny had not come back into the main compound and Liz wondered if he had succumbed to the torture and been killed. Then she dismissed that thought from her mind. Walter Coburn, the burly contactor she had befriended at the same time as Granny, had told her that the prison guards would have talked about it. He understood a little Korean and he would have heard snippets of conversations. Granny was a western prisoner along with the others who were incarcerated there. There were only four of them: Liz Montgomery, Walter Coburn, Granny and a new prisoner named Fredrik Jorgensen, a Dutch industrialist who had been transferred to the prison camp. He was a quietly spoken, introspective man. Liz had only talked him for a few minutes. He seemed shell shocked. She knew how he felt.

Liz had been imprisoned at another prison camp where a mass breakout had freed about one hundred Korean prisoners. Granny and another Black Ops operative named Mickey Kostmayer had led the raid and the hundred captives had been loaded into four helicopters and flown over the Chinese border. The mercenaries who had been a part of this rescue mission had all been killed except for Granny and Kostmayer. The prison camp had been moved to this older facility which was basically falling apart. Liz looked up at the watchtowers where three North Korean armed guards were permanently stationed. She thought they were rotated in eight-hour shifts. And there were the guards who roamed the camp to keep tabs on the prisoners. Most of the captives were incarcerated in the older huts in the front of the camp. This section was used to keep the more high-profile inmates, which included the western prisoners, who had been captured. There were no locks on the doors of the Quonset huts. They were watched day and night. Although Liz knew that Mickey Kostmayer *had* escaped from the camp during a work party when the North Korean prisoners had rebelled against their captors. She did not know if he had made it to the Chinese border or not. He never came back, so she supposed that he had been killed. But she did not know that for sure. She knew that Kostmayer and Granny had been close friends.

Liz's hands clenched into fists. Her captivity had taken its toll on her emotional health. And it had been all her fault. As a photojournalist, she had strayed too close to the North Korean border trying to find a prison camp that the North Koreans insisted did not exist. Liz's intention was to photograph this prison camp. Candid shots sent to the western world to show what kind of conditions the Korean prisoners were enduring. Her sister Deva Montgomery had been visiting her sister in New York City. She had insisted on accompanying Liz on her photo shoot. They had taken off from Jeongseok Airfield in an Air Force WC 135 Phoenix aircraft to make a reconnaissance survey at the North Korean border. They had strayed too far into the trees following some hikers that they had spied from the air. Their Phoenix aircraft had developed engine trouble and they had crashed landed in the dense woods. The pilot had been killed, but Liz and Deva had scrambled out of the crippled aircraft. They found a trail that the Korean hikers had used, but then they had become separated. Liz had lost sight of her sister and had been picked up by a North Korean BTR-152 Armored Personnel Carrier jeep. Liz had tried to explain that she was an American photojournalist whose aircraft had developed engine trouble and crashed landed. She demanded to be taken to a place where she could be flown to the American Embassy in Seoul. If the North Korean guards understood what she was saying she had no idea. They had not said a word. She had pleaded to the North Korean military personnel to find her sister Deva, but her entreaties had fallen on deaf ears. After seven hours Liz found herself in this North Korean prison camp which she knew was an old one. She had no idea what happened to her beautiful sister Deva.

Until today.

When Liz turned away from the fence and its gate her spirits soared. She could not believe her eyes. Her sister Deva had just stepped out of a modified jeep manned by two North Korean guards. She looked weary and disorientated, but she was *alive*! Deva had not seen her sister as yet. Liz ran down the compound and practically threw herself into her sister's arms. Deva just burst into tears. Liz had always been the tougher older sister, edgy and forceful, who swore like a sailor and who had one-night stands more times that she could count. Her sister Deva was more withdrawn, sweeter, wary of affection and other people's motives. Liz was a brunette with a page boy cut. Deva was a blonde with cascades of Farrah-Fawcett hair layered on her head. Liz was dressed in the grey prison uniform all the prisoners wore. Deva still wore her jeans, a turtleneck, a lightweight jacket and laced-up boots, but Liz knew that would change.

Deva was a little unsteady on her feet, so Liz supported her to the large hut where she and the other western prisoners spent most of their time. Liz had been forced occasionally to go outside the prison camp in work parties, always supervised by the guards. She felt Myang-Sook-Jang had wanted these western inmates for a special purpose. Ransom, or to parade them in front of some video cameras so they could be forced to denounce the United States. But so far the prison hierocracy had left the western captives alone. Liz looked up and saw that the two North Koran guards up in two of the watch towers were following their progress with no interest. Liz looked around and noted that the guards in the compound regarded them with disdain. Which was fine with Liz. The less the contact they had with these torturers, the better.

When they reached the wooden steps at the large hut, Deva just collapsed onto them. Walter Coburn jogged over to them. Liz's eyes searched his face for any word on Granny. He just shook his head.

"This is my sister Deva," Liz said. "We got shot down in the forest, but then we got separated. It has been six days since I have seen her. I had lost hope."

"Nice to meet you, Deva, even in these harsh circumstances," Coburn said. He looked at Liz. "There is a reason your sister has been brought here to this camp."

"I twisted my ankle sliding down a steep ravine," Deva said. Her voice, as opposed to her sister, was softer and a little hoarse. "I couldn't find Liz and then North Korean soldiers spotted me and picked me up. I was held at another prison camp for six days, then I was transferred here. They let me keep the clothes I was wearing. I don't think they knew what to do with me."

"You're here, that's all that matters," Liz said, and hugged her sister again. "We'll get you inside. There are no locks on these huts. We are watched all the time. But there are beds and even some furniture, a couch and a couple of chairs and a writing desk."

The Dutchman Fredrik Jorgensen moved up to them. His voice had a melodic quality to it. He held out his hand, as if they were being introduced at a garden party. "Fredrik Jorgensen."

"I'm Liz Montgomery."

Fredric Jorgensen smiled in spite of himself. "But not the Liz Montgomery who was on our telly screens and who could twitch her nose to make magic happen?"

"Not that Liz Montgomery," Liz sighed. "Or I would have twitched my nose a lot earlier than this and made all of these fuckers disappear. No offence, Mr. Jorgensen."

"None taken, I assure you."

"My sister has a colorful vocabulary," Deva said, and laughed, probably Liz thought for the first time in days. "You should have heard her when she is dealing with other photojournalists who give her crap. She can swear with the best of them."

"Especially in this godforsaken place," Liz said.

"Best to remain circumspect and deferential in the camp," Coburn warned them. "A wrong word could mean the difference here between life and death."

Coburn had turned toward the rusting gate and took a step forward. "Granny is back!"

Liz turned and saw Granny, barely able to walk, pushing his way through the gate that led back to where the huts were lined up for the Korean prisoners. Two of the Korean prison guards were behind him. They watched him stumble and almost fall. Coburn leapt down from the wooden porch steps and ran forward. Liz jumped to her feet to follow.

"Wait for me here, Deva," she said.

Then she was racing to catch up with Granny.

Walter Coburn reached him first. The contractor pulled him up to his feet. The two prison guards watched dispassionately. By that time Liz had reached him and took his other arm.

"I'm all right," Granny said in a halting voice.

Liz could hear the strain in his voice. She clutched him tighter. "We got you, Granny."

Granny looked at her with his lopsided grin. "You're an angel come down from heaven."

"I've had boyfriends who have described me in less glowing terms, but I'll take the compliment."

"Lean on me," Coburn told him.

They half-carried Granny the rest of the way to the large hut. When they reached it, Granny nodded, as if he were fine now, which could not be further from the truth. Liz and Coburn lowered him to the lower porch step.

"This is my sister I told you about," Liz said. "Deva."

Granny nodded, his voice still hoarse, but getting stronger. "I see the resemblance."

"We got separated, but they brought her here," Liz said. "Thank God."

"They want all the western prisoners in one camp," Granny said.

Liz turned to Walter Coburn and said: "Bring him some water, Walter, would you?"

"I'll pass on the water," Granny said, even though the irony was lost on the group.

Deva looked out at the guards who were patrolling the grounds of the compound. There were some North Korean prisoners among them, but they kept to themselves. "What are they going to do to us?" she asked, fearfully.

"Nothing," Granny said. "Yet. They'll make their intentions known to us."

"I thought we had lost you," Liz said, with genuine affection in her voice. She glanced at Deva to see if she had caught the implication in her voice. "Granny is very precious to all of us."

Deva had not missed her sister's tone. "I'm sure he is."

"What did they do to you in that metal coffin?" Liz asked him.

"They made me drink water," Granny said, ironic. "They asked me questions. I had no answers for them. After a while they let me out."

"They could have let you rot in that metal coffin."

"I was too busy working on my motorcycle."

"They allowed you to have a motorcycle?" Deva asked, incredulously.

"It was a beauty. But I had to leave it behind."

Liz was tracking with his logic. "I always said you should have played Steve McQueen in the *Great Escape*."

Granny smiled at that.

"Is that really your name?" Deva asked him. "Granny?"

"It suits me."

"Let's get you inside the hut," Liz suggested. "You need to lie down."

Granny nodded. He allowed Liz and Coburn to help him up to his feet. Then he looked past them. Myang-Sook-Jang stood outside his two-story hut smoking a cigarette. Granny had looked into the windows of the hut before he had been knocked down by two of the patrolling guards. It was nicely furnished inside with wicker furniture, old-fashioned oil lamps, a desk, a sofa, two upright chairs, even a piano in one corner. Two wooden porch steps led down into the compound.

Jang did not move. He did not acknowledge Granny, or Walter Coburn, or the Dutch Industrialist Fredrik Jorgensen who had joined them. He was looking at the two sisters. There was nothing in his opaque eyes and no expression on his face. He smoked his cigarette. Granny allowed Liz and Walter Coburn to support him inside the hut.

He got a fleeting glimpse of Myang-Sook-Jang's face before the hut door closed.

It was impassive, but Granny felt his black eyes were mocking them.

The fight in the playground area at P.S. 119 in Brooklyn had escalated out into the street. A black-and-white police car pulled up to the fence and two Officers jumped out. Both of them were in uniform. The female Officer was Alexa Kokinas, an American of Greek heritage in her mid-twenties, her raven hair piled up on her head. She was backed up by her partner, Tony Palmer, a good-looking, edgy cop.

Alexa Kokinas was *deaf*.

Well, that was not strictly speaking true. Her right ear had no hearing in it whatsoever. Her left ear had some partial hearing, maybe 30 per cent. Which, as far as Alexa Kokinas was concerned, was all she needed to function as a human being and be a good *cop*.

The hoodlums had invaded the playground and had sought out the high students there, some of whom had been wandering into *their* territory when they had been attending a party at some dude's house. The street gang had arrived at P.S. 119 to kick a little ass and generally terrorize the students. Their game plan had been to find the students who had dared to encroach on their territory and teach them a lesson they would never forget. But the students at P.S. 119 were tough and the fight had spilled out quickly through the gate of the playground and into the street which was cordoned off to traffic. The gang members were wielding lengths of chain and knives. Unfortunately for them, Alexa Kokinas and Officer Tony Palmer had been in the neighborhood. In fact, they had just finished settling a domestic dispute at a house around the corner when the call came in on their radio. Alexa and Tony were on the scene of the school playground within two minutes.

The students were giving as good as they got. Anxious teachers who had been assigned to the school playground had already called the police. The gang members scattered when the patrol car pulled in their midst with a screech of brakes and the two NYPD Officers leapt out. One of the hoodlums had a scrappy student on the ground and was choking him. Alexa pulled him off and applied her own choke hold. She dropped him down to the sidewalk, dragged his arms behind his back and shook out her handcuffs. The teenager got to his feet and limped back through the school gate. A cheer went up from the students congregated there. The gangbangers scattered like so many rats deserting a sinking ship. Officer Palmer let them go. He was only interested how his partner was doing wrestling the hoodlum below her into submission. Which she accomplished with ease. She dragged the kid and threw him into the fence. Alexa relieved him of the switchblade knife he had pulled from his belt and had kicked out his length of chain away. By now there was a larger crowd of students, most of them younger than the high school student, standing at the front gate to the playground. Tony moved over to them, making a gesture for them to back off. The teachers at the gate stayed were they were. Tony had caught Alexa's eye and nodded. There was a shorthand they used that worked well.

Alexa faced the youth who was not so cocky now. He had a shock of strawberry blonde hair with white streaks in it for effect. She addressed him in a halting style, but her words were distinct, if a little slurred.

"What is your name?"

"Shaggy Dog."

"Not your street name," she said. "Your real name?"

"Raymond Daniels."

"What is your gang affiliation?"

"Flatbush Greased Devils."

"Catchy title," Tony commented.

"This is what is going to happen, Raymond," Alexa told him. "I am going to uncuff you. You scurry back to your own neighborhood with the rest of the scum."

She glanced at Tony, who had his Glock 17 gun un-holstered, but pointing down at the ground. He released the handcuffs from the youth's wrists, then stepped back.

"If I see one of you back in this neighborhood," Alexa said, "I'll arrest you."

That was enough for the youth, who took off. He turned the corner of the school and disappeared. "You let him off a little easy, didn't you?" Tony asked her.

She shrugged. In her halting, hoarse voice, she said: "If he comes back to harasses these kids, we'll know about it."

Several of the kids approached the cops. One of them, a tall, gangling girl named Kristin who had been shooting hoops with her friends, picked up on Alexa's af-fliction right away. "Are you deaf?"

Alexa smiled. "Pretty much."

Another of her friends, Maddie, said: "But you don't act like a deaf person."

Instead of being offended, Alexa's smiled broadened. She responded to both teenagers by using her voice and sign language. "What do deaf people sound like"?

"Like anyone else," a third girl said, a willowy blonde named Taylor who was glaring at her friends. "Duh, you guys." To Alexa she said: "I took some sign language courses last semester."

Alexa signed for her. "How did you like them?"

"They were really cool!"

"But you can hear us, right?" Kristen asked.

"I have no hearing in my right ear at all," Alexa said. "Completely dead. I've got 30 per cent hearing in my left ear."

Alexa's partner was getting impatient. "We've got to go," Tony said.

Alexa continued signing as she spoke. "There is a Deputy Sheriff in Arizona who has partial hearing. I think we're the only ones in the country to serve as Peace Officers."

"You've got such striking raven hair!" Maddie said. "It's gorgeous!"

Alexa smiled. "Thanks."

One of their teachers, who did not look much older than the high school kids, whose nameplate said *Mrs. Alvarez*, stepped in. "That is enough, guys. These Officers do not want to be given the three-degree. We've had enough excitement for one morning." She turned to Alexa. "I'm sorry for all the intrusive questions."

"I don't mind," Alexa said.

Kristin said: "What if someone tried to sneak up on you?"

"They'd be very sorry they did," Tony said and grinned.

Alexa looked at him with some affection that was not lost on the other kids.

"Did you attend the police academy?" Mrs. Alvarez asked her.

Tony answered for his partner. "She passed her exams with honors."

"You cope with your disability very well," Maddie said.

Alexa signed and said: "I don't think of it as a disability."

"What should we do if those hoodlums come back?" Mrs. Alvarez asked.

Alexa noted she did not use the word "gangbangers." She looked at her partner.

Tony said: "You should call the 76th precinct. A patrol car will be here within five minutes and make arrests. It was an isolated incident. The *Flatbush Greased Devils* didn't like a bunch of high school jocks showing up at their party."

"But let us know if they *do* come back," Alexa said.

"Thanks for talking to us," Maddie said. "It was cool."

"You kids have a good day now," Tony said.

Alexa and Tony walked back into their black-and-white police car and climbed inside. Tony sat behind the steering wheel. Alexa slid into the passenger side and slammed the car door

"The *Flatbush Greased Devils*," Palmer said. "Give me a break. What happened to the good old-fashioned *Greenwich Village Motherfuckers*? Let me know when you are going to wrestle an asshole like Raymond Daniels to the ground. I'm here to back you up."

Alexa grinned. "No sweat."

"Don't take chances."

Alexa looked at her partner and signed: "Because I am deaf?"

"No, because you're reckless."

"Don't worry."

A radio echoed through to them. "10-21," Alexa said. "Burglary in progress."

Tony picked up the radio, setting their vehicle in motion. "Responding," he said.

The patrol car pulled away from the schoolyard.

▶ 4 ◀

McCALL WALKED INTO the extensive grounds that housed the six eight-story buildings in the small industrialist park in Washington D.C. The last of the buildings were the headquarters of The *Company*, a shadowy, black ops spy organization. There were no signs, of course, nothing to say what it was. McCall entered the marble lobby where one of the uniformed Security Guards moved over to him. McCall had known the older black American for over ten years. Harvey Nichols never changed. *Company* agents came and went over the years, and Harvey had known them all. He had a soft spot for Robert McCall who had helped him solve a personal dilemma years before with his daughter. That was right before McCall had travelled to St. Petersburg in Russia to try and rescue another *Company* agent named Serena Johanssen. That had not gone well. He had been able to rescue Serena from Kresty Prison by impersonating a notorious Russian interrogator named Vladimir Gredenko and brought her to the city of Yaroslavl. She had been felled by sniper's bullet from the top of the Spaso-Probrazhensy Monastery. McCall had finally caught up with the assassin outside Prague on a heavy wooded slope overlooking a magnificent chateau where a summit meeting was taking place.

Jovan Durkovic put an epic fight, but eventually McCall had killed him. But that did not bring Serena Johanssen back. Nor the beautiful Russian *Company* agent Elena Petrov who had been the love of McCall's life.

"Nice to see you again Mr. McCall," Harvey said with a smile. "We've been expecting you. I will escort you up."

The Security Officer gave McCall a badge and rode up the elevator to the sixth floor. Walking down the corridor, Harvey said: "That problem you helped me with last year. It got sorted out. My sister and that no-good husband of hers have parted ways. Thanks to you. I saw Mr. Kostmayer here a few days ago, but I have not seen Granny for a long time. Is he coming back to the *Company*?"

"Need to know, Harvey."

"You will bring him back."

"You may have too much faith in me," McCall said.

"No, sir. If anyone can do it."

Harvey opened a glass door. There were several offices on the floor. Control's office was in the corner. "You will know your way to the small boardroom, Mr. McCall. They're all in there waiting for you."

Harvey closed the door behind him and walked back down the corridor. McCall moved past two shut doors where he knew fifty *Company* analysts sat at computer consoles, two big screens in front of them, one of them showing hot spots in countries around the world. When he entered the small, oak-paneled boardroom there were three people sitting at the round cherrywood table. A desktop computer was in the center with files strewn around it. There were large glass panels in one of the walls, plus television monitors running constant news feeds from CNN, Fox News, MSNBC, BBC and Al Jezeera. Control stood in the center of the room. Across from him was a

Syrian analyst in his early forties whom McCall had met once before named Assad Malifi. He had swarthy good looks and deep gray eyes and that looked somewhat sorrowful. Beside him was Emma Marshal, Control's secretary, dressed today in a clinging skirt, a man's white shirt unbuttoned almost to the waist where her cleavage overflowed in an alarming manner. She jumped to her feet and greeted McCall as only Emma Marshall could, with a kiss on his lips that would take down a lesser man.

McCall smiled. "I wasn't sure if you had been summoned back."

"Oh yes, Control rescued me from a life of purgatory living with my cankerous mother who is in her eighties who can't believe I haven't found a nice boy to marry." Emma looked at Control. "It's good to have him back."

Control said: "You remember Assad Malifi, Robert. One of our top analysts. He's got some got some intel for you."

Assad shook McCall's hand. "It's not much for you to look at, Mr. McCall."

"I'll take whatever you can give me."

McCall sat down at the round table beside Emma who had returned to her notes. She lowered the lights in the small boardroom and fired up the lighted panels on the wall. She nodded to Assad. "This is your dog-and-pony show, Assad. I'll just bring up the images."

The first lighted panel showed a North Korean prison camp. Emma Marshal added some aerial footage in the other lighted panels around it. "This is the North Korean prisoner camp that the mercenaries hit," Assad said, "which included Mickey Kostmayer and the agent you call 'Granny.' Do you have a real name for him?"

"I am sure Control has a file for him on his desk," McCall said. "But 'Granny' is fine for me."

Emma's fingers flew over her computer keyboard as she brought up more images, but there were not many of them. "A clandestine raid was carried out in North Korea," Assad continued. "It had the backing of this spy agency, but the details of the raid were kept under wraps. The foray into enemy territory was devasting in the North Korean prison camp. One hundred Korean prisoners were freed, loaded into three AVC AC 391 helicopters and flown across the border into China. Where they landed is in the briefing notes we have for you. The mercenaries were all casualties of war. All of them were killed except for Mickey Kostmayer and Granny. Using aerial surveillance some drones flew over the North Korean camp, but it had been totally destroyed and abandoned."

"Mickey Kostmayer reported to me for his briefing three days ago," Control said. "He said that the North Korean military had moved the prisoners to another prison camp. From what I can gather, it was a very old facility. Badly in need of repair. Go on, Mr. Malifi."

"Mickey said there were three watchtowers," Assad said. "A fourth had been swallowed by the jungle. When Kostmayer managed to escape from the facility, he took a circuitous route to flee from his captors. Eventually that led him to the Yalu River at the Sino-Korean Friendship Bridge. He swam to an island in no-man's-land to the port at Dandong and hitched a ride in a truck into the city. Then a regular scheduled American Airlines flight took him home to New York City. But sitting at this very table, Kostmayer had no idea how he had gotten away from his captors and where he had left this prison camp."

"Remember, Kostmayer had been beaten, starved and tortured," Control said. "His memories of the camp are hazy at best. All he knows is that the guards took one of the western prisoners into the forest, a man with butter-colored hair, and killed him."

"Which could have been Granny," Emma said, "but we can't be sure of that."

"So, you have no idea where this older North Korean prisoner camp is located?" McCall asked.

"We haven't got the faintest idea," Assad said. "Take a look at this."

Emma's fingers flew over her keyboard again. McCall leaned forward. There was aerial footage of forests in North Korea as far as the eye could see.

"This aerial footage goes on for miles," the Egyptian analyst said. "If there *is* another older prison camp in these woods, we haven't found it yet."

"But it would have been within striking distance to the Yalu River and the Sino-Korean Friendship Bridge," Control said.

"That could cover a hundred miles," Assad said. "We're still compiling aerial footage for you, Mr. McCall, but I am not optimistic. It's a very large area and we can't send a strike force anywhere near it."

Emma put a series of slides on the four lighted wall panels.

"Elizabeth Montgomery," Assad continued. "Not the famous actress who could twitch her nose and make things appear and disappear." The Egyptian analyst smiled, but no one at the table was smiling, so he pressed on rapidly. "She's a photojournalist in her thirties whose plane developed engine trouble and went down in the forest just over the Korean border. Her sister Deva Montgomery was with her. She is four years younger. She lives in New York City and had been visiting Liz Montgomery in Seoul where Liz had been taking photographs for her New York City magazine."

"Our intel says they both survived the crash," Control said, "and were picked up a North Korean patrol. But that is *all* we know. They could be both dead now. Or they could be rotting in one of the North Korean prison camps."

Emma lit up more panels. Assad continued: "Walter Coburn is a contractor in South Korea. He also disappeared. There's one more slide, isn't there, Emma?"

She brought up the lighted panel on one of the walls. "Fredrik Jorgensen is a Dutch businessman who disappeared almost nine months ago. The North Korean Government has vehemently denied any knowledge of him."

"We do have two young men to show you," Control said.

Emma hit a couple keys on her computer. The faces of two young Korean men brightened on the lighted panels. "The first one is Kyu-Chul, about thirty-five. He escaped from North Korea ten years ago. He has been working at the American Embassy in Seoul. The second one is Yo-Han, same age, a mercenary who hires out to the highest bidder, which happens to be *us*. They will be your liaison in North Korea."

"That's all intel we can give you, Robert," Control said. "Not much to send you halfway across the world. Even with their assistance it could take you six months or more to find this new North Korean prisoner camp. But I know you are going there anyway."

Emma powered down the computer. The lighted panels in the wall died. Control stood up. "Thank you, Emma and Assad."

"I have your new passport and travel papers for you," Emma told McCall. "Or I will have them for you tomorrow morning."

"Emma will bring them to you in New York City," Control added. "Walk back with me to my office."

McCall stood and looked at Assad Malifi. "You may think you haven't been helpful, but you have been." He looked over at Emma Marshal, who was standing awkwardly. "Thank you, Emma."

He walked out of the boardroom after Control.

Emma sighed heavily. "Well, that briefing sucked."

Assad said: "Robert McCall may find himself in South Korea for a long time before he could ever get *into* North Korea."

"You don't know him like I do," Emma murmured.

McCall moved toward the glass door where he could see Harvey's figure waiting for him. Control paused in the doorway of his office. "You know I could stop you from leaving. I can have you placed under arrest as a security danger to the country."

McCall kept walking. "You could try, but you won't."

Emma had reached her desk. She pushed a buzzer. McCall pushed the glass door open. Outside in the corridor, Harvey said: "Ready to leave, Mr. McCall?"

"Yes."

McCall stepped into the elevator with the Security Officer and it descended. Control's hands clenched to fists. Emma was subdued. She touched her boss's arm gently.

"Does he have a chance of finding Granny and the other American prisoners?"

"Not a hope in hell," Control said.

He walked back into his office and slammed the door.

Granny and Liz Montgomery walked around the prison compound. The Western prisoners were not restricted by anyone because there was nowhere for them to go. There was no escape. Granny glanced at the three watchtowers that towered above them. Two of them were at the front of the prison compound. The third one was at the back of the camp. A fourth tower had been demolished and the rubble had been strewn for a hundred yards in both directions. The North Korean guards above Granny and Liz kept an unrelenting vigil both day and night. Granny had timed them. They had eight-hour shifts. There was something unnerving about their constant surveillance. They did not move their positions. They carried standard issue KPA type 58 rifles, although Granny noted some type 88 rifles among them. Most of the prisoners were housed away from the main compound where the bigger huts were located. It was as if these huts were for show only. The North Korean prisoners were herded in small huts which housed as many as ten families. They were given an hour to exercise before they were directed back to their Quonset huts. In constant, the Western prisoners had free rein to go wherever they liked, except there *was* nowhere them to go.

Liz Montgomery stopped at a small, abandoned hut and leaned against the dilapidated porch. Beyond her was the large hut where she could see her sister Deva talking quietly to a new prisoner who had been captured and brought into the camp the night before. His name was Daniel Blake, a reporter for Associated Press who had been captured when he strayed too far over the border. His vehicle had gone off the road and ploughed through a fence. It had taken the North Korean patrol all of ten minutes to surround him. He had protested that it had been a genuine mistake, but the North Korean guards had not listened to him. Twenty hours later he had found himself in this prison camp. He was scared and disoriented, but at least he had recognized a face from the Western prisoners in Deva Montgomery. They had become friends when he had been living for a time in South Korea.

Granny stopped beside Liz. He followed her gaze to the hut where Deva and Daniel Blake were sitting. Deva coughed repeatedly, her hands shaking slightly.

"How bad is that cough of your sister's?" Granny asked.

"It's bad," Liz said. "But there's nothing I can do about it in here. She had bronchitis when she little and it comes back sometimes to haunt her. The medical facilities here suck and that goes for the Korean prisoners as well as the Western ones. The doctors here are butchers. They beat the North Korean prisoners as viciously as the guards do."

"I'm going to get you all out of here," Granny told her, his voice quiet and reassuring.

Liz was not buying it. "Like hell you are. You blasted apart that first North Korean prison camp and rescued I don't know how many prisoners, but there's no escape from this place."

"Mickey Kostmayer escaped from here."

"You know that won't happen again," Liz said. "Myang-Sook-Jang lost face when your mercenaries came storming through the last prison camp. He has tightened up security in this camp. It is an old one, falling into disrepair, but that is why he has doubled the guards. If Deva does not get to a hospital where she can receive proper medical attention that cough is just going to get worse."

"You have to trust me, Liz." Granny said. "One way or another, I will get you out of here. I promise you."

Almost unconsciously, she reached out for his hand. Granny took it and squeezed it. He thought his voice sounded hollow but giving her some hope was all he could do right now. He felt that the relationship between them had blossomed into something more than friendship, although neither of them had acted on it in the circumstances. It was a glance up, a look that held between them when no words were needed, a touch of her hand that spoke volumes.

Liz turned back to him. "Your friend Kostmayer talked about a fellow agent at your spy agency who he said would get him out of here."

Granny nodded. "I know exactly the man you mean."

"What was his name again?"

"Robert McCall."

"That was it. Kostmayer said nothing would stop him from rescuing you from this place. But in the end, that did not happen, did it?" she said, bitterly. "Kostmayer escaped from here on his own."

"He got lucky," Granny said. "How far he made it to freedom I don't know. None of the prison guards will talk about him. Probably for fear of being executed on the spot. Then, of course, Myang-Sook-Jang moved the prison camp to a new location here in the forest."

"I remember Kostmayer had a peculiar name for this agent," Liz said.

"The *Equalizer*."

"That was it. Someone who would be there for you when all else had failed."

Granny nodded. "That sounds like him."

"Catchy name, but it does not mean a Goddamn thing. There is no 'Equalizer' here to rescue us. He was just a figment of Mickey's imagination. He doesn't exist."

"Don't be too sure of that."

Liz turned back to Granny, not quite into his arms, but close. "*You're* the only one in here that I trust."

"Keep that thought."

Liz kissed him, just a tender kiss like you would give to an old friend. There was no passion in it, but there was an intimacy that was implied. She looked at the big main gates of the prison compound which stood open. Prisoners in their drab grey uniforms were moving through it, prodded occasionally by the North Korean guards.

"Work patrol?" she asked.

Granny nodded. "Sent out to work on the forest roads clearing tree stumps and fallen tree limbs. Kostmayer escaped from one of those work parties, but the guards in here have doubled since then."

One of the Western prisoners, Walter Coburn, detached him from the others and headed to where Granny and Liz Montgomery were standing. Granny noted that Myang-Sook-Jang had walked out of his two-story house. He lit a du Maurier cigarette and took a long drag on it, his attention going from the guards and the prisoners to where Granny stood with Liz. His eyes betrayed nothing. Walter Coburn paused at the hut without turning around. "Is the Commandant still looking this way?"

"He is," Granny said. "Don't let it unnerve you."

"It would take more than that jumped up tin soldier to do that," Coburn retorted. "No one around us to hear me?"

"The guards don't speak anything but Korean. As far as Myang-Sook-Jang is concerned, neither do we."

"Bloody good." Walter Coburn looked at them both. "I may have found a way for us to get out of this hellhole."

► 5 ◄

MICKEY KOSTMAYER FOUND Emma Marshall at the Park Lane Hotel on Central Park West. It was her favorite hotel in the city with an impressive view of Central Park outside the massive windows on the second floor. She had just finished her breakfast and was sipping her coffee when the brash Company agent slid into a chair opposite her. She was not surprised to see him.   It was a meeting she had been dreading ever since she flew into New York. She had seen Kostmayer when he had come into the *Company* building to be debriefed about the United Nations evacuation. She knew he been down in a parking facility beneath the U.N. buildings holding a homemade device filled with C4 explosives waiting for the bomb disposal squad to arrive. The device had been defused by Colonel Michael G. Ralston—*Gunner* to friends and foes alike—but there had been a secondary device and Kostmayer had had to wait for twenty agonized minutes for the bomb squad to find him and declare that the secondary fuse had not been triggered. Emma knew it had left Kostmayer shaken. He and Gunner had saved everyone's life that night at the United Nations, but she understood that the experience had weighed on Kostmayer. He usually kept his ironic, edgy persona in check, but right now his nerves were frayed. She recognized the signs. She had seen enough *Company* agents while being Control's secretary to know when they were still recovering from trauma.

But she smiled at him and said: "Good morning, Mickey."

Kostmayer came straight to the point. "I talked to Assad Malifi at the *Company* last night. I know that there is a classified mission running. Assad wouldn't give me more intel that that, and I had to threaten him with thumbs screws before he would tell me that the mission concerned Robert McCall."

"Control hasn't authorized any new missions that are running at this time.," Emma said.

"Doesn't matter if it's sanctioned or not. It is in motion or Assad Malifi would have not been in a briefing room giving McCall what intel he had. I am guessing it is a mission for him to fly to North Korea and rescue Granny from the prison camp there. The same one that I escaped from. I need whatever intel you can give me."

"I can't discuss sensitive information with anyone, even one of *Control's* top agents. You know that."

"Just tell me if Granny is alive or dead?"

Emma took a deep breath, looking out the window at the carriages pulling tourists down Central Park West. Finally, she said: "We don't know what has happened to Granny."

"But McCall must have reason to believe that he's still alive."

"He believes it is a possibility." Emma looked back at Kostmayer. "But it is a solo mission."

"That's what I wanted to know." Kostmayer got to his feet. "Sorry to interrupt your breakfast, Emma. Good to see you back in the fold. Take care of yourself."

Kostmayer walked away from the table. Emma looked at him with concern in her eyes. "This is going to end badly for you, Mickey," she said, quietly

Granny and Walter Coburn waited until midnight before they left the large hut. There were the usual North Korean guards patrolling, but not as many as during the daylight hours. They had to time it just right, avoiding the sweeps of the searchlights on the three high watch-towers. Granny had reconnoitered the shed where the guards kept their Hurricane Lamps. While Coburn stood guard, Granny broke the padlock on the door, which was rusted, and found two large Vintage style Black Hanging Hurricane Lamps, battery operated with a Dimmer Switch. Granny put the padlock back on the door, handed one of Hurricane Lamps to Coburn who led the way to the front of the prison camp. There they had to avoid the third watchtower which only intermittently swept the area. The wooden huts that housed the Korean prisoners were grouped close together. Nothing stirred in any of the windows. Granny followed Coburn through the heaped-up rubble that was scattered across the ground to where Coburn knelt down. There was an old storm drain buried in the debris of bricks and steel. Coburn lifted a rusting manhole to reveal a metal ladder leading down into the darkness. They waited until the next sweep of the searchlight which came in just two minutes. Then Coburn climbed down the metal rungs, carrying the Hurricane Lamp. Granny was right behind him. With Coburn's help he lifted the heavy metal manhole cover back into place.

They stepped down into rank, ankle-deep water that had pooled in the storm drain. They lit their Hurricane

Lamps which provided a wan radiance at best. Their voices echoed in the confined space.

"There is a series of tunnels down here around the storm drain," Coburn said. "I think North Koran inmates of this prison tried to dig their way out at some point. Let us see where this leads to."

"No talking," Granny said, softly. "Use hand signals."

Coburn nodded and moved down the storm drain. They came to the first tunnel which branched out into two more, but the ceilings were no more than eight feet above their heads. The Hurricane Lamps illuminated their way like they were in a maze. More rubble was strewn everywhere. They had to climb over piles of bricks until finally they came to a tunnel that opened into a larger space, maybe twelve feet long and six feet deep. Dust drifted across the tunnel and more of it sifted down from the ceiling. Coburn gestured to Granny that he was going to go to the end of tunnel to see where it led to. No sense of them both reconnoitering it. The tunnel walls looked like they could collapse at any moment. Granny indicated that he understood. Coburn moved further into the tunnel, the Hurricane Lamp leaping in front of him as it splashed light on the rocky walls. Then his figure disappeared into the murky gloom.

Granny hefted his Hurricane Lamp and splayed the light across another tunnel that led off the main one. It only travelled about ten feet before branching out into two more narrow passageways. Granny backtracked to the first tunnel and found it branched off into two more. Obviously, whomever had dug these tunnels had been fueled with despair. They led a few feet and then collapsed into the rock wall. Granny found one last tunnel, wider than the others, but not higher. The ceiling above Granny's head must have been four feet high. He had to stoop down to crawl along it. Then the tunnel opened to twelve feet, but there was barely enough space to turn around. Granny looked up at the earthen roof of the tunnel. Then he retraced his steps back down the tunnel to where it joined the first one. The height of this passageway was ten feet. He had to transverse back to the main tunnel where he had left Coburn. He set down his Hurricane Lamp on the ground. He heard the sound of the contractor returning. He stumbled into the smear of white light that streaked the tunnel and collapsed on one of the rocks that studded the interior. He was breathing heavily and, Granny thought, asthmatic.

"No bloody good!" he panted.

Granny moved his hand down to shush him.

"You think the gooks can hear us down here in this bloody coffin?" Coburn asked.

Granny had not heard the phrase "gooks" since Vietnam. It made him smile. "Take it easy, Walter."

"These tunnels lead *nowhere!*" Coburn said. "They just bloody stop! So, whoever built them, they hit bedrock or sheet metal, so they downed tools and turned around and hacked out another tunnel that led bloody nowhere too! I came to six tunnels and all of them petered out after a few feet at rock walls. I will give them an A for trying, but it was obviously a futile exercise. I cannot image how long it took them to burrow down here and then to come to dead ends. They never got out of the labyrinth. They just went back up top, closed up the main tunnel and resigned themselves to their fate. Bloody idiots. They should have kept digging. There is forty feet to the fence here. Poor bastards never made it even that far."

Granny had given up trying to shush the Aussie. He waited until he was finished and had nothing more to say. Then he looked at Granny. "You find anything in the other tunnels?"

"Just dead ends, like you found."

"Bloody hell!"

"But that's okay," Granny said, and smiled lopsidedly.

"How can it be okay? You want to have a picnic down here? Maybe I should have brought down some bloody sandwiches and soft drinks and potato chips?" Then he looked at Granny's blue eyes and it pulled him up short. "What's that look for?"

"I know where we are," Granny said, softly.

McCall was waiting for Kostmayer at the Upstairs Bar at the Dead Rabbit Grocery & Grog in the Financial District. It had the feel of an Irish American saloon named after the group in Scorsese's *Gangs of New York*. It was packed with tourists and locals, the ambience rowdy and friendly. Warm wood framed the walls around the booths along one wall with their high stools. McCall sat beside the fearsome eagle at one end of the bar, sipping a Glenfiddich 21. On a flat screen above the bar the Knicks were playing the Pacers, the sound turned down low.

Mickey Kostmayer entered and slid onto a vacant bar stool beside McCall. A tall, gorgeous brunette moved over to serve him, but he shook his head.

"What makes you believe Granny is alive?" Kostmayer demanded, with no attempt to even say hello.

McCall had been expecting this, even if Emma Marshall had not called him with a head's-up that Kostmayer would be looking for him. McCall took out his cellphone from his pocket, scrolled down and turned it around so that Kostmayer could see the screen.

Odds against me. Still a prisoner in NK. Come and get me and others. Granny.

Kostmayer looked back up at McCall. "That means that Granny is still alive."

McCall returned to the full screen and slipped the phone back into pocket of his leather jacket. "No, it doesn't. Someone else could have sent that message. Maybe the Commandant of the prison camp. Maybe it was traded by one of the guards for a package of cigarettes. Maybe one of the North Korean children stole it to play with it. Whatever the truth is, I'll find out."

"I'm going with you," Kostmayer said.

"Not this time," McCall said.

Kostmayer leaned a little closer to McCall. He had been drinking. His eyes were bloodshot from lack of sleep and stress. His voice had a husky quality to it that took McCall by surprise. The raucous atmosphere in the bar masked anyone else hearing them. This was for McCall's ears alone.

"Granny was my friend long before he was *your* friend, McCall. I could not take him with me when I escaped from that North Korean prison camp. I did not go back for him and left him for dead. I am not going to do that again. What do you always say? Leave no one behind."

McCall's voice was quiet and measured. He knew how much Mickey was hurting, but that did not matter when it came to the safety of the mission.

"It was a miracle that you managed to escape from that North Korean prison when you did. No one else could have done that. Good thing for the sake of your country you did, or the United Nations buildings might be a pile of burnt-out rubble right now and all of those innocent people you saved would be dead. You cannot do it all, Mickey. I know how Granny's presumed death has eaten away at you. But you would not be any good to me on this mission. You would be a liability. You would only slow me down. Granny deserves a better chance than that."

The harsh words were spoken in the same quiet tone, but they had the desired effect. Kostmayer looked like he was going to throw a punch at the man he idolized. Then he settled back, his hands clenching, staring at Robert McCall with fury in his eyes. McCall noted that Emma Marshall had just walked into the bar, but she held back, watching the two men she knew so well.

"I could fly to North Korea without you," Kostmayer said, his words a little slurred.

"You could," McCall said, "but you won't. There has been too much history between us. You know I'm right."

"Go to hell, McCall," Kostmayer said, and slid off the barstool. He slammed out of Dead Rabbit bar, clattering down the stairs to the ground floor. Emma took his place.

"That didn't sound good," she said.

"It was the way I knew Mickey would react. I would have done the same thing in his place."

"Where can we talk?" Emma asked him.

McCall slid off the barstool and moved with Emma to one of the booths. She took an envelope out of her bag and slid across to him. Once again, their voices were lost in the overall ambiance of the place.

"From Control," she said. "New passport with papers to enter South Korea. Here is as much as we can give you on the aerial footage on North Korea. Some of these photographs will give you a broader picture of the terrain, but it is all pretty much the same. The drones we sent up have yielded some grainy shots, but none of them show a prison camp shrouded in the forest. The camp that Mickey Kostmayer escaped from must still be there, of course."

"He doesn't know where it is," McCall said. "He was disoriented and lost his way in the forest. NK patrols were searching for him. He does not know how he made it to the Yalu River at the Sino-Korean Friendship Bridge.

That prison could be five miles from that location or fifty miles. I can use the Sino-Korean Friendship Bridge as a landmark, but that's all."

"So, what are you going to do?"

McCall shrugged and smiled. "Improvise."

She put another envelope on the booth table. "This is more intel on your two contacts in South Korea. Kyu-Chul is still working at the American Embassy in Seoul. He knows you are coming, but he does not know when. Yo-Han is out of country right now, but he is expected to return tomorrow. By the way, they call him 'Harry'. Both of them hate the regime in North Korea, but that is no guarantee that they will help you. People have their own agendas. But there is a meeting arranged with them as soon as you can get there. That's as much as I've got for you." Emma glanced over to where Kostmayer disappeared down the steep stairs from the Dead Rabbit Grocery & Grog bar to the street. "Is Mickey going to be okay?"

"He will be," McCall said, "if I can come back with his friend alive and in relatively good condition."

"What are the chances of that?"

"Not good," McCall said.

Emma looked back at him. "Are *you* going to be all okay?"

"Ask me in five days."

Emma took McCall's hand in both of hers. "No point in my telling you that what you're contemplating here in madness?"

"No."

She leaned over and kissed him gently on the lips. When she broke from him, she said softly: "Take care of yourself, Robert. You are very precious to me. You saved my life in that pub in London. I won't forget that."

She slid out of the booth and was swallowed up by the crowd. McCall glanced up at the television above the bar. The Knicks-Piston's game was over. The Piston's had won by a score of 107-101. Tim Hardaway Jr. for the Knicks had scored 37 points, one rebound and one assist. A valiant effort, McCall thought. He finished his Glenfiddich 21, slid out of the booth and headed down the stairs of the Dead Rabbit bar to the street.

He hoped that his Korean grocer had something for him.

If not, then he was hoping for a miracle.

Granny had emerged from the debris around the manhole cover below the first watchtower careful to not be seen. He narrowly missed a patrol of North Korean guards who would have crossed their path if Granny had not pulled Walter Coburn back underground and heaved the manhole cover over their heads. They waited five minutes before they ventured out again. They came around the rubble-strewn area, timing the sweep of the searchlights from the two remaining watchtowers. They ran in the darkness to where the large main huts were constructed. Granny climbed fast onto the wooden porch and threw open the door for them.

As soon as entered the hut, he knew something was wrong.

Deva Montgomery was at one of the cots, with Fredrik Jorgensen and Daniel Blake, the new AP correspondent whom Granny had met briefly before he and Walter Coburn had left under cover of darkness to get to the underground tunnels. They tended to stay together as one group for fear of reprisals.

Liz Montgomery was not with them.

Her sister Deva rushed over to Granny, distraught and shaking with fright. "They took Liz about an hour ago! Just dragged her out of here with two of the Korean guards. They took her to the Commandant Jang's hut. There was nothing any of us could do."

"We've been checking every few minutes for Liz to be returned," Jorgensen said.

"Stay here," Granny said. "All of you."

Walter Coburn offered to stay with them. Granny left the hut and jumped down the porch steps. He saw Liz Montgomery immediately. She was moving from Commandant Jang's two-story hut with some difficulty. He ran toward her. Two of the North Korean guards had opened the gate for her and closed it again. She stumbled before Granny caught up with her. She had been beaten. Angry purple welts and bruises were on her face, arms and presumably her legs. Her tunic had been ripped open, exposing her large breasts. Her left eye was almost closed. Her lip was swollen. She was soaking wet. Her dark hair was a rat's-nest that hung down her back and in her face. The four Korean guards watched Liz's progress but didn't impede it. Another set of guards were patrolling the perimeter of the compound watching them.

Granny steadied her. "I've got you!"

"I can walk," Liz said in a hoarse whisper.

"What did Jang do to you?"

"He let me live," she said, and tears flooded her eyes.

Granny knew what had happened. "Jang had you waterboarded."

"I am sure that was coming next. He stripped me and threw me to the ground of his hut. One of his guards threw a bucket of cold water over me. Then Jang held me down while the guards watched. He raped me repeatedly. Every time he pulled out of me he had one of his guards pour more freezing cold water over my body while the other guards held me down. Then Jang would enter me again. I did not struggle. It was like he had picked up a sopping little mouse from the floor and was playing with it. I was a dead thing. I felt nothing. Must have driven the fucker crazy. After about thirty minutes he got tired of me and motioned to the guards to let me go. My prison uniform was thrown at my feet. I put it back on and the two guards dragged me onto my feet. Jang just gestured to the door. I wanted to walk out of there without help. Jang let me. Not because he was concerned with my dignity, but because he wanted to see if I could make it through the hut door. I walked down the porch steps. His two guards came out behind me, but they did not follow. I made it as far as fifty yards before I could not stand anymore. That's when you got to me."

Granny looked instinctively behind them. Rage coursed through him. Myang-Sook-Jang stepped out on the wooden porch, shook out a du Maurier cigarette and blew out a cloud of smoke. Liz clutched Granny's arm to spin him around. He saw that Deva Montgomery and Walter Coburn were sprinting toward them. Behind them was Fredrik Jorgensen and Daniel Blake.

"Don't tell Deva what happened to me," Liz pleaded. "I was beaten by Jang's guards. Because I had no intel to give Jang. After half an hour he let me go. *Please*, Granny. It would destroy her."

Granny nodded. With trembling hands Liz buttoned up her prison tunic. The others had reached them at this point. Deva took one of Liz's arms and Coburn the other. Fredrik Jorgensen and Daniel Blake supported her.

"What did that monster do to you?" Deva asked her sister, her face as white as a sheet.

"I guess I don't respond well to assholes questioning me," Liz said, her voice still a rasping whisper. "I'm all right. I really am."

"Let us get you back to the hut," Fredrik Jorgensen said, very concerned.

Walter Coburn let them take Liz's weight as she walked. He looked at Granny and their eyes met. The contractor knew immediately what had happened to Liz. But he moved after the others. Granny turned back to Myang-Sook-Jang's quarters. The Commandant was watching him with a quizzical expression on his face. As if he excepted him to charge past the two North Korean guards and leap up onto the porch with his hands around Jang's throat. The look was meant to mock him.

"Don't worry, Commandant," Granny said, softly. "I am going to kill you."

Then he moved after the group reaching the main hut in the compound.

Myang-Sook-Jang watched him with dead, cold eyes.

► 6 ◄

MCCALL PARKED HIS Jaguar on Crosby Street a couple of blocks from Broome Street and walked back toward Greenwich Village. The convenience store was located on a corner that backed out to a narrow alleyway. The Asian owner and his wife would still be up. But when McCall turned down the street he saw that the shades were pulled down at the windows. It was late, after midnight. McCall thought the convenience store probably closed at eleven o'clock. He had wanted to get there right after it had closed but dealing with Mickey Kostmayer had delayed him. A padlock was on the front door and a sign said: *CLOSED*. He tried knocking on the glass, but there was no response.

McCall examined the padlock. It had been broken and left on the door. He pushed inside and found the convenience store shrouded in shadows. He paused to look at the alarm panel at one side of the door. It had been bypassed. He heard small sounds coming from upstairs where he knew the old Korean couple lived over the store.

McCall moved through the overlapping shadows to the back staircase. It was narrow, no carpet on it, one wooden handrail. McCall climbed up soundlessly. At the second floor there was a short corridor in darkness that led to a living room. The door was ajar. McCall could see a kitchen off another doorway. There was a door to a very small office space. Someone was searching it. More than one person. There was not a sound from the living room.

McCall moved right up to the ajar door. A young Korean gangbanger was pulling out drawers in a desk, dumping the contents onto the floor. He was dressed in gang colors, wearing sandals on his feet. His cheeks were sunken, his complexion sallow, a chicken neck protruding from his open shirt. His eyes were slits with no color to them. On the other side of the desk, a second gangbanger was throwing books and papers from a floor-to-ceiling bookcase onto the floor. He looked like a carbon-copy of the first hoodlum except he was marginally taller, wearing the same clothes, sandals on his feet, his eyes a dingy dishwater color. McCall had seen them before from when he had lived in the neighborhood. They were members of a Korean street gang called the *Yellow Death*. Cold, detached, emotionless.

McCall knew exactly what they had been looking for.

The first Korean gangbanger whirled. With no hesitation he leapt right across the desk, kicking out at McCall with lightning martial arts moves. McCall avoided the blows like they were landing in slow-motion, moving under them, then time speeded up again as he grabbed the youth around the throat and snapped his neck. The second gangbanger at the bookcases grabbed a pair of heavy-duty nickel-plated steel scissors from the desk and stabbed at McCall's eyes. McCall wrenched the scissors out of his hands. His hands wrapped around the gang-banger's throat. The youth pulled out a Schrade Viper 3 switchblade knife with a black handle which McCall might not have seen except he was looking at a grimy mirror hung on the office door. McCall disarmed the youth who was spitting at him in a frenzy. He broke McCall's stranglehold. He whirled to gouge his eyes out when Mc-Call brought him down to his knees and broke his neck. He dropped him down beside the other gang member. McCall heard a third assailant pelting down the narrow stairs. He ran to the open office door in time to see the other gang member, dressed in the same clothes, sandals on his feet, turning the corner on the stairs. McCall went after him, but when he reached the turn in the staircase the assailant had thrown open the door to the convenience store and run out into the street. He was carrying nothing with him. McCall did not think he had searched the office or the store as yet. He climbed quickly back up the staircase and ran down the short corridor into the living room.

Kung-Jae and his wife He-Ran were tied up in front of a leather armchair where a television was playing *Late Night with Stephen Colbert* with the sound muted. McCall turned off the flat-screen television and untied them. He helped up the old Korean woman into the armchair. She was defiant and did not want his help. The old Korean grocer looked at McCall.

"There were three of them," he said.

"The third one went down the stairs and ran out in the street," McCall said. "Did recognize them?"

The old Korean shrugged. "I have seen them in the neighborhood. They come in for sodas and ice cream bars. They are animals. I am glad you took care of them."

"I didn't have a choice."

McCall felt for He-Ran's pulse. It was weaker than it should have been, but she did not seem to be in any distress.

"They did not come here to harm us," Jerry said. "They were looking for maps they thought I had. They did not find them. I have been waiting for you, Mr. McCall." He turned back to his wife. "We have business to discuss."

He-Ran just nodded. The old Korean grocer moved out of the room. McCall put a gentle hand on the old woman's arm. "I am sorry this had to happen to you."

She nodded again. As if she had no interest in the conversation. She did not turn back on the television. She sat in the leather armchair which completely swallowed her up and stared out at nothing.

McCall walked down the short corridor, past the office door, which Jerry had closed. He climbed down the stairs. The convenience store was still in shadows. The old Korean grocer motioned for him to join him behind the counter. He had moved the lottery tickets to one side. There were several maps he had laid out for McCall to see. They were old and grainy. McCall could see the shape of North Korea on them.

"A friend of mine called me from Kanggye where I was born." Jerry said. "He still lives there. He sent them to me by fedex. I got them tonight. What are you looking for?"

"An old prison complex that was buried in the forests."

"There are several prison facilities listed here. Most of them are in the north provinces."

"I am looking for one in the southern region," McCall said. "Close to the Yalu River."

Jerry searched through more faded maps until he came to the one he was looking for. "Here, just outside Yonganp'on. Not far from Donggang across the Chinese border. You can see the outline of the Yalu River snaking through the forests." Jerry tapped it. "Right here. An old prison facility. It has been abandoned for years."

"How reliable is this map?"

The old grocer shrugged. "Who knows? Nothing much has changed there. The jungle may have reclaimed it."

"It's the closest thing to aerial drone footage that I've got, Jerry."

Before he could say anything more, the first fire-bomb smashed through the window of the convenience and exploded in a rage of heat. A second and a third Molotov cocktail were lobbed into the store and erupted into flames. McCall grabbed the old Korean grocer, pulled him out from the counter and propelled him toward the shattered front door.

"Get out! I'll get He-Ran."

Jerry staggered toward the door which was already buckling in the heat. McCall ran toward the back stairs. Thick black smoke was everywhere. Fire crawled up the stands of cookies and donuts and individual fruit pies. Shelves of bread and croissants were ignited. Another explosion rocked the interior as an old heater erupted, sending more flames shooting through the store.

McCall reached the narrow wooden staircase and ran up it. Two more Molotov cocktails exploded upstairs, one through the study window and one through a bedroom window. By the time McCall reached the living room it was blazing. He staggered through the dense smoke to where he had left the old Korean woman sitting in the leather armchair. She had passed out from smoke inhalation. McCall lifted her up in his arms and ran with her to the living room window. From there a skeletal fire-escape led down to the alley below. McCall reached up and heaved at the window.

It did not budge.

He heaved up one more time, but the window looked as if it had not been lifted since the Korean couple had moved in. McCall turned in the choking smoke, his eyes streaming. Black smoke filled the room. Furnishings were going up and pieces of the ceiling had started to come down. McCall laid the unconscious Asian woman back down on the armchair and picked up a heavy chair from a dining table. He was coughing as the smoke clawed at his lungs. He ran back and threw the chair at the window.

It bounced off.

McCall tried again.

This time the window smashed out.

McCall punched out the glass fragments that had splintered away, then ran back to the old Asian woman. He lifted her onto his shoulder in a fireman's lift. She was a husk. He did not think she could have weighed more than ninety pounds. He climbed through the shattered window and reached out for the edge of the fire-escape. He caught it, steadying He-Ran in his arms and stepped across the gap between the window and the fire escape. Still holding the fragile Asian woman on his shoulder, McCall went down the fire-escape to the ground floor. He pulled the skeletal ladder down and climbed the rest of the way to the street.

McCall came around the corner to see Kyung-Jae sanding outside his burning convenience store. Flames were shooting through the windows. The interior had been blackened and more smoke was pouring through it. McCall laid the old Asian woman down onto a square of coarse grass and made sure she was breathing. Neighbors had congregated on the sidewalk in their pajamas. The sound of the fire engines was getting closer, sirens wailing. Two of the neighbors rushed over to He-Ran and knelt beside her. Her husband turned to McCall.

"Go now. Before the EMT's and the fire department get here."

McCall looked at the conflagration that was engulfing the convenience store.

"This is on me," he said.

"I am been here long enough," Jerry said. "You have what you came here for?"

McCall felt in the inner pocket of his jacket for the folded maps he had taken from the old Korean man's counter. "I've got them. The firefighters and the police will find two charred bodies in your study."

"They were there to rob me. I did not see their faces. I managed to free myself and my wife and came down the stairs. We ran outside as the fire started. I hope you got what you needed, Mr. McCall."

He extended a limp hand and McCall took it. There was not time for anything more. McCall crossed the street just as the first fire engine pulled up. By the time he had run down to his Jaguar, the fire truck had been joined by two police cars and more were on their way. McCall jumped into his car and pulled away.

McCall would find a way to thank the old Korean couple.

Right now, they had given him hope.

Alexa Kokinas liked the bar she had found on the Lower East Side. It had wooden booths and a long mahogany bar with brass trimmings and bottles stacked up in front of a gilt mirror. The place was called *O'Grady's Saloon* and served pub-style food with the specials being traditional Irish Beef & Guinness Stew and Dublin Bay Prawn Bisque. It was always packed to the rafters, but inside Alexa's cone of silence the raucous ambience meant nothing. There were four pool tables laid out in the bar. Alexa was prowling around one of them with a cop from the 16th Precinct in Manhattan named Pete Hightower. He was a tough, no-nonsense Officer with a reputation for never cracking a smile, on or off-duty. Which suited Alexa Kokinas just fine. She was not looking for validation or for a buddy on the force.

She was also creaming his ass.

She had four shots lined up that were winners. She just had to give Hightower time to show her what a hot shot he was before she performed the coup de grass that sent him reeling. She had a cheering section around the table. Her biggest champion was a powerfully built, stocky cop named Frank Macamber, also from the 16th Precinct, a Detective First Grade who was the unofficial leader of the squad. They called themselves *The Elite*, a nickname they had had since they graduated from the Police Academy. Alexa thought it was an anomaly that the members of *The Elite* all had found themselves at the 16th Precinct in Manhattan as detectives. She figured some strings had been pulled, but it did not matter to her. She was a rookie cop. They had made her feel welcome at their precinct house. Frank Macamber was encouraging her to "put Hightower away", although she was not catching all of his banter because his voice came through only sporadically. She kept looking to see if his mouth was moving, and right now she had other things on her mind. Like how she was to humiliate Pete Hightower and beat him into submission.

Hightower missed his next shot. That sent up another cheer from the amassed police officers, although she really did not hear it, just the vibrations it sent up. Alexa took a hefty swig from the Corona bottle she had in one hand. She set it down, picked up her pool cue, came around the table, lined up her shots and just like that, the balls rocketed into the pockets. When the last one disappeared, she held up a clenched fist. Now there was no mistaking the cheer that went up from the patrons who had been following the game. Alexa held out her hand, palm up. Pete Hightower had a wry expression on his face.

"You sure you're not a pool hustler, patrolman?"

Frank Macamber moved over to him and pummeled him on the back. "She beat you until your eyes bled. Pay up, Hightower."

The Officer peeled off some dollar bills and dropped them into Alexa's hand. She felt another cheer go up. Macamber took Alexa's arm, still grinning, and propelled her through the tables toward the bar. She caught sight of a lanky, raw-boned cop she had not met yet, Jerry Kilpatrick, who was also a member of the *Elite*. He had just transferred from another precinct. He was a good-looking Police Officer with close-cropped blonde hair. Alexa thought he was watching Macamber with an intensity that she found momentarily unnerving. Then Jerry picked up a Samuel Adams Boston Ale by the bottle and moved to where Hightower was sitting at one of the booths. His fellow *Elite* cops were Tom Graves and Saul Cooper. Alexa could not remember the name of the last Police Officer, but she knew he was nicknamed "Moose" because of his size and weight. When Alexa reached the bar, Macamber remembered to turn fully around to her, which she appreciated.

"What can I get you?"

Alexa used a mixture of sign language and her own voice. "Corona. Bottle is good."

Macamber signaled to the bartender. "How are you adjusting to the precinct?"

"Fine."

The bartender brought over the Corona. Alexa picked it up, expertly flipped off the bottle cap and took a swig. Macamber glanced over at Pete Hightower who was deep in conversation with the other members of the squad, glancing a couple of times over at Alexa with unconcealed scorn.

"Don't pay any attention to Hightower," Macamber said. "He can be an asshole, but he's a good cop. You humiliated him in front of his guys and that won't sit well with him."

Alexa shrugged and took another swallow of the Corona. Macamber looked around the raucous bar. "Where's your partner? What is his name again?"

"Palmer."

"Yeah, right, I've seen him around the stationhouse. Good guy?"

"The best."

"It's important to trust your partner on the streets. He couldn't be here tonight?"

Alexa signed a little more frenetically, punctuating it with a few words: "Home problems. His wife. Going through a divorce."

"I think I got most of that!" Macamber said, grinning. "Your signing is too fast for me! But I will catch on if you give me the chance. It is really amazing what you have accomplished. You are the first patrolman who has ever been assigned to the NYPD. Are there other Peace Officers in the country like you?"

"Deputy Sheriff in Arizona," Alexa said.

"Is that right? So, just the two of you? Outstanding. How to do cope with the silence? The Lieutenant at the 16th Precinct said you can hear some sounds and speech."

Alexa waggled her hand, come se come sa. She indicated the booth where Jerry Kilpatrick and joined the *Elite* group of Pete Hightower, Tom Graves and Saul Cooper.

"Who is he?"

Macamber followed her gaze. "Jerry Kilpatrick. Transferred to the 16th Precinct about six months ago. Comes from a family of cops. The jury's still out on him. He does not fit in, but maybe he will come around. The other guys at the booth are Saul Cooper, been at the 16th the longest, a good guy, Tom Graves, I call him the *Rat Catcher* cause he knows where to find the rats that crawl out of the sewers, and the big one on the end is Detective Rabinski, we call him the 'Moose'. If you are a perp, you don't want to tangle with the 'Moose.'"

Alexa signed again, slowing her hand gestures significantly. "You all graduated from the Police Academy at the same time?"

"Yeah. It just worked out that way. All of us wanted to be assigned to the NYPD. I was the first on the squad, then Hightower and Saul Cooper got transferred to the 16th Precinct. Tom Graves, the *Rat Catcher*, had been a uniformed patrolman for four years, but then he got moved up to detective. Moose just got his promotion and his shield last week."

"The six of you are detectives?"

"That's right. I'm a Detective First Grade," Frank Macamber said. "Hightower is a Detective Second Grade and so is Saul Cooper and Tom Graves. Tell me, when you look around at this bar, what can you hear?"

Alexa shrugged. "Noise. Like white static."

Macamber nodded. "Okay, I got that! You can hear people when they are talking right at you. That is outstanding."

Alexa shrugged.

"If I have not said it before," Macamber said, "welcome to the 16th squad, Alexa."

She smiled and took another swig of the Corona. One of the patrons had racked up the balls on the pool table nearest to the bar. He called out to Alexa, but she could not hear him. Macamber gently touched Alexa's arm.

"Guy at the pool table wants to tango with you." Alexa turned and followed Macamber's gaze. The pool player, a heavyset, bearded guy, shouted at her. Macamber took a step forward. "Doesn't that asshole know you can't hear him?"

Alexa put a retraining hand on Macamber's arm. She signed for him. "Not everyone in here knows I am hearing impaired."

Macamber said: "I don't think this asshole knows who he's dealing with!"

Alexa grinned, stepped away from the bar and moved to the pool table, her Corona in her hand. In the noisy ambiance the bartender brought Macamber another Bud Light. He shouted: "You're going to have your balls handed back to you, buddy!"

Alexa put her beer on an empty table and picked up one of the pool cues.

At the back booth where the *Elite* were sitting, Detective Jerry Kilpatrick was watching Frank Macamber. Something in the way he was checking out Alexa Kokinas bothered him. He had been wary of the man ever since he had been introduced to him at the 16th Precinct.

Alexa broke apart the balls which skittered across the pool table.

Jerry Kilpatrick watched Frank Macamber gazing at Alexa Kokinas as he drank his Bud Light at the bar. His look to her was almost predatory.

▶ 7 ◄

WHEN CANDY ANNIE awakened it was to the sound of smashing plates and crockery. She pulled out of bed, wearing only a t-shirt, and padded to the door of the bedroom. It was a warm night and she usually kept the windows open. She opened the door. Kostmayer had opened cabinets in the kitchen and hurled the dishware onto the floor. He had smashed a bone-china plate with a rose pattern with gold trim that lay in porcelain splinters. Candy Annie was relieved that he had spared the western candle holders and the turquoise floral Wall Cross that hung on the wall. Kostmayer had given her that as a gift. But a San Juan Great Plains pottery table lamp had been smashed and a black fireplace tool set was strewn in front of the low coffee table.

Kostmayer stood at the window looking out onto Fifty-Fourth Street and Second Avenue. The traffic along the boulevard was reflected off his face. His rage and had been spent. He heard Candy Annie approach him. He wondered briefly what she was wearing to bed these days. It would not be much.

"Go back to bed, Annie," he said, quietly.

She loved that he called her "*Annie*" and not "*Candy Annie*". Tentatively she reached out and put her hand on his shoulder.

"What's happened?" she asked him.

"Nothing that concerns you."

"Everything you do concerns me."

She turned him around to face her. He had forgotten how strong she was. She looked into his face and saw the pain in his eyes. She had seen it there before. It had been there ever since he had returned from North Korea. He had left a comrade behind there, that much she knew. It had been eating away at him. She had wanted to reach out to him, but he had put a wall around his emotions. She had seen that happen in the world beneath the Manhattan streets. People kept to themselves. Whatever pain they had experienced that had caused them to dwell in the sub-world of the subway sewers they kept close. But Candy Annie had escaped from that suffering. She had been given a new lease on life. Because Robert McCall had taken a chance on her. It was time to give back.

Candy Annie took a step back from Kostmayer and pulled the t-shirt over her head. She let it fall to the hardwood floor. She moved naked into his arms and kissed him. There was the barest hesitation on Kostmayer's part, then he kissed her back. When they came up for air, he lifted her and carried her back into the bedroom. He set her down on the bed, all the while kissing her and caressing her body. Her kisses were the sweeting things he had even known. He pulled off his clothes and laid down beside her.

Candy Annie was transported to a world she had never known. It was raw and carnal, at the same time gentle and arousing. She had longed for these moments ever since she had known Kostmayer's gentle spirit. But when she awoke sometime later, shadows wreathed the room,

Kostmayer had gone.

It had been easy for Granny to find the armory in the prison camp. It was an older brick building set apart from the other corrugated huts with an iron door that was padlocked at all times. Two armed North Korea guards stood outside in three work shifts. Granny had watched two of the guards unlock the padlock on the doors and enter the armory at least twice during his incarceration. There was no way for anyone except the guards to gain access.

At least through the iron door.

Granny was working underground with Walter Coburn. Fredrick Jorgensen had apparently had a seizure in the prison yard brought on by an epilepsy attack. He had been carried into Commandant Jang's office while the guards had brought the doctor of the camp, such as he was. Jorgensen had only been left alone for a few minutes, his epilepsy attack faked, although he *did* suffer from a mild form of epilepsy. He had found the blueprint in a bottom drawer of the Commandant's desk. He had stuffed the blueprints into his shirt and was back on the oversized leather sofa when the so-called doctor came to see him. He protested that he was recovered now. The doctor allowed him to return to the main compound. Jorgensen had passed the blueprint to Granny and Walter Coburn. When night came, Granny and Coburn headed to the third watchtower, carefully timing the sweep of the searchlights there. When it had left them in blackness, they had scrabbled through the bricks and the pieces of sheet metal and accessed the manhole. They had climbed down the metal ladder and had lifted the manhole back into place. Their Hurricane Lamps had illuminated their way into the first black tunnel.

It had taken most of the night, but they had managed to build a crude scaffolding from scrap metal and discarded bricks up to a height of ten feet. It was a precarious affair, but it would do the job. Granny sat at one end of the makeshift platform and Coburn at the other, a foot separating them. They dug up into the earth roof of the tunnel. Again Granny felt like he was channeling Steve McQueen, whom he bore a striking resemblance to, digging one the tunnels below the Nazi prison camp in *The Great Escape*. Fredrik Jorgensen's stolen blueprint was only a rough guide, but Granny thought that the earthen floor was about two or three feet above their heads. The chances of them breaking through and climbing up into the armory into the waiting arms of the Korean prison guards were slim. But they would have to be quiet.

Granny looked above his head where the earth had crumbled around them. Maybe another two feet up. They did not have much time. Fredrik Jorgensen had heard the North Korean guards talking. They did not know he spoke Korean and so did Granny. The prison camp was going to be closed any day now and the prisoners would be moved to a new facility.

Granny did not believe any of the western prisoners would make it out alive.

Sam Kinney had built the Library Bar in the Liberty Belle Hotel in an annex off the main lobby. It had gilt fixtures with rose panels where the bottles were stacked. There were floor-to-ceiling bookshelves on either side of the marble bar with leather-bound books. Classic editions, including *Charles Dickens, Lord Jim, War and Peace, Don Quixote, Faust, The Three Musketeers* and *Moby Dick.* Robert McCall approved of the annex's collection. He had been meaning to starting his own library of classics, but something always happened to delay that. Usually when an assassin came at him with a gun. He suspected Sam Kinney had slipped a couple of thrillers on the shelves: Tom Clancy and Lee Child and James Rollins. Deep leather armchairs were placed in front of the bar. A fire roared constantly in the brick fireplace. Chloe was the bartender tonight, mixing cocktails the way Sam taught her, serving the few patrons who ventured in. She was in the uniform of the Liberty Belle Hotel with its name stitched on the breast pocket. Sam Kinney kept the Library Bar as one of his little secrets. For old spymasters like himself. He looked older to McCall these days, his hair getting greyer, his hands shaking ever so slightly. McCall had thought it was an affectation, but the palsy had worsened in the time he had been staying at the hotel. Sam was drinking a brandy sifter of Armagnac, plum brandy, sweet vermouth and a dash of black Strap Rum. McCall sipped at a Glenfiddich scotch.

"I heard from Brahms in Jerusalem," Sam was saying. "Did you know the city was besieged twenty-three times and captured and recaptured forty-four times since the days of the Canaanites? I think Brahms was there during all of that time," he added, dryly. "He did all the tourist things like visiting the Wailing Wall, the Old City, the Church of the Holy Sepulcher in Bethlehem. Then he took the cable car over the Snake path where King Herod built his palaces and visited the caves at Qumran where the two-thousand-year old Dead Seas Scrolls were discovered. But long do you have to stay in the Holy Land before the weight of history makes you crazy?"

"He's missing Helga," McCall said.

"Sure he is. We all miss her. She centered Brahms. She was his muse. Now it is time for him to come back and rejoin the living. Too much antiquity and grieving are not good for his soul."

"I think Brahms' soul is doing just fine," McCall said, wryly.

"Which is more than be said for mine, tarnished as it may be," Sam said. "I hear that Isaac Warnowski is going to be indicted in court Monday for setting that apartment fire and nearly killing everyone in there. We still got Norman Rosemont here, holding court with his apartment pals, the Weinbergers, nice folks, Miguel Vasquez, Linda Hathaway and her rugrat Gemma. I detected a romance brewing between Linda and Norman. I think there are going to move out to another hotel pretty soon, closer to Norman's office building. More customers I will lose to the Plaza."

"I'm just glad you're all okay."

"Warnowski was one sick puppy."

McCall took another sip of the Glenfiddich and waited.

"You're going to North Korea," Sam said.

"What gave you that idea?"

"An old Spook's instincts. And Kostmayer was here looking for you at the hotel. I sent him over to the Dead Rabbit Grocery & Grog in the Financial District. He probably wanted to tag along."

"He did."

"You told him no?"

"I did."

"I'm told it's a suicide mission," the old spy said. "Might have been good to have a backup with you."

'Not this time."

"No way I can stalk you out of this?"

McCall just smiled. Sam Kinney nodded as if the weight of the world was on his shoulders. "Do you have a plan?"

"I won't know until I get there."

"In that case, I'll drink to that."

Sam finished off his sweet cocktail.

Jimmy Murphy entered the Library Bar. He was a slight man, tipping the scales at five-ten, green eyes in a sharp face. He was wearing a dark green track suit and orange Nikes. He had long since retired from the covert spy organization known as the *Company* at the insistence of his wife Sarah who had not wanted to identify him in some back alley in Chetna or Berlin where he had been found shot to death. Enough already! Jimmy had gone into the security business and was doing very well from it. He ran—well, truth be told, he jogged—every day, came home to a loving wife and two precious children and did not miss the cloak-and-dagger traumas in the slightest.

But that did not include Robert McCall.

Jimmy had known McCall for years at the *Company* and after that he had resigned and gone off the radar. But Jimmy had known that would not last. He knew people would seek him out because he helped people. That was just the way it was. When McCall called him to do a job for him, Jimmy never refused. Robert McCall had saved Jimmy's life at least three times while he was a spook for the Spy Organization. McCall had got out after that, and so had Jimmy, but he was always there for Robert McCall. It was an unwritten law in Jimmy's mind. His wife Sarah did not like it, and she was always worrying that McCall would still find a way to get her husband killed, but that had not happened yet. McCall had also declined Sarah's many invitations to come over to their house in Brooklyn for dinner. Secretly, Sarah was glad. It was dangerous just knowing Robert McCall and she did not want Jimmy pulled back into his old way of life. She had long ago stopped arguing with her husband about this association that he would not let go. In the end she just told her husband to be careful.

She knew that Robert McCall had his back.

Sam Kinney was fond of Jimmy, but he knew he would not be visiting the Liberty Bar here in the hotel unless he was here to see Robert McCall.

"What brings you out of the shadows, Jimmy?" Sam asked him. "This isn't your usual jogging route."

"I sometimes go home to my wife and children, Sam," Jimmy said, dryly. "You might try it sometime."

"Twice married, twice divorced," Sam Kinney murmured. "But give Sarah my love."

Jimmy nodded. "I'll do that."

McCall could feel his tension in the bar. He finished off his glass of Glenfiddich. "What's happened?"

Jimmy looked at him and sighed. "Mickey Kostmayer is in trouble."

Jimmy pulled his Lexus up to a one-story biker bar in Prospect Heights. A neon sign above the two glass-fronted doors said: *HOG HEAVEN*. There were at least two dozen Harley-Davidson motorcycles and some Buells parked outside. Loud music echoed from inside. McCall got out with Jimmy and moved to the front door.

"Going anywhere with you is an adventure, McCall," Jimmy remarked.

McCall did not respond. He was anxious to make this trip to North Korea and did not have the time to make a pit stop in Brooklyn to nursemaid Mickey Kostmayer.

He opened the door and was greeted with a cacophony of sound. A jukebox was playing old 50's hits at ear-splitting levels. Some bikers were crowded inside wearing their signature insignias of a skull on a white background with the name *Hell's Angels* on their jackets. Above the bar there was a painting of a demon holding a pitchfork with white horns and wings crouched over three skulls of fire with the words: *New York City* at the bottom. Another sign in black and white said: *God Forgives, Outlaws Don't.* The numbers "81" were placed at intervals. The bikers were sitting at tables and booths or shooting pool. A biker with sleeves rolled up her arms and myriad tattoos was dispensing drinks at the bar as fast she could make them. Cigarette smoke hazed through the interior.

Kostmayer was standing at one of the pool tables, making a tricky shot, taunting a group of Hell's Angels who had moved from one of the tables. McCall could see he was pretty drunk and spoiling for a fight. McCall turned to Jimmy.

"Stay outside," he advised.

He moved further into the bar. Jimmy did not retreat, but he gauged the distance McCall would have to travel with Kostmayer to get to the front door. A biker chick turned from the bar as McCall passed her, drinking an Anchor Brewery Steam Beer. She was clad in black and red leather with a ring through her nose and diamond studs embedded in her face in several places. Her breasts spilled almost out of the leather shirt she was wearing. Her long red hair was splayed down her back. She caught McCall's eye and obviously liked from she saw. She toasted him with the bottle.

McCall kept going until he was at Kostmayer's pool table. The *Company* agent still held onto his pool cue, but it was more like a weapon now in his hands. McCall could not hear what he had said to the four Hells Angels who surrounded him, but it was already too late. Kostmayer had thrown the first punch. One of the bikers, a monster in leather, staggered back. McCall caught Kostmayer's arm in a vice-like grip.

"Time to go, Mickey."

But the other three Hells Angels who had been crowding Kostmayer now turned their attention to McCall. One of them lunged. McCall avoided the blow and brought the biker to his knees. The second biker threw a punch that connected with McCall's jaw, sending him into the pool tables. The third biker grabbed McCall's leather coat, but at that point Jimmy got into the fray with a couple of shots to the third biker's solar plexus. McCall blocked the second biker's fist, picked him up and hurled him over his shoulder, slamming him onto the pool table. His opponent missed his shot and the balls careened around the table. Another of the Hells Angels slammed a fist into Kostmayer's face that would have brought him down if McCall had not been holding onto him. McCall kicked out the legs out of the bruiser, who outweighed Kostmayer by two hundred pounds. Kostmayer went slack in McCall's arms as he dragged him away from the action toward the front door.

The fight had reached into the bar area where the bikers were throwing punches with no idea who they were fighting with. The Bartender came over the bar hefting a baseball bat and wielded it with some precision. She had obviously broken up frights in this bar before. McCall turned in the melee to see that Jimmy was heading toward the front door.

A massive biker came at McCall with murderous intent.

The gorgeous redhead at the bar swung a bottle at his head. It connected and sent him down to the sawdust floor. McCall had noted her long raven hair, the ring in her nose and the studs that were etched on both sides of her face.

"Thanks."

The babe grinned. "Just another quiet night at Hog Heaven."

McCall crumpled up some bills and dropped them onto the bar. The redhead leaned closer to him, whispering: "You better get your friend out of before he gets hurt."

"Good thinking," he said.

McCall hauled Kostmayer over his shoulder as if he was a sack of potatoes. The redhead staggered against him and McCall steadied her. "You all right?"

"I'm doing fine and dandy. When your friend sobers up, come back and buy me a drink."

"It will have to be another night."

"Sure." She smiled at him. "It's a date."

McCall carried Kostmayer over his shoulder through the brawl to where Jimmy had the bar door open. Jimmy's antagonists had lost interest in him and had turned their attention to some other bikers who used this excuse to break a few heads. McCall carried Kostmayer through the open doorway and Jimmy slammed it shut behind them. McCall dropped a barely conscious Kostmayer onto the back seat of Jimmy's Lexus and climbed in. Jimmy slid behind the wheel, fired it up and hauled ass out of there.

Inside *Hog Heaven* the fight stopped as quickly as he had started. A couples of the Hells Angels picked up some chairs. The players at the pool tables resumed their games. The Bartender deftly hauled herself back over the bar and dropped the baseball bat at her feet. Business as usual. The redheaded biker had rescued her Anchor Beer from the bar, toasted McCall's memory and took a swallow.

McCall gently dropped Kostmayer onto the couch in his Manhattan apartment. He had come to briefly in Jimmy's Lexus, but then had passed out again. Candy Annie had hurriedly put on some clothes when she heard Kostmayer's key in the lock. Which meant she was wearing panties and a *Buffy The Vampire Slayer* T-shirt two sizes too small for her. Jimmy lingered in the doorway, a little embarrassed by Candy Annie's state of undress. Candy Annie knelt down solicitously beside Kostmayer. Her expression was a mixture of exasperation and concern.

"What happened, Mr. McCall?"

"He got into a fight."

"Where?"

"It's not important. He is banged up, but he will live. Let him sleep it off."

Jimmy cleared his throat. "Okay if I go home now, McCall? I want to rehearse my story for Sarah when she finds out I have been brawling in a biker bar in Brooklyn."

"Blame it on me."

"That thought had occurred to me. At the hotel, Sam told me you were planning a trip to sunny North Korea?"

"Need to know, Jimmy."

"I don't need to know. But I don't like it and neither does Sam."

"Thanks for your help, Jimmy."

"I live to please. Take care of yourself, McCall." He turned to Candy Annie. "I didn't get your name?"

Candy Annie straightened. It was only then that she glanced down at herself and realized that she was wearing practically no clothes. She blushed. "It's Candy Annie."

"Nice to meet you," Jimmy said. "Don't be too hard on Kostmayer. He's been through a lot."

Jimmie closed the apartment door. Candy Annie glanced back down at Kostmayer, who was sleeping. She gripped McCall's arm. "Please let me know what is going on with Mickey."

"You know what Mickey does for a living."

"I do. It sounds very dangerous."

"It can be. He left a friend behind in enemy territory."

Candy Annie nodded, as if McCall had lifted a great weight off her shoulders. "You will bring Mickey's friend back, Mr. McCall. I know you will." She looked back down at Kostmayer. "I will look after him until you return."

There was no doubt in McCall's mind that the girl loved him with all of her heart.

"I know you will, Candy Annie," he told her, gently.

He gave her a kiss on the cheek and let himself out of the apartment.

The redheaded biker let herself into her apartment in SoHo which was about the size of a closet she had once rented when she had lived in Washington D.C. A bed, a table and an unravelling cane chair, a kitchen counter, a bathroom. She unpinned her hair and shook off the red wig and dropped it onto the bed. She stripped off her leather outfit, stepped naked out of it and just let it fall to the floor. It had served its purpose. She moved into the kitchen and lifted a brandy glass filled to the brim with Hennessy XO Cognac and walked to the narrow window that overlooked the street six floors below. She savored the raw sensation of the brandy. It had been worth the wait of many days. She knew that eventually McCall would follow Mickey Kostmayer out to *Hog Heaven*. It had been a favorite haunt of his for years. It all been a ruse to get McCall there. She cast her mind back to the bar. McCall had practically stumbled into her in the midst of the melee. It had given her the perfect opportunity to plant the tracking device on him. He had not even felt it when the tiny blade had severed his skin. She took another swallow of the brandy and walked to where the neon splashed across the window. She picked up her cell phone from the decarded leather and tapped out a number. When the man answered she had said five words.

The first words were: *Memento Mori.*

Her next words were: "It is done."

She hung up the cell phone and fished out the small receiver out of her leather jacket. She pressed a button and the little receiver turned on.

She would have no trouble tracking Robert McCall wherever he went.

▶ 8 ◀

IN THE NORTH KOREAN prison compound, below in the tunnels, Granny and Walter Coburn finally broke through the floorboard at the bottom of the armory. Granny removed two of the wooden floorboards and handed them down to Coburn. The hole they had dug was wide enough for one person to climb up. Granny left Coburn on the wood platform they had built and pulled himself into the armory. He reached down and Coburn handed him the black LED Hanging Hurricane Lamp. He set it down on the floor of the corrugated hut and hit the Dimmer Switch to low, so that it barely illuminated the small hut. Then he waited for a sign that one of the North Korean guards had unlocked the iron hut. He heard nothing. It would be a chance occurrence that one of them would decide to check on the armory at that moment which was virtually the middle of the night. Nor would they see the wan light that the Hurricane Lamp generated unless they opened the door. But Granny gave it another five minutes.

There was no sound outside the hut.

Granny got up and moved to the steel shelving and he found what he was looking for: explosives, nitroglycerin and powdered shells of clay and stabilizers. He knelt down and had Coburn hand him up a crowbar they had been working with. He pulled a crate from the bottom of the steel shelves and broke it open. Inside, dynamite sticks had been placed in sealed plastic bags. On the next shelf were boxes of C4 explosives. He lifted the top off the box. The C4 explosives were composed of explosives, plastic binder, plasticizer to make them more malleable and odorizing taggant chemicals. They were stored in the form of modelling clay. Granny found sixteen of the malleable clay in the box. They were insensitive to most shocks. They could not be denotated by a gunshot or by dropping them onto a hard surface.

Granny dragged the crate of C4 explosives over to the hole they had made in the floor. He signaled Coburn. One by one, Granny passed the C4 explosives down to the contractor until the crate was empty. Granny shoved the empty crate underneath the shelving and dragged the box of sealed bags of dynamite sticks with wire and fuses and detonators over to the hole in the wooden flooring. He passed that down to Coburn. Carefully. One sealed bag at a time. When he had passed the last bag down, he slid the empty box onto the steel shelves.

He heard sound of footsteps outside.

Keys jangling.

Two North Korean guards talking,

Granny grabbed the black LED Hurricane Lamp and handed it back down to Coburn. Granny forced himself down through the jagged opening.

The door the armory was unlocked.

Granny fitted the wooden floorboard back in place. Coburn steadied him on the makeshift scaffolding. Neither of them moved or breathed. Up in the armory they heard the sound of the guards moving through to the shelving. Granny could see them in his mind's eye. They would give the small, corrugated hut a cursory glance to make sure that nothing was out of place. After a few seconds they moved back to the armory door. The heavy keys jangled in the lock, the door was closed and the padlock outside was locked.

Granny figured it would take him and Coburn an hour to get the explosives into the tunnel at the ladder. They would have to be very careful hauling them up into the prison camp.

They did not have much time.

Hayden Vallance landed the Bombardier Global 6000 Vista 9H-VJJ jet at the Iljin Airfield in Seoul, South Korea. The mercenary had flown McCall there at night, taxiing to a break in the fence where a Hyundai Genesis V8 sedan was waiting for him.

"The airfield will be deserted at this time of the night," Hayden said. "Iljin Airfield has a pilot training course located here, certified by South Korea's Ministry of Land Transport and Maritime Affairs. They also operate two CE-56 and two CE-525 aircraft here and a CTN-11 simulator. I took the course once. Pretty impressive."

McCall was carrying a lightweight backpack with him. As usual, Hayden Vallance had not asked McCall why he needed to go to South Korea, but he was pretty sure McCall's final destination was somewhere in North Korea. How he would get there, Vallance did not know or particularity care. He lowered the steps on the Global 6000 Vista Jet. Control would have provided everything McCall would need, but, maybe from force of habit, Vallance said: "You've got a first-aid kit, a timetable of the trains in South Korea, not that you'll need them, a radio, a trauma kit with a small amount of pain drugs, including Toradol and a small amount of morphine with a IV drip and anti-nausea meditation. Which will not do you much good if you are picked up by a NK patrol and thrown into of their prisons. You have a Canadian passport and a Bulgarian Makarov 9-by-18 MAK semi pistol and a pair of EES Profile NVG Foliage Green binoculars, three-times magnification. Everything the well-prepared tourist would need. You know how you're going to get into North Korea?"

"I have a meeting in Seoul with two mercenaries who will get me there."

"Have you met them before?"

"First time."

"You're taking a chance they have been compromised," Vallance said, "but you already know that. The intel I got from Kostmayer was that Granny was dead. He was taken out into the woods around the prison camp and left there with a bullet in his brain."

"Kostmayer went through an ordeal to escape," McCall said. "His recollection may be suspect."

"He wants Granny to be alive. But that may be wishful thinking on his part."

"I have to go there to be sure."

"If you find him, tell from me not to get caught this time."

McCall smiled. "I'll be sure to pass that massage on to him."

"What was your Control thinking sending you on a suicide mission like this?"

"I didn't give him much choice."

"I figured." Vallance held out his hand. "Good luck, McCall."

McCall nodded. He climbed down the Global Vista jet stairs and jogged to the break in the chain-link fence. He found the keys where Control had said he would find them, under the right-wheel of the Hyundai, and slid inside. When he turned his head the Vista jet was already taxing down the runway and was up in the air.

Hayden Vallance was not one for long goodbyes.

McCall fired up the Hyundai and drove it through the trees down the airport road.

When he got to Seoul he ditched the Hyundai and took a subway train to Hapjeong where he took the first right from the exit down a side road, walked down it about two meters, turned northwest and walked down the street for another 90 meters until he came to the *Get & Show Lego Café*. It featured a huge *Giant Lego Man* in a red shirt on the storefront. McCall pushed into the café where young people were sitting at tables strewn with pieces of various Lego sets. A counter served up teas and cakes. Lego sets were displayed on plastic shelves that ran the whole length of the café. There was a huge Lego street on one counter with stores and restaurants rising three stories topped off with a clock tower. McCall walked up some stairs to a second balcony in the café where more young people were drinking tea and devouring various cupcakes. South Korean waitresses moved down the tables with more pieces of the Lego puzzles to be handed out to the players. The café had a festive atmosphere that McCall would have found charming in other circumstances.

He found Kyu-Chul and Yo-Han seated at one of the tables overlooking the street. Kyu-Chal was a dour, laconic South Korean man about thirty-five, six foot, with sallow features and heavy-lidded brown eyes. He was eating a *Patbing* pastry with milky shaved ice topped with red beans and fruit and was drinking honey Pomegranate tea in a plain mug. His companion, Yo-Han, looked like a Korean version of *Howie Doody* with myriad freckles on his face and green eyes. He was about thirty with an engaging personality and a kind of manic effervescent that was infectious. He was sipping an Ethiopia Kochare coffee and eating a carrot-layer cake with nutmeg and cinnamon topped by cream cheese. Beside him on the table was a partially completed Star Wars Millennium Falcon with intricate exterior detailing, upper and lower quad laser canons, landing legs, four mini cockpit figures with a detachable canopy and a highly detailed main hold and gunnery station. It was manned by Han Solo, Rey, Finn and BB-B, and included Han's blaster pistol and Chewbacca's stud-firing bow caster. Kyu-Chal gestured to McCall to join them.

When he did, Yo-Han glanced up with a grin and said: "Mr. McCall, right? The description fits. That's Kyu-Chal sitting beside you. He is not much on small talk, but he will have your back. I am Yo-Han, but everyone calls me 'Harry'. I am finishing off a Star Wars First Order Heavy Assault Walker to be used against Poe, Rey and the Resistance allies. I was just dropping in head-mounted spring-loaded-shooters. I can drop in mines from the back. Should finish it in about an hour. Then I get a free Sabayon Caramel Roll. Just delicious."

He went back to his Heavy Assault Walker Lego that was slowly taking shape. McCall looked around the tables on the second-floor balcony. "Can we talk here?"

"The decibel level in here would drown out a Black Sabbath concert," Harry said, wryly. "Three dudes talking about Star Wars and making Lego's? No one will be giving a rat's ass about our conversation."

Both of the mercenaries glanced up from time to time, however, to make sure no one was overhearing them. McCall opened his backpack and removed two SanDisk Cruzer Glide USB flash-drives wrapped in plastic. He handed the first one to Kyu-Chal.

"One-hundred-thousand dollars will be transferred to your personal account at the Shinhan Financial Group bank here in Seoul." He handed the other flash-drive Yo-Han. "One-hundred-thousand dollars will be transferred to your personal account at the Woori Bank here in Seoul."

Kyu-Chal pocketed his flash drive. Harry barely glanced at his flash drive before stuffing it in his jeans pocket and making some minor adjustments to the Star Wars Heavy Assault Walker Lego he was constructing. Kyu-Chal looked at McCall.

"What did you bring for us?"

McCall unfolded one of the maps from his backpack. Harry grudgingly made room for it among the debris of his Lego game and spread it out on the table. Kyu-Chal looked the map of North Korea closely.

"Where did you get this?"

"An old Korean grocer friend of mine in New York City gave it to me," McCall said. "The prison facility is an old one. The North Korean prisoners were moved there when their location had been compromised and overrun."

"We heard about that," Harry said, his Lego pieces momentarily forgotten. "Some kind of a clandestine un-sanctioned raid. I heard that a hundred prisoners were ferried across the Chinese border on four Chinese AVIC AC391 helicopters. Awesome!"

"The survivors won't last long," Kyu-Chal said. "I know the Commandant of this prison camp. He has moved the prisoners, including some journalists, into a new prison camp."

"Well, not exactly *new*," Yo-Han said, his infectious grin flashing. "Falling apart is more like it."

"The prison camp in an old one," Kyu-Chal conceded, "buried in the forest. The Commandant's name is Myang-Sook-Jang."

"You forgot the best part," Harry said, fitting together more Lego puzzle pieces.

Kyu-Chal said: "Myang-Sook-Jang is a sociopath and a serial rapist."

Harry was still grinning. "I love that part." He looked up. "You never told me how your paths had crossed?" Kyu-Chal just looked at him. Harry grinned. "Kyu-Chal doesn't say much. Still waters run deep. But he would like to slit that motherfucker's throat if he got into that prison camp." He shrugged. "Just a guess."

Kyu-Chal looked back at McCall. The North Korean maps were still spread on the table. The mercenary tapped one of them. "You believe that the new prison camp is located here just outside Yonganp'on?"

"That's where my Korean grocer friend said it was located," McCall said. "You can see the Yalu River marked here snaking through the forest. The prison camp is right outside it."

"How reliable is this map?" Yo-Han asked, dubiously. "The jungle might have swallowed it whole."

"My friend thinks it's still there," McCall said. "But it could be abandoned at any moment."

"How many North Korean prisoners are in the camp now?" Kyu-Chal asked.

"Maybe fifty, but that number is suspect. It may be more."

"How many Westerners are in the camp?"

'I'd say from the intel I have received maybe a half-a-dozen," McCall said.

"Including this covert agent you call Granny?" the mercenary asked.

"That's right."

"Bitchin' name!" Harry said. "What's his real name?"

"Need to know," McCall said.

"He may not still be alive." Kyu-Chal objected. "If he led the clandestine raid on the NK prison facility, and once the prisoners were moved to a new camp, Myang-Sook-Jang would have taken your colleague into the woods and executed him."

McCall took out his cell phone, tapped the buttons on it and turned it around so the two mercenaries could see the screen.

Odds against me. Still in NK. Come and get me and others. Granny.

"That means nothing," Kyu-Chal said. "Commandant Jang could have used the cell phone to lure you into a trap."

"He doesn't even know that I exist."

"But your spy organization might have sent someone to rescue him."

"They wouldn't do that," Harry objected. "Too dangerous. A covert spy would have to take his chances. The American Government would leave him there to rot in the jungle."

"But *I* wouldn't," McCall said.

A silence followed that.

Kyu-Chal said: "Tell me about the other Western prisoners that are being incarcerated in this camp?"

McCall took some photographs out of his backpack and spread them out on the table, making a space in the Lego clutter. "This is drone footage we managed to obtain in Washington D.C. There is no way to verify that these prisoners are still at the prison camp with Granny. Liz Montgomery is a photojournalist working mostly for the New York Times. Walter Coburn is a South African contractor. Fredrik Jorgensen is an industrialist and Daniel Blake worked for Associated Press before he was captured on North Korean soil." McCall slid another picture in front of the mercenaries. "This a picture of Liz Montgomery's sister, Deva, a real estate broker working on Fifth Avenue in Manhattan in New York City. She had been visiting her sister in Seoul. She came on a joyride with Liz Montgomery who had been taking covert photographs for the New York Times. Their plane got shot down. My intel says both sisters are together now in this North Korean prison camp, but I can't be sure of that."

Yo-Han suddenly looked grim. "Both sisters are American, beautiful and vulnerable. How long will it be before Myang-Sook-Jang rapes them both?"

"We can't do anything about what has happened to them in the prison camp," McCall said, somewhat curtly. "We need to rescue them before they're killed."

"Are you sure these are odds you can equalize?" Harry asked. McCall looked at him. Harry shrugged. "Read your ad online. Bitchin' concept. But we are we are not in the mean streets of New York here. This is South Korea and your altruistic ideals could get you killed."

Kyu-Chal said: "Shut up, Harry. Mr. McCall came here on a mission. We're a part of it unless you want to back out."

Yo-Han looked chastised. "I would never do that, bro. You have a history with the Commandant of this prison camp. But I am with you. Always." He looked back at McCall. "The money you're paying us buys a lot of loyalty and a lot of respect. I can see you are a man of honor."

Kyu-Chal turned the North Korean map around. "And the prison facility is not far from Pongang across the Chinese border?"

"That's the intel I got from my grocer friend in New York."

"Which could be highly biased," Harry pointed out.

Kyu-Chal looked up at him. "Once we had those flash drives in our hands, we were committed. Are you in, or not?"

"How badly does Commandant Jang want to cut your balls off and roll them into the jungle?"

"We left on bad terms," Kyu-Chal admitted, irony in his voice.

Harry shrugged. "Then I'm in." He looked at McCall. "When do you want to fly out?"

"Tonight. You'll need to steal a helicopter."

Kyu-Chal folded up the North Korean map and put it into his backpack. "That won't be a problem."

Harry flashed what McCall thought of now as his signature grin. "Perfect."

▶ 9 ◀

GRANNY SAT THE ROUGH-HEWN table in their hut with the blueprints that Fredrik Jorgensen had stolen from Myang-Sook-Jang's office spread out before him. Walter Coburn sat with him. Liz Montgomery was the lockout at the window that overlooked the compound. Granny had thought it was better for the Western prisoners not to be seen huddled in their hut. Jang was paranoid that they were conspiring against him. Liz watched as Fredrick Jorgensen chatted with some of the North Korean prisoners near the main gate. Her sister Deva was sitting on the porch outside the hut on the top step with Daniel Blake, the reporter for Associated Press who had been incarcerated a few days before. Liz would make a sign if Myang-Sook-Jang emerged from his office hut or if any of the North Korean guards made a sudden move toward their hut. Granny himself had just come back through the main gate with some of the North Korean prisoners. They had been chopping down Dogwood and Korean Evodia trees to clear some roads that were impassable. Granny liked some of the Korean prisoners he worked with under the watchful eyes of the North Korean guards, but he could not acknowledge them. No one knew he spoke fluent Korean except Fredrik Jorgensen. Liz looked back at Granny who was in deep conversation with Walter Coburn. She remembered the kiss they had shared, tender, almost chaste, but it stirred in her feelings she had thought were long forgotten. She wanted the promise of that kiss, but not in these circumstances. When they escaped from this awful place.

Which Granny told her was going to happen *that night.*

Liz looked back out of the window and saw there was a small commotion among the prisoners. A helicopter was descending into the prison camp, its rotors whirling, creating a downdraft as it landed.

Liz said: "You should see this, Granny."

Granny looked up from the blueprints, instantly on guard. "Guards on their way to the hut?"

"No. We've got a visitor."

Granny rose and moved to the window beside Liz. Outside, the chopper was coming to a stop in the compound. He saw it was a MD-500 helicopter with North Korean markings. It would have a Hug 30-mm Hughes Chain Gun, four Tow missiles and probably Stringer missiles as well.

"Well, what have we got here?" Granny murmured. To Liz he said: "Stay inside."

Granny opened the hut door and stepped out onto the wooden porch. Deva and Daniel Blake had already moved off the steps into the compound for a closer look. Granny jumped down the porch steps to join them. He noted Fredrik Jorgensen had broken away from his group and was looking at the chopper. Granny saw Myang-Sook-Jang emerge from his hut and walk briskly toward the helicopter as if he were expecting his visitor.

A commanding Korean figure stepped out from the helicopter. He was tall, maybe six-foot-one, dressed in civilian clothes, in a trench coat, gray trousers and high boots. He had high cheekbones and a sallow complexion. Granny recognized him from a mission he had taken when he was still with the *Company*. The man's name was Ji-Yeon, a one-time enforcer with Al-Qaeda who still had ties to the terrorist group. Granny understood that affiliation was carefully disguised now. Ji-Yeon had a high profile with several NATO countries as an expert negotiator with terrorists. He was urbane and deadly. Granny watched as Myang-Sook-Jang and Ji-Yeon met up and shook hands. They walked through the compound. The North Korean prisoners who had been milling in the compound dissipated at the sight of the Commandant. But Ji-Yeon suddenly stopped. He was looking at Deva Montgomery intently. Myang-Sook-Jang followed his gaze with mild interest. He said something that Granny could not hear. Jang made an off-hand gesture to two of his guards who had accompanied him from his hut. They moved forward and grabbed Deva before she could even move. Daniel tried to free her from their grasp, but two more guards ran forward and clubbed the journalist to his knees.

The door to the small hut flew open and Liz Montgomery ran down the wooden steps into the compound. The first two North Korean guards continued to manhandle Deva toward Jang's quarters. Ji-Yeon watched dispassionately as Liz ran toward her sister. Granny grabbed her and held her tightly. His voice was low.

"If you go after her, they'll kill her. There is nothing you can do. Jang is catering to his guest. He won't interfere."

Liz's voice was hoarse as she struggled in Granny's arms, but she allowed him to subdue her. "Who the hell is he?"

"His name's is Ji-Yeon. He is a mercenary I tangled with a long time ago. A dangerous man. Working with NATO the last I heard."

Liz calmed down as much as she was able to. Granny relaxed his grips on her arm, but he did not trust her not to run. The two North Korean guards shoved Deva up the wooden porch outside Jang's quarters and moved her inside. Ji-Yeon walked up the porch steps and followed the guards. He paused on the steps, looking intently where Granny stood with Liz Montgomery. Walter Coburn had run to Daniel Blake's side and helped him back onto his feet. Granny turned Liz to face him.

"Ji-Yeon is a predator like Jang. What he is going to do to your sister he is going to do whether you try to go in there or not. He will not rape her. That is not his style. He will intimidate her. He will try break her will. He will allow her to live. But not if you go rushing in there."

Liz's breathing was coming fast, like she had been running a marathon race. She was shaking violently.

"He'll let her go when he's had his fun with her," Granny said. "Then she'll be escorted back out into the compound."

"But in what condition?" Liz said, and her voice was barely a whisper.

"I don't know, but you'll be there for her." Granny tightened his grip on Liz's arms again. "You've got to listen to me, Liz. We are getting out this prison *tonight*. If Deva is still in Jang's hut when the fireworks start, I will get her out of there. Look at me, Liz. That is a solemn promise. You understand that?"

Finally she nodded and sank down into his arms, trembling.

"Don't let Commandant Jang see your emotion," Granny said. "Don't give him the satisfaction."

By that time Daniel Blake, Walter Coburn and Fredrik Jorgensen had moved over to them. Daniel put his arms around Liz and supported her back to the hut. She did not look back.

Coburn said: "Jang and his buddy will both rape the sister."

Granny shook his head. "Ji-Yeon has a code of honor. He will not violate that. Jang is a different matter."

"So what do we do?"

"We need to get Deva out of that hut tonight."

Fredrik Jorgensen lowered his voice. "I heard some of the North Korea guards talking on the way back to the camp. The camp is going to be evacuated before dawn. We're out of time."

"In that case," Granny said, softly, "we'll set up the explosives as soon as it gets dark."

In Myang-Sook-Jang's hut, Deva was sat down on a hardbacked chair by the two North Korean guards. Jang had brought out two cut glasses and poured himself and Ji-Yeon a shot of Stolichnaya Elit Vodka 750. They clinked glasses.

"Please let me go," Deva pleaded. "I need to be with my sister."

Ji-Yeon said something to Jang in Russian. The Commandant gave Deva a hard look, then downed his vodka, picked up a sheaf of papers and walked out of the hut. Ji-Yeon shook out a pack of *Belomorkanal* cigarettes from his jacket pocket and lit one. He gave a nod to the two North Korean guards. They grabbed Deva from her chair and held her between them. Ji-Yeon settled back as the guards stripped her and threw her down to the floor of the hut. She was on her hands and knees, trembling. The guards stepped back, expectant. Ji-Yeon let the smoke drift up to the ceiling from his thin lips and nodded.

The two guards struck the naked young woman in the face, on her breasts and her stomach until she was bleeding, humiliated and demoralized. Ji-Yeon lit another *Belomorkanal* cigarette, his face impassive as the smoke curled around him and he watched the beating continue.

Kyu-Chal and Yo-Han picked McCall up in a Kia Sorrento Silver SUV two streets away from the Lego Store. Both of them were dressed in black. Kyu-Chal was driving, Harry sitting beside him. Neither of them said a word to him. McCall slid into the back and Kyu-Chal drove off. Twilight was descending fast on Seoul. Two hours later Kyu-Chal pulled up to a chain link fence at Yangyang Airport where several hangers were clustered. Harry jumped out, unlocked a gate in the fence and swung it open. Kyu-Chal drove through. Harry closed and locked the gate behind him and got back into the Sorrento. Kyu-Chal drove around the hangers until he came to a hanger hemmed in by trees. He killed the engine. There was nothing but silence around them. The two mercenaries got out of the Kia and opened the trunk. They took out two lightweight Nike Sport III Duffel bags. Harry ran ahead to the hanger which was fitted with Bifold Schweiss doors. He lifted the lift-strap and opened up the hangar.

Inside the cavernous space was a CH-47F Chinook helicopter with twin rotors. Kyu-Chal removed the chocks and wheeled it out onto the tarmac. Harry gestured to the chopper like it was a prized possession. "The CH-47F Chinook helicopter! Isn't she a beauty? You can buy them in Japan and Italy. It can carry as many as fifty-five passengers and a payload of 27 700 kg of cargo."

"Where did you get it?" McCall asked, amazed.

"It's kind of on loan," Harry confessed.

"A friend of mine in the South Korean Air Force flew it here to Yangyang this afternoon," Kyu-Chal said. "He owed me a favor. He has to pick it up before dawn. How many North Korean prisoners do you think are in this North Korean camp?"

"My intel on that is sketchy," McCall admitted. "Maybe sixty, maybe more."

"We'll fit them in," Harry said. "The more the merrier, right?"

"You'll get clearance from the tower?" McCall asked Kyu-Chal.

"Yangyang Airport had twenty-six passengers through its terminal building last year being serviced by one-hundred-and-forty-six airport staff," he said. "The last commercial flight took off in November. The South Korean press described it as a 'ghost airport'. We will have no trouble taking off or landing. Once we are in over North Korean air space, that's when we'll have a problem."

No kidding, McCall thought.

He had to admire the chutzpah of the two mercenaries

Yo-Han helped McCall climb aboard. Kyu-Chal climbed behind the controls. It took him a few minutes to go through the pre-flight checks. Then without another word from either of them they took off in the elegant CH-47F Chinook helicopter. Kyu-Chal angled it over the abandoned airport hub and headed to North Korea.

In Commandant Jang's hut Ji-Yeon lit another *Belomorkanal* cigarette. The two North Korean guards had stood back, awaiting the man's pleasure. Deva lay the floor of the hut. Her breathing was labored, coming out in small gasps. She was waiting for the next blow to be struck. Ji-Yeon moved to where the guards had stripped her of her prison clothes. He carefully picked them up and lay them down beside Deva's naked body. His tone was matter of fact, but there was a gentleness to it

"Get dressed now," he said in English.

Deva looked up at him, expecting a trap. He shook his head. "It's all right."

Ji-Yeon helped her to her feet. The two North Korean guards immediately moved forward. Deva flinched, but Ji-Yeon waved them away. Deva faced the soft-spoken Chinese man defiantly. Her left eye was swollen almost shut. Her lip had been split. There were bruises on her face, on her breasts, down her stomach. The blonde triangle of her pubic hair was matted, but untouched. There were angry welts down both of her legs and over her buttocks. Deva put on her gray pajamas with trembling hands. Ji-Yeon blew a plume of smoke from the cigarette, then blew it away from her face.

Every inch a gentleman.

"You know of course that Commandant Jang would have raped you," he said, again in English. His voice was silky soft. "I have watched him have his fun with western prisoners. Not my style."

Deva was dressed now, still trembling. Ji-Yeon helped her to a couch on the other side of Jang's desk. She sank down into it. He offered her one of his cigarettes, but she shook her head.

He nodded, as if he were concerned about her health. "They are very strong. I should give them up, but..." He shrugged and gave her an ironic smile. "My one vice."

Deva did not move from the couch. She wondered where the next humiliation would come from. Ji-Yeon nodded, as he if understood, and moved back to his chair beside Jang's desk.

"Tell me your name?" he asked her. Deva shook her head, as if that would be a betrayal to her sister. Ji-Yeon glanced at Commandant Jang's papers on the desk and found the one he was looking for. "Deva Montgomery. Your sister is Liz Montgomery, the famous photojournalist. Too bad she has ended up here. You have a choice to make now, Deva," he said, lighting another *Belomorkanal*. "The prisoners will be leaving the camp before dawn. You don't want to be here with them."

"I need to see my sister," Deva said, her voice shaky, but gaining strength.

"That will not be possible. Your sister will not leave this camp. None of the western prisoners will. Your choice will be to come with me when I leave."

"I won't do it!" Deva said, said through her split lips.

Ji-Yeon nodded, as if he had expected this "It is not a choice to be made lightly. Think it over. You have until dawn. Till then, sit here, relax if you can. No one will harm you."

Deva looked at the two North Koreans with a mixture of loathing and fear. Ji-Yeon dismissed them with a wave of his hand. For a moment they hesitated, then they opened the door of the hut and closed it behind them,

Ji-Yeon sat back and looked at Deva. There was the ghost of a smile on his thin lips.

Deva thought it was the scariest thing she had ever seen in her life.

Kyu-Chul set the CH-47F Chinook helicopter down in a clearing where the forest surrounded the chopper on all four sides. McCall saw some of the trees had been recently cut down, presumably by the prisoners in the prison camp. He had noted a moonlit road about a quarter of a mile from the landing point when they had descended. Harry had one of the maps unfolded on his lap as the twin-rotors powered down.

"I'd say the prison camp is located six miles from Ponggang across the Chinese border," he said. "If this map is accurate, which it may not be, but it is the only rough guide we have, so we'll go for it. The road you saw as we landed is a quarter of a mile from this landing site. It is regularly patrolled by NK troops, usually a two-man affair. I got their schedule down to a twenty-minute window, but that is all guesswork."

Kyu-Chal said: "I figure we have maybe less than twenty minutes to be on the safe side. They will not be looking for any traffic on the road. But this close to the prison camp they will have instructions to watch for escaped prisoners."

"Not like that will be a priority," Harry said.

McCall climbed out of the helicopter, hefting his backpack on his back. Harry dumped down the Nike Sport III Duffel bag and unzipped it. Kyu-Chul lifted out a Daewoo Precision K2 assault rifle with a K201 grenade launcher. Yo-Han brought out a Daewoo 5.56 light machinegun. Kyu-Chul fitted a holster on his hip with a North Korean type 70 pistol. Harry wore a Pusan Jin Iron Works 1911-style pistol. McCall took out the Bulgarian Makarov 9x18 pistol that Hayden Vallance had given him. He swung the Ees Profile NVG Foliage Green binoculars around his neck.

"Let's do this," Kyu-Chul said.

Granny and Walter Coburn split up in the darkness beneath the prison complex. Coburn carried the C4 explosives which were stored in what looked like modelling clay in plastic sleeves. He had detonators with long fuses and blast caps. Granny had lost sight of him, but he knew he had run to the base of the second watchtower. Granny knelt down in one of the abandoned huts in the prison camp. Moonlight filtered through the grimy glass where several cots had been stacked to one side. Granny tore open the crate of dynamite sticks in their sealed plastic bags. He inserted the long fuses into them which took him twenty minutes. He had to be watchful for the sweep of the searchlight atop the first watchtower. He had timed it out at seven minutes. In the end, he had eight dynamite sticks in bunches with their long fuses sticking out of them that were red or green. He wrapped the dynamite sticks in plastic sheets and carried them to the door of the hut.

He stepped out into the night.

There was movement through the compound, just vague sounds, muffled commands. The camp was getting ready to evacuate. Granny waited. In five seconds the sweep of the searchlight flared across the huts and the compound and swept on across the main part of the prison. Granny sprinted across the shadows to the base of the first watchtower and knelt down in its shadow. He dug down into the shallow dirt that covered the compound, but the ground was harder than he had anticipated. He had brought a rusty trowel he had also liberated from the armory and buried the sticks of dynamite with their red-and-green fuses trailing out from them. He was still at it when the searchlight swept back across the abandoned huts. Granny squeezed behind the metal support of the first watchtower and remained as still as possible, his heart pounding. The bright flare of the searchlight swept past his hiding place and moved on. Granny let out his breath out soundlessly and knelt down beside the shadow of the watchtower. Now he had to dig a shallow trench to hide the fuses. He used the trowel to dig up the ground, moving the red-and-green fuses into a little shallow trench and then covered them with dirt. It was slow going but he kept at it. He could not afford for one of the North Korean guards to come upon the watchtower and disturb the dynamite.

He was rapidly running out of time.

McCall had set down his backpack onto the ground in a dense part of the wooded area. He took out the Heckler & Koch MP5 submachinegun and fitted it with one of the magazines. The stretch of lonely road gleamed in the moonlight. Kyu-Chul had told McCall to wait for him and Harry on the other side of the road. The wind moaned through the foliage, stirring it. McCall noted there was a steep gradient up to the road made up of loose shale and gravel.

He heard the sound of the vehicle before it saw it.

It was a BTR-152 six-wheel North Korean armored personal carrier, built on the chassis of a Zis-151 utility truck. It was open at the back and carried a driver and a single passenger who used the radio. The vehicle had a pintle-mounted 7.62mm SG-43 Goryanov (SGMB) machinegun which could transverse 45 degrees and elevate between -6 and +24 degrees. McCall noted the wooden benches jammed into the vehicle which looked like a throwback to another era.

The vehicle slowed. McCall saw a flash of movement to his right. A figure staggered out from the shelter of the trees and collapsed onto the steep gradient, displacing flurries of loose gravel and shale. It was Harry, disheveled and hurt, crawling up onto the moonlit ribbon of road. The BTR-152 vehicle ground to a halt and the North Korean guard leaped out. The radio operator had his hand on the machinegun, ready to swing it up into action. Harry was sprawled out on the road, blood seeping down one side of his face. The North Korean guard moved closer, carrying a North Korean Type 73 machinegun. Suddenly Harry raised up on his arms, swinging the Daewoo K3 machinegun into his hands and firing a short burst. The North Korean guard keeled over. Before the gunner in the BTR-152 could even raise up the 7.62mm machinegun, up Kyu-Chul stepped out of the trees and fired his own K2 assault rifle, riddling the gunner's body with bullets. Yo-Han was already up on his feet, wiping the blood off his face. He dragged the dead Korean gunner into the trees at the side of the road. Kyu-Chul dragged the body of the radio operator into the same copse of trees, dumping his body in the underbrush. McCall noted they had relied on hand signals only. He jogged out of the trees to the road. Neither of them said a word. McCall pulled himself into the BTR-152. He dropped his backpack down onto the wooden bench. Harry joined them. The ambush had taken less than twelve seconds. Kyu-Chul fired up the armored vehicle and moved down the road through the forest. Harry unfolded his map and tapped the spot where McCall's old grocer had indicated.

"We need to get off this road," he said. "There's a turning marked here. It cannot be more than a mile in front of us. According to the map, it's the road that leads to the prison camp."

Kyu-Chul nodded.

There were no more talking.

McCall was glad that these two mercenaries were on *his* side.

Granny finishing burying the long fuses into the hard-packed earth fifty yards from the first watchtower. He did not think one of the Korean prison guards would see the fuses unless he was looking right at them on the ground. Granny turned in the shadows and stepped back into the shelter of the abandoned huts, waiting for the searchlight at the top of the watchtower to wash over him. He did not have to wait for long. The Korean guards on their high perch had a routine they kept to. No deviation. Ingrained in them with their training. Four minutes later the sweep of the searchlight flared past the abandoned huts. There was no sign of Granny or anyone else out in the compound. Granny knew Walter Coburn would be wiring his watchtower with C4 explosives and should be heading back to the large hut where the other western prisoners were waiting.

Granny jogged toward the porch of the hut.

Kyu-Chul could see the prison facility now surrounded by dense trees. McCall pulled the EES Profile NVG Foliage Green binoculars out of his backpack. There was a main gate which was closed. Within the compound were huts stretching back to the three watchtowers. A searchlight swept from them intermittently, flaring brightly, then sweeping on. There was some movement within the compound, uniformed North Korean guards moving to some of the huts. It looked to McCall that the activity was coordinated. He swept the glasses to where three drab green buses stood parked along the main gate. He lowered the glasses, keeping his voice to barely a whisper.

"It looks as if the camp is being readying to be evacuated."

"You are calling the shots," Harry said. "What do we do?"

"Turn around," McCall said. "Get to the back of the facility."

Kyu-Chal nodded and followed the road where it branched off through the densely packed trees, finding another track that skirted the camp. He came onto the back of the facility where the fence was practically right against the trees. Kyu-Chul pulled up three hundred yards from the compound. McCall jumped down to the ground. Yo-Han leapt out with him. McCall pulled back the Chronograph Diver's watch on his wrist. Kyu-Chul and Harry did the same with their watches, all of them state-of-the-art.

"Ten minutes from now," McCall said.

Kyu-Chul and Harry coordinated with him. "We'll keep in touch via the walkie-walkies," McCall said. He looked at Kyu-Chul. "How close can you get to the front gate?"

"I'll wait on the road we just came down. It's screened in the trees right outside."

Kyu-Chul turned the BTR-152 armored vehicle around on the dirt track and made a wide sweep of the prison until he was lost to sight.

McCall and Harry ran through the trees toward the back of the prison fence.

Granny made it back to the porch on their hut where Liz Montgomery, Daniel Blake and Fredrik Jorgensen waited for him. He saw a shadow and caught a glimpse of Walter Coburn heading back to the hut by a circuitous route. Fredrik Jorgensen's voice was hoarse with suppressed emotion.

"I heard some of guards talking when you were gone. The camp is being evacuated within the hour. The North Korean prisoners will be loaded into those buses at the main gate, but I fear not all of them. The prisoners were forced to dig a mass grave a mile from the gates."

"Before then the fireworks will start," Granny promised him.

"My sister..." Liz said, her face ashen.

Granny took hold of her hand. "I'll get Deva out of Jang's office. As soon as the explosives are set off."

There was no time for more. Four of the North Korean guards turned the corner of the hut and climbed up onto the porch. Daniel Blake, Liz and Fredrik Jorgensen were herded inside. The two other guards grabbed Granny's shoulders and marched him off the wooden porch. Granny caught Walter Coburn's eye as he rounded the corner. He spread his fingers.

Ten minutes before the fuses were lit.

Coburn nodded and faded back into the shadows.

The two North Korean guards hauled Granny across the compound toward Commandant Jang's hut.

At the back fence of the compound, McCall and Harry waited until the sweeping searchlight had passed them. Harry took out a small multitool from his Nike Sport Duffel bag and cut through the fence. He and McCall pulled back a section of the fence and crawled out through it, heading toward the hut at the foot of the first watchtower.

As he was marched up the porch steps outside Commandant Jang's hut, Granny heard a heated exchange between Jang and Ji-Yeon, in Korean. Myang-Sook-Jang had returned to his quarters with the intention of raping Liz's sister Deva, but Ji-Yeon had urged him to exercise caution. The Americans were aware that the North Korean soldiers were holding Western prisoners. They should be used as bargaining chips. To threaten to molest one of them was folly. Jang retorted that he had already raped the photojournalist Liz Montgomery. Ji-Yeon's tone was condescending. All the more reason not to harm her sister. Ji-Yeon had plans for Deva. He was going to take her with him when he left the prison. At that moment Granny was hauled into the hut. He saw Jang dismiss Ji-Yeon with a wave of his hand.

He said in Korean: "Do what you like with her."

At which point Myang-Sook-Jang turned around and Granny was thrust before him. He waved that dismissive hand again and one of the North Korean guards clubbed Granny to his knees. Blood ran hot down his face, matting in his blonde hair. Ji-Yeon took a step forward. He made a gesture to one of the North Korean guards to lift up Granny's head. Granny looked up at the terrorist through pain-filled eyes.

"I know this prisoner," Ji-Yeon said.

Jang looked at him in surprise.

"He is a mercenary," Ji-Yeon said. "I met him when he was attempting to airlift some missionaries out of Kenya years ago. A dangerous adversary. Did you attempt to break him?"

Jang's eyes were fixed on Granny's face. "He has been resistant to interrogation. He has conspired with the other western prisoners against me. His defiance is of no conscience."

Jang said something guttural to the two North Korean guards who dragged Granny up to his feet. Granny knew enough North Korean to know that he was going to be taken out and shot. Ji-Yeon stepped closer to Granny, his expression ironic.

He said, in Korean: "I don't remember your name. Something obscure. A western name." Granny shrugged, as if he could not understand him. "I remember that you speak Korean fluently. No matter. I cannot do anything to help you. This prison camp is not, as you Americans would say, my bat and ball. Commandant Jang calls the shots. He is unforgiving. You must have tried his patience."

Jang said something more to the two guards who turned Granny around and marched him out of the hut and down the wooden stairs. Ji-Yeon lit another *Belomorkanal* cigarette.

"Make an example of this one prisoner," Ji-Yeon advised. "Don't harm the others."

"I will consider it. I have to prepare for my departure," Jang said, tersely.

He started to dump papers from the drawers of his desk into a leather briefcase. Ji-Yeon shrugged, settling back into the armchair, turning his attention back to Deva.

"We will be leaving shortly."

Deva just shook her head, cowered into herself, her face a mask of pain and betrayal.

▶ **10** ◀

THE TWO NORTH KOREAN guards had marched
Granny to one of the abandoned huts in the compound. He
dragged his feet, as if barely able to walk. Beyond them, the
chain link fence glistened in the moonlight. The rest of the
huts were wreathed in shadows. Granny suddenly came to
life, trying to wrench the SKS rifle from the guard's hands.
He was slammed with the butt of the rifle, sending him
down to his knees. He tried to crawl to his feet, but the second NK guard kicked him back down. Off-balance, Granny
could only turn back to his executioners.

The first North Korean guard leveled his rifle at
Granny's head.

McCall moved out of the shadows, knocking the SKS
rifle from the man's hands. He twisted the man's head and
snapped his neck. At the same time, Harry emerged from
the shadows outside the abandoned huts and slipped an
Italian 5mm Stiletto blade into the North Korean's back.
He crumpled to the ground. While Harry dragged the
two dead guards behind the first abandoned hut, McCall
grabbed Granny and brought him to his feet. Granny noted that McCall was carrying a Heckler & Koch MP5 submachinegun. Granny looked at him and just nodded. "I
knew you would come for me."

"You would have come for me," McCall said.

"Yeah, I would have."

"You're okay?"

"I'm okay."

"Where are the other western prisoners?"

"In one of the main huts," Granny said. "There are five of them. One of them, a contractor named Walter Coburn, has wired up explosives with me that we stole from the prison armory. There is a photojournalist named Liz Montgomery. Her sister Deva only came to the prison camp two days ago. She is being held in Myang-Sook-Jang's hut. He is the Commandant of the prison. There is also a mercenary who just arrived at the compound named Ji-Yeon. Used to work for various terrorist organizations, but he has gone legitimate now. Hires out to various NATO countries."

"Who else?"

"Fredrik Jorgensen, a Dutch entrepreneur and Daniel Blake who worked for Associated Press," Granny said.

Harry returned from disposing the bodies of the guards. McCall said: "This is Yo-Han, a mercenary who is on this mission with me. He has a partner Kyu-Chul who is waiting in a BTR-152 armored vehicle outside the main gate."

Harry gave Granny a cavalier wave. He had two sets of heavy keys in his hands. McCall turned back to Granny. "Where are the North Korean prisoners located?"

"In the back huts behind here."

"Set them free, Harry," McCall said.

"Perfect."

Harry disappeared back into the deeper shadows around the abandoned huts.

"Where did you pick up the kid?" Granny asked. "He doesn't look older enough to shave yet."

"He's got my back," McCall said, curtly. "How much time do we have?"

"I've got explosives wired under the three watchtowers and more of them in the abandoned huts throughout the compound. Dynamite sticks tied together. The fuses need to be lit. There is some C4 explosives also, but they could have been compromised. Nothing in this place is exactly state-of-the-art. I need to get back into Commandant Jang's hut and pick Deva up. Ji-Yeon is going to take her with him when he leaves the camp."

"How is he going to do that?"

"He has a North Korean pilot waiting for him in a MD-500 helicopter. North Korean markings. The prison is being evacuated within the hour."

McCall looked out into the night that surrounded them. Granny seemed stronger to him now, more in command of his emotions. He would need him to get himself together if they were going to have a chance of survival.

"How long before the fireworks start?" McCall asked.

"As long as it takes me to light the fuses."

"Do it," McCall said.

Granny grabbed both of the 58 AKS rifles from the fallen guards. McCall set down his backpack and took out the walkie-talkie from it.

"Kyu-Chul."

Kyu-Chul's voice echoed from the walkie. "Here, Mr. McCall."

"Two minutes to breach the prison gate."

"Copy that."

The mercenary clicked off the walkie.

McCall looked back at Granny. "Light your fuses."

Harry used his stiletto knife on two of the North Korean guards, collecting two more sets of keys. He unlocked the door of the first hut. Bleary faces looked back at him from the cots inside. The North Korean prisoners were dressed in their drab olive prison uniforms. Harry picked up the first few of the prisoners, helping them to stand. He spoke to them in Korean.

"You are leaving this place. Come with me! All of you!"

There was confusion and fear etched on their faces. Harry roughly brought the rest of them to their feet, herding them to the open hut door.

"Outside! Stay together!"

Harry unlocked the next three huts. He grabbed the prisoners, some of them old, infirm, but Yo-Han was not going to leave any of them behind. By the time he got the last of the dilapidated huts open, there were more than forty people milling around him, shivering in the bitter cold. Harry grabbed the arm of one of the younger men.

He asked in Korean: "Where are the others?"

The young man pointed to another row of huts. Harry dumped a set of large keys he had taken from the body of the North Korean guard. "Get them out! But come right back here!"

The young man ran for the first row of huts. Harry aimed his 58 AKS rifle into the glowing darkness, acutely aware that more North Korean guards could come upon them at any moment.

McCall ran onto the rotting porch on the main hut where Granny had directed him. Liz Montgomery had been at the grimy window overlooking the compound. She turned at his entrance. Daniel Blake and Fredrik Jorgensen joined her.

"My name is Robert McCall," he said. "Come with me."

Liz stared at him as realization of who he was flood-ed through her. "Granny talked about you! The guards just dragged him out of here."

"He got away from them."

"He was going to set off explosives!" Fredrik Jor-gensen said.

"I'd say he's doing that right now. Anyone else here with you?"

"Just us! They keep us together," Daniel Blake said.

Liz grabbed McCall's arm. "I'm not leaving without my sister! She's been taken to Commandant Jang's quar-ters."

"I'll get her," McCall said.

He moved out onto the porch. The other Western prisoners followed him. The compound seemed eerily de-serted. McCall took out his walkie-talkie. "Ten seconds, Kyu-Chul!"

"Copy that!" the mercenary said.

At the back of the abandoned huts, Granny knelt down and grabbed up the fuses that were protruding from the ground. He took out a matchbook that he had carefully hidden for months and lit the fuses. They roared along the hardpacked earth, shaking free, burning bright-ly toward the first watchtower. Granny ran to the next set of fuses and lit them, and the next, until all of them were burning through the loosely packed ground. The search-light on the tower swung around, blazing a white light across Granny's figure. He leapt away as bullets kicked the earth around him. He reached the porch of one of the abandoned huts, looking across into the darkness where he knew Walter Coburn waited. He would be lighting the fuses for his C4 charges

Granny counted down the seconds: "Four… three… two… one…"

He looked up at the intimidating watchtower where the searchlight arced down to him. He saw the first fuses reach where the dynamite was buried.

A huge explosion rocked the watchtower, followed by two more eruptions. The watchtower blew apart and started to fall toward the ground, taking the North Korean guards with it. Granny turned to where the second watchtower was precarious perched. For a moment he thought that Coburn had not been able to light his fuses. But the fuses ignited the C4 putty, sending fire exploding across the second watchtower. It collapsed with a rage of light and heat. A moment later the third watchtower exploded, not falling yet but sending its North Korean guards screaming to the ground.

Kyu-Chul smashed through the main gates of the prison, sending them flying. North Korean guards ran from huts, unslinging their rifles. Kyu-Chul mowed them down, his machinegun exploding hot in his hands. More guards were running from the shadows, firing at the armored vehicle.

McCall led the small group of Western prisoners off the porch, firing his Heckler & Koch submachinegun at the North Korean guards who poured out of the wooden huts ringing the compound. They were cut down by the crippling gunfire. McCall saw Granny's figure running through the swirling clouds of choking smoke heading toward Commandant Myang-Sook-Jang's quarters. Liz Montgomery clutched McCall's arm.

"My sister is in there!"

Before McCall could even respond, the door to Jang's hut flew open. Ji-Yeon dragged Deva Montgomery down the porch steps, firing a heavy Colt Python .357 Magnum revolver into the mayhem. He held onto Deva with an iron grip. At the same time, his pilot in the MD-500 military helicopter had started the rotor turning. Ji-Yeon propelled Deva toward the chopper. Walter Coburn came running up from the dust cloud of the decimated third watchtower, firing the 58 AKS rifle he had picked up from one of the fallen guards. He strafed the remaining guards, sending them to the ground. Kyu-Chul swung the BTR-152 armored vehicle around, aiming the grenade-launcher at Myang-Sook-Jang's hut. It exploded in a fireball, sending more clouds of dust swirling into the air. Granny reached the shattered porch steps.

McCall pulled Liz Montgomery out of harm's way as Ji-Yeon fired more rounds with the .357 Python Revolver. In the chaos, Daniel Blake was disoriented, blinded by the acrid smoke. One of the North Korean guards fired at him. He was hit by two bullets and stumbled to the ground. McCall put four bullets into the guard's body. Deva suddenly wrenched out of Ji-Yeon's grasp, running to Daniel's side. He looked up her, his body in shock. Ji-Yeon reached them and pulled both of them to their feet, firing his heavy Revolver. He propelled both Deva and Daniel to the MD-500 helicopter. Liz cried out in anguish. McCall shielded her body as he fired more rounds from the submachinegun, decimating the North Korean guards coming at them.

Ji-Yeon reached the chopper. He hauled Deva up into the arms one of the North Korean guards who had accompanied him. Another of his guards thought that Daniel was also a hostage and dragged the journalist inside the helicopter. Ji-Yeon climbed aboard, emptying his Pylon Revolver at Walter Coburn, who ducked down beside one of the demolished huts.

McCall took aim on the chopper, but it was too late. The helicopter rose and banked steeply over the shattered main gate. Beyond McCall, Kyu-Chul's vehicle slewed around again, firing the grenade launcher at the next set of buildings. They exploded in a fiery inferno..

Yo-Han led sixty North Korean prisoners past the ruins of the smoking first watchtower, heading for two of the buses parked along the perimeter fence. McCall held on to Liz Montgomery. She was distraught in his arms. He could not do anything about Ji-Yeon's retreat from the prison camp. It had happened too fast. He needed to get the prisoners to the two buses parked against the chain link fence. He motioned Fredrik Jorgensen to head for them. Behind him, Walter Coburn kept firing on the Korean guards who had taken refuge from the blistering attack.

Granny ran into the shell of Commandant Jang's headquarters. Two walls had collapsed in the RPG attack. Debris was strewn through the office. The couch and the two high-backed chairs were still standing. A wall-to-ceiling bookcase had fallen, smashing apart. Heavy books, small glass knickknacks and framed pictures had crashed across Jang's desk. The piano had been blown apart. Smoke hazed through the office, obscuring details.

Myang-Sook-Jang came out of the devastation, aiming his Tokayev pistol at Granny. Granny leapt across Jang's shattered desk and kicked it out of his hands. Jang snarled at him, hurling what was left of the desk to one side. The Commandant was a skilled martial artiste, striking Granny with punishing blows. Granny countered them, but barely. The blow to his head by the North Korean guard had almost blacked him out. Jang kicked out, his steel-tipped toes slamming into Granny's body, staggering him. Jang's had religiously practiced body hardening through a Korean style of fighting called *Taekkyon*. The nerves in the Commandant's body were deadened. Jang met Granny's counter blows on the inside of the arm between the elbow and wrist. Granny knew it was called the "iron bridge", attacking the soft underbelly. Granny kicked at Jang's shin, but it was hard as a rock. Jang came back at him with a spinning back kick and then a spinning back fist.

Granny ducked away from the deadly barrage. Large splinters of glass were strewn over the floor. He dived down, grabbed one of them, cutting his right hand as he wielded it. Jang turned, too late. Granny stabbed him in the leg, the dagger penetrating right to the bone. At the same time, Granny used a technique he had taught Robert McCall. He struck his rigid right-hand fingers in an upward move at Jang's chest, forcing him to expel air from his lungs. It was an "air dimmak point." Granny grabbed Jang's right wrist and gouged the pressure points there which made the Commandant believe for a split-second that his whole body had been hit. Granny followed it with an attack on the colon points on the Commandant's upper forearm, using his own version of the "iron bridge".

Myang-Sook-Jang staggered back. Granny hit him with his full weight and sent him against the back wall, smashing another bookcase. Jang was off-balance and slipped on the shards of broken glass that littered the floor. Granny brought the Commandant down to his knees. He noted Jang's swagger stick on the floor just under the debris of the desk. Granny picked it up and brought it to Jang's throat, pressing back, his knee against the back of his spine.

"This is for Liz Montgomery," Granny hissed to the Commandant. He pulled back on the swagger stick against Jang's throat. The Commandant writhed and foamed at the mouth, biting through his lower lip and his tongue. Granny exerted more pressure on Jang's throat, pulling his hair back, then he put his fingers into Jang's eyes. The Korean screamed, but he was writhing so violently that it was all Granny could do to hold onto him. More glass showered over them as knickknacks from the shelves rained down.

Jang's face turned blue as the blood and oxygen drained out of his neck.

Myang-Sook-Jang gave one last, convulsive gasp, then slumped down. He was dead before his body hit the floor. Granny released the swagger stick from the Commandant's throat. He staggered to his feet and kicked Jang to one side, forcing air into his own lungs. He heard more gunfire outside. Granny ran through the demolished office, leaving Myang-Sook-Jang's swagger stick beside his body.

Robert McCall and Walter Coburn were firing on the North Korean troops who had taken shelter behind the wooden porches of the huts. More explosions rocked the prison camp, blowing gaping holes in the remaining huts. Kyu-Chul slewed his BRT-152 around and fired on the North Korean troops. He sent a grenade screaming at a hut which exploded in a fireball. Liz and Fredrik Jorgensen had made it to where the first two drab buses stood at the chain fence. Yo-Han had started loading the North Korean prisoners onto both of them. They were frightened and disoriented, but Harry kept them together, shouting to them in Korean.

"On the bus! No stragglers! Everyone gets a free ride today!"

Granny picked up a fallen 58 AKS rifle and knelt down beside McCall who looked at him. "Did you get what you came for?"

"Yeah. Jang's dead. What happened to Ji-Yeon?"

"He took Liz Montgomery's sister in the helicopter," McCall said. "There was nothing I could do to stop him.

He also took one of the hostages with him, Daniel Blake. He had been wounded. Ji-Yeon will already have radioed the North Korean authorities."

"There was nothing you could have done to stop him," Granny said.

"Leave no one behind," McCall said.

Kyu-Chul launched another grenade, rocketing into more of the North Korean huts and obliterating them. Then he turned the BTR-152 around and raced toward the shattered main gate.

McCall motioned to Walter Coburn to fall back. He and Granny gave him covering fire as they ran toward the parked buses. A fusillade of bullets struck Coburn as he ran from the protection of one of the huts. He pitched over to the hardbacked earth in the compound. McCall fired into the compound, sending more of the North Korean troops scrambling for cover. Granny came back for Coburn. He looked to be badly hurt. Liz Montgomery was looking at the barbed wire fence as if willing herself to see beyond it. She clutched Granny's arm.

"He took Deva! Ji-Yeon took my sister!"

"I'll find him. Get onto the bus, Liz! You've got to go right now!"

Shaking with emotion, Liz staggered away from him as if he had betrayed her. Granny lifted Walter Coburn onto on his shoulders in a fireman's lift. He carried the wounded contractor to one of the two buses. McCall followed, raking the submachinegun across the decimated North Korean troops. Liz climbed up into the first bus. Granny gently laid Walter Coburn across three of the seats. Liz moved over to him.

"How bad is he hurt?"

"I'd say pretty bad," Granny said. "We need to get him to a hospital right away. Stay with him."

Liz sat down beside Coburn. He was sweating profusely, but he nodded. "Don't worry about me," he said through gritted teeth. "Get us out of here."

Harry got the North Korean prisoners loaded onto the two buses. He climbed into the driver's side of the first bus. Fredrik Jorgensen sat beside him. McCall pulled himself onto the bus and moved directly to Walter Coburn. His eyes were closed. McCall moved Granny away from him.

"Walter Coburn has lost of blood," McCall said. "We need to get him to a hospital in Seoul."

"I wouldn't made it without him."

"Sit tight."

Granny sat in the front seat. The North Korean prisoners were crowded into both of the buses. "Where do you want to go?" Harry asked them as he slid behind the driver's seat. "Disneyland or Harry's Potter's Wizarding World?"

McCall jumped out as Kyu-Chul screeched to a halt beside him. More bullets were flying around him. "Did the old guy get it?"

"Walter Coburn will live if we can get out of here," McCall said.

"Follow me," Kyu-Chul said.

McCall nodded and climbed onto the second bus, sliding into the driver's seat. Kyu-Chul launched another grenade into one of the huts, totally obliterating it. Debris rained down. Then he turned the BTR-152 around and raced to the shattered main gate. More explosions ripped apart more buildings in the prison compound. McCall drove out through the wide-open gate onto the glowing road. Harry followed him in the second bus, crowded with the rest of the sixty North Korean prisoners. Kyu-Chul fired one last RPG shell which erupted into the demolished building that once had been Myang-Sook-Jang's quarters. Then he was through the buckled prison gate.

In the first bus, Liz held Walter Coburn's hand. Fredrik Jorgensen came over and sat beside her. Behind him the Korean prisoners were silent and traumatized.

"You are leaving this place," Liz said softly to Coburn. "The cavalry is here."

Coburn just nodded, his eyes far away.

In the second bus, McCall followed Kyu-Chul down a back trail that cut through the woods. He guessed it had once been a logging road, but now it was overgrown with vegetation. The mercenary seemed to know where he was going. McCall had seen him accessing more maps on the helicopter trip into North Korea. In less than twenty minutes McCall found himself on the ribbon of moonlit road where Kyu-Chul and Harry had commandeered the BTR-152 armored vehicle. That led to another back road where they could see the ghostly shape of the CH-47F Chinook helicopter shrouded in the trees. McCall pulled the bus as close to the densely packed trees as he could and cut the engine. He pressed the switch to open the doors. At first the North Korean prisoners did not move, looking at each other as if expecting a new humiliation to befall them. Then one of them, a woman in her sixties with iron-gray hair, stepped down and held out a hand for a frail old man. He climbed down from the bus with her.

Yo-Han drove the second bus through more trees a little closer to the chopper. He brought it to a halt and opened the doors. He started helping the North Korean prisoners down the steps. Fredrik Jorgensen and Liz Montgomery carried Walter Coburn down the steps to the muddy ground. They held him up between them.

Kyu-Chul pulled up in the BTR-152.

McCall ran up to him. "Get the helicopter fired up. I'll give us some back-up."

Kyu-Chul just nodded and jumped out. McCall took his place. The North Korean prisoners were moving through the trees to the chopper in an orderly fashion. They had all of the hope squeezed out of them. They were more than willing to be herded together one more time. Liz Montgomery and Fredrik Jorgensen were moving among them, gingerly carrying Walter Coburn. Kyu-Chul and Harry had reached the helicopter and climbed inside. By the time McCall was almost out of the trees the rotor blades were turning.

A Wheeled Improvised Fighting Vehicle flashed down the moonlit road, bristling with North Korean soldiers. McCall fired the grenade launcher on the BTR-152. The RPG exploded into the IFV, sending it down the steep ravine. It was immediately engulfed in flames. Behind it a UAZ-3151 Utility Vehicle appeared out of the trees, also loaded with Korean army personnel. McCall fired another rocket grenade at them. This time the vehicle swerved away from the road and crashed down the incline where it turned over.

McCall turned the BTR-152 around and drove back the way he had come. By the time he reached the copse of trees, the chopper's rotors were turning at speed. He saw that the last of the North Korean prisoners were now coming aboard. He knew the Chinook 47-F could seat as many as fifty-five passengers, so it would be a tight squeeze, but all of the prisoners, including the western prisoners, would be aboard. McCall jumped out of the BTR-152, took out his Makarov pistol and aimed at the gas tank. The vehicle exploded, sending flames through the trees. McCall ran to the helicopter and climbed onboard.

The North Korean prisoners were jammed into the chopper. Liz Montgomery and Fredrik Jorgensen had found a spot where they could lay Walter Coburn down. Granny was in the cockpit. McCall slid behind the pilot and co-pilot. Kyu-Chul lifted the helicopter off the ground. It banked over the trees and into the night sky.

"How long will take the North Korean military to scramble their F-35 Stealth fighters?" McCall asked.

"There is a contingent of antiquated and obsolete aircraft in the North Korean air force," Kyu-Chul said. "Also the Shenyang J-5, a Chinese version of the 1950's era Mikovan Gurevich MiG-17."

"The Wright Brothers were flying better planes," Harry said.

"Some F-35 Stealth Fighters were delivered to a military base at Cheogju in North Chungcleong Province, but they won't be delivered to North Korea yet," Kyu-Chul said. "The North Korean military will never find us."

Harry said: "We're below their radar. We'll be over the border into South Korea in under fifteen minutes."

Granny made his way through the crowded helicopter to where Liz Montgomery was sitting. Fredrik Jorgensen was still sitting beside Walter Coburn. Granny slid down beside Liz. Tears glistened on her face. Granny held one of her hands tightly. Then she just collapsed against him. Granny put his arm around her.

"I am going to find Deva," he whispered to her. "I am going to bring her home."

If Liz heard him, she did not acknowledge it. She just held onto to Granny, sobbing uncontrollably. Up on the cockpit of the Chinook there was no more conversation until Kyu-Chul turned to McCall twelve minutes later and said: "We're in South Korean air space."

"That's outstanding," McCall said.

"Your friend 'Granny,'" Harry said. "We did rescue the right dude, didn't we?"

McCall looked at him and smiled. "You did good."

Harry grinned. "Perfect."

▶ 11 ◀

ALEXA KOKINAS HAD stopped in at O'Grady's Saloon right before it closed to drop off some homemade oatmeal raison cookies she had made to give to Max, her friendly bartender, who was having a birthday party for his eight-year-old daughter tomorrow. She was in uniform, but she was just going to be in and out. It was a promise that she had made to Max before calling it a night. Max, for all of his rough edges and sawdust-blarney, had been very grateful to receive it. His wife Beth would be thrilled. Alexa had looked around O'Grady's, but it was almost closing time and the place was emptying out. There were the usual suspects in the bar, most of them Police Officers, but she did not see any of the *Elite* cops among them. She was relieved. She had had enough of Frank Macamber's forced camaraderie to last her a lifetime. Max came around the bar and told her to be *careful* out there, which she thought was from some old TV show. He said it to her every time she entered O'Grady's, but she had found it was kind of endearing. She promised she would be and moved to the door.

Outside a light drizzle was falling. Alexa climbed into her police car and pulled away from the curb. Her partner Tony Palmer did not like it when she took the patrol car when she was alone, but he could be a little over-protective. She would report back to the squad and then go home.

As a matter of course, Alexa glanced over at the abandoned warehouse on the corner of the street. She always checked it when she was passing to make sure it was secure. This time the chain-link fence at the derelict building was slightly ajar. She made a U-turn and parked in the street next to the building. She got out of the patrol car and saw that the padlock that usually held the gate closed had been broken off. She knew that several of the homeless tried regularly to get into the warehouse from time to time. It was a cold night and she did not blame them. But she would have to move them if the warehouse had been broken into. She thought of calling for back-up, but she thought she could handle the situation, if there *was* a situation. She did not want Officer Palmer to babysit her.

Alexa moved through the gate to the exterior of the warehouse.

That was when the alarm bells went off in her head.

There was a light on the ground floor at the front of the building which had not been on when she had done her usual tour of the place.

She pulled her gun out of her holster.

She moved to the warehouse door. The padlock had been broken off some time ago. She pulled it open and stepped into the dark, shadowy interior. The windows were grimy, but there was enough moonlight to see by. The darker recesses of the building receded into blackness. There was litter strewn across the floor, empty cartons of Chinese food, Macdonald's cartons, discarded candy bars, used condoms, congealed paint cans and broken crates stacked along the wall. The sign on the warehouse said: *Tristate Moving and Storage – Brooklyn NY.*

Alexa heard what sounded like rats scurrying through the debris in front of her. Shapes moved in the shadows. She raised her 9mm Glock, aiming into the darkness.

"Police Officer!" she called out.

The scuttling sounds of the rats scurried toward the back of the massive warehouse area. There were several open oil drums spaced at intervals where fires had been lit, but they had burnt out. There were empty glass offices in the gloom, all of them abandoned, some where the glass bad been smashed out. It made a mosaic of the refracted shadows coming through the moonlit windows. Alexa had her back turned to the first derelict office, turning her gun in a small semi-circle.

She was deaf and she did not hear them coming.

She sensed a presence behind her and tried to whirl, but it was too late. A dark figure rammed something into her chest. She realized in that split second that she had been shot with a taser. Not the kind that shot out darts but with a Drive Stun capacity. It caused an Electro Muscular Disruption in her body without the perpetrator having to actually shoot the darts. All he had to do was hold the Drive Stun gun against Alexa's chest. She collapsed to the ground, writhing in pain, her nerves on fire.

More of the dark figures surrounded her. Hands unhooked her belt with its holster and radio in it and tossed it away. Her belt was pulled out and her uniform trousers were lifted off her legs. One of the attackers pulled her black Danner black boots from her feet leaving the white socks she had been wearing. Another of the assailants, also wearing black and a ski mask, ripped Alexa's police blue tunic open. He pulled her bra right over her head, leaving her large breasts exposed. A third attacker took hold of her white panties and pulled them over her legs, revealing the triangle of blonde pubic hair beneath. She now had only her white socks on and the torn blue tunic that clung to her body.

The effects of the Drive Stun taser had not worn off. Alexa felt woozy and disoriented. The blood roared in her head. She tried to stand, but one of the assailants sat on her legs and smashed a fist into her face. It almost took her head off. She gasped, blood gushing from her nose. The same man, who must have been two hundred pounds, hit her again and kept on hitting her. Alexa spit up more blood. Her right eye was swollen almost shut. Someone took over for the big guy and hit Alexa in the solar plexus, doubling her over. Then hands were all over her body, gripping her breasts, scratching at her stomach and her legs, digging into her blonde crotch, lifting up her ass and thrusting fingers inside it. Alexa moaned, trying to turn over, fighting them off, but the jolt from the taser had almost left her unconscious. Her strength was gone. Finally she could not move at all, lying naked on the filthy floor.

The attackers backed off a little bit, relishing the respite. She was their plaything. They could do anything to her that they wanted. One of the men held down Alexa's right arm, another of them her left arm. There was no feeling in them. They were deadened. A third man held her head still so she would stop thrashing.

Then the attackers systematically raped her.

They took their time about doing it, fondling her breasts, squeezing her face, lifting her up so she was on her side so they could knead her buttocks. One of them held her head so that she could see what each of them was doing to her. The assailants entered her while the others held her down, taking turns. There was no conversation. It was the nonchalance with which they raped her. There was no passion to it, no emotion, no fulfillment. It was carnal and brutal. She had been violated and she could not make a sound. Only her breath rattled in her throat as she gasped repeatedly.

There was a respite, which Alexa had been waiting for. One of the black-clothed figures knelt down beside her. It looked as if the attacker was trying to make sure that she was still breathing. She reached up suddenly and dragged the black ski mask off his face. She was delirious with pain and the effects of the taser which had stunned her. She saw a glimpse of the man's face, but it was just a blur. Whoever he was, he had not taken part in the rape. He had stood off to one side, out of the circle of darkness that encircled Alexa, but he did nothing to stop the others from continuing to fondle and slap her and slide into her.

Alexa knew who her rapists were.

The Elite.

All of them rogue cops. Tom Graves, Saul Cooper, Marvin Rabinski, Pete Hightower and Jerry Kilpatrick. Their leader was Frank Macamber. He was sweating like a stuck pig. She could smell his BO from a mile away, just as she had smelled it when he was talking to her at O'Grady's Tavern. He straddled her and the other members held the rookie cop in place. Macamber entered her. But all of the life had gone out of her. She was a lifeless doll that they could play with. She would not give Frank Macamber the satisfaction he needed. She lay with her chin pressed up and her breasts swinging as Macamber raped her. It was all over quickly. Then he pulled out of her. The others had let go of her face. She opened her eyes and stared up at Macamber. He did not like that. He slapped her hard twice, then three times. Blood gushed again from her split lip. Her left eye was now closed and would not reopen.

Macamber got to his feet. The other members of the squad crowded around him, including Jerry Kilpatrick who had quickly put back on his ski mask. Alexa lay back on the hard floor, not making a sound, her silent world filled with the pain and rage she felt inside. She wondered if they would rape her again, but she heard nothing now.

She pulled herself up into a sitting position. Her uniform had been tossed to one side. She found her panties that had been ripped off and put them into the pocket of her uniform. She pulled herself upright, hanging onto one of the iron poles that were scattered throughout the warehouse. She pulled her trousers of her uniform back onto her hips and buckled her belt. There was nothing she could do about the uniform tunic that had been ripped open. The bra was beside her, but she left it there. Her belt with the holster and the radio lay in an oblique shaft of moonlight. She leaned over and picked them up, putting them back on her hips. She moved forward, trying to regulate her breathing. She found her Glock 19 in a corner. It had been emptied of bullets. She put the gun back into her holster.

Her world was made up of shadow and silence and pain.

Alexa took two more steps toward the warehouse door before she collapsed to the floor again, allowing the darkness to flood in.

Officer Tony Palmer knelt beside his partner. She was conscious now, disoriented, looking up at the shadows that surrounded her.

"I called for back-up," he said, gently. "The ambulance will be here in five."

Alexa nodded, but even doing that brought a wave of nausea. Palmer held onto her. He could see the evidence of the beating she had sustained. Her left eye had been closed and her right eye was a slit. The blood had stopped flowing from her nose and had concealed. She reached up and pulled her uniform tunic around her exposed breasts with a trembling hand. She looked up into her partner's face and just said: "Okay."

"Who attacked you?"

She swallowed hard, trying to force herself to form a few words, which was difficult at the best of times.

"Six men."

"Did you recognize any of them?"

"Wore ski masks."

"They jumped you?"

"Taser."

Palmer heard vehicles pulling up around the warehouse. The EMTs had just arrived. "I left the door of the warehouse open. Just hold on."

"Couldn't do anything," Alexa said. "Too many." She reached up and gripped Palmer's arm. "Waiting for me."

"They were waiting for you here in the warehouse?"

Alexa nodded, the fingers of her left hand digging into her partner's arm. "Planned it. Knew I would investigate. Padlock broken."

"You should have called in for back-up."

"I know," she whispered. "Wasn't thinking."

"Can you describe these men, even though they were wearing ski masks?"

Alexa knew who they were, but she had no proof. She looked up into Parmer's face, the humiliation and betrayal in her expressive eyes.

"*Elite*," she said, softly.

Officer Palmer was stunned. He murmured: "You've got to be kidding me," but Alexa could not hear him.

The EMT's arrived, wheeling a gurney right up to where Alexa was lying with her back at one of the empty offices. Uniformed patrolmen moved into the warehouse, accompanied by detectives from the 35th Precinct at Midtown South. Two EMT's had answered the emergency call. One was a no-nonsense paramedic whose named badge said *Croselli*. She was a little older than Alexa. Her partner's name badge said *Whitford* and looked like he should be surfing in Malibu or Hawaii. Tony Palmer straightened up from Alexa. The EMT's started dealing with Alexa right away, not realizing at first that she was deaf. It was Croselli who made the connection. She needed to know that Alexa could hear what she was saying.

"I can hear you fine," Alexa said in her halting way.

"You're doing great," Croselli said.

Whitford was on the same page. "We need you to…" Alexa was turned away from him, so he touched her arm to bring her attention back to him. "We're going to put you on the gurney. We'll lift you up."

"What's your name, Officer?" Croselli asked her.

"Alexa."

"We're going to lift you up between us, Alexa," Whitfield said.

"Just let us do all the work," Croselli said.

Officer Tony Palmer had backed away further. The two EMT's lifted Alexa up and placed her onto the gurney. Croselli was careful not to touch Alexa's uniform blouse which she held together at her chest even though the buttons on it had all been scattered on the warehouse floor. Whitfield put a blanket over her. She nodded her thanks.

Alexa turned her head so she could see her partner Palmer. He was talking to the detectives from the 35th Precinct who had caught the call. She felt ashamed of the state which they had found her. While Whitfield secured her to the gurney, Croselli gripped Alexa's hand and held it tightly. Her voice was filled with compassion. She looked over at her partner..

"These animals did a real number on her."

Alexa laid her head back on the gurney and whatever strength she had left drained out of her. She closed her eyes and sense-memory took over. The beatings and the violations to her body surged inside her head. There were images of the men, but disjointed, ill-defined, just impressions of brutality.

Then the darkness seeped through the memories and she passed out.

▶ 12 ◀

DAWN WAS BREAKING in vivid splashes of color when Kyu-Chul landed the CH-47F Chinook helicopter on the roof the eight-story, block-long US Embassy building at 188 Sejong-daero. Jonguo-gu in the heart of Seoul. Immediately Yo-Han started gathering the North Korean prisoners and moving them out of the chopper onto the flat roof. They were frightened and disoriented, but McCall jumped out and moved among them, telling them that they were in a safe place. It did not take long before yellow-jacketed guards had surrounded the helicopter with automatic rifles. Fredrik Jorgensen spoke Korean to them, explaining that these were prisoners who had been liberated from a North Korean prison camp. Granny lifted Liz Montgomery out of the chopper. By that time Ambassador Harry Harris, U.S. Ambassador to the Republic of Korea, had been summoned. McCall had been briefed on him by Control. Ambassador Harris was the first Asian-American to hold a four-star rank in the US Navy and the first to head USPACO. He held the State Department's Distinguished Honor Award, the Defense Distinguished Service Medal, plus 3 Navy Distinguished Service Medals, 2 Bronze Stars and the Air Medal. McCall recalled that he had also been awarded the Republic of Korea's Tong-il Medal in 2014. As startling as their arrival on the roof of the US Embassy had been, the Ambassador swiftly took charge of the situation. McCall gave him his passport. Granny gave him his passport that he had stolen back from Myang-Sook-Jang's desk, along with Liz Montgomery passport. He also handed the Ambassador Fredrick Jorgensen's Dutch passport and Water Coburn's South Africa passport. Harry carried out Walter Coburn from the chopper.

"This man needs urgent medical assistant," McCall said. "He's been shot. The wounds are life-threatening."

The Ambassador quickly ordered a wheelchair up to the roof of the Embassy. He handed the four passports back to McCall. He left Fredrick Jorgensen's passport with the US Ambassador. Harry had now evacuated all of the North Korean prisoners, doing a head count: Sixty-six in all. More US Embassy staff had made it up to the roof now, accessing the situation for themselves. McCall made sure all of the North Korean prisoners were beneath the rotors. Then he turned and gave Kyu-Chul the high sign. The helicopter lifted up off the roof before any of the guards had a chance to bring their weapons on it. The mercenary banked steeply over the building, heading back to the Yangyang Airport where the chopper would be picked up by Kyu-Chul's "friends". The US Embassy staff escorted the North Korean ex-prisoners to four conference rooms on the third floor of the building, supervised by Granny and Liz Montgomery. McCall elected to go with the wheelchair down to the street level. The EMT's lifted Water Coburn onto a gurney and closed the back doors. McCall hitched a ride with the ambulance to the Korea Univ Guro Hospital at 148, Gurodong-ro, Guro-gu in Seoul.

The ER doctors worked on Coburn and then sent him up to the OR. McCall waited for him in a spartan waiting room until one of the doctors came to tell him that Coburn was out of danger. It had been touch-and-go, but the bullets that had struck him had missed vital arteries. The physician said that Coburn was conscious and had been asking for Robert McCall. McCall showed the doctor his passport. The physician said he would have to make out a report about the gunshot wounds. McCall had been expecting that. He would be happy to sign any paperwork he was given. He did not mention the fact he was going to be leaving South Korea that night.

McCall found Walter Coburn in his private room on the second floor. He pulled a chair over to Coburn's bed. He had been instructed by Coburn's doctor that he had only a few minutes with him. The South African contractor looked pretty good to McCall after all he had been through. His voice was rough, but strong.

"How are you feeling?" McCall asked.

"Like I was dragged backwards through a meat grinder. Do these doctors know where I came from?"

"They only know you were shot multiple times," McCall said, "and were brought to the Univ Guro Hospital here for treatment. Whatever else you tell them is up to you."

"Have all of the western prisoners been accounted for?"

"They have. Liz Montgomery is with them at the U.S. Embassy. Fredrick Jorgensen has been translating. When I left there was a mob scene in four conference rooms where the North Korean prisoners were being processed. I think it was just getting through to them that they were free and on South Korean soil."

"Did Granny make it out alive?" Coburn asked.

"He did."

"Bloody good." Coburn squinted at him through the sunlight reflected through the window. "Your name's McCall, right?"

"That's right."

Coburn nodded. "Granny talked about you. He said if there was one person who could get us out of that hell-hole it was you."

"I had help."

"Yeah, a couple of Korean mercenaries were with you. One of them didn't look like he was old enough to shave."

"They got the job done."

"Too right they did.:

He handed Walter Coburn back his passport which he left on the bedside table.

"Thanks. I figure you aren't going to be staying around for long."

"I have a ride back to the States tonight," McCall said.

"Going to take Granny and Liz with you?"

"That's the idea. What will you do once they tell you can leave the hospital?"

"I'm a South African contractor," Coburn said. "I haul goods all over Europe. I have a missionary school I look out for in South Sudan. Government forces have been killing and decimating the people for years. President Salva Kiir got booted out and that left the country under martial law. The UN has 7500 troops on the ground there. I need to get back to my missionary parish, make sure they are all right. I would like to look Granny up one of these days. We bonded. That happens when you are blowing the shit out of a prison camp. Where I would find him?"

"Probably in Central Park in New York City playing chess."

"I'll keep that in mind."

Coburn were getting heavy-lidded. McCall stood up. "Get some rest. That missionary school in South Sudan needs you."

Walter Coburn opened his eyes again, looking at McCall with a sudden fierce intensity. "Any idea where that asshole Korean mercenary took our beautiful Deva Montgomery and Daniel Blake?"

"Not yet."

"What was his name?"

"I don't know."

"But you're going to find him?"

"Count on it," McCall said.

"Are you going to take Granny with you?"

"I would have a lot of trouble keeping him away," McCall said. "It's a safe bet they flew out of North Korea, so they could be anywhere by now."

Walter Coburn looked back up at McCall's face with some intensity. "Granny said that you don't give up. He had a nickname for you. Something about the odds being in your favor."

"That sounds about right. You saved a lot of lives today, Walter. Get out of this hospital. Those missionaries are counting on you."

"Too bloody right."

Walter Coburn had closed his eyes again. One of the nurses came into the room at that moment. She looked at Coburn's vital signs as McCall was leaving.

McCall took a cab to Tapgol Park on 97 Jongno Street in the center of Seoul. Kyu-Chul was sitting on the steps of a ten-story stone pagoda in the park. A high-rise towered over it. There was another glass-encased monument of Wongaksa which had been built in 1471. Tourists and locals strolled through the park. Kyu-Chul straightened when McCall approached. He glanced around them.

"Where's Harry?"

"Trapped in the US Embassy making sure the North Korean prisoners are getting treatment for the horrors they suffered in Commandant Jang's prison," McCall said. "The Embassy are making calls to various family members who are enroute to the Embassy. All the North Korean prisoners were suffering from malnutrition and dysentery."

Kyu-Chul nodded. "Harry will disappear from the Embassy as soon as he can and meet me here."

"You had no trouble returning the Chinook CH-47F helicopter back to Yangyang Airport?"

"My friends were waiting for me," Kyu-Chul said. "I owe them. It's a debt they will call in at some point."

McCall and Kyu-Chul strolled away from the stone pagoda through the trees of the park.

"Where do you go now?" McCall asked him.

"Kashmir in India. The conflict there has separatists attacking the existing Indian government. There have been hundreds of casualties, mainly among children. There is a train in Bannu Station that has been filled with two thousand refuges meant to hold no more than a thousand. Five thousand lie on the station platform suffering from pneumonia and cholera. They sold everything they carried with them, umbrellas, pots, pieces of clothing, to pay for food. I have to reach that station and get the refugees onto that train."

"Do you know any of them?"

"Not a soul."

"Then why do you do it?"

Kyu-Chul shrugged. "Why not?"

McCall nodded. It was the answer he was expecting. "Will you take Harry with you?"

"Just as soon as he finishes his latest Lego game."

"You've been together a long time."

"He would not survive without me."

At that moment McCall saw Harry jump out of a cab and hustle through the park toward them. He was out of breath when he reached them.

"Man, getting out of the US Embassy was tougher than getting into Commandant Jang's prison. I left Fredrick Jorgensen doing his interpreter thing. The US Ambassador had already called the CIA who will want to question all of us, but that was the time I bailed. I gave the Ambassador a description of that Korean hitman who visited Jang. What was his name again?"

"Ji-Yeon," Kyu-Chul said.

"Right. Your dude Granny had already given Deva Montgomery's description to the Ambassador, along with the Associated Press journalist, Daniel Blake," Harry said. "God knows where Ji-Yeon took them. As far as the North Korean government is concerned, there *was* no prison camp located just south of the Yalu River. The North Koreans were holding no western prisoners. I wanted to tell the Ambassador that the prison camp was no longer in existence because we blew the shit out of, but I did not think it was my place to mention that. Liz Montgomery, the photojournalist babe, is pretty distraught about her sister Deva, but she is keeping it together. I believe agents of the CIA are on their way to the Embassy."

"They are going to want to interrogate you about what happened at that prison camp," McCall said.

"There's nothing we can tell them," Kyu-Chul said. "We were never *in* North Korea."

McCall nodded and held out his hand. "I would never have made it without you."

"It's what we do," Harry said, and his signature grin flashed.

The two Korean mercenaries shook hands with McCall, somewhat somberly. He left them walking through the little park arguing about the final *Games of Thrones* episode.

McCall called Granny on his cell phone and his cab pulled up outside the Seoul Ace Tower near Jonggak Station where Harry had told him there was a fabulous Starbucks. He found it on the second floor, a triangular bar filled with various coffee drinks and welcoming baristas. Granny and Liz Montgomery were seated at the end of the bar on low, cloth-covered stools. Both of them were sipping Teavana Blueberry Bliss tea and were holding hands. Liz looked about at the end of her emotional endurance. Both of them had changed from the North Korean prison uniforms to western clothes which consisted of jeans, dress shirts and lightweight jackets which one of the Embassy assistants and gone out to purchase for them. Liz was wearing a Nike running shoe in a light blue. Granny had been given a Nike Vapor Max in pink. McCall handed Granny two passports, one for himself and one for Liz.

"I handed Water Coburn his passport and he kept hold of Fredrick Jorgensen's passport to give to him. Walter is out of danger, resting comfortably."

"The Ambassador at the US Embassy was good enough to get us new clothes," Granny said. "He asked us to wait until the cavalry had arrived at the Embassy along with several CIA agents. I did not want to seem ungrateful, because the Ambassador was compassionate and savvy, but I knew we were not going to stay long. He wanted to hear our story from the beginning, but I didn't think that Control would appreciate that."

"Control was out of the loop," McCall said.

Granny nodded. "I figured as much, but I wasn't taking any chances. Do we have a ride home?"

McCall nodded. "Waiting for us at Incheon International Airport, but we won't be travelling on a regular commercial flight. Are you both ready to go?"

Liz reached out for Granny's hand and held it tightly. "Granny took care of Myang-Sook-Jang," she said. "He did that much for me. But it is not enough. I need to know where my sister Deva has been taken."

"Granny and I will find her," McCall said.

"You can promise me that?"

"I can."

Liz nodded her thanks. "Then get me the fuck out of this country."

McCall and Granny slid off the bar stools, leaving their teas behind. Outside McCall had already called for a taxi to take them to the airport. The cabbie dropped them off at the far end of the airport where the hangers were located. Hayden Vallance was waiting for them on the tarmac in his Global 6000 Vista 9H-VJJ jet. He had flown to Seoul in the hope that McCall had got out of North Korea. He had not been surprised to get the call on McCall's cell phone. His other passengers were Granny, a friend of McCall's, and Elizabeth Montgomery, a photojournalist whom Vallance knew by reputation. She looked exhausted and shaky, but she walked up the steps with Granny into the Vista jet.

Vallance looked over at McCall. "When I didn't from back from you I didn't know if you were lying in a mass grave somewhere in North Korea."

"It was touch and go for a few hours," McCall admitted.

"Did everyone at that prison camp get out in one piece?"

"I lost two of the prisoners to a terrorist mercenary named Ji-Yeon."

"I know of him," Vallance said. "He has got quite a reputation. A nasty piece of work."

"Liz Montgomery is a photojournalist. It was her sister who was kidnapped. The other captive was a journalist working for Associated Press named Daniel Blake. They were hauled onboard a MD-500 military helicopter by Ji-Yeon and taken out of North Korea."

"Where are they now?"

"I don't know," McCall said.

"But you're going to find out." Vallance said. "I'd like be on that rescue mission when you find them."

McCall looked at him with some irony. "I thought you didn't get involved in missions that have nothing to do with you?"

"It must be associating with you," Vallance said, wryly.

"You did come back for me in Syria."

Vallance nodded. "I did. It was against my better judgement. Let us get of here before the South Korean police take a good look at your passports."

McCall climbed the steps into the Vista jet. Hayden Vallance climbed after him and closed the jet door. Five minutes later the Bombardier Global Vista 9H-VJJ lifted into the sky and headed back toward New York City.

Tony Palmer stood in Alexa Kokinas's darkened hospital room. She was asleep. Her doctors had her hooked up to an EKG machine to monitor her heart and an IV had been inserted into a vein in her hand. The bruises on her face and arms were purple where they had crushed small blood vessels under the skin. Her right eye had closed almost shut. Her left eye was still a slit. There were lacerations on her face and one of her cheekbones and been fractured and surgery had been required to replace the bone chips. She was breathing on her own, but a respirator was standing by.

Palmer felt a rage inside him that had not subsided since he had first looked at her.

There was a soft knock on the hospital door that made Palmer turn. Detective Frank Macamber stood in the doorway, motioning for him to join him. Palmer took one last look at Alexa's face, then he exited the room and closed the door behind him. Small, muted sounds came down from the nurse's station where several of the nurses were accessing laptop computers. There was a sense of suppressed urgency to the activity in the ward. Two more detectives, Pete Hightower and Saul Cooper, were talking in muted tones to a doctor at the nurse's station. Detective Macamber took hold of Palmer's right arm in a vicelike grip. His florid face was flushed with color and his eyes were dark, grey chips.

He lowered his voice tersely. "What the hell happened to your partner?"

"She checked out an abandoned warehouse on Fremont Street."

"I know the one. Down the street from O'Grady's Saloon."

"That's the one," Palmer said. "She routinely checks there on her way home. This time the gate was ajar and the padlock and been smashed. She went inside with her weapon drawn."

"Didn't she call for backup for Christ sake?"

"She did, but not right away. In the darkness she was attacked by six men wearing black clothing. All of them were wearing ski masks. She was disarmed and thrown to the warehouse floor. One of them used a taser on her, drive-stun capacity. It incapacitated her to the point where she could offer no resistance."

"Son of a bitch! She should have waited for back-up! Jesus Christ! I knew something like this would happen to Alexa. She is deaf, for God's sake! She should not have been on patrol alone. A deaf cop is a liability. It was only a matter of time before she would turn the wrong way and let a perp disarm her!"

"She was brutally attached, Frank," Palmer said. "They used a stun gun on her. There were six of them."

"Any descriptions that Alexa could give you?"

"She said she only saw shapes and shadows."

Macamber nodded, as if he were tracking with this logic. "A street gang using the warehouse for drugs. Your partner happened to be in the wrong place at the wrong time."

"Alexa said they were waiting for her." Palmer said.

Macamber looked at him. He looked back at Alexa's hospital room. "Did she say that?"

"That was my impression. They were expecting her."

Frank Macamber looked back at him. "How could they have been expecting her?"

"She checks out that warehouse every day. Routine. They were lying wait for her in the shadows. She said it as a coordinated assault. They knew what they were doing."

"I guess they could have jumped her in any dark street."

"They chose a place that was abandoned, where no one could disturb them except maybe a homeless person taking shelter from the cold."

"All speculation. We need a description! Height, weight, any distinguishing marks or tattoos."

"She was drifting in and out of consciousness," Palmer said. "I couldn't get much out of her. I thought I would go back to that warehouse and take another look around."

"Fuck you," Macamber said. "That's a crime scene. I have got several of my Officers in there right now. The last time I checked, Palmer, you were not a detective. You were a patrolman. I already had a meeting with my Captain at the precinct. You are going to be assigned a new partner until we see how Alexa pulls through. Even if she does recover, she's finished as a Peace Officer."

Palmer was keeping a tight rein on his emotions. He had wanted to give Macamber the chance to make a mistake. Get caught out in a lie. But he was too smart for that.

"Alexa will recover from this assault."

"You don't get it, do you, Officer Palmer," Macamber said. "Your partner is toast. It was terrible what happened to her, but it was her own fault. She should not have gone into that warehouse alone. Rookie mistake. A costly one. She is lucky these animals did not beat her to death. We are going to find the men responsible for this cowardly assault. But leave that to us. I am mounting a full-scale inquiry. The *Elite* are going to be beating the sidewalks and turning every rock over. We are going to find these assholes and bring them in. You stay out of it. Are we clear here? Let me and my squad do their job. We got this." He put a meaty paw on Palmer's arm. "Anything Alexa needs, we'll be there for her. You can tell her that."

Macamber let Palmer go and moved over to where his two detectives were talking to Alexa's doctor in subdued tones. Officer Palmer moved back into Alexa's room and stood looking down at her bedside. She had still not moved from her fitful sleep. He leaned over her.

"I know who was responsible for this attack," he said softly.

Alexa did not stir. Two nurses came into the room with a doctor Palmer had not seen before. He left them to it and existed the room. Detectives Hightower and Cooper had left. Frank Macamber was standing at the nurse's station staring at Palmer. His expression was as empty as his eyes. Officer Palmer walked down to the bank of elevators. He knew in his heart who the perpetrators were.

But proving it was something else.

▶ **13** ◀

SAINT-LUKE'S LUTHERAN church was located at 808 W Forty-Six Street in Hell's Kitchen. If you did not know it was there, you could miss it. Mickey Kostmayer liked going to Joe Allen's between 8th and 9th Avenue. It was a theatre restaurant with a lively ambiance with a great bar and posters on the brick walls of Broadway shows. Kostmayer always had the same entrée: Steak Tartare with toast points, arugula, sautéed spinach and banana cream pie. He ate by himself, usually up at the bar, where he knew all of the waiters. Today he was waiting for Candy Annie to join him. She had the late shift at Langan's Irish Pub and Restaurant off Seventh Avenue, but she did not have to be there until 4:00 PM. Kostmayer had told her that he was going to introduce her to someone that he thought she might like to meet. He was still angry with Robert McCall for excluding him from his mission to North Korea, although he understood the reasons. McCall had not returned and Kostmayer had heard nothing of his fate. He could not even go and find Brahms who always had his ear to the ground because he was still in the Holy Land.

When Kostmayer emerged from Joe Allen's he saw Candy Annie striding down the street toward him. She had on her black outfit for work at Langan's and was wearing open-toed sandals. She brightened when she saw him. It was still a little scary for her to be out in the streets of New York City. She was still not used to the constant barrage of people in her face. Her quiet, silent world beneath the Manhattan streets had been a sanctuary for her for many years. She had been grateful that Robert McCall had rescued her from that life, and even more grateful that she had met Mickey Kostmayer. But it was still daunting for her to be accosted by so many people whom she did not know and would never know.

Kostmayer took her arm and propelled her down 46th Street toward 8th Avenue.

"Your phone message sounded mysterious!" Candy Annie said. "Where are we going?"

"To church," Kostmayer told her.

They walked down the street and came to 8th Avenue where imposing limestone stairs led up to St. Luke's Lutheran church. Candy Annie looked up in some awe at the neo-Gothic building and the adjoining parish house and rectory. Kostmayer opened the church for Candy Annie and they stepped into the cool, hushed interior. He noted there was no service until the evening. It was quiet inside in the old-style pews. Kostmayer remembered the free-standing organ and the stained-glass panels and the nave with its wood roof. He and Candy Annie walked down the center aisle past the holy water throne to the front pew where the organist sat. The pastor had been playing a few isolated chords. Behind him the main altar was shrouded in cloth and there was a lone crucifix of wood placed in the center. The pastor got to his feet and approached them. He was a slight man in his late fifties wearing a white shirt with no tie and a pair of dress pants. He smiled when he saw Kostmayer, although the smile was tinged with some sadness. Kostmayer did not shake hands with the pastor.

"Candy Annie, this is my brother, Father David Kostmayer."

Candy Annie saw the resemblance immediately between the two brothers. The pastor was at least ten years older than Kostmayer. He had a ready smile and a way of making his congregation feel like they belonged. He shook hands with Candy Annie.

"So you're the young woman that Mickey has been telling me about. Where does the 'candy' come from?"

"I used to eat a lot of candy when I saw younger. Gummy bears, jelly babies, nougat, chocolate frogs and bunnies. The name kind of stuck."

"My brother told me you haven't been living in New York City for long."

"Actually, Annie has been living here for over ten years," Kostmayer said. "But that was when she resided *below* the streets of the city. In the subterranean tunnels and passageways. She came back to the *Upworld* to start a new life. My friend Robert McCall was responsible for making that happen."

"You have mentioned this friend of yours more than once to me," Father Kostmayer said. "Is he still in the same business?"

"You mean is he still a spy for a clandestine organization like me? No, he resigned. Or so he says. I am still operating in the shadows, but you knew that was never going to change."

There was an edge to Kostmayer's voice when talking to his brother that Candy Annie immediately recognized. A deep-seated hurt that he could not disguise. Candy Annie knew that kind of resentment from when she had lived in the subway tunnels with the Subterranean dwellers. They did not allow people into their lives. Father Kostmayer just shrugged off the abrasive tone with a smile which Candy Annie thought would probably infuriate Kostmayer even more.

"What brings you to this place of worship?" he asked.

Candy Annie was suddenly tongue-tied for a response. "Well, it's just… I have been wanting to do some good… not that I have anything to show for it, but…"

"She's meaning to do some kind of charity work since we got together," Kostmayer said. "I thought you might have a place where she could accomplish that."

"I have the just the place," David said. "I have been ramping up the care packages that the congregation are sending out each month. They are shipped to children's hospitals and clinics around the world. In fact, my volunteers are putting together a new shipment right now heading for the South Sudan which we are liaising with UNICEF. Children are experiencing violence and exploitation as never before. Their survival depends on life-saving denotations. Would that be something you could get involved in? It would only be part-time."

Candy Annie's face lit up. "I would be honored to part of something like that!"

"I have a community space just few doors from the church on W 46th Street," he said, "where the care packages are being organized. I was just heading there. Would you like me to show you around? I can introduce you to the volunteers."

Candy Annie looked expectantly at Kostmayer. Some of the rancor had left his attitude. He nodded. "You're in good hands."

David Kostmayer turned to his brother. "Will you accompany us?"

"Not my thing, Father," Kostmayer said and smiled.

"It has a been a long time since you visited this church. It's always good to see you."

"Even if I am still battling my own personal demons?"

"Your work for the Lord is not done yet."

"Knowing the parish priest gets me in the door at least."

Now it was Father Kostmayer turn to smile. "Good to have friends in high places."

"Since I haven't been in your beautiful church in quite a long time, I wanted to spend some quiet moments here."

"Take all the time you need. I'll escort your girlfriend to the community center."

"I am not really his girlfriend," Candy Annie protested, a little embarrassed. "Just a good friend."

"For a 'spy', as my brother likes to describe me, I don't keep secrets very well," Kostmayer said, wryly. He turned to Candy Annie. "You go on, Annie. There's a candle I need to light for someone."

Candy Annie kissed him on the cheek and then accompanied Father David Kostmayer to the doors of the church. When they had exited, Kostmayer stood for a moment in the stillness. He walked to the vestibule, picked up one of the unlit candles, lit it and placed in on the railing in front of the likeness of Christ's image, which in this case was a statue of the Savior on the cross. Kostmayer knelt down to say a silent prayer in the hushed ambiance.

Someone moved out of the shadows.

Granny said: "If you're lighting that candle for me, you might say a prayer for both of us."

Kostmayer got his feet and whirled around. Granny stood in front of him, smiling his lopsided grin. The two friends embraced, then Kostmayer held Granny at arm's length.

"Damn, it's good to see you." he said.

"Likewise."

"McCall got you out?"

Granny shrugged. "Who else?"

"You've lost a lot of weight."

"North Korean food didn't agree with me."

"You look like shit."

Granny smiled. "I'll take that as a compliment."

"Did McCall make it out himself?"

"He did. Dropped me off right here in the city. Take a walk with me?"

Kostmayer and Granny took a stroll through Central Park where the chess tables were located. Granny told him everything that had happened in the North Korean prison camp. Kostmayer listened, injecting an occasional response, but he was happy to let Granny tell his story. Finally there as a lull between them. Granny looked over at the chess tables where he recognized a couple of players, including Mike Gammon.

"Feels good to be back."

"Where is Liz Montgomery now?" Kostmayer asked.

"At her apartment in Gramercy Park," Granny said, "She has got an office at CNN. I will be picking her up for dinner later. I tried to get her go to a doctor, but she is headstrong. Almost bit my head off."

Kostmayer smiled. "That sounds promising." After a moment, he added: "You've got no idea where this mercenary Ji-Yeon took Liz's sister when he flew that MD-500 chopper out of the North Korean prison camp?"

"None whatsoever." Granny said. "I talked to Control about Ji-Yeon as soon I got back here. He has got quite a reputation in Europe and Russia, but he is a phantom. He is going to put the word out through diplomatic channels. I know that Ji-Yeon had been working with al Qaeda."

Kostmayer glanced over at the softball games being played in the park. "Once he's finished with Deva Montgomery he'll put a bullet in her head."

"Not his style. But he might keep her as a pet."

"Now there is a charming thought."

"I cannot allow Liz to believe that is true," Granny said. "One way or the other it would destroy her."

"So you're going to look for her," Kostmayer said, "and this AP journalist Daniel Blake?"

"That's the plan."

"Not a plan sanctioned by our Government?"

Granny just looked at him. Kostmayer nodded. "What's McCall's take on this situation?"

"He doesn't have one," Granny said. "He came to North Korean to rescue an old friend and get him out safely. He did that. Liz Montgomery and her sister Deva were not on his radar."

Kostmayer smiled. "I don't believe that and neither do you. Once McCall becomes involved in your life, he does not leave anyone behind. He will be looking for Deva Montgomery and Daniel Blake wherever they have been taken. He will rescue them. Count on it."

"Rhetorical question," Granny said. "I understand you have a new girlfriend?"

Kostmayer nodded. "You'd like her. She is feisty and very sweet. She lived *under* the New York streets most of her life. McCall brought her back into the *Upworld*. She's with my brother David right now doing some charity work for him at his church."

"I look forward to meeting her."

Kostmayer glanced across the park again at the chess tables. "I wanted to go North Korea on the mission. McCall stopped me."

"You escaped from that hellhole once." Granny said. "McCall didn't want you to do that again. He was looking out for you. The way he always does. You know where to find me."

Granny moved over to where Mike Gammon was standing now at one of the chess tables. Granny shook his hand, said something that Kostmayer could not quite hear, then they both sat down at the chess table and Granny pinged the timer.

"Good to have you back, Granny," Kostmayer said, softly.

▶ 14 ◀

MCCALL WAITED FOR Stavros Kokinas outside the entrance to Loi Estiatorio's Greek restaurant at 132 W. 58th Street, just down from Central Park West. The proprietor was Chef Maria Loi and she was the finest Greek cook in New York City in McCall's opinion. Her establishment was cozy, the staff were outgoing and accommodating in an atmosphere that called for the finest of Greek hospitality. Marie Loi was the heart of it. She hailed from Nafpaktos. McCall often stopped late at the restaurant when the crowds had gone to sample Chef Loi's spreads: Tzatziki, Tyrokafteri, Melitzanosalata and Hummus, followed by Tiger Prawns, arugula, cauliflower, lemon and olive oil. Marie Loi had published 36 cookbooks and was a celebrity who had catered to President Obama and Vice-President Joe Biden and 250 guests at the White House. A group of Greek men exited the restaurant with Marie Loi in their midst. The carefree ambiance had not carried out onto the sidewalk. The mood was somber. The center of attention was a stocky, good looking man in his early sixties, Stavros Kokinas, who was Alexa's father. He shook hands with the waiters and gave Maria Loi a hug. She glanced over at McCall and nodded, as if she understood now who he was. Stavros walked over to him. McCall held out his hand.

"I'm Robert McCall."

Stavros shook his hand. "Stavros Kokinas. You know Maria Loi?"

"Best Greek restaurateur in the city."

"She is. Walk with me into the park."

They crossed 59th Street outside the Plaza Hotel and entered Central Park. Stavros's voice was clipped and terse. "Detective First Grade Steve Lansing at the 7th Precinct told me you help people. That you are some kind of a knight errant. Sounds like a vigilante to me who takes the law in his own hands."

"When I have to."

"As a Police Officer I can't condone that."

"I have rules," McCall said. "Why don't you tell me what has happened to you?"

"Not to me," he said. "To my daughter Alexa."

McCall waited. There was so much rage bottled up in the man that it threatened to explode. They walked through the trees, heading toward the Pond. Finally Stavros was able to contain his wrath and bring it down to an acceptable level, but it simmered just below the level of violence.

"I'm a cop. I have been teaching at the Police Academy for thirty-two years. We used to be located at 20th Street in Gramercy Park but in 2014 we moved to West College Point in Queens. A 750,000 square-foot facility that covers three buildings. I train the police recruits in communication skills, safe tactics, intelligence gathering and shooting training. I teach counterterror methodologies, counter surveillance technology and education to protect the lives, rights and dignity of all New Yorkers and their visitors."

They skirted around the Pond and headed in the direction of the baseball diamond and the chess tables. Stavros was on a roll. "We have numerous locations with-

in the facility that can be utilized. We got a precinct stationhouse, a multi-family residence and a convenience
store that gets robbed every day. On purpose, of course.
We got a bank and a subway car and platform. It's a great
facility."

They passed the Zoo and headed down The Mall toward the Sheep Meadow.

McCall waited.

Stavros said: "My daughter Alexa had wanted to
be a Peace Officer since she was five years old. She was
a grade-A student who graduated high school with honors. She joined the Police Force when she was twenty-two
years old. She is volatile and fiery and conducts herself
with dignity and compassion. She has had to deal with
a major handicap. She is hearing impaired. Which is the
polite way to say that she is deaf. Not totally. She has hearing in her left ear. But it is like being underwater for her.
She says she hears a whooshing sound like static on an
old transistor radio which comes in and out, but she cannot hear the music. But she copes with it beautifully. She's
tough and she's strong."

Stavros seemed to run out of words. He stopped and
looked through the trees toward Strawberry Fields and
the John Lennon Memorial.

Finally McCall said: "Is your daughter the only hear-
ing-impaired Police Officer on the force?"

"There's only one other, a Deputy Sheriff in Arizona.
About the same age as Alexa."

"Tell me what happened, Stavros."

The tough Greek took a breath and slowly let it out.
"Alexa was alone in her patrol car down on the Lower East
Side. She has got a partner, Officer Tony Palmer, a couple
of years older, who swore he would look after her, but he
did not. She entered an old warehouse building down the

block. The gate had been left open. A padlock had been broken off. Alexa approached with all due caution, but she did not immediately call for back-up. She had her weapon drawn. She entered the warehouse and was attacked out of the shadows. Alexa said that the perps were all wearing black clothing and ski masks. They used a taser on her to bring her down to her knees." Stavros paused, collecting himself. He said: "They raped her. When it was all over, they left her on the floor of the warehouse barely able to breathe. Officer Palmer found her and radioed it in. They took her to Bellevue Hospital."

"Can she give a positive ID on the men who assaulted her?"

"I know one of them," Stavros said. "A NYPD homicide cop out of the 16th Precinct named Frank Macamber. I taught him at the Police Academy. He is a foul-mouthed, bigoted asshole who graduated at the top of his class. He is a dirty cop who takes graft and distributes heroin to the street gangs. The 16th Precinct has trying to make a case against him for harassment and intimidation, but they have never been able to prove anything. He has a clean record."

"So Alexa can't say for certain that Macamber was one of her attackers?" McCall asked.

"No," Stavros said. "But Officer Palmer believes her and so do I. There were six of them altogether that graduated from the Academy. Unusual for all of them to get assigned to the 16th Precinct, but that was calculated. Frank Macamber had markers he cashed in. They had a nickname at the Academy. They called themselves *The Elite*. They were fighting crime. Cleaning up the streets of New York. They are scum like you would wipe off your shoe. We have a word in Greek. It is *Viasmos*. It means *ravishment*. That was what they did to my little girl. They ravished her and left her unconscious on that warehouse floor with the filth and the rats."

The man's hands were shaking. He stopped amid the trees to try to compose himself.

"Who is leading the investigation at the 16th Precinct?" McCall asked.

Stavros looked at McCall with savage irony. "The *Elite*, of course. They will ask all the right questions, get statements from eyewitnesses, of which there were none. The crime will be swept under the rug and life with go on. Except that Alexa will be finished as a Peace Officer. She will he traumatized by this for a long time."

"You can't be sure these Police Officers were the rapists?" McCall objected.

"I would bet money on it, but that never will be proven. Macamber is the ringleader. So unless you get a better idea, Mr. McCall, one of these dark nights out in the streets I will put a bullet into Frank Macamber's brain."

McCall shook his head. "You'd be throwing your career and your life away."

"Only if I got caught. Are you going to try and stop me?"

"If you corner Macamber in a dark alley somewhere, that's game, set and match. You cannot do that, Stavros. You asked me my help. Let me see what I can do."

"Frank Macamber will hunt you down and kill you."

"I'll take my chances."

Stavros looked away again toward the John Lennon Memorial. "John Lennon was gunned in the street for no good reason. I've got a reason."

"You're a better man than that," McCall said. "In Greek, the term '*Philotimo*' means doing something with pride, with love and respect of oneself and one's family. The Greek word *psuche* is the aftermath of God breathing his life into a person. If you take someone's life, you will be losing your soul. Let me take care of this."

Stavros slowly nodded. "I will give you three days, Mr. McCall. Then I will be coming for Frank Macamber."

Stavros Kokinas walked away without another word toward Bow Bridge and The Lake.

Leaving Robert McCall to think about Frank Macamber and the *Elite*.

Alexa's doctors only gave McCall ten minutes alone with her. She had been moved from the ICU ward to a private room on the fourth floor of the hospital. She was hooked up to various machines monitoring her heart rate, blood pressure, an IV drip. McCall had sat beside her for five of those minutes. Her beautiful face was a mess. Her right eye had opened up a little, but her left eye was still a slit. Her face was heavily bandaged. She looked bleary and disoriented when she turned around to look at him.

"My name is Robert McCall," he told her softy. "Your father came to see me."

When Alexa spoke her voice was a hoarse whisper. "Why?"

"He wants to find justice for his daughter. I am going to help him do that."

She focused more on his face. "You are a cop?"

Her speech was more halting than usual. McCall shook his head. "No. But I am here to help you. You can read my lips. I will go slow, but we do not have a lot of time. I read the police report that your partner Tony Palmer made out for the precinct. You were in an abandoned warehouse. Six men attacked you. They were all wearing black?"

Alexa nodded.

"And black ski masks?"

Alexa nodded.

"But you didn't know who they were?"

She hesitated.

"I know you know who there were," McCall said. "But you can't be sure of their identities. Not unless you can identify them. Can you do that?"

Alexa shook her head. Unwanted tears came into her eyes and spilled down her face. Gently McCall wiped them away. "You can do this, Alexa. You know what you *saw*."

The soothing quality of McCall's voice reassured her. But she shook her head.

"Dark."

"Yes, it was dark, and the shadows were crowding in on you. I am not trying to cause you any more grief, but you could hear what these animals were doing to you. You have those images ingrained in your head. We can reconstruct what happened to you. I know it will be painful, but you are the only eyewitness to what happened. Close your eyes. Give me your impressions on a visceral level. Try to see back to that night."

Alexa searched his face for reassurance. Then she nodded and closed her eyes.

"You don't need to be able to see me, Alexa." McCall said, still very quiet in the hushed room. "Everything I need is in your subconscious. I know one of the men used a taser on you. That was how they were able to incapacitate you. Did any of them talk to you? Telling you to lie there, be still, don't fight them."

"No talking," she said haltingly.

"All right, that's good. These attackers were big men. Would that be right?"

"Yes."

"You can see that in your mind's eye."

Alexa nodded. "Yes."

"They held you down." McCall said. "Probably two or three of them at a time."

"Yes."

"Do you remember how they held you there? What was it an effort for them to keep you from struggling?"

"Taser."

"Yes, they used a taser. That is how they subdued you. Think of their breathing. What was it coming easily or were they grunting for breath?"

Alexa kept her eyes closed, reliving the nightmare. She said: "Heavy breathing."

"From all the attackers, or just one of them?"

"One of them."

"Like he had to catch his breath?"

Alexa nodded.

"Was he wheezing?"

Alexa nodded emphatically.

"Maybe he coughed a lot?"

Alexa nodded.

"A heavy smoker, probably. Prone to asthma attacks. Think about the order of the men who attacked you. When one of them climbed onto you, was there anything that set him apart from the others? I know this is hard for you to have to remember this trauma. But you were right there."

"Took turns."

"Were there any mannerisms you can remember?"

"Third attacker," Alexa said. "Had a laugh."

"He laughed at you?" Alexa shook her head, as if McCall did not understand. "But he had some kind of a laugh that resonated with you. Try to remember it. Was it deep-set or was it high-pitched?"

"A giggle."

"So this attacker had a nervous giggle."

"Peculiar," Alexa said. "A kid's laugh. When he was agitated."

'Had you ever heard it before?"

Alexa nodded. "Pool hall."

"You heard it when you were playing pool?"

Alexa nodded.

"Where was that?"

"O'Grady's Saloon."

"Where is that?"

"Lower East Side. Near Gramercy Park."

"Who were you playing pool with?"

"Cops."

"From your precinct?"

"16th."

"Were you beating this guy at pool?"

"Creaming his ass."

"How tall was this cop?"

"Over six feet."

"So he stooped over the pool table?"

"Yes."

"Were any of the others tall?"

"One was short."

"Maybe five feet six?"

"Taller than that."

"Five eight?"

"Like that."

She clenched her hands into fists on the bedcovers. More of the tears fell from her eyes.

"You're doing great," McCall said. "Take your time."

Alexa said haltingly: "One of them hit me. In the face. He made a sound when did that."

"What kind of a sound?"

"Humming."

"A distinct tune?"

"Just humming."

"The tall one or the short one?"

"Tall one."

"Did any of them have a lot of weight to him?"

"Yes. Big man. He was sweating."

"How do you know that?"

"I felt it on his hands."

"Who was the last attacker?"

"Another big man."

"But not bigger than the one who was sweating?"

"Not that big."

"But you felt this man's weight when he climbed on top of you."

"Yes. He smelled."

"What did he smell of?"

"Body odor. Made me nauseous."

"Where did you smell this body odor?"

"At the pool hall."

"One of the haunts of these cops?"

"They're there most every night."

"Anything else you can remember?"

Alexa shook her head, trying to bring the memories to the forefront of her mind.

"Did they just climb on you and climb off again?"

"Yes." Then she said: "Saw one of them standing up."

McCall moved closer to her. "One of them stood up?"

"Yes." Alexa was struck with the sudden sense-memory. "He took off his ski mask."

"Did you see his face?" McCall asked, urgently.

"Just profile."

"Did you see his eyes?"

"Cornflower blue."

"What color was his hair?"

"Fair hair. Sideburns."

"How long were his sideburns?"

"Long. His eyebrows were not there."

"What do you mean?"

"They were very fine. Like…"

. "Like an albino's eyebrows?" McCall asked her.

"Like that."

"What else could you see?"

"He turned from me right away. Embarrassed. Looking down at my naked body."

"Then what happened?"

"One of the others told him to put back on his ski mask."

"Did you recognize his voice?"

"Yes. From the pool hall. With the bad breath."

"What was his name?"

"Frank Macamber. Detective First Grade."

"Go back to the blonde cop with the sideburns," McCall said. "Was he one of the rapists?"

"No. He didn't want any part of it."

"But he let it happen."

"Yes."

McCall could tell that the rookie cop was exhausted. He put a gentle hand on her shoulder. "That's enough for now."

Alexa opened her eyes and looked up at him.

"I did okay?"

McCall smiled reassuringly at her. "I would say you were outstanding. You gave me detailed descriptions of your attackers, including the ringleader."

Alexa motioned toward a small table standing in front of the window. "Piece of paper."

McCall rose, picked up the pad from the table and brought it back to her. Alexa's hand flashed over the page. When she had she finished, she turned the page back so McCall could read it.

FRANK MACAMBER – PETE HIGHTOWER – TOM GRAVES – SAUL COOPER – MARVIN RABINS- KI – JERRY KILPATRICK

"The *Elite*," she said, softly.

"Not elite anymore," McCall said with an edge to his voice. "We know who they are. Your father knew also. Now I have to prove it."

Alexa shook her head. "Can't. These are corrupt *cops*. They will kill you."

"They can try." McCall took a card from wallet and put it beside the bedside table. "Call me anytime you need to. Day or night. Especially if Frank Macamber comes to see you. He is heading the investigation into your attack."

She took McCall's card with trembling hands. "Nothing you can do."

"Let me worry about that."

Her voice had a new hope in it, but she shook her head. "What can you do?".

"I can lower the odds against you."

McCall left her in her shadows. She looked again at his card. "You can't," she said, very softly. Then she said again: "They will kill you."

▶ 15 ◀

MᴄCᴀʟʟ ᴋɴᴇᴡ ʜᴇ ʜᴀᴅ picked up a tail as soon as he had left the Bellevue Hospital at First Avenue and 26th Street. He crossed uptown in the cab, lost the tail in the traffic, then picked it up again after passing Central Park, heading up to the West Side. They were NYPD unmarked Hondas, one in a Crystal Black, the other in a Lunar Silver, older models, red lights that could be mounted on the dash when they wanted to be identified. The cabbie turned onto Broadway where McCall redirected him to Amsterdam Avenue. He kept going until he was at the corner of the New York Public Library for the Performing Arts and told the cabbie to drop him off. He paid the cab, moved down Amsterdam Avenue, then cut through a building site toward the Good Shepherd Faith Church. High rise apartments towered above him.

He did not have to wait for long.

The black Civic pulled up to some trees overhanging the churchyard. Frank Macamber climbed out. Tom Graves, the *Rat Catcher*, backed him up. Behind him the Lunar Silver pulled into the alleyway beside the church and cut off any exit that way. Two more of the *Elite*, Pete Hightower and Marvin Rabinski, climbed out of their unmarked cars with their hands resting on the 9mm Sig Sauer guns in their holsters.

McCall turned to face Macamber who had taken out his NYPD wallet and flashed the tin. He was carrying a Glock 17 in a holster on his belt.

"Robert McCall?"

"That's right."

"Detective First Grade Frank Macamber, 16th Precinct. I am going to cut through the bullshit and get down to it. You visited Alexa Kokinas in her hospital room at Bellevue. I know you are not a relative and she does not have any friends here in New York City. She is a rookie Police Officer who just joined the force a few weeks ago. So who the hell are you?"

"I heard what happened to her."

"Where did you hear that?"

"Her father talked to me. Stavros Kokinas."

"I know who he is," Macamber said. "He's a cop who teaches at the Police Academy. A good guy who is dealing with grief right now. That does not answer my question. What were you doing seeing my patrolman Alexa Kokinas in her hospital room?"

"Trying to get some answers."

"What does her attack have to do with you?"

"Nothing yet."

"So what did my officer tell you?"

"She didn't remember much."

"Alexa doesn't remember *anything* about the assault." Macamber said. "It all happened too fast and it was brutal. She's lucky to be alive."

He took another step to McCall, getting right in his face. Behind him, Detectives Hightower and Rabinski had not moved, but their right hands hovered over their open suit jackets. McCall stood his ground.

"I know who you are, Mr. McCall," Macamber said. "You've got quite a reputation. A vigilante who likes to patrol the streets taking on lost causes. Someone who wants to take the law into his own hands. But you know what, Mr. McCall? That is *against* the law. I hear you have a fancy nickname. They call you 'The Equalizer'. That does not mean jack shit to me. You are a private citizen. You do not know Officer Alexa Kokinas and you are not going to get to know her. I will have you barred from her hospital room because right now she needs to rest and to heal. If you visit her again I will arrest you as a potential witness and lock you up. Am I talking too fast for you, Mr. *Equalizer*," he said with a sneer, "or have you got that message?"

McCall did not respond.

He thought Macamber would like nothing better that to bring out the handcuffs and snap them over his wrists.

"You're impeding an ongoing police investigation," Macamber said. "This is very personal to every detective, cop and patrolman at the 16th Precinct. One of our own was brutally assaulted and left lying bleeding in that deserted warehouse. We are going to find the perpetrators of this assault and bring them to justice. My detectives are fielding leads, phone calls, maybe over a hundred of them right now. That is the way it works, Mr. McCall. You interfere with that process and you are going to jail. It's as simple as that."

McCall basically ignored Macamber's harangue. He said: "What happens to Alexa Kokinas now?"

That seemed to piss off Macamber even more. "As far as you are concerned, *nothing* happens to her. Her doctors have upgraded her condition to serious. After that, her odds get better. But that does not mean didly squat to me right now. Alexa Kokinas is finished with law enforcement. She will never be a Peace Officer with her affliction to overcome. She is *deaf*, for Christ sake! That would be a liability for her in any circumstances. She should never have been hired for the NYPD in the first place! She had fellow Police Officers who rallied around her, but that does not mean crap either. Sooner or later she would been in a life-threatening situation and this would have happened. She dodged a bullet and that is the way it should be. We are going to move heaven and earth to find her attackers. Take your bleeding heart someplace else. Alexa Kokinas is nothing to you. You do not know her. You are not going to get to know her. Are we clear on that?"

McCall did not say anything more.

He waited for Macamber to get out of his face, or he would have to hurt him badly. The detective stood back from him, as if he sensed that, even with his back-up at the other police car. They had not moved their positions. Macamber nodded, as if he thought he had made his point. He looked at McCall and smiled a shit-kicking smile.

"You have yourself a nice day now."

For the first time, Macamber looked over at Officers Hightower and Rabinski. They took his signal and climbed back into their Honda LX. Macamber and Detective Graves got back into the Civic and did a U-turn. The cops headed back the way they came.

McCall let out his breath slowly. It had been painful putting up with Macamber's bombastic in-your-face approach, but it told him everything he wanted to know. He continued on past the Good Shepherd Faith Church toward 66th Street. Above him the windows of the Liberty Belle Hotel towered over the trees. He knew without a question of a doubt now that the *Elite* cops had been Alexa Kokinas's rapists.

Now he would have to prove it.

Samantha Gregson had found her *Memento Mori* mercenaries sitting around the several pools that surrounded the grounds of the Tangiers Al Havara resort Spa Hotel located on the beach on the ocean. She had made a signal to one of them, Scott Renquist, a powerfully built, edgy mercenary who had been Tom Renquist's brother. Robert McCall had killed him at the West Texas Regional Treatment Plant in Boerne, Texas. The pools were shaped like small lagoons beneath the palm trees. The sandy beach stretched across the ocean a few yards in front of them. Renquist acknowledged Samantha and got to his feet. He made an imperceptible nod to the other mercenaries seated outside under the palm trees. They took their time finishing their cocktails and proceeded toward the staircase that climbed to the second-floor level.

Samantha allowed time for her soldiers-of-fortune to reach the balcony of the hotel, then she climbed up the staircase after them. They were seated at small, marble tables. Ten of them were accounted for. There was an eleventh man, Jack Roslin, a big bear of a man, who was now in the Greek Islands where he made his home. He was an explosive expert and would wire the C4 explosives at the Greek concert.

Samantha had inherited her "boys", as she fondly called them, from Malcolm Goddard who had generated a list she knew many beleaguered countries would kill for. Her gaze swept past them: Jaak Olesk, who had a way of hooding his eyes that reminded Samantha of a cobra. Bradley Stafford was a laconic arms dealer who had fought with the guerrillas in Malaya and North Greece. Terence Soul, her *Soul Man*, who had previously worked for Defion Private Military Company and who was a specialist in Sarin pharmaceuticals and their derivates. Mace O'Brien was an Irishman with great stories to tell, none of them true but he had a whale of a time telling them. Harry Brandt who had murdered his father, his uncle and both of his cousins in one night, but Samantha had never had the nerve to question him about it. Damien Malinov took great pride in his appearance. He had worked for Halliburton before joining the rarefied ranks of the *Memento Mori* elite. Aleksanteri Karjala was so very quiet that Samantha wanted to feel for a pulse when she was with him. Then there was Gabriel Del Castillo, a heavyset man whom the other mercenaries called 'Patriot'. He had once been known as 'Putin's Chef', although Samantha had never where the nickname came from. He was her most silent killer.

She had come to respect these men. Their loyalties had belonged to Matthew Goddard, before he had been knifed by Robert McCall in his Manhattan apartment. She would have her revenge on that savage act, but not yet. She had business to take care of first. She had inherited these mercenaries, and she loved them, but did not mean that she trusted any of them. They were men who could be brought and paid for. She has no illusions about their true loyalties. But as long as Samantha was straight with them, they would put their lives on the line for her. That was the way it was. Matthew Goddard had seen to that.

Which made her next action all that more reprehensible.

Samantha had picked the hotel in Tangiers because it was quiet and not crowded with tourists at this time of the year. The group of mercenaries were the only people seated on the balcony overlooking the ocean. In front of each of them was a folder which they had not yet opened. They were waiting for their leader. Personally, Scott Renquist questioned how Samantha Gregson had managed to commandeer so many killers in one place. Mathew Goddard had hand-picked these men for their ruthlessness and efficiency. He did not know their identities and he did not want to know them. They were shadow operatives, all of them killers. They were expensive and loyal. For now, Scott Renquist waited to see what Samantha Gregson's next move would be. He had no doubt that it would be covert.

Samantha Gregson stepped up onto the terrace. No one acknowledged her. She moved down to the second table where the last of the of the mercenaries, Lars Karlsson, had been sitting looking out over the ocean. He was a dour, sullen killer with very pale eyes and a nervous habit of clenching and unclenching his hands. Samantha paused beside the man's chair, as if she were going to look out at the surf crashing onto the sandy beach.

Then she stabbed a syringe she had been carrying in one hand into his carotid artery.

Lars started pumping blood immediately and was dead before his head hit the tabletop. No one at the table moved a muscle. Samantha said: "Lars betrayed my trust. He reached out to people who are not in our deal. Unless you have an objection to his demise, get rid of his body. Carry him between you and dump him where he won't be found."

Two of the other mercenaries, Damien Malinoy and Aleksanteri Karsala, stood up at the table. One of them lifted the dead man over his shoulder while the other steadied him. They carried him away from the table and down the marble stairs. Samantha took his place at the table and opened her folder.

"Matthew Goddard was working on the end game of this mission when he was murdered," she said, calmly. "His killer was a one-time member of a covert spy organization called the *Company*. His name is Robert McCall. I will deal with him personally." She glanced over particularly at Scott Renquist. "Does anyone here have a problem with that?"

Scott Renquist remained silent. He would seek his own revenge on Robert McCall when this mission was successfully concluded. Right now, he met Samantha's gaze steadily.

She nodded and said: "Does anyone here have a question he wanted to ask me before we get started?"

No one did.

McCall walked down 7th Avenue from the Old Navy Store into Times Square. A marque for *Good Morning America* was prominent next door to the *Citizen* sign. McCall found Detective First Grade Steve Lansing at one of the tables shaded by red umbrellas. He was looking at a manila folder and eating a hot dog with all of the trimmings. He had a weather-beaten face with high cheekbones and grey eyes who had seen the depravity that human beings could sink to with some resignation. He had been a cop for years and nothing surprised him anymore. But the photographs of the beating that Alexa Kokinas had received had at the hands of the *Elite* had shaken him. He had obtained them from Stavros Kokinas who should not have access to a file like this, but he was a fellow cop teaching at the Police Academy and had connections within the department.

McCall sat down at the table. He noted that Lansing had bought him a hotdog. McCall picked it up and ate it while Lansing reviewed the file in his hands.

"Did you see Stavros Kokinas?" Lansing asked.

"This morning. And I visited his daughter Alexa at Bellevue this afternoon."

"Did you get anything from her?"

"More than I had expected," McCall said. "She didn't see her attackers, but she gave me a detailed description of them as far as she could. One was short and asthmatic. One of them had a distinctive laugh. One of them was very tall and stooped over. One of them liked to hum. One of them Alexa actually saw for split second. Young, fair hair, sideburns. The ringleader was sweating like a pig. You can fill the blanks, like Alexa did."

"That is a pretty good description from an eye-witness," Lansing said. "Doesn't get any better than that."

"She is a very special young woman. I was rousted by four cops out of the 16th Precinct on the way here."

Lansing looked up from the folder. "Led by Frank Macamber?"

McCall nodded. "He read me the riot act."

"So he and his *Elite* cops are running scared."

"They're not running anywhere," McCall said. "They're protected by the code of silence. Except I'm thinking that doesn't work well for you?"

"Not as far as the *Elite* are concerned," Lansing said. "Frank Macamber is a dirty cop. He has been on my radar since he joined the 16th Precinct. I heard a lot of rumors and innuendos, but nothing ever stuck to him. He is well-connected in the force with a lot of powerful friends. You go up against Macamber, you are heading right into the lion's den, but you already knew that. Here is their file."

Lansing turned the manila folder around to McCall. He went through photographs of the six Police Officers: FRANK MACAMBER – PETE HIGHTOWER – TOM

GRAVES – SAUL COOPER – MARVIN RABINSKI – JERRY KILPATRICK.

"Where did their nickname come from?" McCall asked.

"Frank Macamber. It was the rep they had at the Police Academy. Somehow it just stuck. You know how that can happen."

McCall looked Lansing ironically. "Macamber made it a point to call me 'The Equalizer' at least twice to show his contempt for the name and the persona. A lot of cops react to the name in the same way."

"Not *these* cops," Lansing said. "They're dangerous. The next time they will not just roust you. Macamber will make sure you are found in an alley somewhere with your throat cut."

"I'll keep that in mind." McCall picked out one of the pictures and turned it around to Lansing. "This Police Officer in the lineup seems to be out of place."

Lansing picked it up. "Yeah, Jerry Kilpatrick joined the 16th Precinct six months ago. Comes from a family of cops. I would not be surprised to hear if he were having a tough time adjusting. The *Elite* can be very intimidating. I heard he asked for a transfer to another precinct, but that was still under consideration. If Macamber wanted you to leave the unit, you could leave. But if he wanted you to knuckle under and toe the line, that was the bottom line. Macamber shoots deserters."

"You've compiled quite a file on this *Elite* unit," McCall said.

"Knowing they're corrupt is one thing," Detective Lansing said. "Proving it is a new ballgame. Macamber is smart and vicious. Don't underestimate him."

McCall nodded and handed the file back to Lansing. "This is all I need."

"I presume there's no sense in my telling you you're going against a stacked deck?"

McCall smiled. "None at all."

Lansing nodded. "If you could prove that these were the cops who raped Alexa Kokinas, you would need her statement, and that would be highly suspect. She's hearing impaired and a good defense attorney would blow holes through her testimony."

"She won't be testifying," McCall said. "Macamber will confess to their crime."

Lansing smiled as McCall finished his hotdog and stood up. "How are you going to get him to do that?"

"He'll make a mistake. If I need you, I know where to find you."

"You know I can't condone vigilante behavior out on the streets, Robert."

"You won't have to," McCall said. "Good to see you again, Detective."

McCall walked away from the table. Detective Lansing watched him as his figure disappeared into the crush of humanity in Times Square.

► 16 ◄

JERRY KILPATRICK ENTERED his ground-floor apartment in Murray Hill near the Empire State Building. He snapped on a lamp that sat on a coffee table beside the worn couch. He moved into the kitchenette and pulled out a beer. He unclipped his holster with the Glock 19 gun in it and dropped it on the coffee table. He sat on the couch, took a swallow of the Budweiser and let his head rest back. It had been a long shift of duty and Jerry was tired. He had a migraine that had started in his temples and got worse. He had been getting a lot of them these days.

He did not hear the small sound behind him.

It had not fully registered with him, but it should have. He knew that most cops had a sense of jeopardy installed in them, but he thought that was just a myth. He had not heard anyone entering his apartment. The front door was locked and latched.

An arm snaked around Jerry's throat. Before the young detective could even move the intruder had him in a headlock, pressing down tightly against his forehead. Jerry writhed under the choking hold, but he was completely incapacitated. His eyes flicked to the coffee table where his Glock 19 sat in its holster.

McCall said softly: "Don't even think about it. You'd be dead before you got as far as the end of the couch."

For emphasis, McCall jammed the headlock tighter. Jerry would lose conscious quickly if he did not ease up on him. McCall noted Jerry's pale eyebrows, quite startling in the shadows. Another detail that Alexa Kokinas had nailed for him when she had described her attackers.

"I am going to talk to you," McCall said quietly, "and you're going to listen. Or I can snap your neck. Your choice."

Jerry writhed some more, but there was no way of breaking the stranglehold on his throat. He stopped struggling, breathing hard.

"I'm going to ease off on you now," McCall said, "but you won't be able to move. If you do, I will tighten the hold and you will pass out. Do you understand? Just nodded if you do."

Jerry nodded. McCall eased up on the pressure on Jerry's throat. He made sure the young detective was breathing again. "Deep breaths. Calm your nerves. Can you do that?"

Jerry nodded again. He found his voice, which was raspy with his throat constricted.

"Who the hell are you?"

"No one you would want to know. Here is the part when I talk. I know that you are a police officer at the 16th Precinct in Manhattan. Transferred there maybe six months ago. You come from a long line of Police Officers. Your father was a cop for thirty-six years and your grandfather as well. That is a proud tradition. You were the newest recruit of Frank Macamber's *elite* force. But there was nothing elite about them. They are dirty cops who take graft and are dealing drugs and paybacks. But maybe not you. You were along for the ride. Would that be true to say?"

Jerry Kilpatrick did not respond, just listened the sound of McCall's soft voice, as if he were telling a child a bedtime story. "There was a new recruit who joined your squad. Alexa Kokinas. An attractive, no-sense kind of Peace Officer who followed the rules. She suffered from a handicap that left her virtually deaf, but that did not slow her down at all. She was sassy and spirited and you probably liked her for that. But that did not matter. Frank Macamber had plans for this rookie cop. You and your fellow Officers cornered her in an abandoned warehouse on the Lower East Side and raped her. You left her battered on the floor barely clinging to life. Her partner found her and called for an ambulance that took her to Bellevue. She came out of ICU a couple of days ago. That was where I talked to her. She gave me a description of the *Elite* as best she could. Which was quite a lot, even though they wore black clothing and had on ski masks. My question to you Jerry is this: Did you rape Officer Alexa Kokinas, or were you there in that warehouse and you allowed it to happen? This is where you can answer."

McCall knew that young detective was dealing with the guilt and shame he felt. He was also probably intimated by Frank Macamber. Finally Jerry said: "I can't betray the trust of my fellow Police Officers."

"I know all about the thin blue line." McCall told him. "So we will try this again. You need to tell me if you were in that warehouse, wearing a black ski mask, the night that Alexa Kokinas was attacked?"

It took Jerry another moment to answer. McCall increased the pressure on his throat a little, but not too much. Finally the young detective said, his voice barely audible: "I let it happen. There was nothing I could do to stop it." McCall thought that is was quite an admission for him to make, but it was only his word against McCall's, nothing that would stand up in court.

But it was a start.

"And you couldn't go to your Captain at the precinct about the corruption you have witnessed out in the streets."

"No."

"Wrong answer, Jerry." McCall increased the pressure on his throat another notch. "Were you intimated by Frank Macamber?"

"Yes."

"That was the answer I was hoping to get from you."

McCall eased off on him. Jerry started to breathe again. McCall said: "Frank Macamber has quite a hold on these cops."

"He keeps them in line," Jerry said. "I can't go against him. Frank talked about you. Robert McCall. He called you 'The Equalizer', or some name like that. You are out of your league. Macamber will hunt you down. He will handcuff you and throw you into the back of an unmarked car somewhere in the city and take you out to Long Island. It is a killing ground that Macamber sometimes uses. Even the other cops do not know where it is. He'll bury you in the gravel pits out there."

McCall felt that the young detective had been wanting to get that off his chest for a long time. He said: "Macamber might want to do that, but he won't."

"Frank won't let this go."

"Neither will I. I can deal with him. You have to decide is what you're going to do about Alexa Kokinas."

"I know that Officer Kokinas's career with the NYPD is finished."

"Not if I have a say in it."

Jerry looked down at the floor. He shook his head again, anguish clearly in his voice. "I couldn't stop it."

"I know that. But this is the decision you have to make. Do the right thing, Jerry."

McCall did not say anything else. Jerry Kilpatrick waited for him to move away from the couch, but there was no sound. In a sudden rush, Jerry reached out for his Glock 19 in its holster on the coffee table and whirled around.

McCall's figure was gone.

Jerry leapt up to his feet and ran to his front door. The latch and been lifted off. Jerry opened the door and moved out into the street. There was some light traffic past the Empire State Building and a few pedestrians. There was no sign of McCall. Jerry shut his front door, still with his gun in his hand, moved to the kitchenette and picked up his cell phone. He jabbed at the buttons, then paused. Slowly he disconnected the line. He picked up a bottle of Jim Beam whisky on the kitchen counter and poured himself a stiff drink. He sat back down on the couch. His hands were shaking.

But the words that Robert McCall had said to him had resonated.

On the terrace of the Tangiers Al Havara Hotel, Samantha Gregson had directed the *Memento Mori* mercenaries at the marble-topped tables to open their folders. Inside were innocuous travel brochures, maps and detailed descriptions.

Samantha said: "Your mission is to infiltrate three 'concert sites' in three different countries. The free concerts are being given to raise awareness of the refugee problem throughout the world. All of you will travel to these countries. Each of you will be given impeccable documentation to become part of these events without raising any suspicions. You will be contacted by the terrorists at these rock concerts. That part of the plan was initiated while Matthew Goddard was still alive."

One of the mercenaries looked up from his travel folder. His name was Jaak Olesk. Samantha knew his reputation was as a merciless killer and she did not trust him. She did not trust any of them, but Jaak Olesk had a way of hooding his eyes that reminded Samantha of a languid cobra. The image sent a shiver down her spine.

She knew she was in the company of dangerous men.

Jaak Olesk asked: "How many innocent civilians will be killed at each venue?"

Samantha did not hesitate with her answer. "Maybe fifteen thousand. Maybe more."

If Jaak Olesk had a comment on that, he kept it to himself.

Scott Renquist sorted through the various travel brochures in his folder. "Which countries do we travel to?"

Samantha said: "The sites of the rock concerts will be at the Rockwave Festival in Malakasa, Athens, the Terme di Caracalla baths and ruins in Rome and at the Royal Albert Hall in London. It will take a lot of organizing to pull this mission off. I will be meeting with the Taliban in the next three days. All of you will all be traitors to the United States of America if you are caught. Which you will not be. The five of you will walk away with ten million dollars each which will be wired to your bank accounts in the Grand Cayman Islands."

She had been holding her breath throughout her speech. She needed not have worried. The mercenaries exchanged glances.

They were *in*.

Sam Kinney came around the reception counter at the Liberty Belle Hotel as soon as McCall walked into the hotel. He grabbed McCall's hand and steered him around a throng of people who were waiting to check in. Chloe and Lisa, a languid blonde, were handing the weary and fractious mob with aplomb.

Sam said: "Who have you pissed off this time?"

McCall smiled. He was used to Sam's bombastic moods. "There's probably a long list."

"A couple of off-duty cops were in here about 7:00 P.M looking for you."

That stopped McCall. "How do you know they were off-duty cops?"

"I'm an old spymaster. They had that cop aura about them."

"What did they look like?"

"The skinny cop had lost most of his hair and squinted a lot. The heavyset cop called him the *Rat Catcher*. The heavyset cop sweated a lot and kept wiping his face with a handkerchief."

"They did ask for me specially?"

"They kept a low profile. They hung around here for a while, then they left, but they did go far. They are parked out on 66th Street. What do they want with you?"

"Nothing good. Thanks, Sam."

"You know I've always got your back."

"What would I do without you?"

"You might live a little longer," Sam muttered, but the crowd surging in the lobby had swallowed McCall up.

McCall walked out of the Liberty Belle Hotel and hailed a cab. He did not look down the street to where the off-duty caps were sitting in an unmarked Silver Honda parked at the curb. He climbed in and gave the cabbie a destination. The cab pulled away and the Silver Honda followed behind them.

McCall had the cabbie take him down to the garment district on Thirty-First Street. Tall cranes towered into the sky near Penn Station. McCall had the cabbie take a side street and then pull over. He paid him and got out and strode through a narrow alleyway until he was at a construction site. The Silver Honda drove fast down a side street, but it could not turn there and had to go to 30th Street and turn around. By the time the cops had pulled over to where the streets were cordoned off, McCall's figure had disappeared. Detectives Graves and Rabinski got out and hustled after him.

The site was cordoned off with temporary high fences and barricades. McCall broke the lock off one of the wooden doors and slipped through. A sliver of moon hung in the sky. A six-story building was going up with the framework in place. There was another smaller building under construction next door to it. The construction site was littered with steel pipes, oil/waste drums, mesh lockers, cinder blocks, piles of dirt, huge orange cones and platform ladders. Three huge construction cranes towered into the sky. A backhoe lay beside the first six-story building with a smaller crane. There were two works lights rigged up across at the construction site, but their radiance did not spill into the myriad shadows.

McCall felt like he was entering an intricate maze in the darkness.

He heard the detectives entering the construction site behind him. The cops had drawn their weapons. They split up, giving them a better chance to cover the area they were searching. McCall shook his head. Not a good idea. They were better off staying together. But they were after one man. They had had guns and purpose. They had McCall cornered and there was no help coming for him.

Marvin Rabinski was unnerved by the silence and the sense of dread that had come over him. McCall's figure was a shadow among the other shadows. He had no shape, no substance, a wraith who merged in and out of the darkness. The moon had gone behind the cloud cover.

When McCall came at him he no idea where he had come from.

McCall slammed a length of pipe against the big detective's back. He folded up like an accordion. McCall checked to see if he was still breathing. He was, but barely. McCall dragged the big man behind some oil drums. Tom Graves ran from the side of the construction site, but there was no sign of his partner. The *Rat Catcher* moved closer to the six-story building under construction. All he could hear were the small sounds of traffic around the site.

One of the immense cranes, a hydraulic crawler, swung around almost on top of him. Detective Graves whirled but the boom of the hoist slammed into him, sending him down to the concrete. McCall climbed out of the immense crane and knelt beside him. He was out cold. McCall dragged him over to the oil drums where he had left his partner.

McCall moved back through the overlapping shadows and let himself out of the construction site. He moved back toward Penn Station, dialing his cell phone.

Jimmy was in O'Grady's Tavern on the Lower East Side. He was sitting at the bar nursing a beer. The place was hopping. The four pool tables were all in use. Jimmy was keeping an eye on a couple of cops that McCall had wanted him to watch. He did not ask why. If McCall had called in the favor, there was a damn good reason. That was good enough for him.

Jimmy could see Detective Frank Macamber in the gilt mirror over the bar. He was shooting pool with one of his detectives attached to the 16th Precinct, Pete

Hightower. They were in high spirits. Jimmy's cell rang in the noisy bar. He picked it up. He looked at the text message, deleted it and wrote a message on the back of a beer coaster. He passed it to the female bartender who was mixing cocktails as fast as the waitresses ordered them. Jimmy had already established a rapport with her, having been in the place several times that week for McCall.

"You know which one of these cops in here is Detective Frank Macamber?" he asked.

The bartender, whose name was Mary Lynn, looked over at the pool table with a sour expression. "Uh huh, I know him."

"Can you give him this note? Just wait until I have gone, okay?"

Mary Lynn shrugged. "Sure. But you do not want to have anything to do with Detective Macamber, Jimmy."

"Just delivering a note for a friend."

Jimmy finished his beer and made his way to the door of the bar and restaurant. He glanced back once and saw that Mary Lynn had gotten one of her waitresses to deliver the note. Jimmy watched Frank Macamber's reaction.

All of the color had drained out of his face. It was almost white with rage.

Jimmy nodded. Time for him to leave before Macamber had time to look around to see who had delivered the message.

Robert McCall sat down at the bar area at the Liberty Belle Hotel. Sam Kinney immediately put a Glenfiddich in front of him.

"What happened to the two cops?"

"They ran into trouble when they came after me," McCall said. "I left them in a deserted construction site in Chelsea. The EMT's were called and transported them to Lennox Hill Hospital with severe headaches. Frank Macamber is going to think twice before he sends any of his Officers after me."

"What happens now?"

McCall shrugged. "I'll wait until Macamber plans his next move."

"Which may be lethal."

"Possibly, but I don't think so. I bought myself a little breathing room. One member of the *Elite* is conflicted about what he has done. I am betting he will get in touch with me."

"Without Frank Macamber knowing about it?"

"That would be the idea."

The old Spymaster shook his head. "You're playing with fire, McCall."

"I'm trying the save two people's lives," he said, quietly. "Alexa Kokinas and Jerry Kirkpatrick. They're worth the risk."

"As if you'd ever listen to me," Sam muttered.

McCall looked at him fondly. "Would I do without you, Sam?"

"You might live a little longer."

McCall finished his Glenfiddich and got to his feet. "I've got a date."

That brightened Sam up. "With that babe from the Dolls Nightclub? What was her name?"

"Melody."

"That was it. A voice like spring rain. Marilyn Monroe kind of curves."

McCall smiled. "She's a very special girl. But it was not that kind of a date. If any more cops come looking for me, let me know."

He exited the bar. Sam watched him walk across the lobby toward the hotel doors. "One of these days you're going to skate a little close to the edge. McCall."

But McCall had already left the lobby.

▶ 17 ◀

GRANNY WAS WAITING outside the Liberty Belle Hotel for McCall. They took a cab to Cleopatra's Nightclub on Broadway and 92nd Street. The club was packed with jazz patrons. McCall and Granny found a table at the back. McCall did not have to look for Hayden Vallance. He was jamming with a Jazz Trad Band called *The Midnight Follies* in the front of the raised stage. Vallance played a pretty hot piano. The rest of the band consisted of a cornet, a clarinet, trombone, guitar, banjo, ukulele, bass sax and drums. McCall had never known Hayden Vallance to be anything except a mercenary, but in Cleopatra's Needle he saw another side of the man. He was in high spirits, enjoying the camaraderie of his fellow musicians. They were right at the end of a set. The trad jazz tunes were unfamiliar to McCall, with names like *Vo Do Do De O Blues*, *Louisiana*, *Singing the Blues* and *You're Driving Me Crazy*. They finished off the set with an old jazz tune called: "*That's A Plenty*", including vocals by Vallance. There was a rousing cheer from the boisterous crowd and the band moved to other tables before their next set.

Hayden Valance had seen McCall and Granny at their corner table and slid in beside them. One of the waitresses brought them menus. Vallance looked at Granny.

"You like trad jazz?"

"When it's played sweet and hot."

McCall said: "The Trombone player, Keith Nichols, who also doubles on piano and banjo, is the foremost stride pianist in Europe. He is here in New York City for some gigs. I usually sit in with him when he's here at Cleopatra's Needle."

"But you're not here to talk with me about great trad jazz bands," Valance said. "So I figure you're here because of Granny."

"Liz Montgomery was one of the western prisoners in that North Korean prison camp," Granny said. "She is a renowned photojournalist. Myang-Sook-Jang allowed her to carry a cell phone to take pictures of the camp. It was his private little joke. The phone would be taken away from her when Jang decided to abandon the camp, but that never happened. "

"Yeah, because McCall and those two young mercenaries he was with…" Hayden looked over at McCall. "What were their names again?"

"Kyu-Chal and Yo-Han, but everyone calls him Harry," McCall said.

"Yeah, that's right. They came in with guns blazing and blew the crap out of the place. Not many inmates ever escape a prison camp in North Korea like that. You were lucky."

A waitress arrived at that moment to take their orders. Granny ordered hummus and stuffed grape leaves and a chocolate martini which was served with vodka and Dark Crème de Cacao. Vallance ordered stuffed mushrooms and a Cleopatra's Martini, which was made with vodka, Banana Liqueur, Frangelico with a splash of Vanilla Schnapps. McCall ordered some garlic bread and a Sam Adams beer. The waitress went off and Granny leaned forward.

"Myang-Sook-Jang was joined on that last night by a Korean thug who obviously knew him well. Liz Montgomery took a picture of him."

Granny turned his cell around to show Vallance. He nodded. "I know him. Ji-Yeon. Like I told McCall, he is a nasty piece of work. He is a mercenary who works with various terrorist organizations including the Taliban in Afghanistan. He has been known to work with NATO countries on their security measures. He had no alliances to anyone. No one knows where he lives. He comes into a country to do a job and then he disappears. The man is a phantom."

"But you *do* know him?" Granny said.

"Our paths have crossed a couple of times," Vallance said. "I was in the Southern Cameroons after Amazonia declared its independence and Paul Biya and Idriss Deby of Chad had declared war on the Boko Haram. Ji-Yeon was brought in to negotiate with the local separatists. I ran into him again in the South Sudan where a truce is holding between Salva Kiik and the rebel leader Riek Machan until 2022. Ji-Yeon was offering the olive branch, which was ironic to me because he is no more than a glorified hoodlum."

"Ji-Yeon liked the look of Liz's sister Deva," Granny said. "She had been brought to the prison camp only a few days before. Ji-Yeon dragged her into Myang-Sook-Jang's quarters. I don't know what happened, but he may have assaulted her."

Vallance shook his head. "That wouldn't be Ji-Yeon's style. But he would have enjoyed watching her being beaten by Jang's guards."

"There was another western prisoner being held in the compound named Daniel Blake," Granny said. "A journalist who worked for Associated Press. When all hell broke loose, Ji-Yeon dragged Deva Montgomery and

Daniel Blake to his helicopter and had his pilot take off. The State Department and the United States Government has no idea where Ji-Yeon took them."

"Presumably out of North Korea," McCall said.

Vallance nodded. "So they could be anywhere right now."

Their appetizers arrived and their exotic drinks were served. The waitress smiled at Vallance. "Enjoy."

Vallance watched her sashay away. "Great ass. Eat some food, Granny. I figure the cuisine in the prison camp left something to be desired. And the chocolate martini is like nothing you have ever tasted."

Granny took a swallow of the chocolate martini. "Not bad." He leaned over again to Vallance. "I need to locate Deva Montgomery and Daniel Blake."

"That won't be easy."

"I have to try."

"They could both be dead," Vallance said.

"They're not."

"You can't be sure of that."

"I'm sure," Granny said with some passion. "It was the way that Ji-Yeon looked at Deva Montgomery. Like he had special plans for her."

McCall handed Vallance some photos that Granny had given him of Deva Montgomery and Daniel Blake. The mercenary put them away as if they were afterthoughts.

"I don't make personal commitments, McCall. I don't get involved in other's people's lives."

"I made a promise to Liz Montgomery to find her sister," Granny said. "And to locate Daniel Blake. I aim to keep that promise. But I can't do it without your help."

Vallance sighed and glanced over at McCall. "Only for you would I do this, McCall." He put the photographs of Deva Montgomery and Daniel Blake into the pocket of his suit jacket and handed the cell phone back to Granny. "I'll see what I can find out."

"Any idea where Ji-Yeon could be now?" McCall asked him.

"Not in North Korea, that's for sure." Vallance sat back, glancing critically at Granny. "I guess you had a pretty rough time in that North Korea prison camp. Good thing for you that you've got a friend like Robert McCall to come to your rescue."

Granny flashed his signature Steve McQueen smile. "A very good thing."

"I'll have some kind of answer for you tomorrow," Vallance said. "Right now I need to play another set. We start off with *Exactly Like You, Blue Room* and then swing into *Back In Your Own Backyard*."

He slid out of the booth. The trad jazz band was forming around the piano again. After a cue from Vallance they started in on *Exactly Like You.*

Granny looked at McCall. "How far can you trust him?"

"Vallance got me out of Syria with that American US Army Captain Josh Coleman," McCall said, quietly. "He came back for us when all hell was breaking loose. He didn't have to do that."

"If there is a chance of finding Deva Montgomery and Daniel Blake, I need to take it." Granny said. "This means a lot to me."

McCall nodded. "If anyone can locate a phantom like Ji-Yeon, it's Hayden Vallance."

McCall met Emma Marshall for breakfast before she flew back in the afternoon to Washington D.C. Her thoughts were suitably chaotic, as always. She had been up half the night fielding calls for Control and getting to know a cool guy who looked like Matt Smith from Dr. Who. She was hoping he would call her before she left. She was dressed in a chic suit and high-heels and her white shirt was unbuttoned as far as decorum would permit. She knew from experience that if McCall had sought her out, there was a reason for it. She was on high alert because Control had called for a meeting to take place on that Friday morning. Emma knew that McCall was invited because the name Samantha Gregson had come up in the briefing. She had been Malcolm Goddard's assistant and was, in Emma's words, a slut and a viper. McCall told her that her instincts were probably correct, but that was not the reason he had wanted to see her. He had a job for her. It had to be discreet and be accomplished before the end of the day.

"Now I am really intrigued," Emma said.

"This has nothing to do with Control," McCall told her. "This has to do with a rookie cop in the NYPD whose life is in danger."

"So, this is kind of an 'Equalizer' thing?"

"You can call it that. You have the day to organize what I need. Can you do that?"

Emma looked at him over her bacon-n-eggs and shook her head. "Are you actually asking me that? You saved my life in that pub in London. I would run over hot coals for you. What do you need?"

McCall told her. She listened carefully, wolfing down her breakfast. McCall paused and took a swallow of coffee. Emma said: "I'll have to make a few calls. Find the right place. It won't take me long. Consider it done."

That afternoon Granny met Liz Montgomery in Central Park. She had walked down from the CNN building where she worked. They hugged briefly, then strolled together over the magnificent Bow Street Bridge.

Granny asked: "How are you doing?"

"I'm back at work with photo deadlines to meet as if nothing ever happened. All my follow co-workers are very excited that I'm back and in one piece, but they whisper behind my back as if I'm some fragile doll that is going to break."

"Those are the kinds of scars that do not heal. Not for a long time. What Myang-Sook-Jang did to you in that prison camp was vile and an act of terrorism."

"I'm dealing with it," Liz said, shortly.

"No, you're not," Granny said. "But you will."

"You never told me what happened to the Commandant."

"He's dead," Granny said, somewhat tersely. "Leave it at that."

"You said you would come for him," Liz said. "You did that for me. I know that. But that doesn't get me closer to finding my sister."

"Robert McCall has a client," Granny said. "She's a rookie, about twenty-two years of age, just started out at the NYPD. She was assaulted by her fellow cops, although there is no proof of that yet. McCall is going to find some justice for her. He will do the same for you. Tell me what happened at the State Department."

"I besieged them with demands about my sister Deva and that photojournalist Daniel Blake," Liz said. "They told me they were investigating the entire North Korea incident. I spent four sessions with the CIA being questioned. They were concerned and sympathetic, but it was so much bullshit. Basically they have no idea where Ji-Yeon took my sister and Daniel Blake. That Korean thug just walked away from that prison camp, took off in his helicopter and disappeared into thin air. Tell me you have found out something."

"The pilot who flew us out of South Korea is a merce-nary named Hayden Vallance," Granny told her. "McCall knows him. Says he is an honorable man. Vallance knows Ji-Yeon and his reputation with terrorist organizations. He has also worked for NATO countries and brokered several deals with other terrorists when it suited him. Vallance got a one-time location for Ji-Yeon."

Liz stopped on the bridge. Her voice was suddenly filled with hope. "What else did this mercenary tell you?"

Granny glanced out at the tranquil lake. "It's not much to go on, but last night Vallance made some phone calls. He found out that Ji-Yeon lives somewhere in Fin-land in a town called Lappeenranta on the tip of Lake Saimaa. It is thirty kilometers from the Russian border. Ji-Yeon had been a student at the Saimaa University of Applied Sciences at Lappeenranta at one time. Maybe someone from the town or the University will remember him. It's a long shot, but I have to start somewhere."

Liz looked into his face, then kissed him. When they broke the embrace, Liz stood back. Granny was surprised by the kiss, but it had felt good to him.

"This intel could all come to nothing," he told her.

Liz shook her head. "It won't. I know it won't."

They moved on down the Bow Bridge which gleamed in the morning sun. Liz took Granny's arm. "When will you leave?"

"Tonight."

"Will Hayden Vallance fly to Finland with you?"

Granny shook his head. "Solo mission. If I find out anything, I will call McCall. Hayden Vallance doesn't be-lieve in getting involved with other people's crusades, but I think he made an exception for McCall's sake."

"Thank God he did."

Granny shrugged. "McCall has that effect on people."

Liz held onto his arm. "This the first time I have truly believed that Deva will be found alive and safe."

Granny did not want to tell her that the chances of that happening were slim to none.

▶ **18** ◀

FRANK MACAMBER ENTERED Alexa Kokinas's hospital room and closed the door behind him. It was late, around four o'clock in the morning. He had already flashed the tin for the nurses on duty, told them who he was and that he was checking on his patrolman. They had no problem with that. He had already cleared any visits with Alexa's doctor.

The room was dark. Alexa was asleep in the bed, turned away from the window. Macamber had to be careful. There would be a record of his visit, in the line of duty, but that did not matter. No one had actually seen him going into the hospital room. He had told the night nurse he would only be a minute to look on his rookie patrolman. He was not going to unplug any of the machines she was hooked up to. He would just push a pillow over her face. He did not think there would even be a struggle. If she did awaken, it would be over in seconds. The night nurse would not come in until six o'clock in the morning to take blood from her and check her vital signs. By that time Macamber would be long gone.

Macamber took a step to her bed and looked down at her. He had to admit that she was pretty messed up. The bruising and lacerations to her face and arms were extensive. She should not have resisted so violently. She could have walked out of that abandoned warehouse under her own steam, but she had chosen to flail and writhe like some wild thing. Macamber thought it was too bad. Looking down at her now, he thought she could easily have had a cardiac arrest in her sleep.

He reached down for the pillow under her head.

A man's voice said quietly: "Checking up on your patrolman?"

Macamber froze, his hands nowhere near the pillow yet, and whirled around.

Detective Steve Lansing displayed his CITY OF NEW YORK POLICE – DETECTIVE wallet with the number 7 in gold beneath the shield. "Detective Steve Lansing, 7th Squad."

Macamber moved forward immediately, shaking Lansing's hand. "Frank Macamber, 16th Precinct. I wanted to know how Alexa was doing. Maybe we should let her get her sleep."

Detective Steve Lansing opened the hospital room door. Macamber saw at once that there was a uniformed Police Officer stationed outside. He closed the door behind him. They stood together in the ward while the small, muted sounds echoed from the nurse's station. Lansing indicated the uniformed police officer.

"My Captain offered to authorize some added back-up for Alexa Kokinas. Three Officers on eight-hour shifts."

"What does this have to do with the 7th Precinct?"

Lansing shrugged. "A little added protection. Until she gets stronger. Patrolman Kokinas is one of our own. What happened to her was despicable."

"Yes, it was," Macamber said, recovering quickly. "Glad to have the help. I'll make sure my Captain at the 16th and your Captain are brought up to speed."

"Making any progress on the identity of the perps?"

"We're making headway, Steve. My guys are hunting down every possible lead. We have established a hot line into the precinct. We have had over a hundred tips on it in the last forty-eight hours. Nothing substantial yet but we are chasing down every lead, no matter how small. We are going to find these guys. It is only a matter of time. I've got my best men on it."

"You call them the *Elite*, don't you?"

Macamber shrugged, his expression wry. "A label we seemed to have picked up right out of the Police Academy. It is a little embarrassing, and my guys take a lot of ribbing about it, but they are the best. As soon as I get something solid, I'll pass it over to you at the 7th Precinct." Macamber weighed his next words carefully. "We rousted a guy who came here to the hospital to see Alexa. His name's Robert McCall. Have you ever heard of him? Some of an urban vigilante."

"I haven't come across him," Lansing said, deadpan.

"A total psycho. I am going to nail this asshole. He attacked two of my cops in a construction site and sent them to the hospital."

"You can prove it was this guy?"

"Neither of them could provide a description," Macamber said, "but I'm going to take him down. Thanks with the help for Alexa. I'll call on her in a couple of days, see how she's doing."

Macamber shook hands with Lansing, as if he were preoccupied, and headed down to the nurse's station. He had a quick word with her, professional and clipped, then rode the elevator down to the ground floor.

Detective Lansing was ironic. "Good luck with arresting Robert McCall. Let me know how that goes for you."

McCall found the Kilpatrick house on the banks of the Hudson River in Millerton, a quant old-world town steeped in history and culture. It was a mansion built with Vermont marble, tall colonnades, with a flagstone porch and rolling hills that ended in the woods on the river. He had heard back from Emma Marshall the night before. She had said that everything was in place for him. McCall had thanked her and disconnected. He had parked his Jaguar off to one side of the maple trees and found a meandering flagstone path that led up the house. Tables had been placed on a gorgeous terrace for a buffet spread. There were small tables with fruit punch and bottles of wine on them and wine coolers on the nearby lawn. There must have been at least sixty people crowded around the tables or strolling through the trees that led down to the banks of the river. It looked like a gathering to McCall of aunts and uncles and family friends. A dozen children were racing around, most of them under the age of six, but there were several teenagers in attendance as well. The party had a festive, celebratory feel to it. Everyone was in good spirits and conversations were punctuated with laugher.

McCall stepped up onto the terrace. Immediately a stocky man with a shock of red hair, greying at the temples, walked up to him, putting out his hand. He had chiseled features, piercing blue eyes and a ready smile.

"Welcome! I am Joel Fitzpatrick. I guess I am in charge of this mob of unruly renegades. Most of them are family, although there a few of them I expect are imposters just here for a good time. But that is the cop in me."

McCall shook hands. "Robert McCall."

"I am going out on a limb here, but I figure you must have something to do with my son Jerry."

"He invited me to your family get together," McCall said, noncommittally.

"Well, you're most welcome. I think Jerry just went into the house."

"I'll find him."

McCall stepped off the patio and walked up the sweeping lawn to the imposing house. Joel Fitzpatrick watched him as he disappeared inside. Something about McCall's intensity, although understated, had bothered him. But then he was assailed by some cousins and friends and found himself being the gracious host again.

A hallway faced McCall leading into a living room and a study which was open, revealing floor-to-ceiling bookcases and white coaches. A narrow marble staircase wound down from the first floor to the basement. McCall took the stairs and stepped out into a long corridor. Every inch of the wood-paneled walls was lined with framed photographs of the Fitzpatrick family. Prominent was a massive painting in muted oil colors of *Joel Fitzpatrick* in a dress uniform with a cap and white gloves. To one side of it was another oil painting of an older man also dressed in a dress uniform of the NYPD. A brass plaque below it said the man was *Nicholas Kitzpatrick*, Jerry's grandfather. The older man looked like a carbon-copy of his son with the same piercing blue eyes, the same chiseled features, maybe more of a twinkle in his eyes. To complete the family was an oil-painting in rich colors of *Gordon Fitzpatrick*, Jerry's great grandfather, also in the dress uniform of the NYPD, with cap and white gloves. At the time when the portrait was painted the old man must have been in his late nineties. He had gray slate-colored eyes and the rugged features of the Fitzpatrick family. His dress uniform, complete with cap and white gloves, came from another era.

There were framed pictures of the elder Kitzpatricks with politicians, including the Mayor of New York and various officials throughout the tri-State area. There were photographs of New York City from the sixties through the eighties, including a homage to the Twin Towers. There were exquisite oil paintings of St. Patrick's Cathedral, Grand Central Terminal, the Empire State Building, the Statue of Liberty and Rockefeller Center. There was a montage of Central Park including the Pond, the Central Park Zoo, Bethesda Terrace and the Fountain, the Ramble and Strawberry Fields.

Jerry Fitzpatrick was standing in front of more glass-fronted photographs of the three generations of his family. He was casually dressed in jeans with open-toed sandals with no socks and a gray New York Yankees T-shirt.

McCall moved over to Jerry and indicted the montage. "Three generations of Police Officers. That's quite an achievement."

"I can't take credit for that. We have these parties twice a year," Jerry said. "Gives us a chance to get the family all together in one place. It can get a little chaotic at times. Did you meet my father, Joel Fitzpatrick?"

"I did. He was very cordial."

"He's tough as nails and big-hearted. He would give you the shirt off his back or stake you to a meal and a beer. In his day he took no prisoners. He is a strict disciplinarian and used to rule this family with an iron fist. He has mellowed out some. My grandfather is also here. My great-grandfather should be somewhere too, holding court with the ladies even though he is pushing ninety-eight. He is a rascal. I lost count of how many cousins, aunts and uncles come to these shindigs at Fox Haven.

That is the country name for the house. Probably maybe a hundred when they all finally arrive."

"Quite a gathering."

Finally Jerry looked at McCall. "I didn't know if you would come."

"You invited me."

Jerry nodded. "There's a back way out of the house at the top of these stairs. Follow me."

McCall followed the young NYPD Officer to another narrow staircase at the end of the basement that led up to the main floor of the house. Jerry moved into an oak study which had more pictures on the walls in front of a desk and floor-to-ceiling bookcases. The pictures in the study were mainly baseball photographs from another era, including signed autographs from Phil Rizzuto, Whitey Ford, Derek Jeter, Yogi Berra, Joe DiMaggio, Lou Gehrig, Mickey Mantle and a special shrine of the Great Bambino himself, Babe Ruth.

Jerry let himself out to a patio area where a wrought-iron bench sat shrouded by greenery. McCall followed him. Jerry walked out onto the rolling lawn at the side of the house. More family members were arriving, slamming car doors, children scrambling out and greeting people. *Joel Fitzpatrick*, Jerry's father, was the official greeter for the family. *Nicholas Fitzpatrick*, Jerry Fitzpatrick's grandfather, was embracing his daughter-in-law whom McCall recognized as a high-fashion model. At one of the picnic tables McCall noted the patriarch of the family, *Gordon Fitzpatrick*, Jerry's great-grandfather, sitting alone, sipping what looked like a Black Russian. McCall thought that no one escaped the old man's intense scrutiny. He had noted McCall and Jerry strolling over the lawn to disappear into the red maple trees and Douglas firs that marched down to the bank to the Hudson.

In the dense trees, McCall waited for Jerry Kilpatrick. The bursts of laughter and camaraderie did not quite reach them here. Jerry's voice was subdued. Finally he said: "I don't know what to say to you."

"Yes, you do," McCall said.

Jerry took a deep breath. "Frank Macamber had it all planned out. He followed Alexa Kokinas when she left O'Grady's Tavern. He had made sure that the padlock on the fence of the abandoned warehouse was broken. There were six of us waiting in the warehouse when she entered. We were wearing black turtlenecks and ski masks. Pete Hightower tasered Alexa. That brought her down to the floor. She was paralyzed." For a moment Jerry could not go on. McCall let him get through it in his own time and did not interrupt. Jerry took another deep breath. "The *Elite* all took turns raping Alexa. Except for myself. I lost my nerve. The horror that was happening finally got through to me. I pulled off my ski mark. Frank Macamber grabbed me and whispered that we were all in this together. There was no backing out now. I think he would have killed me right there and then, except one of the *Elite*, Marvin Rabinski, we call him the Moose, he said to let me go. I put back on my ski mask. I stood in the shadows while my fellow Police Officers assaulted Alexa. Macamber was the last one. He took his time with her. He slapped her around and punched her in the face. When he was through, he climbed off her. He said she was conscious. She would find her way out of the warehouse. If she wanted to be a cop, she could start acting like one. We left her on the floor and walked out."

"Macamber would have had the last word," McCall said.

"He did. He cornered me the next day at the precinct and made sure that I understood about the code of silence. No one does anything without his blessing. If any of the *Elite* were implicated, I would have been found in an alleyway with my throat cut. Frank Macamber is a cop you do not want to mess with. He's vicious and brutal." Jerry looked at McCall for the first time. "But he's right. I can't cross over the line and confront my fellow Police Officers."

"You've got three generations of your family sitting at those tables on the patio," McCall said, quietly. "Your father, your grandfather, even your great grandfather has made an appearance. All of them were Police Officers you have looked up to your whole life. What are you going to say to them?"

Jerry shook his head. "They would be mortified by what happened. Especially my Pappy, that is what my father calls my great grandfather. He would never recover from the shame of it."

McCall said: "You have to do the right thing, Jerry. Alexa Kokinas did not deserve what happened to her. You've got a chance to make that right."

Through the trees Jerry saw more family members arriving onto the grounds of the magnificent house. His mother, a gorgeous redhead, brought out more fried chicken, baked potatoes, corn-on-the-cob and salads to the picnic tables. She had help from other family members and the children who were ready to pitch in.

"Macamber told the *Elite* that this will all blow over," Jerry said. "Don't sweat it. None of them will ever be caught."

'Don't bet on that," McCall said.

Jerry looked at more family members arriving onto the grounds. There were snatches of laughter, hugs and more fried chicken set up on two more picnic tables.

"What can I do?" Jerry asked, his hands clenching into fists. "I can't get a confession out of Frank Macamber or any of the others."

"There may be a way," McCall said. "But you will have to own up to your part in the assault. Maybe the Distinct Attorney will cut you a little slack. There will not be a way to spare your family the humiliation of what is coming. That's on you."

Jerry was quiet for another moment. Then he said: "Frank Macamber knows about you. Mr. McCall. He'll come after you."

"He already has," McCall said. "He sent two of his Officers to kill me on a construction site late at night."

"Which ones were they?"

"Detectives Graves and Rabinski. They are now in Lennox Hospital recovering. Their injuries were not serious, but it will give Frank Macamber food for thought. You are going to break the hearts of three old-time cops, but I believe they will forgive you when the time comes. But there cannot be a cover-up. That decision is up to you."

Jerry looked back through the maple trees and slowly nodded. McCall thought he had reached a decision.

"What happens now?" he asked.

"Macamber will confess to his crime," McCall said.

"Not going to happen."

"I think it will. I want you to contact Frank Macamber tonight. Give him the impression that everything with you is back on track. You have moved on like nothing happened. Tell him you have new intel about Alexa Kokinas. Will he at the 16th Precinct?"

"Today he'll be off-duty," Jerry said. "He'll be shooting pool at O'Grady's Tavern on the Lower East Side. Probably with Detective Hightower and the other members of the *Elite* squad."

'Make sure that all of them are at O'Grady's together."

"How will you know that?"

"I'll know." McCall handed Jerry a card. "Call me at this number. Let me know when you are at O'Grady's. Do not lose your nerve, Jerry. Be convincing. You are doing this for Alexa Kokinas. Can you do that?"

Jerry nodded.

McCall said: "I'll be in touch."

He made his way back out of the woods to where his Jaguar was parked on the edge of one of the lawns. He caught the patriarch of the family, "Pappy" Jerry had called him, watching him intently. The old cop knew something was very wrong. Jerry emerged from the woods and joined him at his table where a slew of cousins and a lovely looking older woman, who must be his mother, joined them. Jerry was all smiles and forced camaraderie.

McCall knew what the revelation was going to do to this proud family of ex-cops. Maybe there would be a way for him to ease the suffering they were going to experience.

It was the suffering that Alexa Kokinas was experiencing that concerned him the most.

McCall slid into the Jaguar, fired it up and drove away from the Fitzpatrick mansion where it was swallowed up in the elm and spruce trees.

► 19 ◄

JIMMY MURPHY SAT at the bar in O'Grady's Tavern nursing his second Corona Extra, watching the action in the place in reflection in the mirror over the bar. O'Grady's was hopping tonight. Three of the pool tables were in use and all of the booths had been taken. Detective Soul Cooper sat at the booth with an order of nachos in front of him. He greeted Tom Graves and Marvin Rabinski who slid into the booth next to him. Both of them were a little worse for wear having tangled with Robert McCall. Tom Graves, the *Rat Catcher*, had a cut above his right eye that had had to have stitches. Marvin Rabinski had been knocked unconscious and dragged twenty feet behind some oil drums in the construction site. He was bruised and was walking with a pronounced limp. Frank Macamber was playing pool with Pete Hightower. Jimmy could see that Macamber's mood was murderous. He sank two balls that rocketed across the table. He acknowledged his fellow *Elite* members with barely a glance.

That was when Jerry Kilpatrick entered the pool hall.

Jimmy had expecting him sometime during the evening. McCall had not said when he would arrive. He was casually dressed, as were the other members of the squad. He made a signal to Macamber and slid into the booth with his fellow cops. Macamber sank the last ball with a vicious swipe and headed for the back of the bar. Pete Hightower followed him. Macamber gestured to the booth behind the *Elite* table. Jerry nodded and sat down there. Pete Hightower slid in opposite him. McCall had warned that there might be bad blood between Macamber and Jerry Fitzpatrick, but in the gilt mirror over the bar Jimmy had no hint of that. Jerry was talking earnestly to Macamber.

Jimmy jumped up and moved to the restrooms. He passed Macamber's table. He only heard a fragment of their conversation. Jerry's voice was low, almost drown out in the rowdy atmosphere. He was saying: "… moved her from Bellevue to a private facility called Rosewood Clinic outside of Trenton, New Jersey."

There was no time more because Jimmy was past them. He washed his hands in the restroom, allowing the minimal time he figured he needed to be away from the booth and went back through the door into the small corridor. A blast of sound greeted him as he walked to the first booth where Macamber was saying: "… finish this once and for all."

The *Elite* were all standing up now. Jimmy watched them moving to the doors of O'Grady's Tavern. He noted that Jerry Fitzpatrick went with them. By the time Jimmy reached the bar and slid back onto his stool, the rest of the cops were gone. Jerry was the last one left standing with Frank Macamber. He looked around for a moment as if trying to get a glimpse of McCall, but he was not in the tavern. Macamber said something to Jerry who nodded and both of them moved through the door out into the street.

Jimmy gave it a few more seconds, then he dialed his cell. McCall's voice picked up.

Jimmy said: "They're on their way."

Then he disconnected and took another swallow of his Corona Extra.

The rest would be up to McCall.

The *Elite* Officers arrived at the Rosewood Clinic in Trenton, New Jersey just before nine o'clock in the evening. The clinic was on its own grounds with pewter driveway gates assessing the property. It was a five-story building with ivy crawling up the walls and several wrought-iron balconies. Red oak and silver birch trees sheltered it amid stretches of manicured lawns. There were lights on in several of the windows. The cops walked up a flagstone path that led up to the main entrance. Frank Macamber led the way. Inside was a foyer in heavy oak paneling. Several lithographs were displayed in muted colors on the walls of Autumn Trees, a sunset seen through Acacia Trees and a magnificent cherry tree in full bloom. A brunette receptionist sat behind a pine desk in front of a desktop computer. She looked up as Macamber strode to the desk. The rest of the squad waited behind him. Macamber opened his wallet to show his badge and ID.

"Frank Macamber, 16th Precinct in New York. You have a new patient who has just transferred here from Bellevue in Manhattan named Alexa Kokinas. She would have arrived about six o'clock."

"I'll check for you, Officer," the receptionist said in soft tones. She checked the computer screen. Macamber was tense and felt the weight of the others behind him. He was stressed, but tonight was the night it would all end. Finally the receptionist looked up. "Yes, the patient is here at the Clinic. Room 419." She stood up. "I'll escort you."

Macamber put away his wallet. "Official police business. We will find our own way up. Thank you for your time."

He motioned to his Officers and strode to the elevator. Detective Pete Hightower accompanied him. Tom Graves, Saul Cooper, Marvin Rabinski and Jerry Kilpatrick pushed through a door and climbed the stairs.

Macamber punched the button for the 4th Floor. The doors closed and the elevator ascended. He was aware of Hightower's tension immediately.

"You got something to say to me, Pete, spit it out."

"Assaulting Alexa Kokinas was one thing," Hightower said. "The bitch had it coming. Murder is another whole ballgame. You do this, there's no going back."

"She's already spilled her heart to that vigilante, McCall," Macamber said. "Forget the fact that she's deaf. *He* heard her! He took two of our guys out at that construction site and wiped the floor with them. We will take care of Alexa, then we will deal with McCall. We are in this together, Pete. You got that?"

Hightower nodded. He did not like it, but Macamber made sense. Alexa had to be silenced. Macamber and Hightower stepped off the elevator and entered the ward on the fourth floor. It was quiet, the ambiance restrained. Macamber moved to the nurse's station and flashed the tin.

"Detective Frank Macamber, 16th squad. You have a patient that has been transferred here from New York named Alexa Kokinas. I need to see her."

The night nurse, a willowy blonde whose name badge said *Holloway*, smiled at him. "Yes, Alison said you were on your way up. Alexa Kokinas is in room 419. The doctor just left her. I believe right now she's sleeping."

"I need to have a word with her," Macamber said. "It won't take long."

The others of the *Elite* had filed into the ward. Macamber turned to Hightower.

"Secure the floor," he murmured. "No one goes in or out until I'm finished."

Saul Cooper made sure the way into the ward was blocked off. The other rogue cops took positions around the nurse's station. Macamber looked at the other patients in the ward whose doors were all open. In one room a patient was watching a re-run of an old *NCIS* episode on television. He was wearing pajamas and a terrycloth robe. He was alone. In the next room, a man of forty was playing scrabble with another patient, also in his forties. Both of them were in pajamas. In the third room a man in his thirties was on the bed watching a ballgame with the sound low. He had a pallor to his face, as if all of the blood had drained out of it. Macamber thought we looked pretty sick. Maybe cancer.

Macamber reached the last room on the floor. He noted that there was no longer a uniformed Police Officer stationed outside. Detective Steve Lansing had obviously pulled the police detail when Alexa had transferred to this facility. Macamber paused, listening to the subdued sounds of the far-away television, the soft murmur of the patients, all of it low-key, barely audible, which suited him just fine.

The third floor of the facility it was eerily empty except for one suite in the center where Detective Steve Lansing sat with headphones watching four monitors. At the nurse's station, Nurse Holloway was typing on her laptop on the television screen. Lansing noted the old man in room 413, the two men playing scrabble in Room 415 and the sick man in Room 417. The only door that was closed was at Room 419. He watched Frank Macamber approach it. Behind him uniformed SWAT Officers crowded around the monitors.

"Wait for McCall's signal," Lansing said, tersely.

Macamber opened the door to Room 419 and closed it behind him. The room had only one bed in it. The bathroom door was ajar, the light off. The room was filled with shadows. There was no sound except for the incessant soft bleeping of one of the heart monitors to which Alexa was hooked up to. Her figure was under the covers, turned away from the door. Her distinctive raven hair glowed in the dimness. Macamber paused once again, listening for any telltale sounds he could not identify. There were none. Alexa was hooked up to two cardiac heart monitors and to an electrocardiogram machine. Macamber unhooked the two machines. He reached into the pocket of his overcoat and brought out a silver garrote wire.

A figure stepped out from the shadows of the ajar bathroom door behind him.

In the third-floor suite, the scene on the last monitor was blurry and grainy. Macamber's lone figure took a step toward Alexa's bedside. The strangling garotte caught a flash of light in the shadowy room as Macamber moved forward.

"That's the signal," Steve Lansing said. "Move out! Go! Go!"

The SWAT Team were already on the move into the third-floor corridor, moving quickly toward the door leading to the stairs.

In the ward, the nurse came around the counter at the nurse's station and tackled Saul Cooper, bringing him down to the ground. She pulled handcuffs from her white coat and put the bracelets on him before he could even move. At the same time, the old man in Room 413, Sam Kinney, who had lost interest in his *NCIS* re-run, was galvanized into action. He flung Detective Tom Graves to the floor. The two other patients in Room 415 and Room 417 tackled Pete Hightower and Marvin Rabinski respectively. Neither of them had idea what had hit them.

The door to the ward was flung open and the SWAT team surged in, all of them with their weapons drawn. Sam Kinney was struggling with Tom Graves, but the fight was over before it had begun when Graves realized he was surrounded by SWAT Officers. The other "patients" both had their men on the ground. One of them produced a pair of handcuffs from his robe and pulled Tom Graves's hands behind his back. The other patient had no trouble with Marvin Rabinski who was still recovering from the beating he had received at McCall's hands. Steve Lansing entered the ward right behind them, his Glock 19 in hand, but he did not think he would need it.

In Room 419 Frank Macamber moved to Alexa's bed holding the garotte taut in his hands. The figure's raven hair was splayed across her face. She turned over, as if restless in her sleep.

The figure was *not* Alexa Kokinas.

An attractive Police Officer held a Sig Sauer .9mm pistol in her hands.

"You're under arrest, Detective Macamber," she said, calmly.

The Police Officer threw back the covers, revealing she was wearing jeans, a dark blue t-shirt, and bare feet. But she was slightly off-balance. Macamber's reaction time was lightning fast. He hit her in the face with a fist that stunned her, at the same time knocking the Sig Sauer pistol out of her hands. He grabbed her long raven hair and slammed her back against the wall. He kicked her legs out from her. He brought the strangling garotte around her throat and pulled it taut.

McCall moved out of the darkened bathroom.

He aimed a vicious punch at Macamber's kidneys. He grunted, taken completely by surprise. McCall ripped the strangling garotte out of his hands. The female Police Officer slumped to the floor, gasping for breath. McCall dropped the garotte to the floor, hitting Macamber as he turned toward him. The blows struck Macamber in the solar plexus and his face. McCall followed it up with what was called in *Muay Thai* a *Buffalo Punch*, designed to take down a *charging Buffalo* in one hit. That move brought Macamber down to his knees. McCall found the notch right above the collar bone at the base of Macamber's throat and pressed with his knuckle. But Macamber was stronger than McCall had anticipated. He lashed out at McCall, hitting him below the belt, sending him back against the heart monitor equipment which crashed to the floor. McCall came back with a *Kao Tone* straight knee strike. Two elbows to Macamber's face finished him. He collapsed to the floor.

McCall grabbed the young Police Officer who was still trying to get air back into her lungs and deposited her on the bed. He picked up her fallen Sig Sauer pistol and dropped it beside her. Macamber tried to crawl back onto his feet. McCall grabbed him and threw him against the opposite wall with uncharacteristic rage.

"Alexa couldn't hear you!" McCall shouted at him. "She had to deal with shadows and shapes she didn't even recognize!"

He grabbed Macamber and threw him against the wall in front of the bed. "She was helpless once you had tasered her! But you were counting on that, weren't you?"

Macamber was groggy, trying to function. McCall did not give him a chance to recover. He grabbed his shoulders and threw him once again against the far wall.

"Did that pump you up?" McCall raged at him. "Knowing Alexa couldn't hear where the blows were coming out of the shadows?"

Macamber put up his hands to ward off more blows. McCall grabbed him and connected to his shin. He doubled over and went down to the floor. This time he did not move. McCall stood over him, breathing fast, his hands held loosely at his sides.

From the doorway of the room, Steve Lansing said calmly: "Try not to kill him, McCall. I need him to testify."

McCall looked up from the shadows and saw Lansing standing in the open doorway of Room 419, a Glock 19 in his hand. Slowly the rage that had been building inside McCall had dissipated. He turned to the bed and lifted the Police Officer back to her feet. She was pissed that Macamber had got the jump on her. She shook out the handcuffs and cuffed his hands behind his back.

"You have the right to remain silent, Frank. Whatever you say may be held against you in a court of law. You know the speech. Try to walk so I don't have to carry your ass."

She dragged Frank Macamber through the open door of Room 419. Detective Steve Lansing holstered his weapon.

"Policeman Jessica Daniels. She usually works vice for me at the 7th Precinct. I think her feelings were hurt. She is used to dealing with drug dealers and street gangs. Macamber was tougher than she realized. You okay?"

McCall slowly nodded. The fury that had taken over him had subsided.

"Remind me to never piss you off," Lansing murmured. "Don't worry about the smashed heart equipment. Just props."

McCall followed Detective Lansing out of the room, closing the door behind him.

He looked out at the chaos in the ward.

It had all been a set-up.

The Rosewood Clinic in Trenton, New Jersey and not been officially opened as yet. The building was going through extensive repairs and had been closed for four months. The Receptionist who had greeted Frank Macamber and his *Elite* cops worked as a Security Consultant. The staff in the ward on the fourth floor had been assembled with Detective Steve Lansing's help. The computers were new and never been used. Nurse Holloway was in fact Detective Linda Holloway of the 7th Precinct. The two Scrabble Players in their thirties were vice cops named Chris Fellows and Bobby Stevens who also worked at the 7th Precinct with Steve Lansing. The sick man was Detective Ray O'Quinn who worked vice at the 7th Precinct. The old man who had been watching the *NCIS* re-run on his television, which had been just hooked to cable that day, was Sam Kinney. He looked triumphant, although McCall could see he was wheezing from tackling Detective Tom Graves. McCall had been worried about Sam, but the old spy had jumped at the chance to get "back into the action". He gave McCall a thumbs-up sign.

The SWAT Officers had rounded up all of the *Elite* cops and taken them into custody. Officer Jessica Daniels handed Frank Macamber over to the SWAT team. McCall noted that Jerry Kilpatrick was handcuffed with the others. McCall took Steve Lansing arm and nodded at Jerry.

"Jerry Kilpatrick helped me set up the sting on the *Elite*. He comes from a prestigious family of cops. Three generations. I have already talked to the Assistant District Attorney, who happens to be my ex-wife, Cassie Blake, about Jerry Kilpatrick. She is going to consider a plea-bargain for him. He never actually raped Alexa Kilpatrick, but he allowed the assault to happen. That in itself was bad enough, but Frank Macamber was a powerful influence on all of them. Jerry feared for his life and the lives of his family."

Lansing nodded. "I already talked to Cassie," he said. "Macamber is being arrested on attempted murder and the other members of the *Elite* are looking at rape and conspiracy charges. She is working out a deal for Jerry Kilpatrick. He may not have to serve any jail time."

"Let me know how that goes."

McCall looked at the rogue cops being hustled out into the corridor to the elevators. Frank Macamber turned around to look back at McCall with murder in his eyes. Then the *Elite* were being taken down the stairs by the SWAT Officers.

"I didn't think anyone could bring down these rogue cops," Lansing said. "I alerted the Captain at the 16th Precinct as to what was happening. He was appalled by the magnitude of the crime his detectives had committed. He is my next call. He will not be sorry to hear about Frank Macamber. He had been trying to nail him for two years."

Lansing held out his hand and McCall shook it. "No parting words about vigilantes taking the laws into their own hands?" McCall asked.

"Not this time," Lansing said. "Just watch your back, McCall. One of these days you're going to come on a situation you can't get out of."

McCall glanced over at Sam Kinney wryly. "You've been speaking to my conscience."

Lansing smiled. McCall headed out of the fake ward and disappeared down the stairs to the lobby.

► 20 ◄

McCALL FOUND STAVROS Kokinas at Loi Estiatorio's restaurant on 58th Street. There were twenty people at the ornate curved bar and at five of the tables, all of them drinking Boutari Grande Reserve Naoussa wine or Nemea Boutari. They were boisterous and talking over each other in high spirits. Maria Loi had closed the restaurant to the public. McCall realized it was not truly a celebration because of the heinous nature of the circumstances. He had let Stavros know what had happened to Frank Macamber and the other *Elite* Officers who were now in Federal prison. He was ecstatic with the news.

And his daughter Alexa stood right beside him in the boisterous ambiance.

When Maria Loi had opened up to let McCall in, Stavros had come right over and hugged him. He had tears in his eyes. He ushered him to where Alexa stood, surrounded by friends and, presumably, colleagues from the 16th Precinct. Her partner Tony Palmer was beside her. She looked a little shaky but was holding her own with some style. Her voice was stronger than he had heard it before. She reached out a hand and clasped McCall hand in hers. Her grip was firm, although McCall detected a tremor in her fingers. He had been told that Bellevue

Hospital had released her that afternoon. Her face still had the scars from her beating, but they had been skillfully covered with make-up. There was a small bandage on her right cheek where Macamber had repeatedly hit her. McCall had called ahead to tell Stavros about what happened to the rogue cops. He did not think it had sunk in yet, but Alexa bestowed a smile on him that he would remember forever.

"Over?"

That one word said everything that needed to be said.

"Yes," McCall said.

"The *Elite* are in jail?"

"Yes."

She suddenly moved into McCall's arms and hugged him.

She did not let him go for a very long time.

When they did break, McCall said: "This will be a trying time for you. The perpetrators will be arraigned tomorrow. The Assistant District Attorney, who happens to be my ex-wife, is going to throw the book at them. They will be in Rykker's for a long time. You have my word."

"Good." Alexa chose her words carefully in her halting fashion. "My Captain at the 16th Precinct wants to see me when I have fully recovered. I guess I am no longer going to be a Peace Officer."

"Don't be too sure of that," McCall said. "Leave that to me."

Alexa actually smiled, which took her an effort. She said haltingly: "Do you leap single buildings in a single bound and wear a cape?"

McCall smiled. "Not yet."

"I'd like to thank you also," Officer Palmer said. "On behalf of my partner."

"No thanks are necessary," McCall said.

"I think they are."

Stavros grabbed McCall's hand. "You must join us for dinner! This is as much your celebration as ours. I insist!"

McCall shook his head. "I'll have to pass." He looked back at Alexa. "I just wanted to make sure you were okay."

She said: "Fine… now."

"I'll be in touch."

McCall moved through the door of the restaurant and was swallowed up into the shadows outside.

Samantha Gregson felt apprehensive when she the left the series of caves in the mountains in Afghanistan. She had met with the leaders of the Taliban, particularly the Deputy Minister of Foreign Affairs, an Egyptian named Khalid Rehman Mohammed. He had been cordial and attentive as Samantha had laid out her plans for the European concerts that Matthew Goddard given to her. But there was an unnerving ambience to Mohammed's manner in the way he looked at her. Like she was a bug he had just seen crawling out of a rock and had stepped on. Khalid Rehman Mohammed was in his forties, a swarthy, handsome man with jet black hair, who, incongruously, had a livid scar on his face three inches in diameter where he had been knifed in a street brawl. It gave his obsidian eyes an unnerving, sinister quality. He had been educated at Oxford in political science and graduated with honors. But he had never given up his heritage. Khalid Rehman Mohammed had returned to Pakistan and then to Afghanistan to fight the infidels of the Far Enemy. Mathew Goddard had coached Samantha on the religious teaching of these students of Islamic law and the religious precepts from the Quran and the Hadith. They were members of the Sunni Islamic fundamentalism political organization. All of them were Pashtun tribesmen except for Khalid Rehman Mohammed who was their leader. Samantha had s smattering of Pari, Tajik and Uzbek that Malcolm Goddard has taught her which the Taliban tribal leaders spoke incessantly. Samantha had laid out notes, maps, design graphs and intel she had stolen from the *Company* before she left. The Taliban Leaders had greeted this intel like it was the Holy Grail. Samantha caught a few words here and there. The meeting broke up and Khalid Rehman Mohammed had escorted her through the series of caves until they emerged into the watery sunshine outside. He noted her tension with some irony, but he said: "You impressed the tribal leaders with your passion."

"I'm gratified to hear that," Samantha said. "Where were you educated?"

"In Oxford in England."

"Where you graduated with honors?"

"You did your homework."

"Yet you returned back to this hot, Godforsaken country."

"It was my density," the Terrorist Leader said. "Our faith has sustained us against the false prophets of the Infidels. Life can be very fragile. But we will triumph over the Far Enemy. You will help us achieve that goal."

Khalid Rehman Mohammed accompanied her to where a Russian utility light helicopter was waiting ringed by mountains. Scott Renquist and Jaak Olesk were waiting beside it. Mohammad took Samantha's arm when she stumbled on the uneven ground.

"Allow me to escort you, Ms. Gregson. The terrain here can he treacherous. My colleagues are not accustomed to a woman dictating terms to them, but I think they were impressed with your determination and tenacity."

"I am gratified to hear that, Mohammad," she said, but she was clearly unnerved by him.

"I will go over your diagrams and maps with them to make sure there were no misunderstandings. This plan will strike at the very heart of the western world. You have my word that the Taliban will carry out this audacious attack."

"You talk as if you were not one of them."

"I have my own reasons for the lifestyle I have chosen," Mohammed said, urbanely. "What is your reason for betraying the ideals you have embraced since childhood? It is not just a question of ideology or hate for the western world. It is something fundamental in your character. You have no qualms about the innocent lives that will be sacrificed in this bloodbath?"

"I also have my reasons for carrying out this act," Samantha said, tersely. "I don't feel compelled to share them with you."

Suddenly Mohammad grabbed Samantha's arm and pulled her close to him. The livid scar on his face was highlighted by his proximity. His tone was filled with menace.

"Matthew Goddard should have not sent you to a place where you could be harmed. One of these Taliban tribesmen could slit your throat for daring to speak to us like equals as you did."

"That's why the two mercenaries standing at the helicopter have my back."

"Are you sure of that?" he asked "Mercenaries can be bought. They have no loyalties to anyone but themselves."

Samantha was being held tight in Mohammad's arms. But the look on her face belayed the momentary panic she had experienced. "This is a stiletto blade," she hissed at him. "If you so much as twitch I will slide this knife into your ribcage. You'll bleed out before any of your Taliban buddies could reach your body."

For a moment Khalid Rehman Mohammad locked eyes with her, then he took a step back. Samantha had not been bluffing. She clutched a large Peacock switchblade knife with a red hilt that opened up to 3:5" inches. The Chieftain Taliban smiled.

"You won't need that," he said, his tone mocking. "This is a great moment for us. I will make sure that your wishes will be followed to the letter. It is a mistake to look too far ahead. Only one link of destiny can be handled at one time. You know who said that?"

"I haven't the faintest idea."

"Winston Churchill. May the mercy, peace and blessings of Allah be upon you. Ms Gregson."

"Wa alaikam salam we rahmatullah wa barakatuhu," she said.

She pocketed the switchblade in her coat and moved from him over the rocky ground to where Scott Renquist greeted her. She practically fell into his arms. "Get me the fuck away from here," she said, hoarsely.

Renquist put arm around her and motioned to Jaak Olesk to fire up the chopper. By the time Samantha and Renquist reached it, the rotors were turning with Olesk at the controls. Renquist lifted Samantha up into the helicopter, climbed in beside her and strapped them in as the copter lifted off the ground. Olesk navigated between two mountain peaks and was swallowed up in the valley behind them.

Below, Khalid Rehman Mohammad watched Samantha's departure with expressionless eyes.

McCall took the phone call from Hayden Vallance when he arrived at the nondescript building complex in Herndon, Virginia. He paused in front of the building and listened to what Vallance had to say. He was terse, but Hayden Vallance had never been a good conversationalist. McCall did not interrupt except when Vallance said: "What do you want me to do about this?'

"I'll take care of it," McCall said and disconnected the line.

He entered the building with its marble floors and its subdued ambience. Harvey, the uniformed African American security guard, got up immediately from his desk. He did not need to see McCall's ID. He had been around since the days of Kennedy and Nixon. He escorted McCall up to the sixth floor, through the glass double-doors and to the conference room. The room was crowded. Emma Marshall was laying out slides at the circular table. There were manila files at the table and a water decanter. Emma was wearing a lilac blouse with a black skirt and high-heeled pumps. McCall thought her look was subdued for her until he looked closer and noted that the blouse was being held together by one stalwart button that threatened to expose her voluptuous figure. Most of the *Company* agents seated at the circular table were strangers to McCall. He did recognize one figure, Jason Mazer, a *Company* agent who was standing beside Control. There was no love lost between McCall and Mazur who regarded him with undisguised disdain. His supercilious manner and pedantic logic had grated on McCall for years. Mazer had been behind a coup that had threatened to oust Control when he had disappeared from the Spy Organization. McCall had rescued him from a secluded cabin in the Virginia woods being guarded by terrorists and returned him home. Nothing had been said about his incarceration, but McCall always felt that Jason Mazer was just biding his time until a more viable opportunity presented itself. He glanced up now and gave McCall a curt nod. Control glanced up. The elegant spymaster was wearing his usual grey Saville suit, a pink striped shirt, a red tie with small chess pieces on it and his signature gold cuff links with his initials on them. He acknowledged McCall and went back to his intense conversation with Mazer. Assad Malifi, a good-looking Egyptian analyst who had been with the *Company* for ten years, moved over to McCall and shook his hand.

"Nice to see you back with us, Mr. McCall."

"A temporary arrangement."

"You're looking well."

The Egyptian then moved across to Emma Marshall to help her sort out the slide presentation. Mickey Kostmayer took his place. "You could slice the tension in this room with a scalpel," he said. "Jason Mazer still thinks you're lower than pond scum."

"He is entitled to his opinion."

"Don't turn your back on him."

"I wasn't planning to."

"Granny and I got things squared away," Kostmayer said. "He doesn't blame me for not coming to his rescue, but he should."

"Let it go, Mickey."

The young Company agent nodded. "Did Control give you any heads up about the meeting?"

"Only that it has something to do with Samantha Gregson. I gather she is no longer working for Malcom Goddard," McCall said.

"I believe you stabbed a throwing knife into his right eye," Kostmayer said, conversationally.

"He tried to kill a friend of mine."

"I didn't think you had friends."

"You and Sam Kinney should get together and compare notes," McCall said, wryly. "The intel I have is that

Samantha Gregson has taken over Malcolm Goddard's network of mercenaries."

"What is she doing with them?"

"That's what we're here to find out."

At that moment another Security guard opened the door to the conference room. Colonel Michael G. Ralston, *Gunner* to his friends and enemies, entered. Kostmayer moved over to him immediately, shaking his hand. He dragged him over to where McCall was standing.

"McCall, this Colonel Michael Ralston who kept me company in that underground parking lot at the UN building while I attempted to defuse a bomb. Well, Gunner did the defusing. I just gave him some moral support."

"I heard it all about it," McCall said, shaking his hand. "You're retired from the army now?"

"Last week," Gunner said. "I told my wife it was time for me to spend time with all the 'honey-do' chores around the house that I have been avoiding for thirty years. Then I received a call from my old CO to report here to this facility at 0900 hours. I had already met your Control at a fund-raiser for wounded vets last year." Gunner glanced around the crowded room. "I gather this Back Ops outfit doesn't officially exist."

"It doesn't," McCall said. "But if Control has sent for you, there'll be a damn good reason for you to be here."

Gunner looked back at McCall. "But I didn't expect you to be here. Mickey Kostmayer brought me up to speed about you. You reigned from the spy business some time ago?"

"I did."

"Control can be very persuasive," Kostmayer murmured.

Gunner nodded, still looking at McCall. "So there's a good reason for you to be here today also."

"A rogue agent named Samantha Gregson has gathered some dangerous mercenaries around her," McCall said. "They were handpicked by her mentor Malcom Goddard who had been the head of this spy agency for a short while. He was also a dangerous man and a traitor. His protégé Samantha Gregson is planning a terrorist attack. She should not be underestimated."

"What happens to you when the dust clears?" Gunner asked.

"Then I'm done in the spy business." McCall looked back at Mickey Kostmayer. "Got anything to add to that, Mickey?"

"Like Michael Corelone in the *Godfather II* movie." Kostmayer said. "Every time I think I am *out*, I get dragged back in again." McCall looked at him. Kostmayer shrugged. "I'm just saying…"

Control called the meeting to order. Emma Marshall turned out the lights with a flick of her wrist and lights seeped onto the circular table. The other *Company* agents grouped around the screen.

"*Memento Mori*," Control said. "Mercenaries who have been organized into a lethal force by the late Malcolm Goddard. The phrase they use is: '*Remember that you must die*.' They wear *silver demon's claws* on their right hands and a second silver ring beside it. They've been organized by Samantha Gregson." Emma's fingers brought up a recent photograph of Samantha Gregson. "This was taken at a fund-raising for the Lymphoma Foundation in D.C. After that, and the demise of her boss, she has gone completely off the radar. She has been gathering her own army of dangerous mercenaries. We believe she is planning to strike at the heart of Europe to fulfill her boss's directive."

Emma brought up six countries in Europe on the circular table. The agents spun it around so that the various countries were highlighted. Assad Malifi stepped in. "The six European countries are Barcelona, Spain—Rome Italy—Stockholm, Sweden—Prague in the Czech Republic—Athens Greece—and London, England. There is a credible terrorist threat to these six European countries. Samantha Gregson is coordinating these potential terror attacks."

"These *Memento Mori* mercenaries are also involved in protecting the terrorists," Control added.

Assad nodded at Emma and she brought up the travel brochures that been provided for them. "These travel brochures were found in Samantha Gregson's apartment when we initiated a search there. They could just be brochures that Samantha Gregson had been collecting in preparation for going abroad. They might not mean anything at all, but we are taking them very seriously. Our intel has been that these six countries are at a high level of alert and the chatter on the dark web is significant. You can take it from here, Emma."

Emma spun the circular table again for the agents. "All six of these countries will be hosting rock concerts to benefit the worldwide refugee relief efforts. The countries have been passionately involved with this cause, including the Vatican. These terrorist threats are going to happen in one or more of these six countries. Or they may not happen at all."

"You'll all be assigned to your respective countries," Control said. "You will coordinate with the Government of all six countries. Read through the brochures. Take them seriously. You all leave in the next forty-eight hours. Any questions, liaison with Assad or Emma. Good luck, gentlemen."

▶ 21 ◀

THE MEETING BROKE UP with Emma bringing the lights up and killing the illuminated table. The respective agents took their folders with the travel shots of their locales and the intel on the *Memento Mori* mercenaries. McCall picked up his folder with travel arrangement in London, England. Colonel Michael Ralston moved over to where McCall was standing with Assad Malifi.

"Where do I fit it in this?" Ralston asked. "I seem to be odd man out."

Control moved over to the ex-Army Colonel. "I understand that you spent a lot of time in Greece, isn't that right?"

"That's right. Maybe eight, ten trips. I fell in love with the country. The heritage, the antiquity, with the people I met. Where is the rock concert being held?"

"Under the stars at the Rockwave Festival at Terra Vibe Park in Malakesa in Greece," Assad said. "Emma will be giving the flight tickets and intel to you before you leave. I am going to be researching facial recognition profiles on several terrorist organisations."

Assad departed with some of the other analysts. Gunner said: "I don't know that I am cut out to be a spy."

"You've spent your life as an army man," Control said. "You've been flighting al Qaeda and ISIS attacks for years. If you will go to Greece I can't think of a better man for the job."

"Good enough." Gunner turned away from the group, then swung back. "There was a mercenary on my radar when I worked with Captain Josh Coleman. His name was Jack Roslin. The last time I heard from him he was running a bar in Rhode Town called the Melete Craft Beer Bar and he had gone to ground in Greece. A very bad guy. He wore a signet ring on his right hand of a *silver skull*. I can look him up."

"See if you can find him." Control said.

Gunner shook hands with him and left the room with Mickey Kostmayer. When McCall was alone with Control and Emma Marshall, he reached down for the manila folder which had been handed out to the *Company* agents and said to Emma: "Bring down the lights."

Emma was surprised by the request, but she moved immediately to the circular conference table and killed the overhead lights. Control returned to his chair at the table, also curious, and sat back down. McCall handed Emma one of the pieces of intel that had been handed out to the *Company* agents. She brought up a grainy black-and-picture of one of the Security Officers in the folder.

"I received a call from Hayden Vallance before I arrived here," McCall said. "You know him."

"Only by reputation," Control said. He looked over at Emma. "He's a mercenary who was with me during the shootout in San Antonio at the Riverwalk Hotel. He saved my life."

"Don't take it personally," McCall commented, dryly.

"I won't. You keep in touch with him?"

"From time to time. This photograph won't mean anything to the other *Company* agents," McCall said, "but I know this man."

The face that glowed in the subdued lights around the conference table belonged to Ji-Yeon.

Control swung the photograph so that it faced him. "He is a Korean who is charge of the security arrangements for the refugee concert in Rome. It will he held in the Terme di Caracalla ruins which were constructed between AD 214 and 216 and are now a tourist attraction. Where do you know him from?"

"He was at the North Korean prison camp," McCall said, "when I rescued Granny and the western prisoners who had been incarcerated there. He was visiting Commandant Myang-Sook-Jang before all hell broke loose. He kidnapped a young woman named Deva Montgomery who happens to be Liz Montgomery's sister. Liz is a photojournalist who befriended Granny in the camp. Another journalist, Daniel Blake, was taken at the same time. I watched Ji-Yeon's helicopter take off and disappear into the night. Granny has been making inquiries at the State Department that got him nowhere. Thanks to Hayden Vallance we may have a location for Ji-Yeon. He is a specialist in terrorist organizations, especially when it comes to al Qaeda."

"But you're saying Ji-Yeon is a known terrorist?" Control asked, incredulously.

"That's never been proven. If anything, he is an anti-terrorist specialist who hires his services to countries who are alerted to terrorist activities."

"Like this refugee rock concert."

"That's right."

"But you are certain you saw him at that North Korean prison camp?" Control asked.

"It was only a fleeting glance," McCall said. "There was a lot of confusion when the C4 explosives were detonated. Granny would know him without question."

"Where is Granny these days?" Emma asked.

"He has been following a lead to Ji-Yeon's whereabouts in Stockholm that Hayden Vallance led him to. But there is a credible scenario that Ji-Yeon will be attending the rock concert in Rome as a terrorist expert."

"Unless you keep that intel from Granny," Control said.

"I can't do that," McCall said. "Granny is like family. He may have resigned from the *Company* a long time ago, just like I did, but he has always kept in touch with me. From what I gather he went through hell in that North Korean prison camp. He deserves to know if Ji-Yeon will be in Rome."

"Granny doesn't work for the Company," Control objected.

"Doesn't matter. You will not be able to keep him away. Better if he makes the trip to Italy for the *Company* than as a private citizen trying to terminate a known terrorist. That will not get Deva Montgomery or Daniel Blake rescued. It will be their death warrant."

Control sighed. "All right. I will reinstate Granny back into the *Company*. What he does after that is up to him. You go to London tomorrow, Robert. The concert will take place at the Royal Albert Hall on Saturday night. Nothing may come of these terrorist threats in these six countries, but we have to take them seriously."

"Samantha Gregson is looking for payback" McCall said. "She has a score to settle with me. She gathered these *Memento Mori* mercenaries for a reason. She is every bit as dangerous as her ex-boss Malcolm Goddard. If innocent American citizens are being put into harm's way, the death toll at these rock concerts will skyrocket. We can't allow that to happen."

McCall got to his feet, handed his manila folder to Control and exited the conference room.

The bar in the Liberty Belle Hotel had just opened. McCall had set up a slim laptop computer on the bar when Mickey Kostmayer walked in. He sat at one of the bar stools and McCall turned the computer around to face him. It was set up for a Skype call. Kostmayer looked at him quizzically.

"Did you get a further debriefing from Control?"

"In a manner of speaking," McCall said.

He jabbed at the buttons on his cell phone.

"Who are you calling?" Kostmayer asked.

"Granny. He has been on the trail of a mercenary named Ji-Yeon who was at the North Korean prison camp before all hell broke loose. He rescued Liz Montgomery, the photojournalist, and others from the camp, but Ji-Yeon escaped in a helicopter and disappeared. He took with him Deva Montgomery, Liz's sister and an Associated Press journalist named Daniel Blake. Granny flew to Stockholm, which turned out to be a dead end, but he got some intel that took him to Russia. He is now in the scenic town of Pylos searching for records pertaining to Ji-Yeon, who once lived there, but Granny's hit another dead end."

"But Control's intel has found him?"

"Could be if it's the same man. Ji-Yeon is coordinating the security at the Terme Di Caracalla ruins in Rome for the rock concert. His reputation against terrorist organizations is stellar. The fact he is a known terrorist himself is only known to Control and the *Company*. According to our intel, Ji-Yeon arrives in Rome tomorrow morning." McCall gave Kostmayer a searching look. "You've been beating yourself up because you couldn't go to North Korea to get Granny. This is your chance to put that right."

McCall connected to Skype. The screen on the laptop brightened to show Granny sitting at an outdoor café in the town of Pylos nursing a black coffee. The quaint cobbled streets around him were crowded with locals. Granny looked at Kostmayer sitting at the bar with McCall.

"In case you're wondering where I am," Granny said, "I am in Pylos in Russia having a grand time. There must be two hundred tradesmen dressed in medieval costumes in the Old Town Christmas market where the locals are selling everything from pewterware, blown glass and intricate wood carvings. There is supposed to a cannibalistic old witch who lives in the woods outside the town in a Hansel and Gretel house which would make my day. There are great taverns and homages to the mood landscape painter Isaac Levitan and old churches including the renovated Church of the Resurrection and a wooden church circa 1699 that is to die for. But there is no sign of Ji-Yeon."

Kostmayer said: "I've just come from a debriefing meeting at the Company with Control."

"Not interested."

"There were a lot of people you know there."

"Still not interested."

"Your quarry, Ji-Yeon, will be in Rome tonight or tomorrow morning."

Granny stared at his laptop screen on the table beside him. "Is McCall with you?"

Kostmayer turned the laptop around slightly to include McCall.

"You were at that same debriefing meeting?" Granny asked.

"I was," McCall said, "but I won't be going to Rome. Control has reinstated you in the Company for the time being. Do you want this assignment or not?"

"Damn right I want it."

"Mickey can bring you up to speed. Take it slow, Granny. If you're forced to kill Ji-Yeon you won't find out where he has taken Deva Montgomery and Daniel Blake."

"Where do I go?"

McCall turned the laptop back to Kostmayer who said: "Meet me tonight at the La Fata Ignorante Restaurant in Rome at 9:00 P.M."

"I'll be there."

McCall hung up the cell phone and slid out from the barstool. "Give Granny all the intel you can on Ji-Yeon."

"Where will you be?"

"In London, England."

McCall walked out of the Liberty Belle Hotel bar and was lost in the crowd in the lobby.

The next morning Granny stood in the Piazza del Popolo in the heart of Rome, looking up at the twin churches and the giant Egyptian obelisk that dominated the neoclassical square. He had met Mickey Kostmayer at the La Fata Ignorante restaurant the night before at Via Guiseppe Givlittt 5 which was an intimate, gorgeous restaurant for dinner. Granny had been very taken with some large oil paintings of what was surely the same person, a brooding blonde woman with dark, hypnotizing eyes. Kostmayer had brought him up to speed about the rock concert that was going to be held at the Terme di Caracalla baths and ruins. Kostmayer had already met with the concert promoters where they had discussed a proposed schedule for Saturday and how many security staff would be laid on. The Rome promoters were leaving nothing to chance. A raised stage had been erected with lights rigged up all around it. There was an impressive array of security personnel on the grounds and a hundred strong workforce already assembled.

Granny did not care about the details of the rock concert. Kostmayer told him that the head of Security, an expansive Italian named Benedetto Lombardi, had advised him that they were going to be working with an elite Security Officer who would be coordinating the concert. He had a stellar reputation working with European countries who required a high level of expertise. He was somewhat of a legend, but Kostmayer did not get a name for hm, except that he was known throughout the security circles as *Ragnvard*, a *silent wolf.*

"The name comes from Sweden and means a powerful fighter," Kostmayer had said. "The man has incredible strength and self-control, according to Benedetto Lombardi. He described him as completely soulless and emotionally devoid of any personality."

"My kind of guy," Granny had murmured.

But he had to be sure that this phantom *was*, in fact, Ji-Yeon

Granny was positioned among the throngs of tourists surging through the Pizza del Popolo. The organizers of the rock concert had not emerged yet. Granny had found a place in front of a restaurant which was crowded with people. Across from him were the twin churches and the imposing obelisk that dominated the piazza. He was standing at an angle to them, watching the people who emerged from the churches. The size of the crowd was something of a problem. It surged back and forth like an amorphous being. Granny had a Fujinon KF8 x binoculars with him with phase correction-coated prisms for enhanced resolution for a linear field of vison for 1000 yards. He had been in the square since early morning. The rock concert promotors had gone to an address in the Piazza where they had been sequestered. They had visited the twin churches, the Santa Maria dei Miracoli and the Santa Maria di Montesanto, in the Piazza with their new Head of Security in the late morning. Granny had not been able to get a good look at Ji-Yeon in the crush of people who had emerged from the three-story building, which was when he had bought the compact pair of binoculars from a Fuji store. Now it was after 12:00 PM and his patience had been finally rewarded. The rock concert group spilled out of the twin churches, heading to a side street on the Via de Corso. Granny put the binoculars to his eyes in one swift motion, adjusting the center focus wheel.

Their Head of Security was, indeed, Ji-Yeon.

Granny adjusted the focus on the glasses and twisted the center focus wheel. If he had been looking for Ji-Yeon he might not have recognized him. The man's face had been altered, and drastically. The cheekbones were still prominent, but they had blended in with skillful plastic surgery. The scarring was subtle. His eyes had also been worked on so that the Oriental look of them had been greatly reduced. The skin in his face was noticeably stretched and smoothed out. But Ji-Yeon had not been able to disguise his eyes. They were black and opaque.

They were terrifying.

Granny recognized him without a question of a doubt.

He put the binoculars back into his jacket pocket. He had to time it just right. He crossed the Via de Corso and took out a hammered silver cigarette case. He was looking over his shoulder at a gorgeous redheaded girl in her twenties. He waved jauntily at her, gauging the distance between her and a white Peugeot which was parked at the curb. Granny swung back, opening the silver cigarette case as he did so, and almost ran right into Ji-Yeon. The cigarettes spilled from his hand to the sidewalk. The three men accompanying the terrorist whirled and one of them reached inside his jacket where Granny was sure a gun was concealed.

Granny was certain that was no way that Ji-Yeon could recognize him. The Korean had never seen him in the prison camp. All of Granny's dealings had been with Myang-Sook-Jang. As far as Granny was concerned, Ji-Yeon did not know him from a bar of soap.

Granny said: "Le Mie Scuca" and "Colpa Mia" in Italian, cursing softly to himself as he reached down for the spilled cigarettes. He was counting on a response from Ji-Yeon if nothing more than a common courtesy. The Korean terrorist leaned down and helped Granny pick up the fallen cigarettes. Granny stumbled a little bit, momentarily holding on to Ji-Yeon, thrusting his hand into the Korean's tailored jacket. Then he knelt to pick up the rest of the cigarettes. When he had them all back in his hammered silver case, he straightened. Ji-Yeon took out a silver lighter from his suit coat and clicked it into flame. Granny accepted the light, nodding his thanks and moving away into the street.

The concert group moved down past the churches to where the white Peugeot was parked. Ji-Yeon climbed into the back seat with three others of the entourage. Behind the Peugeot a 2019 Fiat 500 was parked. The entourage got into the Fiat 500 and the vehicle pulled away after the white Peugeot, scattering the crowd in the Piazza.

Granny watched them leave. The concert promotors would be heading out to the Terme di Caracalla ruins with their new Head of Security.

Granny had got what he had come for.

He had planted the tiny silver bug right under the skin of Ji-Yeon's wrist without leaving so much as a scratch. It had been a pinprick that Ji-Yeon would not have even felt. It was a trick that Granny had picked up from Brahms one time when he and Robert McCall had needed some sophisticated listening equipment. Granny figured that Ji-Yeon had come right from the airport, dumped his bags at the hotel and then he had come with the concert organizers to the building on the Pizza del Popolo. There might be intel that he could gather in Ji-Yeon's hotel room. He would never have a better opportunity to look for it.

Granny took a cab to the Largo Antonio Sarti 4 in the heart of Rome. He got out in front of the Hotel Astrid, a luxurious Best Western with pale pink and cream décor that took up two blocks on a corner. There was a verandah on the 6th floor where Italian flags were displayed. Several wooden balconies were in evidence around the building. Granny pushed through the doors into the hotel. The lobby reception had a pale marble panel where two members of staff worked. Plush red couches stood in front of a green marble slab. A big sweeping staircase led up to the floors above. The lobby was a madhouse. A bus had just deposited forty tourists into the hotel and the beleaguered hotel staff were coping with the weary travellers with charm and grace. But there was a lot of shouting and demanding, which suited Granny's purposes just fine. He wore a badge around his neck on a chain that Mickey Kostmayer had given him saying he was a member of the Terme di Caracalla rock concert staff.

Ji-Yeon had registered under his own name at the Hotel Astrid, which had surprised Granny, but he figured that he had several aliases that he used. His suite was on the sixth floor. Granny took the marble stairs and found suite number 604. There was no one in the corridor outside the suite. He took out a skeleton key that Kostmayer had given him and worked it into the door. The door finally opened. Granny put a *Do Not Disturb* sign on the brass door handle and closed the door behind him.

There were two rooms in the suite. The smaller one had a narrow made-up bed and a glass-topped table. There was a wardrobe which Granny slid open, but there was nothing in it. He moved to the second room, which was larger, although the twin bed took most of the space. There were two more glass-topped tables in it. The bed had been turned down, but not slept in. A Nike Brasilia Duffel Bag that been left below one of the glass topped tables. Granny opened the wooden wardrobe door in the corner. Ji-Yeon had four suits hanging up, all of them silk, black and grey. There was silken underwear in the top drawer along with handkerchiefs, black dress socks and a space for polished shoes. The suite was elegant and minimalist. Granny closed the wardrobe door and hauled the Duffel Bag from under the glass-topped table and placed it onto the bed. He unzipped it. He found it contained blueprints and documents in two glossy folders. He opened the folders.

The blueprints appeared to be a series of underground tunnels.

Granny had a momentary sense of déjà vu.

Had he not just spent a great deal of time in underground tunnels at the North Korean prison camp?

But these tunnels were different. They were hundreds of passageways that interconnected in a way that made Granny's skin crawl. He could almost smell the death in the air of the necropolis.

He realized that he was looking at the ancient catacombs of Rome.

The door to the bathroom was partially open and the mirror above the enamel sink reflected a swathe of light.

Granny saw someone open the hotel room door.

Instantly he had a sense-memory of one of the plush sofas in the lobby area of the hotel. A man had been sitting there reading a copy of *Newsweek*. Granny had only seen him for a second. He had been aware of a dull sheen on the man's right-hand finger which had not registered with him until now.

It had been a *silver death's head* skull.

Memento Mori.

The intruder's reflection flared in the mirror.

Granny stepped from the bed to behind the door in one fluid motion. The mercenary pushed open the door. Granny grabbed his gun hand and disarmed him, but the man twisted the gun out of Granny's hand. It skittered across the marble floor right into the tiled bathroom. The man twisted into Granny and held him in a vicious headlock. The demon's claw ring on his right hand glowed in the light refracted from the window. The mercenary squeezed Granny's windpipe as he writhed in the man's grasp.

He was losing consciousness fast.

An image came into his mind of a trick he had taught McCall years ago for breaking a head lock. McCall had used it when he had fought off Tom Renquist in the Texas Regional Water Plant in Boerne, Texas and broken his neck. Granny struck with his rigid right hand. The muscles contracted violently as they expelled air from the attacker's lungs. It was called an *air dimmak* point. Granny reached down and grabbed the mercenary's right wrist and gouged the pressure points there, then followed it up with a rigid palm strike at the *mind point* on the side of the man's chin. The assassin's grip on Granny's body slackened. Granny jabbed the colon points on the man's upper foreman and wrenched from his grasp. He clubbed him while the assassin was reeling and brought his own arm around the man's throat. In one fierce movement he pivoted and swung the man's neck one way and then back the other way until his neck was broken.

Granny dragged the inert mercenary into the bathroom and dumped him into the shower. He staggered over to the window and opened it. The ambiance of the Rome street echoed around him. He took some deep breaths of fresh air. His throat still felt raw and enflamed. He had not expected an attack, but it told him that Rome was certainly one of the cities where the terrorists were going to strike. Granny closed the window, still dragging air into his lungs. He knelt at the shower and went through the dead man's pockets. He had an ID and a driver's licence in the name of Harry Brandt, but no credit cards or other ID. There was a tattered wallet-size picture of a young child about six years old, smiling self-consciously for the camera in a playground somewhere. The man had a daughter who would never again know her father. It gave Granny a moment's pause. The sins of her father should not be transferred to his child. Harry Brandt had chosen this life of betrayal. He had paid the ultimate price, Granny thought, something all mercenaries paid in the end. He locked the bathroom door and returned to the main bedroom and picked up Ji-Yeon's Duffel Bag. He put the diagrams of the tunnels and caverns that had been in Ji-Yeon's folder and transferred them to his jacket pocket.

The bed in the room had already been turned down. He figured a maid would not be back until nighttime. It would take some time for the security force in the hotel to come up and break the door down.

Granny let himself out of the hotel suite, locked it and put the *Do Not Disturb* sign on the door handle. He went down the ornate staircase, found a side door that led out of the Hotel Astrid and disappeared into the throng of people in the Via de Corco.

▶ 22 ◀

COLONEL MICHAEL RALSTON arrived in Athens and headed immediately out to the Rockwave Festival at Terra Vibe Park in Malakesa. Gunner was greeted by Spiros Alexandros, a big-hearted, expansive Festival director who welcomed him to Greece. Spiros took terrorist threats to his rock concert very seriously, but he confessed to Gunner that he was confident that there was, in fact, no subversive activity that his Security force had encountered. This was the fourth concert that Spiros had put together in two years and he did not see anything to alarm him this time. Everything was under control and the concert was in good hands. He introduced Gunner to his concert promotors, two brothers in their forties, Christos and Niko Lykalos, likeable and gregarious who showed him around the outdoor stadium. Gunner noted the massive stands going up that dwarfed the stage. Myriad colored light stands had gone up above the stage area. The workforce was a hive of activity. Christos and Niko steered Gunner through the frenetic preparations, pointing out safety measures already in place, including several pitched tents where the public were vetted before streaming into the open-air stadium. Gunner asked his hosts what was backstage. He was told there was a basement area with dressing rooms and marble stairs leading down to a lower level. Gunner was appreciative for the impromptu tour, but he wanted to have the chance to look around for himself. The Lykolos brothers had no problem with that and left him to his own devices while even more Security personnel flooded into the stadium.

Gunner climbed onto the stage where the rock band was setting up their equipment. The group was called *Nexus*, whom Gunner had never heard of, but he had not heard of the other mega-rock stars either, except perhaps for the Beatles, the Doors and the Grateful Dead. *Nexus* consisted of Amanda Stevenson, the sole female singer. Beside her were Doc Conrad, Terry Monaghan, Buster Cruz, Ethan Stanwitz and Gonzo Lindsey. Amanda had a voluptuous figure and was dressed in a black t-shirt. Her black hair was cropped short in bangs. She bestowed a smile on Gunner that could have heated up his blood. The other male members of the group were dressed in ripped skinny jeans and a Smiling Apple Hoodie, a long-sleeved Assassin Black Creed shirt, a black *The King of Terrors* Slim Fit t-shirt, and a black knit-weave that had emblazon on it *Do I Look Like a Fucking People Person*? Gunner introduced himself to the band, shaking hands, but they were getting ready for their headlining set.

Gunner walked backstage into the wings where he found a wooden staircase leading down into the basement area. He descended into the three dressing rooms there and, beyond them, several small rooms filled with pipes and electrical equipment under the stage that had been cordoned off. He ducked under the pipes and the heating vents, finding one of the pipes was *very hot* to the touch. There was no sign of explosives being hidden in the basement area, just dusty boxes with more junk and some fairground carnival masks and paraphernalia from some long-forgotten pageant.

Gunner retraced his steps through the basement area and climbed the wooden stairs that led through the Stage Right wings back out onto the stage. *Nexus* were still setting up their equipment which consisted of amplifiers, microphones, keyboards, patch cables and a drum kit with the group's logo on it. There were also several acoustic and bass guitars, a saxophone, violins, electric violins, double bass and two pianos. Christos and Nico Lykalos latched onto Gunner and escorted him from the stage. Above them the tiered bench-like seats were rapidly filling up as the concertgoers were led into the arena. Christos indicated the crowd who were finding their seats.

"After our last experience with crowd control," he said, "we found a way to keep the lines moving rapidly by funneling them through the tents."

"That gave us an opportunity to search for any suspicious backpacks, briefcases or Apple devices," Nico said. "We confiscated a while bunch of them. Cell phones too. The punters moaned about it, but in they realized that we were taking care of them."

"How many Security Staff are on hand in the arena?" Gunner asked.

"We've got about a hundred, give or take," Christos said. "They'll be patrolling the tiers of seats, keeping in touch with walkie-talkies. I am afraid that your intelligence intel may have been for nothing. But we are here for you."

Gunner nodded. "You have a phrase in Greek that I have always liked. 'Don't walk behind me. I may not lead. Do not walk in front of me. I may not follow. Just walk beside me and by my friend."

The two brothers were duly impressed. "You speak our language, Colonel?" Christos asked.

"Halting and not very well. I spent ten years in Greece, on and off. There is an extremist terrorist named Jack Roslin. I came across him in Rhode Town. He frequented a place called the Melete Craft Beer Bar. Ever heard of it?"

Nico grinned. "I thought I knew every Greek dive and bar in a hundred miles! But I don't know that one."

"He may be no longer there," Gunner said. "It's about five years since I last saw him."

"Do you have a description of him?"

"Big guy, soft-spoken, dangerous. Worked as a mercenary for several years. He might he here at the concert. He wears a silver death's head ring on his right hand and another one in plain gold beside it."

Gunner took out one of the folders he had been carrying in his jacket pocket and handed it to them. They shook their heads negatively. Gunner said: "I didn't get a chance to go to Rhode Town, but I talked to my friends in the bar who told me they had not seen him for over a year. But distribute his picture to your security staff."

"We will do that," Nico assured him.

At that point they hustled over to where more Security Officers were having an impromptu conference in front of the stage area. Gunner let them get on with their duties. The ex-Colonel had inspected the backstage area, the warren of small rooms and nooks and crannies in the basement. Security had already gone through those rooms and the backstage area several times. They, like Gunner, had found nothing that pointed to the stadium have been breached. Control had said the terrorist threat could be spurious.

But as he looked around at the stands that were rapidly filling up with young concert revellers, Gunner had a dread in the pit of his stomach that would not go away.

His sixth senses had kicked in big time.

Somewhere in Terra Vibe Park here in Malakesa a bomb was about to go off.

When McCall landed in London it was pouring with rain, sending little fitful gusts into the air. There was a text waiting for him from Control. He had located Samantha's apartment in Kensington Gardens Mews in North London. She had been living there since before she had hooked up with Matthew Goddard. She had never officially moved out, paying the rent ahead. When McCall got to his hotel, which was the Dorchester, he picked up a room key and an envelope that had been left for him at the front desk. There was a single key in it and an address on a nametag. He took a black London cab to the mews address, got out and looked up at a four-story house on a cobbled street which was almost overgrown with ivy that crept up the wall. There was an ornate balcony on the second floor which could be accessed by a sliding glass door. It gave McCall an eerie feeling as is if he had stepped into the past where coachmen and horses were quartered. The mews was sheltered from the rest of the street like it was in its own little world. There was no sound, not even muffled traffic. He inserted the key, opened door to Samantha's apartment and stepped inside.

A narrow staircase led up to the second floor with a floor-to-ceiling library and a small morning room in the back of the house. McCall climbed up to the second floor which in turn opened into a large sitting room with another small room, almost like a carriage room, which overlooked the wrought-iron balcony. Beech and cherry trees were in evidence and a towering elm tree that leaned almost against the mews house. The sitting room was in darkness. McCall could see the shapes of a couch, a couple of wicker chairs, more floor-to-ceiling freestanding bookshelves, a cherry roll top desk, a kitchenette and the sliding glass door that led out onto the balcony. Heavy rain lashed the sliding glass door. Lightning erupted, followed by a roll of thunder. The news house was barely visible in the haze of the storm.

McCall moved quickly to a bedroom. A Hummingbird Percale Duvet cover and sham were on the four-poster bed. There was a rocker in one corner and a maple-wood dresser. McCall opened a wardrobe, revealing dresses and chic suits that Samantha Gregson had worn when she had worked for the *Company*. Rows of men's suits were jammed into the small space as well as men's shoes. They had probably belonged to Matthew Goddard. McCall had a brief sense-memory of Goddard standing in his hotel suite in New York City in a dark blue, three-piece suit. There were several red ties in the closet with small chess pieces on them and a shelf for gold cuff links and several pairs of Florsheim Berkley loafers in Burgundy. He had held a Walther PPK semi-automatic pistol pressed to a young woman's head. She was naked and trembling in the darkness. In the end, McCall had been forced to kill him by sending a slim throwing knife into his right eye.

McCall moved into the bathroom. No soap, no shampoo. There was a wicker hamper full of dirty clothes. He retraced his steps from the living room into the kitchen. There was nothing in the refrigerator except for a few frozen dinners and some left-over pizza. There were some magazines on the low coffee table, Vogue, Harper Bazaar, People, Travel & Leisure and Newsweek. The paperbacks on the bookshelves were all thrillers or romance novels. McCall moved over to the Cherry Roll

Top desk and started opening the drawers. He found the usual assortment of Pilot pens, a ruler, push pins, paper clips, staples and a Montblanc Meisteruck number 149 fountain pen with black ink and an old-fashioned ink-well. He found nothing of interest in the other drawers except for more folded travel brochures. He glanced up. Through the sliding glass door lightning flickered over the mews house. A moment later another explosion of thunder echoed. Rain lacerated the glass balcony window. It might almost have been night. In the sudden cacophony of the elements McCall did not hear someone entering the house.

He turned his attention back to the travel brochures. They extolled the benefits of vacationing in Rome, Spain, Stockholm, Prague, Greece, and the UK. All of them cities where Samantha Gregson and her mercenaries were planning to strike.

The barest of movements swung McCall from the desk.

A cheese-grater looped around his throat.

McCall's vision appeared to narrow down to a slit as the attacker pulled the silver cheese grater tight. He saw the muscles in the assailant's face tighten. His breath was hot on McCall's neck. The sheen of the inkwell on the drawer caught McCall's eye. He reached down, unscrewed the top of the inkwell and threw it back into the assailant's face.

The assassin reached up to claw at his eyes where the ink black had penetrated them.

McCall grabbed at the cheese grater and pulled it from his neck. In the same movement, he went down to his knees and hurled the attacker over his shoulder. He landed hard, his hands trying to claw the stinging ink from his eyes. McCall rolled over and up onto his feet. He saw the assailant was over six feet, wearing a black belted raincoat. McCall's attention was riveted onto the man's right hand. There was a silver ring on his ring finger with the *demon-claws skull.* McCall knew it had etched on it: *Remember That You Must Die.*

Memento Mori.

There was something familiar about the assailant's face. McCall could not place it at first, then he saw a resemblance to Tom Renquist, the mercenary whom McCall had fought at the West Texas Regional Water Treatment plant and sent plunging to his death.

In that instant the assailant was back on his feet.

McCall hit him hard, slamming his head into the open desk drawer. The man caught hold of McCall's coat, getting his arms locked around him. His right eye had almost completely closed up, the black ink staining his face, giving him a bizarre, nightmarish look. Like out of a horror movie. McCall clawed at the attacker's hands, finding purchase, ripping the man's hands away. He came right back at McCall, both of them twisting in various choke holds, trying to find the other's weakness. McCall finally threw the assassin to his knees, but he just came back up again. McCall traded blows with the assassin, parried with fast reflexes while the assassin struck hammer fists at McCall's head. Finally McCall grabbed the man's coat and propelled him past the couch and slammed him against the sliding glass door leading out onto the balcony. The force of McCall's thrust smashed the door, hurling jagged glass shards onto the terrace. The assassin collapsed onto the balcony. McCall followed him outside. Rain sheeted against them, almost blinding in its intensity. Immediately he saw that the assailant had a large piece of jagged glass sticking out from his right leg. McCall knelt down beside him.

"Lie still."

"Go to Hell."

"Tell me your name."

Little bubbles burst from the assassin's his lips as he spoke. "It's Scott," he said.

"Your brother Tom Renquist tried to kill me in Texas," McCall said. "I see the resemblance. I will call for an ambulance. You will bleed out if that glass has severed an artery."

The assassin suddenly reached out a hand for McCall's throat. McCall held it tightly, his face inches from the wounded assassin. "You don't report to Matthew Goddard now. He is dead. Did Samantha Gregson send you to kill me?"

The assailant stared up at him, his right eye obscenely disfigured from the black ink. He was trembling in the driving rain. McCall shook him.

"What is your mission? Who are your targets?"

The mercenary just shook his head, staring up at McCall with ironic eyes. McCall let him go and straightened up. He moved to the shattered door, kicking large fragments of glass from the balcony. He heard a coughing sound behind him and whirled. The assassin had managed to get to his feet and break off the jagged shard of glass.

McCall thought he was about to lunge at him.

Then the mercenary turned around and threw himself over the wrought-iron railing.

McCall heard the sickening fall as he ran to the railing. The man had landed on top of a parked car beneath the massive elm tree. A car alarm had gone off. McCall stared down at the prone assassin, then he ran back to the shattered door into the sitting room.

The cops would be there in within five minutes.

McCall grabbed up the travel brochures and put them into the pocket of his overcoat. He locked the door, ran to the entrance to the secluded mews and disappeared into the elements.

Samantha Gregson stood outside the mews, isolated in the deluge. She was wearing a belted raincoat and a silk scarf at her throat. She watched as McCall's figure ran through the rainstorm and grabbed a passing cab. Samantha was not worried that she would lose sight of him. Her small homing device was still planted beneath McCall's skin. She could track him anywhere he went. She had not realized he had found her mews cottage. That was something she had kept secret. But she did not care. McCall would find nothing in her house that he did not already know about. It would place her in London, but that was all right too. She would be just a face in the crowd at the Royal Albert Hall. McCall would not know she was even there until it was too late. But somehow it irked her that McCall had let himself into her inner sanctum. That was a special place for her. She did not like the idea that her house had been violated in this way. But after tomorrow all hell would break loose.

Samantha heard the sound of the police cars arriving. She felt a momentary regret that her mercenary Scott Renquist had fallen to his death while struggling with McCall. He had been a dedicated follower. He did not deserve to die, but all of her mercenaries were pawns to her. They could be sacrificed when necessary.

Samantha Gregson pulled her Burberry raincoat tighter around her and ran through the downpour where McCall had disappeared.

By this time tomorrow night he would be dead.

▶ 23 ◀

FLOODLIGHTS ILLUMINATED the ruins at the Terme di Caracalla in Rome although the wintery afternoon sunshine had not fully abated. Reds and mauves outlined the impressive Roman structure with its marble tiles that glowed in the oblique waning light. Three tiers of stadium seats had been erected around the stage where work was still continuing. In another three hours the headliners, the *Three Tenors*, would climb up on the stage. A large trailer had been set up on the grounds amid the ruins. The *Silver Bullet*, as it was called, was a 2020 Keystone Premiere 34RI Trailer, measuring 25th feet in length, 8 feet in width, 11th feet in height with two propane tanks. It was fitted with a U-shaped dinette, a mid-size refrigerator and with fifteen television monitors which constantly changed to display the various angles on the Terme di Caracalla ruins. It was the nerve center for the concert.

Kostmayer pulled himself into the *Silver Bullet* where he found Ji-Yeon directing the feeds to the various cameras. He had six assistants crowded around the monitors with him all employed by the rock concert. Kostmayer noted that Ji-Yeon's assistants all wore black with the insignia of the Terme di Caracalla ruins on their shirts. They had small microphones they were speaking into, taking their direction from Ji-Yeon. Kostmayer had never met Ji-Yeon before, although he thought he knew him intimately after Granny's description. He could see for himself that the North Korean terrorist had had a major facelift, although the telltale signs were subtle. The high cheekbones were prominent, but the shape of the eyes were rounder and the scar tissue from the procedure was heightened. If Kostmayer had been forced to pick him out of a line-up, he would have been at a loss. The North Korean could have been an entirely different person. But it was the man's eyes that ultimately betrayed him.

Cold and calculating and utterly without mercy.

Benedetto Lombardi climbed onboard the Silver Bullet trailer behind Kostmayer. He introduced Kostmayer to Ji-Yeon who was concentrated on the video feeds and made no effort to acknowledge Benedetto Lombardi or his guest. "This is one of my concert personnel," Lombardi said, "Mickey Kostmayer who is on loan to us from the US Government. This is Ji-Yeon, our Head of Security."

"Good to meet you," Kostmayer said.

Ji-Yeon gave Kostmayer a curt nod, his full attention still on the various monitors and the images being displayed around the Terme di Caracalla ruins. Benedetto Lombardi quickly propelled Kostmayer out of the trailer. They descended the steel steps to the ground.

"Ji-Yeon is not much of a conversationalist," Benedetto apologized with a self-deprecating grin. "But the man's a true professional. His security arrangements have been first rate. This concert is in good hands."

"Then why does his manner make my skin crawl?" Kostmayer said.

Benedetto shrugged expansively. "Ji-Yeon isn't here to impress you. He is here to do a job and keep these concertgoers safe. If he does not speak more than six words to me during the concert that works just fine for me. I will toast him with an aperol aperitif as soon as I know that the *Three Tenors* have taken center-stage."

Kostmayer took a flier from his jacket pocket and handed a handful of them to Benedetto. "We're also looking for anyone wearing one of these silver demon-claw skulls on their right hands."

Benedetto took the sheaf of fliers and examined them. "What is the significance of a silver skull?"

"Some members of a radical mercenary unit are wearing them."

"I will distribute them to my security force," Benedetto said. "Now I had better get back and see if there is anything Ji-Yeon needs for the performance. Take a walk over to the tents. They are going to start allowing the concertgoers through any minute. Ciao."

Benedetto was already handing out some fliers to other members of his staff, all of them wearing the black outfits with their discreet emblems on the collars. Then he returned to the nerve center of the *Silver Bullet* trailer. Kostmayer took out a walkie-talkie, also labeled for the concert, and spoke quietly into it.

"Where are you, Granny?"

But there was no response.

In Athens at the Rockwave Festival at Terra Vibe Park in Malakesa, the stadium was bursting at the seams. It looked to Gunner that every seat had been taken. Security Staff, all wearing black with the insignia of the Rock Concert logo, roamed up and down the aisles with their telltale hearing aids discreetly placed in their ears. Gunner was standing at one side of the raised wooden stage. One of the entrepreneurs of the rock concert, who looked like a carbon-copy of the *Animals'* singer Eric Burdon, but whose name was Clarence Bishop, was whipping the crowd into a frenzy. Spiros Alexandros moved to Gunner's side, sweating under the bright lights that illuminated the stage area. Gunner noted how nervous the big Greek really was as his gaze was constantly raking across the seats and up the aisles.

"We're about ready to go," Spiros said. "There's been no trouble from your perspective, Colonel?"

Gunner had been watching the *Nexus* group in the wings. He said: "Nexus are comprised of three guitarists, a bass guitarist, a drummer and a lead female singer. That is right, isn't it?"

"Yes."

"I only count two guitarists."

Spiros followed Gunner's his gaze, frowning. "You're right."

A third guitarist moved into the wings in a rush, strapping on his guitar. He was dressed as the same as the rest of the group, in torn jeans, black boots but he wore a waistcoat like an old-fashioned western hero complete with a black string bowtie and gold watchchain glimmering in his waistcoat pocket. He was in urgent conversation with Amanda Stevenson, the lead singer and Gonzo Lindsey who appeared to be the spoken person for the group.

"I'll see what going on," Gunner said. "Check in with your staff. Make sure that what they're seeing is everything that you're seeing."

Spiros strode downstage to the stairs that led into the first rows of seats. The entrepreneur at the microphone was rapidly winding up his spiel. Gunner moved down into the wings stage-right where *Nexus* was waiting. As usual, Amanda did all the talking.

"Hi, there! Gonzo came down with food poisoning this morning and he has been sick as a dog. He could not even get out of bed at the hotel. This is Jack Roslin, a last-minute replacement. I don't know your last name, Colonel."

"It's Mike Ralston," he told her. "But call me 'Gunner'."

"Yeah, that's right, Spiros mentioned that. Cool nickname. Jack here is a hot bass guitarist."

"Hey, man, good to meet you," Roslin said. "I was just sitting in my seat when the goon squad came over and dragged me onstage." He flashed a smile at Amanda. "Happy to jam with you."

"Have you played with *Nexus* before?" Gunner asked him.

"Yeah, he played a gig with us in Florida back in January," Buster Cruz said. "Bitchin' bass guitarist. We're lucky to have him or we would be out of luck."

At the microphone, Clarence Bishop had wound up his spiel. He turned to where *Nexus* were waiting in the wings. "Put your hands together to welcome onto our stage one of the greatest bands of all time!"

"Okay, boys," Amanda said. "Time to put away your dicks and get this show on the road!"

Gunner heard one word over thunderous roar of the crowd.

"*Nexus!*"

The band ran onto the stage and picked up their instruments and guitars. Amanda stepped up to the microphone. The group, including their last-minute replacement, Jack Roslin, rocked into their first song. Particularly Amanda Stevenson, who reminded Gunner of the leader singer of the rock band *Blondie*, whom he had seen in Washington D.C. last year.

He was watching Jack Roslin, whom he had to admit played a mean bass guitar.

But Gunner knew a ringer when he saw one.

The Royal Albert Hall was a magnificent red brick structure in South Kensington in London. Queen Victoria had laid the foundation stone for the building in 1867 in memory of her husband Prince Albert. Around the outside of the building was an 800-foot-long Terracotta mosaic frieze depicting "The Triumph of Arts and Sciences" including 12-inch-high Terracotta letters with the phrase: *"Thine O Lord is the greatness and the power and the glory and the victory and the majesty. For all that is in the heaven and in the earth is thine."* A glass and wrought-iron dome roof had been erected at the top of the structure. The RAH, as is affectionally called, dated back to 1871. There have been 150,000 performances at the venue, including the celebrated BBC Proms, which debuted in 1941 during the World War II, with icons such as Winston Churchill and Albert Einstein, to concerts from Wagner to Frank Sinatra, Cirque Du Soleil, Adele, and the farewell concert of Cream and The Who performing their *Tommy Rock Opera.*

When McCall arrived at the Royal Albert Hall there was a long line that went around the block. The concert promotors had already starting people moving inside the venue. McCall showed his laminated pass which hung around his neck to one of the Security people who, like in the concerts in Greece and Rome, was dressed in black outfits with the logo of the rock concert on their lapels. The Security Officer immediately led McCall through one of the entrances into the massive structure.

The building towered three stories to the mezzanine with an ornate ceiling which supported large acoustic discs that resembled flying saucers. McCall was stunned by the sheer grandeur of the concert hall. It towered three tiers to the mezzanine seats below a magnificent circular roof. Plush red seats had been built in the stalls and circle. More of the Security Officers in black patrolled the aisles with their names badges prominently displayed or hanging around their necks. More of the uniformed staff were ushering people to their seats. A song from The Beatles went around in McCall's head: *Read the news, oh boy, four thousand holes in Blackburn, Lancashire and though the holes were rather small, now they know how many holes it takes to fill the Albert Hall.* Some of the more obscure lyrics that Lennon and McCartney wrote were open to interpretation, but the image of those 4000 holes waiting in the Lancashire landscape to be stepped in somehow had a sinister purpose for McCall. He was more attuned to the lyricism of Lennon and McCartney's *Across the Universe* and *Eleanor Rigby.* Mickey Kostmayer had referred to McCall, somewhat wryly, as the *Nowhere Man*, and McCall had thought had described him accurately.

McCall moved down one of the aisles. The stage area had already been rigged with lights and the stagehands were making final adjustments. McCall found the Head of Security for the Royal Albert Hall standing in one of the aisles, directing people to their seats, coordinating with other front-of-house staff who were doing the same. The laminated name badge that hung around his neck said: *Nigel McGarry.* He was in his thirties with a certain condescending manner. He turned when McCall approached him. McCall showed him his ID and a personal note from Control which was signed: *James Thurgood Cameron.* Nigel glanced perfunctorily at his name badge. He briefly shook hands.

"Good to meet you, Mr. McCall. Nigel McGarry. Quite a place, our RAH, isn't she?"

"I would say specular."

"The venue was opened by Queen Victoria as an homage to her husband Prince Albert," McGarry said. "It receives no grant funding for its philanthropic efforts. Donations only and financial support from the Trustees. The Proms concerts are vital to our survival. None of the Trustees, including the President, is remunerated for their services to the Hall. We just bade farewell to *Cirque du Soleil* after several months of sold-out shows."

"How many seat holders can the Hall accommodate?" McCall asked him.

"There are 329 Seat holders, but the Hall can accommodate another 5900 if needs be. There have been 150,000 performances during that time."

"I saw a performance here at the Royal Albert Hall of *Les Miserables.*"

McGarry nodded. "Twenty-fifth anniversary. A marvellous night at the theatre. Great actors have played the RAH. Judy Dench, Vanessa Redgrave, Harold Pinter, Lawrence Olivier, Dame Perry Ashcroft, the list goes on, including Muhammad Ali and the Beatles. My personal favorite was the farewell concert of The Cream and The Who performing their *Tommy Rock Opera* for the Twenty-fifth anniversary. A fabulous evening."

McCall needed to get the conversation back on track. "And now the grand old lady has to deal with terrorists and a bomb threat."

Nigel looked at McCall as if he bad been slapped in the face. "I would say that threat has been highly exaggerated."

"You don't believe there'll be a strike here by militants?"

"A lot of balls. There has never been a terrorist attack at the RAH in its history. We are taking precautions because your subversive spy organization of doom merchants have taken into their heads there is an imminent threat and we have acted accordingly. I spent the last two days at the Foreign Office at Mi6 accessing the likelihood of a terrorist attack on these shores and I found it is not a credible scenario. But here we all are, racing around like blue-ass flies searching for any sign of covert activity."

"And what did you find?"

"Sweet fuck all. Your Control, whoever he is, has got his knickers in a twist." Nigel spoke softy into the walkie-talkie he was holding in his right hand. "Make a sweep of the aisles, starting at the Circle and working your way down. Punters are coming in."

McCall took out a small, wallet-sized photograph of Samantha Gregson from his wallet and showed it to him. McGarry shrugged, his manner somewhat churlish. "Yeah, yeah, I distributed photographs of her last night to all of the staff here at the RAH. Who is she anyway?"

"She had been a protégé for a spymaster who had worked for the *Company* before her boss was killed," McCall said.

"Right, and I gather from my Mi5 briefing that you killed him?"

McCall's voice had an edge to it now. "I was left with no choice."

"Quite so. I must say she does not look much like a terrorist to me. More like a dolly bird out for a good time with the lads."

"Don't be fooled. She uses her sexuality to maximum effect. She is dangerous and lethal. Several high-profile mercenaries are working for her."

That intel resonated with the Mi5 agent. "Are these mercs here in London?"

"I don't know. They wear *silver-death-skulls* on the right hands."

"What does that signify?"

"*Remember that you must die.*"

"A charming sentiment." Nigel handed back the photograph. "Haven't seen your mystery woman and we've been here at the RAH since last night. The audience is starting to pour in. We will be on the lookout for anything suspicious, but you are going to be bowled for six, old fruit. There is nothing to these threats. Smoke and mirrors, mate."

McCall said: "Where can I find the headliner for the concert?"

"Down in her dressing room below the stage area," Nigel said. "But I would not disturb her if I were you. She is notorious for wanting peace and quiet before a performance. But you go right ahead. You're a spymaster and I'm sure she would like to meet you."

Nigel McGarry moved up to the first row of the Circle where he was met by more of his staff. The doors to the Royal Albert Hall been opened and now there was a flow of people surging down the aisles. No matter what McCall thought of Nigel McGarry, he thought the time had come for him to meet the star of the concert.

Which happened to be *Lady Gaga.*

▶ 24 ◀

IN THE ATHENS ARENA at the Rockwave Festival at the Terra Vibe Park in Malakesa *Nexus* had started their set. Colonel Michael Ralston climbed the aisles of the makeshift seats until he was at the top and looking down at the postage-stamp-sized stage. From there he made his way across eight rows, descending gradually, looking at all the faces of the people who were cheering and hollering. He had a photographic memory which was a gift that sometimes he regretted. In this case it created images of the faces he was seeing that were seared into his mind. None of them were in the least bit threatening. He paused at the hallway mark to touch base with Christo Lykalos.

"Everything is good here," said the burly Greek. "Listen to that crowd! Fantastic!" He accessed his walkie-talkie. "Go ahead, Nico." He listened to his brother's voice and pressed the walkie. "Copy that." He kept the walkie-talkie in his hand. "Nico is dealing with some unruly elements who are causing trouble above us. Nothing to worry about. High spirits, eh? You were on the stage just now?"

"I was," Gunner said. "The new band member of the group seems to be working out."

"That is good." Christo grabbed the walkie, his voice lost in the ambiance of the crowd. "On my way to you, Nico!" He clicked off the walkie. "My brother is going to have a coronary! He will be ejecting people unless I can calm him down. You are good here?"

"I'm fine," Gunner said.

Christo nodded and climbed higher into the stands. The crowd was going wild, but Gunner's attention was fixated on something on the stage. Something about *Nexus'* performance was bothering him. Some anomaly that had manifested itself into his consciousness that was nagging at him. He could not tell what it was. Gunner climbed down the center aisle of seats, checking his walkie where reports were coming in from the other Security Officers. They were all negative.

But the cold trickle of fear that had assailed him was still there.

Gunner made his way to the front rows of seats. One of the Security staff members, who had just come on the scene, examined Gunner's ID and the pass he had hanging around his neck. He waved Gunner on. He skirted the stage where *Nexus* were performing and climbed up into the Stage Right wings. He had a much better perspective from there. Amanda Stevenson, Doc Conrad, Terry Monaghan and Buster Cruz were singing. Ethan Stanwitz, their drummer, kept the beat going at a frenzied pace that would have given Keith Moon of *The Who* a run for his money. As far as Gunner was concerned, the standout performance was Amanda Stevenson who had a kind of raucous, earthy quality that sent a shiver down Gunner's spine. She was a star waiting to happen. But it was Jack Roslin who had joined the group at the eleventh hour who had caught Gunner's attention. All through his time at the Citadel in South Carolina he had played with a rock group, although the military had frowned upon it at the time. He had stopped playing when he graduated from the military school. But it was a skill had had never left him. There was something about the way Jack Roslin played the bass guitar that had started to grate on Gunner's nerves.

Something about it to Gunner's ear was not right.

Granny shouldered his backpack higher as he turned the corner of the Terme di Caracalla ruins. The tiered seats rose several levels where the crowd was swarming to find their seats. The stage area was floodlit from three angles from the iron scaffolding that looked futuristic. The main attraction had not yet arrived, the *Three Tenors*, although they were scheduled to make their first appearance in half an hour. Granny got a glimpse of the *Silver Bullet* trailer in the rows of ascending seats. For a moment he had been tempted to climb down to where the vehicle was parked. There were black-suited staff members moving back and forth on the tiered seats and down the various aisles with their telltale hearing aids in their ears. Granny knew that Ji-Yeon was sequestered in the *Silver Bullet* directing the video feeds from its nerve-center. Granny had the official pass hanging around his neck which listed him as a VIP. He wanted to barge into the *Silver Bullet* and take Ji-Yeon by surprise, but he had promised Kostmayer that he would keep his cool and his emotions in check. He would have been the last person the Korean terrorist would have expected to see at this rock concert. The concert had been given priority because Samantha Gregson was still at large and her mercenaries could be anywhere in the massive crowd, although the organizers thought that was a bogus threat. Granny would not do anything to jeopardise that situation. There would be time for him to deal with Ji-Yeon after the concert had concluded.

In the meantime, Granny needed to check out the perimeter of the ruins. He thought he saw Mickey Kostmayer near the stage area, but he could not be sure. More people were scrambling down the seats from where the large tents had been erected. It would not be long before there was not a seat to be had at the rock concert. Granny had promised Kostmayer that he would maintain radio silence until he had reached his destination.

Granny veered away from the stage area that had been mounted in front of the imposing Terme di Caracalla ruins. More floodlights had been mounted with mauve and purple hues, somehow eerie as they reflected off the stones. He was following the diagrams he had taken from Ji-Yeon's hotel room in Rome. He entered the massive ruins. He passed the Calidarium which was a hall with a dome and ventured into a labyrinth of stone passageways. An ancient entrance led into what had been the swimming pool, the *Nataorio*, then proceeded to the dressing rooms and the Laconica for stream baths. A *hypocoustum* system had been installed which in ancient days had housed the hot air under the floor in the spa complex. Granny came to marble floors and several staircases that appeared to lead nowhere. He heard Kostmayer's voice on the walkie, and tried to answer him, but the signal was faint and then it gave out altogether. Granny put the walkie away. Still following Ji-Yeon's map, he came upon a partial staircase which had collapsed with under the weight of antiquity. Granny lifted some debris away from a hidden staircase. He found an iron door that was recessed in one of the stone walls. It took all his strength just to move it a couple of inches. He pulled harder until there was just enough space for him to squeeze through the doorway.

Another marble staircase descended into the darkness. Granny set down his backpack and took out a black Dominator Lumens Rechargeable LED Flashlight. He hefted it onto his shoulder and switched on the powerful beam. Slowly he descended the marble staircase into the bowels of the earth. It was broken in places and it took him several minutes to reach the last step.

Granny splashed illumination into the darkness of an underground passage. Beneath the Terme di Caracalla ruins was an intricate series of tunnels. He paused a moment to stop his heart from hammering in his chest. Being entombed underground in a dank place had triggered the claustrophobia he had experienced as a child when his father had locked him in a basement room as a punishment for hours at a time. Granny regulated his breathing with an effort and slowly recovered his equilibrium. Then he swung the powerful LED flashlight beam in front of him. It swept a passage which emptied out into the stone catacombs.

Granny moved out into a high vaulted tunnel. The beam wavered in front of the crypts which were piled up one on top of the other. There was a fresco of the *Good Shepherd* painted in the center of the domed ceiling. He held a lamb on his shoulders and two sheep lay at his feet. Granny thought they symbolized the souls that Christ would gather to himself. The catacombs had a musty smell to them that stung Granny's eyes. The stench of death weighed heavily in the stale air. Granny turned a corner in the labyrinth and suddenly the passage widened. Above him massive round lamps had been set high in the ceiling of the tunnel with more marble stairs leading down to them. Granny descended further down into the maze, using the powerful flashlight to illuminate his way. He came to more catacombs where loculi had been cut from the tufa stone in stacks one over the other in the elaborate chamber, or *cubicula*. In places there were frescos painted in bright colors that seemed out of place in this place of death.

Then Granny heard sounds of movement in front of him.

He was not alone in the underground caverns.

When McCall met Lady Gaga in her dressing-room he had a preconceived notion what he was letting himself in for. Instead he found a charming young woman who was completely focused on her performance. He had expected her to be surrounded by a phalanx of make-up people and assistants, but she sat alone in her dressing room before a large mirror. He explained to her that he was a one-time intelligence Officer. He also told her there had been a credible terrorist threat here at the Royal Albert Hall.

"There may nothing to this intelligence," McCall said, "but I need to check it out."

Immediately Lady Gaga was intrigued.

"Does that mean you're a spy?"

McCall smiled. "There was a time. Six countries have come together to host these rock concerts and there is a credible terrorist threat here at the Royal Albert Hall."

"I'm aware of the added security that has been installed," she said. "But if you are going to ask me to abandon my concert, I must decline. I am not going to be intimidated by some threat, real or imagined. I have a duty to my fans and I'm not going to let them down."

McCall nodded. "I felt you were going to say that, but I had to try. There is no immediate danger to you or your entourage. The security forces here at the RAH are first class. This threat may not have been real, but we are not taking any chances. I am leaving you in good hands."

"That is good to hear. My I ask your name?"

"Robert McCall."

"Mr. McCall, I don't know why, but I feel a sense of well-being and comfort talking to you. I know you will keep me safe. Right now, I need some solitude."

Lady Gaga reached out her hand and McCall took it. Her handshake was firm, but McCall sensed the pain which she had to keep at bay. He knew that she had been fighting widespread musculoskeletal pain caused by fibromyalgia which can be accompanied by fatigue and mood swings. The chronic disorder sent pain to the patient's neck, shoulders, hips, arms and legs and it can also affect the joints. There was nothing helpless about Stefani Angelina Germanotta, but she was fighting a valiant battle against her own body. He held her hand for a longer moment than he had intended, then their hands parted.

"What do your friends call you?" he asked her.

Lady Gaga smiled as if she understood. "Stefani. I'm doing fine, Mr. McCall."

"In that case, I won't disturb you any longer."

McCall left this fragile, wonderfully talented artiste to get ready for her performance.

He had resolved to make sure nothing happened to her.

He followed an exit from the dressing rooms that led out into the massive auditorium. The Royal Albert Hall was packed with concertgoers. It looked to McCall as if the 5200 seats had all been accommodated. The crowd was boisterous and rowdy. The opening act was the American country music group *Lady Antebellum,* who had recently changed their name to *Lady A*, which consisted of Hillary

Scott, Charles Kelley and Dave Haywood. McCall entered the auditorium as they were singing their No. 1 hit song *Need You Now*. They were rocking the venue. McCall had to admit they sounded sensational. Screens had been set up around the concert area where they were performing. McCall paused in the aisle, looking up at the immense arena. Blue and white spotlights roamed through the venue. McCall's gaze swept across the stalls, all of them full, down the Arena and the stage area. All he saw were a mass of people, most of them standing, swaying to the music of *Lady A*.

Nigel McGarry was waiting for McCall at one of the aisles. He hustled over to him. "Did you see our esteemed songbird?"

"I did," McCall said.

"What was her mood?"

"She was courteous, quietly-spoken and deferential. But there no way the threat of an Al Qaeda attack was going to scare her off. She was focused and somewhat spiritual in her approach to this concert. No trouble in the Hall?"

"Just the great unwashed masses cheering themselves hoarse." Nigel pressed a button on the walkie-talkie in his hand. "This is Nigel." He listened for a moment, then he said: "All quiet here if you can call this quiet. I can't hear myself think in here." There was another murmur from the walkie. "Copy that."

Nigel hung up the walkie.

McCall's gaze traveled up to the Gallery, the Circle, the Second Tier Box, the Grand Tier Box, the Loggia Box and the seating in the Circle. "How many Security staff have you positioned around the hall?"

"Maybe a hundred."

"Any sign of Samantha Gregson?"

"Not a dickey bird," McGarry said. "If she is somewhere in this mob, she's keeping her head down."

"I'm going up to the Circle and work my way down." McCall said.

"As Frankie Howard would say, he was a comic here in the UK, please yourself. I got spotters looking for Samantha Gregson and no one has seen a bloody thing. But it is a good excuse for a party. It looks as if your *Control*, is that what you call him? Does he not have a name?"

"His name wouldn't mean anything to you," McCall said, somewhat curtly.

"Whoever he is, I'd say his intel was seriously flawed. No mercenaries in black with dark glasses and demon claws on their hands in the crowd. But we are looking all the same. King and Country and Lady Gaga and all that. I need to report in. The lads like to hear the sound of my voice."

Nigel moved over to another of the aisles and answered his walkie, although what he was saying was drowned out in the lively crowd. McCall was in no mood for Nigel's condescending disdain. Somehow, he was haunted by meeting Lady Gaga. Her very fragile quality had resonated with him.

McCall moved into the hallway of the Royal Albert Hall, then climbed up the stairs up to the Circle. He would start at the top and work his way down, looking for any of the mercenaries he might recognize.

If Samantha Gregson were here in the Royal Albert Hall, it would be because she had a denotator in her hand to blow the roof off.

Gunner was standing in the front of the amphitheatre in Terra Vibe Park with his back to the boisterous crowd. It was at the halfway point in the concert. People were connecting with friends, some rushing to the freestanding portable toilets which were located on the grass, others just stretching their legs. *Nexus* had exited into the Stage Left wings. Gunner had been watching Jack Roslyn fiddling with the amplifier that had been left on-stage with the other guitars and the drum kit while *Nexus* took their break. It bothered him that the back-up guitarist had to make some adjustments to the amplifier that been left onstage. Only the members of the band should have been addressing any problems with the equipment. Gunner turned and saw that Christos and Nico Lykalos were coming down the seats some distance apart, watching the crowd which had swelled to capacity. The Colonel brought the walkie-talkie to his lips.

"Christos, come back."

He saw the Greek Security specialist raise up his walkie. "This is Christos, go ahead, Gunner."

"How many explosives experts have you deployed in the arena?"

"Six Officers, all of them trained in demolition."

"Have them make their way to the stage area with you and your brother. Something is not right. Keep a low profile on your guys. I do not want to cause a panic. People would be hurt in a situation like that."

"Copy that, Gunner. We're on our way."

Gunner clicked off the walkie, moved to the seats and climbed up onto the stage. By this time Jack Roslyn had vacated the stage. Gunner did not think he had gone anywhere except to the backstage area beneath the stage. The acoustic guitar that had been left in a shamble of wires in the front of the stage was one Gunner recognized. He had been playing the acoustic guitar from the age of nine. The guitar on the stage was a Gibson Explorer. It was fitted with an angular body and the musician playing it had to be right-handed. The guitar had a angular mahogany body in Antique Natural wood, a Rosewood-topped Slim Taper mahogany neck, Finger Inlay, acrylic Dots, Neck Pickup with a Bridge Pick-up, Burstbucker pick-ups, 2 x volume controls, a 3-way toggle pick-up Switch and an Antique Lacquer finish. It was fitted with digital reverb and it was wired to the amplifier dual master volumes and resonance controls. It was a beauty and it was brand new. It had 12-inch speakers, one of them a "*Vintage*", the other an "*Heritage*". Gunner picked the guitar up. The 1ˢᵗ channel was a classical clean tone, bluesy and a more distorted sound through the orange-and-red mode settings.

By that time Christos and Nico had joined him on stage. Gunner picked up the Gibson Explorer guitar and unplugged it from the amplifier.

"The guitar has been rewired," Gunner said. "A musician like Jack Roslyn would never do something like that. It would blow out the circuits." He turned the guitar over. "The GIF format is standard but here, see those dials, 2 Humbuckers, 2 Volumes, 3-Way Switch, two Spin-a-Splits. The base ground wire wrapped around the braided wires has been removed. See this panel here? It is arched. It has a hollow body with a magnet with fine wire wrapped around it cresting a magnetic field that captures the stings' vibrations and converting them into an electronic signal."

Gunner took a Leatherman multitool from the pocket of his jacket. He slowly unscrewed the back of the guitar. He dropped the last silver screw and removed the backing from the guitar body. Complicated wires protruded from the back where a charge of C4 explosives had been squeezed out like toothpaste.

By now four more demolition experts had jointed the group onstage. Christos took charge, putting the walkie-talkie to his lips. "Start evacuating the area. Let the people know there has been a bomb scare. They can return when the situation has been defused." He clicked the walkie off. The Security detail were grouped in a tight cluster around the explosives. Christos turned to Gunner. "We'll deal with this. It is what we have been trained for. You go after Roslyn."

Gunner nodded and ran down a set of stairs leading down to the basement area. It was in shadows. He found Jack Roslyn putting together a back-up explosive device with sticks of dynamite wrapped in red sleeves which were attached to a blasting cap with blue and yellow wires.

The countdown on the alarm clock was: 00:2:23 seconds and counting down.

An old scuffed duffel bag stood open on the worktable to conceal the device. Roslyn turned at the last moment, sensing Gunner's presence. He pulled a Colt King Cobra Magnum .357 revolver from his pocket. Gunner disarmed him with lightning moves, but Roslyn was incredibly strong. He knocked Gunner to the floor of the basement. He ran out of it into the series the small rooms hemmed in by pipes. Gunner quickly got to his feet, moving to the half-assembled explosives. He accessed an Intermatic ET 1125C hour electronic time switch in a NEMA indoor steel case. He checked that the timer was wired for two circuits at 30 Amps with a 120-277 voltage battery. Gunner had enough Army training to slowly disconnect the wires from the circuits that were protruding from the bomb.

The alarm clock stopped at 00:20 seconds.

▶ 25 ◀

GUNNER RAN ON into the labyrinth of rooms, pulling a P365 semi-automatic pistol from his leather jacket pocket. The small basement room was in shadows, but Gunner had already checked it out. He had a picture of the room imprinted in his mind. More pipes had been installed overhead and discarded boxes were piled up to the low ceiling. Gunner looked around. Lots of hiding places, but there was no sign of his quarry.

Jack Roslyn came at him from the shadows.

He had nowhere else to hide.

Gunner was ready for him, but he had not counted on the man's superior strength. They grappled for the gun which Roslyn knocked from Gunner's fingers. The bigger man put his arm around Gunner's throat, strangling him. Gunner struggled against the terrorist's hold, slowly losing consciousness. He still had the picture of the rooms in his mind. He had one chance to break the man's hand on his throat. Gunner plunged back through the shadows, taking Roslyn with him. Roslyn bore down on his choking hold, both of their legs scrabbling against the uneven floor.

Gunner had a goal he had to achieve to survive.

He slammed Roslyn back into the *hot water pipe*. It seared the back of his neck. He let go of Gunner who twisted out of his grasp, choking, plunging toward the floor where he had seen the gun skittering in his mind. The mercenary came after him, his neck scorched from the contact with the pipe, but the pain had slowed him just a fraction.

He did not see Gunner's figure right away in the darkened storeroom.

Gunner fell to his knees, picked up the fallen Magnum .357 revolver and turned on his back.

The terrorist lunged at him from the shadows.

Gunner fired at him at point black range.

Roslyn was thrown back by the force of the bullets.

Gunner pulled himself up to his feet. He reached Roslyn in three strides, but it was clear he was not going anywhere. Gunner knelt beside the terrorist. Blood seeped down his face and had pooled across his chest. He stared up at Gunner with pale eyes, slightly disoriented, as if he were not quite aware of where he was. Gunner was seized with sudden uncontrollable anger. He lifted the terrorist up, almost shaking him.

"Why did you do it?" Gunner asked him, savagely. "You betrayed your country! You were going to kill innocent people! *Why?*"

Roslyn looked at him uncomprehendingly.

Gunner shook him violently. "I need to hear the reason."

"Chaos theory," Roslyn murmured. "Complex systems. Sensitive to unique changes. Samantha knew that. Random states of order." Roslyn focused on Gunner's face. "Butterfly effect. No stopping it now." The light was fading in his eyes. "Too many of us."

Christos moved into the overlapping shadows behind them. Jack Roslyn gave a final shudder of pain and died in Gunner's arms. Gunner lay him down on the floor of the storeroom and got to his feet.

"What did he tell you?" Christos said.

"He was paid by Samantha Gregson to carry out this act of atrocity," Gunner said. "But it was more than that. These are mercenaries who have been bound together to achieve a world order. They are disciplined and fanatical. Consequences sensitive to unique changes. Chaos theory."

"What did he mean by that?"

"A state of disorder. A butterfly flapping its wings in China can cause a hurricane in Texas."

"So, there's no way of stopping them?"

"There's always a way," Gunner said, softly.

Nico joined them in the small storeroom. "Both bombs have been neutralized. We're leading people back to their seats." He looked down at the dead terrorist. "Do we know his background?"

"Mercenary," Gunner said. "Working alone."

"I will make an announcement when *Nexus* takes the stage," Christos said. "We're saying it was a bomb hoax. No one was hurt as they left their seats. There was no panic. The crowd reacted well."

Nico turned back to Gunner. "We will take care of this. You should go back up onto the stage. Amanda Stevenson wants to talk to you. She is the spokesman for the group."

"You saved a lot of lives today," Christos said. "We're very grateful."

Gunner said: "We got lucky. This was a lone bomber. There will be others."

He turned and exited the storeroom, then climbed up the steel stairs back to the stage area. The guitar and amplifier had been carted away. *Nexus* had picked up their instruments and Doc Conrad, their drummer, was behind his drum kit. Amanda Stevenson introduced Gunner to a mate of hers, Zach Kelley, who had been in the audience for the show. He had offered to step in as a backup guitarist. Doc Conrad was just handing him a new acoustic guitar. The group had several more guitars that the new man could choose from. All of that sounded good to Gunner. Amanda Stevenson grasped his hand.

"Are you all right?" she asked him, anxiously.

"I'm fine."

"What happened backstage? Doc Conrad said that Jack Roslyn attacked you?"

"The man was a terrorist. He had explosives wired up to the Gibson guitar he was carrying onstage, but they were disarmed."

Amanda suddenly cradled Gunners face where the red-hot pipe has seared his skin. "You're hurt."

Gunner was touched by her concern. "A little collateral damage. Rosslyn is dead and the situation has been defused. You can go on with your show."

"Thank God for you." Amanda kissed Gunner on the lips, surprising the hell out of him, then he turned as Nico Lykalos made his way onstage to the microphone. He made the announcement that there had been a bomb scare, but it had been dealt with. He reintroduced *Nexus* to thunderous applause. They took their places onstage, with their new member, Zach Kelley, and the concert continued as if nothing had happened.

Gunner descended into the audience. His gaze swept up the tiers of seats as the sound of the music blasted through the audience. He knew this was not the end of the night. There were at least five more European countries – Italy, Spain, Sweden, Prague and England -- involved in these rock concerts. The Army Colonel wondered if they would include Mickey Kostmayer and an ex-Company agent named, incongruously, *Granny*. And Robert McCall was in London. His life would be also in danger.

Gunner looked out at the raucous crowd and prayed that they found the other explosives in time.

It was claustrophobic in the catacombs beneath the Terme di Caracalla. Granny thought there must be hundreds of passages interconnecting in rectangle niches. Some of the frescos painted in them were vivid in their descriptions of early Jewish, Pagan and Christian citizens. More tombs were piled up right up to the ceiling. It gave Granny an eerie, sepulchral feeling surrounded by the ancient dead. The air inside the catacombs was breathable, but he felt lightheaded the further he proceeded into the labyrinth. The oppression weighed heavily on him in the necropolis. The souls of dead in their crypts had a sinister aurora. Maybe it was because the souls of the dead haunted his dreams. He tried to remember the route he had taken in the tunnels, but he soon lost all sense of time and place. Small spectral sounds assailed him. The feeling that he was not alone in this ghostly mausoleum played on his nerves. The soft, scrabbling sounds that he could hear might have been part of his overwrought imagination. Rats in the tunnels. He tried to rein in the suffocating nausea and took some deep breaths. He paused at the entrance to another of the series of tunnels and took out his walkie-talkie. He was not sure it would work down here in the confines of the catacombs, but he needed to reach the outside world.

He said: "Kostmayer" softly into the walkie.

It took a few seconds, then Kostmayer's voice echoed in the walkie. "I'm here. Come back."

"I thought I lost you. You're my one lifeline."

In the Terme di Caracalla ruins Kostmayer stood on the edge of the stage with a wall of noise behind him. It was hard to hear anything that Granny was whispering. Around him the crowd were at near capacity. Kostmayer felt the excitement in the improvised arena was at a fever pitch. He had had no messages on his walkie of any red flags being raised by the Security Officers who roamed up and down the aisles, earpieces in their ears. Kostmayer was glad he had been the one to had stayed above ground. The thought of Granny buried in the subterranean passages of the catacombs below him held an horrific image,

"I am here right with you, Granny," Kostmayer said. "In spirit."

Down in the sepulchral stillness of the vaults, Granny could hear the irony in his voice. "I take it you don't want to trade places with me."

"Not for all the tea in China."

"It is pretty creepy down here," Granny admitted. "There is mural of skulls behind me that glows in the darkness and more where they came from. What's happening there with you?"

At that moment the *Three Tenors* entered the arena from where they had been waiting backstage surrounded by black-suited Security Officers. The crowd behind Kostmayet started cheering. "The Three Tenors just walked onto the stage. The Security forces around me are in full force. No red flags. I'm keeping in constant touch with them."

"Where is Ji-Yeon?"

"He's taken refuge in a special trailer that has been set up for him," Kostmayer said. "Fifteen monitors, state-of-the-art electronics so that he can watch everyone in the crowd, switching channels constantly. It was why the concert partners had hired him. He has not done anything that would arouse any suspicion about his involvement in the venue. He has not emerged from there, but I have got Benedetto Lombardi, the concert promoter, keeping an eye on him. This concert may have been a false alarm."

"If Ji-Yeon is there, he's there for a reason," Granny said in the hushed confines of the crypt. "It can't be a coincidence. The threat is real. I am going to venture further into the catacombs. Just bale me out if you do not hear from me in awhile. The ghosts of lost souls are clawing at my throat."

"I'll give you an update on the concert," Kostmayere said. "Stay in touch with me every fifteen minutes."

"Will do."

Granny clicked off the walkie-talkie and proceeded further into the labyrinth.

Mickey Kostmyer looked around as the *three Tenors* started their performance. Spotlights in magenta, purple and red crisscrossed each other in dazzling displays of color. The figure of a man making his way away from the stage area caught Kostmayer's eye. He was swarthy with a sallow complexion and his black obsidian eyes were startling. He thought he might have been Egyptian. A livid knife scar three inches long was prominent on his face. Kostmayer pulled out a flyer from his jacket pocket. He had no descriptions of the *Memento Mori* mercenaries, but Control had supplied him with one flyer of a terrorist who was on their radar. His name was Khalid Rehman Mohammad. Kostmayer compared it with the flyer and there was no mistaking the man's face with its distinguishing scar below his right eye.

Kostmayer swiftly pushed through the crowd that was still finding their seats around the arena. The crowd was like a palpable, living organism that kept reforming itself into random patterns. Kostmayer kept Khalid Rehman Mohammad in sight. He was met by three more of the *Memento Mori* mercenaries who made their way out of the melee surrounding the stage. They were all wearing dark clothing and wearing mirrored sunglasses. Three of them were not known to Kostmayer, but the fourth was a soldier of fortune he recognized. His name was Aleksanteri Karjala whom Kostmayer had at one time tried to extradite from Yemen. The three mercenaries talked quietly with Khalid Rehman Mohammad in one of the concert aisles, although Kostameyer could not hear the conversation in the noisy ambience of the crowd. He pulled out a walkie-talkie from his jacket pocket. He was looking for his contact, Benedetto Lombardi, whom he had lost sight of in the crush of humanity.

"Benedetto, this is Kostmayer, do you read?"

There was so response. The *Company* agent pressed the walkie again, keeping Khalid Rehman Mohammad and the other three mercenaries in sight.

"Benedetto, this Mickey Kostmayer, come back."

No response.

Kostmayer had trouble keeping the three mercenaries in sight in the amorphous crowd. There was a sudden surge of people finding vacant seats that had been abandoned. When the logjam finally cleared, the mercenaries were no longer in sight. Kostmayer turned in a three-sixty-degree angle, but he could not see them in the crowd. He ran down the aisle until he was at the beginning of the Terme di Caracalla ruins. He had explored the ruins when he had first entered the ancient baths. He ran over a low footbridge raised over the mosaic tiles. The monument was lit up in red and mauve, creating oblique shadows across the walls and the strewn pieces of masonry. Wherever he looked, images leapt up at him out of the fractured stones: *A Cherub, the tail of a sea-serpent, a pale horse and a partial figure of a woman's naked body.* The landscaped gardens were in shadow.

Kostmayer turned on the verge of the ruins and saw several of the Security Officers patrolling the grounds. But the figures of Khalid Rehman Mohammad, Aleksanteri Karjala and the other two mercenaries had vanished. Kostmayer took out the map that Granny had given him when he had searched Ji-Yeon's suite at the Hotel Astrid. He found an entrance that Granny had marked. He searched the pages until he found another entrance to the catacombs. It emanated from within the ruins, marked in red. Kostmayer made his way through the labyrinth of massive stones, following the map, until he came to a set of wrought-iron doors. He moved through them to the marble floor laid out beneath the makeshift low bridge. He faintly heard the concert reverberating and the sublime voices of the *Three Tenors* raised above the orchestra. He stopped in front of the low bridge. He could see that one of the grey-and-white marble pieces of the floor was loose. He knelt and gripped it in his hands. It moved slightly. He gripped it tighter and swung it out. The piece of flooring revealed a set of marble stairs that descended into the tunnels beneath. The piece of marble floor was on a pivot. Kostmayer was sure that no one at the concert knew of this hidden ancient passageway leading down into the catacombs. He was certain that this was where the four mercenaries had disappeared to. There had been nowhere else for them to go. Kostmayer swung the loose tile back into place and ran through the shadowy interiors of the ruins. He was facing the back of the stage where the light bars and scaffolding was rigged. He brought out the walkie-talkie from his coat and tried to reach Granny. There was no response now. Just static. He was too far down into the tunnels.

Kostmayer changed direction, skirted the stage where he could see the *Three Tenors* performing for the enthusiastic crowd and reached the place where the *Silver Bullet* trailer had been parked. He climbed the steel stairs to the Premiere trailer and pulled on the door handle.

The vehicle was *locked*.

Granny felt the weight of the catacombs pressing down on him like a malignant shroud. The air in the tunnels was rank and smelled of death. Rows of skulls grinned at him where they had been piled up haphazardly in the niches. The passageway he had been following gave out onto a series of tunnels that crisscrossed each other, their putrid odor assailing his nostrils.

But now he knew that he was not alone in the necropolis.

He could hear movement from one of the catacombs. Just vague, rustling sounds. He entered one of the tunnels, reaching for his walkie. He tried to raise Kostmayer, but there was no signal. Granny put away the walkie and took one of the tunnels crowded with upright crypts further into the maze, heading for the place where he had heard the slight movement and a quiet whisper of voices.

In front of the *Silver Bullet*, Kostmayer jumped down from the steel stairs, drew out the 19 Glock pistol from his jacket and blasted off the lock on the trailer. He entered the vehicle. The sight that greeted him was chilling.

There had been six Security Officers in the trailer with Ji-Yeon viewing the fifteen monitors. All of Security Officers were dead. They had been shot through the heart or their throats slit from ear to ear. The monitors had been smashed.

There was no sign of Ji-Yeon.

Benedetti Lombardi entered the Silver Bullet behind Kostmayer and stopped dead. Kostmayer whirled. Benedetto stared down as the shock of what he was seeing resonated with him.

"My walkie had stopped working. I had to go back to base to get another one." He shook his head in disbelief. "My God! What happened here?"

"Ji-Yeon murdered your Security detail," Kostmayer said, tersely. "He must have had help from other terrorists in the crowd. I followed four of them led by a man named Khalid Rehman Mohammad who has been on our radar for some time. Get the *Three Tenors* to vacate the stage immediately along with their entourage, the members of the orchestra and the stagehands. You need to have the entire area cleared. I lost the mercenaries in the ruins, but I think I know where they went." Kostmayer pulled out the map he had been following that Granny had given him and spread it on a table for Benedetto Lombardi. "There is a loose tile in the mosaic here in the ruins just in front of this low wooden bridge. I found a hidden switch that pivoted the tile. Beneath it are marble stairs leading into the catacombs. Take ten of your Security Officers and move down this staircase. The rest of your Security detail should start evacuating the concertgoers as quickly as possible. You are investigating a bomb scare." Kostmayer refolded the map and handed it to Benedetto. "You're taking preventive measures. Tell the concertgoers that they'll be let back into the concert area when your men have secured the site."

"What are you going to do?"

"I'm going after Ji-Yeon."

He pocketed the Glock. Benedetti Lombardi took out his walkie and spoke urgently into it to his Security Officers. Kostmayer ran down the steel stairs to the ground.

▶ 26 ◀

BELOW IN THE CATACOMBS, Granny turned in the labyrinth and heard the murmur of voices. The ceiling was higher in this part of the catacombs with crumbling marble pillars placed at intervals. There was a fresco depicting a mighty figure towering almost to the rocky ceiling. The man was in black silhouette that became a *slithering snake* from which sprouted waving tendrils like some obscene flowering bush. Granny crouched down where the catacombs turned a sharp right angle. Ahead of him were three marble staircases hewn into the ground. Al Qaeda terrorists, all dressed in black, were crouched in the tunnel. There were narrow niches already drilled into the tunnel wall into which the terrorists were stuffing blocks of C4 explosives.

Granny edged back into the deeper shadows in the tunnel.

Above in the Terme di Caracalla ruins the Security Officers, who numbered a hundred strong, were already evacuating the arena in front of the stage, including the *Three Tenors* and their entourage. They kept it very low key, promising to return the concertgoers back to their seats so the concert could resume. Benedetto Lombardi and his ten Security Officers were armed with Taurus 63 9mm Luger semi-automatic pistols. They each carried Delta-5 LED 1300 lumens mode flashlights. Benedetto led them through the floodlit ruins until they had reached the old rickety bridge and found the stairs leading down into the catacombs. Benedetto pivoted the stone, revealing the hidden staircase. He led the way down the twisting staircase into the bowels of the earth.

In the catacombs, Granny took a Steyr A2 9mm pistol out of his backpack. He checked it to make sure it was loaded. It was a reflex reaction brought out by the closeness of the tomb ceiling pressing down on him. Granny remained still, barely moving in the darkness. He did not think any of the Al Qaeda terrorists had seen him. He moved forward until he was at the tunnel entrance. The terrorists were fitting C4 explosives into the niche in the rocky wall. A figure emerged from one of the two marble staircases in the mausoleum. Granny had never seen him before. He was a powerful built Egyptian in his forties. Granny recognized him from the intel he had found in the Rome suite as Khalid Rehman Mohammad. The three mercenaries who Granny had seen with him were also down in the crypt: Terence Soul, Mace O'Brien and Aleksanteri Karjala. The Egyptian carried several diagrams. The terrorists were boring holes into the crumbling tunnel wall where they would place the C4 explosives. Khalid Rehman Mohammad supervised the work, muttering words Granny could not hear.

Granny ducked back into the necropolis cavern where more macabre, leering skulls protruded from the tunnel wall like spectators in a ghoulish carnival. He softly checked his walkie again. He needed to let Kostmayer know the approximate positions on the terrorists.

The walkie was dead.

Granny pocketed the walkie and held up the Steyr 9mm pistol.

There was no time to call in for reinforcements.

Benedetto Lombardi led his Security force through the maze of labyrinth tunnels. He had ventured into the catacombs once before when his nephew, who had been six at the time, had wanted to see the famous crypts. Benedetto had thought they were ghostly and oppressive and the atmosphere in them was suffocating. He had taken a good hour to persuade his nephew that being trapped in the earth with the stench of death around them was not a cool thing to attempt. He had been very happy to find a circuitous route for them to escape back into the fresh air.

Now he was glad for the experience.

It gave him a sense of where he had been in the maze. He led his force down the stone stairs and through the first of the series of tunnels. The Security Force had been trained in stealth, Benedetto using hand signals for communication with them. He consulted the blueprint that Kostnayer had given him which led them into the maze. They came out into the labyrinth of cramped, confined crypts, like the one Granny had encountered, piled up on top of each other until they rose to a height of twelve feet.

Almost immediately Benedetto held up his hand to stop his strike force. He had heard a voice raised in the echoing vaults. He gestured for them to stay close to him as they ran through the sepulchral graves.

Above ground, Kostmayer ran through the surging crowd, looking for any sign of Ji-Yeon and the terrorists who had overpowered and killed the guards in the *Silver Bullet*. He did not see them, but they could not be far behind him. He plunged into the center of the ruins, exiting through a high archway. Ahead of him he caught sight of Ji-Yeon running through the landscaped grounds toward where a helicopter was perched on the grass. His men had dispersed back into the crowd. The rotors were turning on the helicopter. Kostmayer took the Glock 19 from his pocket and sprinted after the terrorist.

In the catacombs beneath the Terme di Caracalla ruins the Al Qaeda terrorists had fitted a dozen explosives into the porous tunnel walls with wires and long fuses hanging down from them. Granny moved closer in the shadows, crouched low. He thought he might find a place to hide in one of the crypts that were jammed into the passageway, but the linen bodies were stacked on top of each other. He took another step forward. It was his shadow that was projected against the tunnel wall that had betrayed him. Khalid Rehman Mohammad looked up that moment and reached for a Heckler & Koch .45 semi-automatic pistol in his belt. Terence Soul, Mace O'Brien and Aleksanteri Karjala drew their own Sig Sauer P229 pistols. The other terrorists were carrying Heckler & Koch Pakistan MP5 submachineguns with 30-round magazines. Khalid and the mercenaries fired at Granny's elongated shadow. He fired back, the rounds echoing explosively around the crypt. The other terrorists opened fire as well, strafing the tunnel walls. Dust clouds raged through the tunnels, which were in danger of collapsing. Granny climbed up into one of the crypts, wedging himself in to get out of the line of fire. The terrorists, given this brief respite, jammed the last of the explosives into the tunnel wall.

Benedetto Lombardi and his team of Security Officers moved quickly down one of the stone stairs that led into the heart of the necropolis. It could not have timed better from Granny's point of view. The terrorists had positioned themselves with their backs to the tunnel where the stairs led down. Benedetto and his Officers fired immediately on the terrorists, sending them to the tunnel floor in the choking dust that was sent up. Granny jumped down from where he had taken refuge with the linen-wrapped corpses and fired. The terrorists were cut down in the crossfire between him and Benedetto Lombardi's Security Officers.

Granny fired at the two professional mercenaries, hitting Terence Soul and Mace O'Brien. They were also cut down. In the confusion in the cramped tunnels, Granny lost sight of Khalid Rehman Mohammad and Aleksanteri Karjala. He thought they had run to one of the staircases that led up to the surface. He ran through the cordite-burning hell to where the terrorists had fallen. In a moment Benedetto Lombardi and his team were beside him. Between them they ripped out the wires and slow-burning fuses that had been placed in the tunnel wall. The dust clouds were slowly clearing. Granny looked in the choking residue of the smoke.

Khalid Rehman Mohammad and Aleksanteri Karjala had disappeared.

Granny kicked out the rest of the fuses that had been dangling from the C4 explosives.

"I don't know who you are," he said, "but Thank God for you!"

"Benedetto Lombardi, head of security for the concert. Your colleague Mickey Kostmayer sent us down here. This entrance to the catacombs had been hidden for centuries. It was only luck that brought us into these tunnels. Mr. Kostmayer didn't mention that he had a colleague down here at the Terme di Caracalla ruins."

"We're kind of a team," Granny said. "I didn't know the terrorists had penetrated the tunnels until I came upon them. What happened at the concert?"

"It has been abandoned," Benedetto said, "and the people are being evacuated. There may be more terrorists in the crowd. We're searching for them." He looked down at the fallen terrorists who lay strewn across the tunnel. "How many of them?"

"I counted at least two dozen," Granny said. "They didn't have time to set their C4 dynamite. They were led by an Egyptian terrorist."

"His name is Kahlid Rehman Mohammad. According Mr. Kostmayer, he is a known radical who had been known on his radar for some time."

"He brought some mercenaries with him. I only saw him for a second before he and his mercenaries opened fire on me. I shot two of them, but Mohammad and these mercenaries vanished in the confusion."

"There are other entrances exits from these catacombs," Benedetto said. "We will search the tunnels, but there is no telling where they have retreated to. There are many places where they could have found a way back up to the surface. These tunnels are a warren that stretches sixty miles. How did you find your way here?"

"I had a map showing a hidden entrance to the catacombs," Granny said. "You must have got hold of one too or you would not have known your way."

"Your colleague Mickey Kostmayer supplied us with a map," Benedetto said. "But there was no guarantee that we would have found our way down here in the catacombs. We just stumbled onto the terrorists."

Granny's smile flashed. "Maybe there's someone up there looking out for us." He looked around the passageways where the explosions still echoed. "I need to get back to the surface."

"We'll take you there, Lombardi said.

Kostmayer was a thousand feet away when the crowded had thinned out. He saw the figure of Ji-Yeon turning from the waiting helicopter. Six men jumped down from the chopper, all of them armed with Sig Sauer P229 pistols. They aimed at Kostmayer who had to fallen to the grassy knoll where the helicopter was perched. He did not dare fire back for fear of hitting some of the innocent bystanders. The retreating crowd, who had avoided going into the main part of the Terme di Caracalla ruins, were panic stricken in the confusion. More bullets whizzed around them making the going treacherous. Kostmayer had his Glock 19 aimed at the figures standing in front of the helicopter, but he still could not fire.

The terrorists made a half-circle around Ji-Yeon, protecting him.

Kostmayer got to his feet as Granny came running up to him. For a moment Ji-Yeon's eyes locked with Granny's. Then he allowed his men to haul him up into the helicopter. It took off and angled over the Terme di Caracalla ruins, the rotor wash blasting both Kostmayer and Granny. The chopper rose higher in the sky until it had been swallowed in the heavy clouds that were obscuring it. Beside him, Kostmayer lowered his Glock 19 pistol.

"By the time we could track the helicopter's speed and velocity it would be long gone," he said. "What happened down in the catacombs?"

"Twenty terrorists were loading explosives into one of the tunnels walls," Granny told him. "Your new friend Benedetto Lombardi and his Security team took them out. They are still down there searching the bodies for anything that might give us a clue as to their identities. I would say these are some of the terrorists that Samantha Gregson recruited along with all her handpicked mercenaries. We might still find some more them in the crowd, but they're just faces here for a rock concert."

Granny took another step away from Kostmayer, staring up at the cloud cover that pressed down on the concert festival. He would not give up on his quest. If Deva Montgomery and Daniel Blake were still alive—and somehow in his heart he believed that they *were*—he would locate them. Granny would be able to track the helicopter with Ji-Yeon and his men onboard. Then Granny would kill Ji-Yeon for the torment and pain he had caused.

Inside the Royal Albert Hall, Lady Gaga had just finished her set to rapturous applause. She wore a scarlet PVC jumpsuit with a flared hemline and cinched waistline. She sat at a piano in the center of the arena in a spotlight while mauve, red and blue spotlights weaved around her. Robert McCall had climbed right up to the circle seats at the highest point at the auditorium. He had ditched his walkie-talkie in favor of a sleek, fitted microphone that fitted into his right ear. It was barely noticeable. He thought that Lady Gaga's performance was electric, her voice hauntingly melodic and soaring. The audience hung on every word that she was singing. But McCall was searching the stalls for any sign of Samantha Gregson or any of her *Memento Mori* mercenaries who could have accompanied her. He was in constant touch with the Security Officers who were patrolling the aisles in the RAH.

Nigel McGarry climbed up to McCall's vantage point overlooking the stage and Lady Gaga's performance. He surveyed the scene with practiced eyes, his manner still sardonic as he approached McCall. His voice was sotto voce in deference to Lady Gaga's performance.

"All quiet on the Western Front?"

"So far."

"She's got a lovely voice this one, doesn't she? Kind of pure and soaring. The audience are lapping it up. You know who got my juices flowing? *Vera Lynn.* Swear to God. She could really touch your heart. You probably don't even know who I am talking about."

"I don't," McCall admitted.

"Singer during the war. Kept the home fires burning and all that. Serenaded the troops in Egypt, India and Burma. I saw her at the Royal Variety Performance in the nineties with my Dad. *The White Cliffs of Dover* and *We'll Meet Again.* Magical stuff. She was over a hundred when she passed on."

"You're keeping in touch with your staff at fifteen minutes intervals?"

"Absolutely. But it looks to me as if your Control got the wrong end of the stick, old fruit. Still, you are being treated to one hell of a great show. Every cloud has it's silver lining and all that."

Lady Gaga finished her piano set to more thunderous applause, stood and bowed. Then the lights on the stage blackout on her.

"I'll hook up with some of my blokes," McGarry said. "See if they have anything to report. I will radio it to you. But don't hold your breath."

He moved across the Top Tier of the balcony, heading toward the exit there.

McCall was no longer listening to him. In the blackout something in the audience far below had caught his attention. He climbed down until he was at the Second-Tier boxes at the front of the balcony. The lights came on the stage in a single spotlight. In the interim, Lady Gaga had somehow changed her PVC jumpsuit to a full evening black dress, elegant and simple with a sparkling necklace at her throat. The audience were all holding small candles that had been distributed to them. They were bathed in a startling phosphorescent radiance. They all had taken infra-red glasses that had been handed to them by the RAH staff before the show had begun. Lady Gaga started on a medley of her hit songs, beginning with *Poker Face and Born This Way*.

McCall pulled out a pair of Zeiss Terra Compact pocket binoculars from his jacket pocket which carried special magnified lenses. Through them he could see in the infra-red blackness. He swung the high-powered binoculars across the stalls below while Lady Gaga performed. The glasses found one of the *Memento Mori* mercenaries about fourteen rows back. McCall knew him, Damien Malinov, a lean, vicious killer whom Samantha Gregson had recruited. His *demon-claw skull* and *silver rings* glowed in the phosphorescence aurora that bathed the audience.

Damien got up from his seat and eased his way out of the row. McCall swept the infra-red glasses down the aisle. He zeroed onto Samantha Gregson walking down the center aisle of the Royal Albert Hall. He had been waiting for her to make an appearance. She passed Damien Malinov without acknowledging him. The mercenary passed something into her right hand. It looked to

McCall through his infra-red glasses that it was a piece of a mechanism, but it was not complete. She pocketed it and kept going down the aisle. McCall swung the Zeiss magnified binoculars back to the aisle where another of the terrorists was waiting in the aisle for her, having edged his way through the row. McCall recognized this man also, Gabriel Del Castillo, a big bear of a man whom McCall had left for dead in a shootout in the market square of Ryenk Glowny in Krakow, Poland. A mistake McCall would not make again.

Gabriel also passed a small object from his right hand to Samantha Gregson who pocketed it and kept going down the aisle toward the stalls exit. Bradley Stafford, another mercenary, moved into the center aisle of the venue. He wore a tailored suit, dark sunglasses with bleached white-blonde hair. He slipped Samantha another piece of the puzzle that she was juggling. Costas Savermento was the last mercenary, handing her the last piece of the puzzle. McCall could not make out just what it was from this distance. The audience for the rock concert was fixated on Lady Gaga's performance and was not aware of anything else that was happening around them.

▶ 27 ◀

MCCALL RAN UP the back of the Second-Tier seats of the balcony, speaking sotto voce into the earpiece in his ear to Nigel McGarry. "You got four mercenaries heading for you. Close all the exits in the stalls."

"I'm on it," McCarry said.

McCall ran into the stalls section G in the Loggia Boxes leading through the large ornate doors leading to backstage. Security Officers summoned by McGarry were already converging on the exit doors to the Royal Albert Hall. Around McCall the audience were wearing their special avant garde infra-red glasses. Lady Gaga was singing in her spotlight at the center of the stage. McCall moved through one of the ornate doors leading to the backstage area. The corridors and the dressing rooms were in shadows. A door led to the Family and Friends Room.

Then he was hit by what felt like an express train.

One of the *Memento Mori* assassins, Gabriel Del Castillo, slammed into McCall and wrapped his massive arms around him. The man's breathing was labored and stressed. McCall's instincts had kicked in at the last possible moment. He half-turned in the man's crushing embrace, stepping sideways, at the same time striking the attacker's arm with his fist. It immediately convulsed. He

314

stamped on the killer's foot with enough force to break it. McCall continued his turn and kicked the attacker's right knee, all but shattering it. The big man started to collapse to the ground. McCall slashed at the man's throat with an openhanded strike. He went down with his legs swept out from under him. McCall grabbed the terrorist's head and snapped it first to one side, then to the other side.

He was dead by the time his head hit the floor.

McCall ran down the deserted dimly lit corridor. Gabriel's embrace had virtually crushed all the air out of him. He noted there were large steamer trunks in the corridor, including an American Dome Steamer Trunk, a Stagecoach 1800's Antique Style Steamer trunk and a Pirate Treasure Chest Wooden steamer trunk. McCall caught a glimpse of Samantha Gregson in the shadows. She was kneeling beside one of the empty trunks lowering something down into it. McCall ran the length of the corridor. Samantha whirled, still on her hands and knees. McCall hit her cheekbone with savage force. The blow jarred her and sent her flying down the polished floor. McCall thought she had lost consciousness. He looked down into the Pirate Treasure Chest Steamer trunk.

Samantha had put together the various pieces of the denotator that had been passed to her by her mercenaries. They fitted together like a jigsaw puzzle with six wires protruding from them. Samantha had not yet fitted the last piece of the three-dimensional puzzle to the contacts. There was a sequential order in which the wires had to be pulled out. There was a detonator with a timer which had started to count down from 1:50 seconds to zero. McCall had spent enough time with Kostmayer and Granny to know his way around these explosive devices. Three of the wires were blue and the last three wires were red.

He carefully ripped out the wires in their correct order.

The timer stopped at 1:20 seconds.

McCall exhaled a breath. He removed the device from the trunk. He set the defunct timer down onto the ground and turned back to where he had left Samantha Gregson lying on the corridor floor. McCall's blow to her head had left her stunned, but not incapacitated.

He had been wrong.

She was gone.

McCall took out his walkie. "Nigel, come back."

Nigel McGarry answered immediately, his voice low. His snide attitude had completely changed. "McCall, we rounded up two of the mercenaries from your description, Damien Milinov and Bradley Stafford. Another of them, Costas Savermento, slipped through the net but we are putting what you would call a Bolo in the States on him. We're still searching for a fourth man, a big brute but he might have escaped backstage."

"He's dead," McCall said shortly. "Samantha tried to trigger an explosive device. I stopped her in time, but she disappeared. You need to send in your bomb detail backstage. I believe I disarmed the device, but I can't be sure."

'On their way to you, McCall."

"Keep the all entrances and exits from the Royal Albert Hall covered."

"On it," McGarry said.

McCall did not wait for the bomb squad to arrive. He ran down another corridor backstage and came out at Row K in the Royal Albert Hall. The lights immediately blacked out. The audience still held the small white candles in their hands. McCall ran for the nearest exit door. The lights came up on onstage and on the audience as Lady Gaga took her curtain call to a standing ovation. The noise within the venue was thunderous. McCall reached one of the exits and ran out of the building. He descended the marble staircase outside. Rain drummed down onto the streets around the massive statue of Prince Albert in the center of the building. McCall stood in the deluge, looking down Kensington Gore which wove around the RAH.

There was no sign of Samantha Gregson.

McCall turned back up the marble staircase and re-entered the building. The audience were calling for Lady Gaga to make one more curtain call. She obliged them, sitting back down at the piano. A hush travelled around the concertgoers. Nigel McGarry ran up to McCall, keeping his voice low, but the cheering for the punters, as he liked to call them, drown any words he was saying.

"The bomb squad converged on the backstage area in seconds. You had dismantled the device. No worries there. They found one of the mercenaries lying dead with his neck broken. His passport said he was Gabriel Del Castillo. I fancy that was your doing. We got the two of the other terrorists locked away in one of the dressing rooms backstage with an armed guard watching them. The last terrorist, Costas Savemento, is still in the wind. Did you catch up with Samantha Gregson?"

McCall shook his head. "She was long gone."

"We shouldn't have let her slip through our fingers," Nigel said. "My fault. But we will pick her up. I have word out to the airports, train stations and tube stations."

"You won't find her."

"But we can try." Nigel followed McCall's gaze that was directed at the stage where Lady Gaga sat in her spotlight. She was singing her *Swallow* song for which she had received an Academy Award. "Do you want me to stop the performance?"

"No need now," McCall said. "Let Lady Gaga finish her show."

"No one in this audience is aware of what has gone on," McGarry said. "We'll keep it that way. No one needs to know how close they came to a bloodbath." He turned back to McCall. "At the risk of sounding like a true Englishman, that was a bloody good call you made. Saved a lot of lives. Forgive my churlishness of before."

McCall did not respond to that. He just said: "Keep in constant touch with your Security Officers. Lady Gaga's show is not over yet."

"Will do."

McCall moved away from Nigel, suddenly feeling that he had accomplished nothing. Samantha Gregson was out on the streets of London. It would not matter how massive a manhunt was launched to find her. McCall knew she would slip their net.

And she would be even more determined now to end Robert McCall's life.

McCall had taken a suite at the Dorchester Hotel in Mayfair in London. He had stayed at the Dorchester on and off for years. There was an old-world feel to the place that had always appealed to him. Granny was there with him. The concerts in the six European countries had been a triumph as far as the public was concerned. The rock concerts in Spain, Sweden and Prague in the Czech Republic had been resounding successes with the public with no hint of terrorism. The concert in Greece had continued once Gunner had found the device loaded with C4 explosives that Christos and Nico had neutralized. The Rome concert had been totally abandoned. The firefight that had raged in the catacombs beneath the Terme di

Caracalla ruins had left twenty Al Qaeda terrorists dead. None of Benedetto Lombardi's Security Officers had been killed. The explosive device that Samantha Gregson had handled in the Royal Albert Hall corridors had been defused by McCall. Lady Gaga had accepted her standing ovation from the sold-out audience in the RAH and the concert had emptied out with no further incidents. Samantha's core group of mercenaries had been decimated. McCall had killed Harry Brandt, Scott Renquist and Gabriel Del Costillo. Terence Soul and Mace O'Brien had been killed in the firefight beneath the Terme di Caracalla ruins. A fourth mercenary, Costas Severmento, had been shot and killed at the Royal Albert Hall by Nigel McGarry. Bradley Stafford and Damien Malinov were being interrogated by Intelligence agents working for Control. The three of the mercenaries who had escaped capture were Jaak Olesk, Aleksanteri Karjala and Khalid Rehman Mohammad. Control had ordered any intel on these men to come directly to him. He wanted what was left of Matthew Goddard and Samantha Gregson's network destroyed.

McCall had had a conversation with Gunner who had relayed to him the events surrounding the Greek concert. How the Security forces there had defused an explosive device found on the stage and that Gunner had been forced to kill a mercenary named Jack Roslyn whom he had confronted beneath the stage area. McCall had thanked Gunner for his timely intervention. He had a lot of time for Colonel Michael Ralston, especially after he had sat with Mickey Kostmayer in the underground parking garage at the UN while another bomb squad had defused an explosive device. Gunner had told McCall that Jack Roslyn had died in his arms without offering any explanation as to what had motivated him to carry out such a potential atrocity. McCall told him it was Samantha

Gregson who had masterminded the list of mercenaries. She had fled the scene at the Royal Albert Hall in London and completely vanished.

McCall took a call from Mickey Kostmayer who had left Rome the day before. He had intel that Khalid Rehman Mohammad, Aleksanteri Karjala and Jaak Olesk had fled from the area and had been seen in Laguardia in Spain.

"It's a very picturesque little town," Kostmayer said. "The stone buildings hide a maze of tunnels and escape routes from when the town was under attack in the Middle Ages. A good place for terrorists to hide out until the heat had died down. There was a sighting on Khalid Rehman Mohammad at the Romanesque church of San Juan Bautista that bought me here. It may come to nothing but tell Granny I am looking into it. Is he with you?"

"He is."

"I presume he told you about planting a tracking device on Ji-Yeon before he took off in that helicopter?"

"He might have mentioned that small detail when we were actively looking for Ji-Yeon," McCall said, mildly, "but Granny has always played his cards close to the vest. He didn't keep it a secret for long. Control is looking into it."

"Ji-Yeon is a thug and a killer," Granny said, as if in his defence. "We had a shot at capturing him in Rome and I let that chance slip through my fingers."

"Let Granny know I am with him all the way," Kostmayer said. "I'll report back if I find any sign of Ji-Yeon."

Kostmayer ended the call. Granny said: "So, you *are* going to go after him,"

"That's why we're here," McCall said, softly. "Leave no one behind."

Hayden Vallance arrived carrying a slim briefcase which he set down on a low coffee table. Granny sat down beside him on a couch. McCall stood as Vallance opened the briefcase and spread a sheaf of maps that he had collected. He pointed to one of them that he had ringed in red.

"This is the town of Plyos in Russia," Vallance said. "One of the Golden Rings Cities. A quaint little medieval merchant town where in the early 1800's Isaac Levitan, the renown classical landscape mood painter, had lived. I have got one of his paintings, a piece called *Twilight Moon*, which had hung in the Tretyakov Gallery. I received it as a gift from the curator for some questionable work I had done as a mercenary. It's got a haunting quality that is memorizing."

"You're always full of surprises," McCall murmured.

"I studied art when I was in my twenties before I found out that dealing with dictators and terrorist thugs was more rewarding," Vallance said, dryly. "We'll have to refuel in Murmansk in Russia which is 24 kilometers outside the city. I have a chopper on call for us. From there it's a short way following the Volga River." He produced another map in greater detail from his briefcase. "This is the rampart of the old fortress. We'll bypass that and that will bring us close to our objective."

"How close?" Granny asked.

"It's on the other side of the lake about a half mile. We will be flying under the radar."

"There's a suspension bridge leading to the Chateau Kharzinski," McCall said. "What you have told me about Ji-Yeon it will be heavily guarded. Men patrolling the grounds, but they won't be on high alert."

"Ji-Yeon has just escaped from Security forces in Rome," Granny said. "He will be on high alert."

"No one else knows where he is," McCall reminded him. "But if he is in that Chateau, we've got a window of opportunity."

Hayden Vallance said: "Here's the floorplan of the Chateau." He spread more maps on the coffee table. "The Chateau Kharzinski has fourteen rooms with balconies above three ornate archways, covered walkways, an elegant courtyard, two libraries, four marble staircases, parquet floors, a mill on the grounds, stables and its own chapel. Stained-glass windows with some interesting scrollwork with rampant lions and the Knights Templar in stone. The grounds are landscaped and surrounded by woods which come down to the lake edge. There is a helipad on the roof."

"A nice fixer upper," Granny said.

"Too isolated for my taste," Vallance said, "but to each his own."

"How many guards will be stationed at the Chateau?" Granny asked.

"No telling, but I'd reckon about twenty or more. Ji-Yeon usually travels with an entourage of at least eight. They are all handpicked mercenaries who would die on their swords if their leader were challenged."

"So it is a fortress," Granny said.

"You got that right. Getting in there won't be easy."

"Leave the floorplan for me," McCall said.

Hayden Vallance lay the floorplan on the coffee table, rolled up the other maps and put them into his briefcase. McCall turned to Granny. "There's a chance that Ji-Yeon and his men are guarding an empty Chateau. There is no guarantee that Deva Montgomery and Daniel Blake are being incarcerated there."

"You want my opinion?" Vallance asked.

"Go ahead," McCall said, but he knew what was coming.

"They're dead," Hayden Vallance said.

"But we won't know that until when go there and find out," McCall said.

Vallance shrugged. "Worst case scenario. I have a date with a blonde tonight with a lot of curves and a bottle of Johnny Walker Black. We will leave in the early morning. I will be waiting for you at the back of Heathrow Airport which you can access from the Western Perimeter Road. I will give you detailed directions."

Granny looked at the mercenary. "You don't have to do this for me."

"Yeah, I do."

"You don't owe me anything."

"I owe McCall," Vallance said simply, and walked out of the hotel suite.

Granny looked at McCall. "What are you going to say to Control?"

"Need to know basis," McCall said, still a little curt.

"He wouldn't sanction this mission."

"He won't know anything about it. What are you going to do now? You can stay here at the suite. The restaurant in the Dorchester is suburb."

"I have a date," Granny said.

McCall nodded. He knew about Granny's date. He put a hand on his arm. "Listen to me, Granny. If there is any chance that Deva Montgomery or Daniel Blake are still alive, we'll find them."

Granny nodded. It was what he needed to hear. Even though he did not really believe it. He picked up his leather jacket from an armchair and exited the hotel suite. McCall poured himself a shot of Glenfiddich Reserve Single Malt whisky and looked out at Hyde Park in the misty morning.

He also thought that the chances of finding Deva Montgomery and Daniel Blake alive were slim to none. He sipped at his scotch as he looked out at Hyde Park.

Hope for the best, he thought, plan for the worst.

▶ 28 ◀

GRANNY MET UP with Liz Montgomery at the Phoenix pub in Central London and they strolled into St. James's Park. Liz was on assignment to do a follow-up piece for the Guardian newspaper about the whistleblower Edward Snowden. She briefly embraced Granny, but she was distracted and aloof. They strolled over into the park. Finally, Liz took Granny's arm as they walked through the gorgeous Buckingham Palace Flower Beds on their way toward the Blue Bridge.

"Please tell me you have news for me about Deva."

"It's nothing definitive, but I may have a lead as to her whereabouts," Granny said. "Ji-Yeon had been coordinating the security for some rock concerts in Europe which took place yesterday. Terrorists struck at three of the venues, but they were quickly neutralized. I came within a hundred yards of him, but he escaped from the grounds outside the Terme di Caracalla ruins in a helicopter. Earlier in the day I had brushed up against him, without him seeing me, and put a tracking device on him."

That stopped Liz dead in her tracks. Her voice had a rising hope in it. "So, you do know where Deva is?"

"If our intel is correct, she is being held somewhere in Russia. At least, that was the last sighting of her. But there's no guarantee I'll find her."

As they walked, Granny brought Liz up to speed about the events that had transpired in Rome and in the other five European countries. He added that even though she was a noted journalist, she could not print a word of the story. She said she understood. Robert McCall had invited Granny to the Dorchester Hotel for a council of war. He told Liz about Hayden Vallance, a mercenary who sometimes did work for McCall when it suited him. He had been at the conference in the Dorchester Hotel with Granny and McCall. He might have the intel to get them to Russia. Hayden Vallance would wait for them on a hilltop overlooking the Chateau, but Granny and McCall would be virtually on their own. Whether he would accompany them after that, that was up to McCall. There was only so far Granny could trust Hayden Vallance, but he would get them as far as Murmansk. They would be flying out early in the morning.

"There's no guarantee we'll find Deva or Daniel," Granny said, "but it's the only shot we've got."

A silence stretched between them as they reached the famous Bow Bridge in St. James Park. Finally, Liz said softly: "You believe Robert McCall will see you through this?"

"He's the only one who could."

"You have that much faith in him?"

"He's the best," Granny said, simply. "But in this case the best may not be good enough. This Chateau may have been abandoned years ago. Or the people living there now could have nothing to do with Ji-Yeon or his mercenaries."

Liz stopped at the bridge. The splendour of Buckingham Palace was seen through the trees. For a long moment she was silent, as the weight of Granny's words resonated with her.

"You might not come back from Russia," she said.

"Let's just say the odds aren't in my favor."

Liz moved into his arms. She kissed him passionately, then broke away and nodded, a far-away in her eyes.

"Then we'd better make this night count," she said, softly.

Control was a member of the Garrick Club which was an exclusive Private Members' Club in the heart of London's West End. It had been founded in 1831 and named after the renown actor David Garrick to tend to the "regeneration to the Drama". Notable examples of the clientele included Charles Dickens, H.G. Wells, J.M. Barrie and A.A Milne. The club was home to some gorgeous paintings, drawings and sculptures. A saying in the club stated that *unobjectionable men should be excluded than one terrible bore should be included*. McCall had liked that sentiment. The Garrick Club remained for "Gentlemen Only", although women guests were welcome visitors in the club these days. When McCall approached the reception desk it struck him that the old porter who was sitting behind it might have been there since 1831. McCall took a folded piece of paper from his pocket which the porter took with due solemnity.

"One of your members here at the Garrick," McCall said, "is James Thurgood Cameron."

The old porter nodded with a smile. "Yes. sir, Mr. Cameron has been a member here for many years. A very courtly gentleman."

"Will you give him this note?" McCall asked. "It's quite important."

The old porter took the folded note and put it in front of him. "I will hand this to Mr. Cameron as soon as I see him, sir. Is there a message I can convey to him, sir? He will be here this afternoon or this evening."

"Just see that he reads it," McCall asked.

"I will most certainly do that, sir."

McCall smiled at the formality of the atmosphere in the club. He left the old porter staring after him as he left the Garrick Club if he had secret knowledge that only he could impart.

Granny gazed down at Liz Montgomery as she lay sleeping naked with her back to him, her legs coiled up in the blanket. He extricated himself from her and covered her with the heavy bedspread. He leaned down and gently kissed her forehead. She did not stir. He straightened, glancing at her watch on the bedside table. It was almost five o'clock in the morning. He picked up his backpack and got it onto his shoulders, checked the Steyr 9mm pistol and put it in his pocket. There was no time for a goodbye. Granny was not big on goodbyes at the best of times. He had only one purpose and that was rescuing Liz's sister Deva and Daniel Blake. Nothing else mattered to him. He moved to the suite door and exited without a sound. But appearances could be deceptive. Liz's eyes were still closed, but large tears spilled down her face.

McCall met up with Granny at the back of Heathrow Airport near the Virgin Atlantic Engineering Hangar where Hayden Vallance was waiting for them. Vallance was once again flying a Global 6000 VistaJet with a 15-passenger capacity. They flew to Murmansk which was a port city sitting on a fjord at Kola Bay near the Barents Sea in Russia. Vallance had equipped them with two Heckler & Koch MPM submachineguns with 6x30mm rounds which Vallance had purchased in Germany. He also provided McCall and Granny with SFP9 Striker single-action pistols in 9mm calibre with high-performance luminescent contrast. Each of them had EES Profile NVG Foliage Green binoculars with three-tie magnification up to a hundred yards. He added two Black Tiger throwing knives. He did not know if they were going to encounter isolated pockets of resistance or if they were going to be facing an armed contingent of Russian troops.

Granny smiled as he laid out the armaments. "Vallance knows how to throw a party."

"He sent me into Afghanistan with everything I needed to rescue that Army Captain Josh Coleman," McCall said. "I didn't get the job done."

Granny glanced over at him, not liking what he was hearing. "I understand you got him almost to Aleppo before the insurgents closed in."

"It wasn't good enough."

Granny had noted these mood swings in McCall before. He had some of the same doubts and fears. But he was glad that he did not have to aspire to such heights of nobility. After all, he thought, McCall was the only man Granny had evet met who was a *real* hero.

In Murmansk they landed at the airport where they switched over to an OH-58 Kiowa Warrior, single engine four-bladed helicopter with advanced visionics, navigation and weapons with integrated systems. It was an older model which why Vallance had acquired it at a bargain price. Both McCall and Granny had changed into Woodland Camo field jackets and hunting insulated jeans. Twenty minutes later they had taken off again. Vallance angled over the town of Pylos in the Privolzhsky District of Russia on the Volga River. McCall could see the old fort in the little town with its market stalls and the magnificent Church of the Resurrection. There was a museum dedicated to the landscape painter Isaac Levitan and the Tree of Love, two pine trees with one branch accreting them. Fourteen minutes later Vallance set down on a grassy slope in the densely wooded forest. Half a mile from them was the impressive Chateau Krarzinski with its elegant courtyard and balconies above three archways, library windows that overlooked the extensive patios, stables, a chapel and several marble fountains. A narrow suspension bridge led to the Chateau on the lake.

McCall and Granny jumped down to the ground. They both held Heckler and Koch submachineguns and carried SFP9 9mm pistols. Hayden Vallance stepped to the cockpit door.

"I'll give you forty minutes," he said. "If you are not back here by then, I'll take off, make sure there are no troops I can see in Pylos, swing back in an arc and land back at the place I left you. After that, I will give it another half-an-hour unless I hear all hell is breaking up at the Chateau. My intel says that the place will be heavily guarded. Get into the Chateau and get out again. Hopefully with Deva Montgomery and Daniel Blake. Or you my find their bodies somewhere buried in the woods."

"Any other words of wisdom you have for us?" Granny asked, ironically.

"I used to like that old Hill Blues TV series," Vallance said, "where the Desk Sergeant would read the roll call and say: 'Be *careful* out there.'"

"Let's go," McCall said, shortly.

He and Granny ran down the grassy slope and plunged into the woods. It took them only five minutes to emerge at the suspension bridge. It was deserted. As far as McCall could see there was no one at the Chateau. He and Granny communicated with hand signals only. They ran across the bridge. McCall crouched down with Granny beside him. They waited in the stillness. No one moved in front of the Chateau. It did look as if it had been abandoned. They gave it another five minutes, then McCall indicated they should split up. McCall went first, following a path in front of the stables and the rose gardens that took him around to the back of the Chateau

Granny consulted his Diver's quartz watch, allowed twenty more seconds to pass, then he ran along the lakefront past the white-framed chapel and the courtyard onto the grounds. He reached the front of the Chateau with its intricate balconies and covered walkways.

A uniformed guard turned the corner of the building.

Granny crouched down beside a three-tier marble fountain where a naked wood nymph was spewing water. The guard was dressed in a Gorka yellow-leaf KLMK oak camouflage Spetsnaz uniform with a Spetsnaz Scorpion patch on one shoulder. On the other shoulder he had a Russian Special Forces Battalion Patch with a fierce lion with bared fangs. Granny realized these were not Russian uniforms but a modified version that the guards wore. The man carried an AK-47 rifle.

Granny tackled him and brought him down to the ground. The rifle skittered along the flagstones in front of the Chateau. Granny tried to grab it, but the guard brought a crushing blow against Granny's face, almost smashing his cheekbone. He wrapped his arms around Granny's throat and applied pressure until Granny was gasping for air. There was a ringing in his ears that was exacerbated by his senses rushing away from him.

He saw a blur of movement and the choking sensation lessened. Granny rolled over, still fighting for breath. The guard slumped over into unconsciousness. McCall reached out for Granny, dragging him to his feet. McCall held him in a steadying grip, allowing him to get air back into his lungs. He gestured to the unconscious guard. Granny nodded. They carried him into the shrubbery at the lake's edge. Granny knew they would be better off just breaking the guard's windpipe, but that was not McCall's style. McCall motioned to the back of the Chateau. *We go in there.* Granny nodded. They ran, crouched low, then pulled up when they heard the unmistakable sound of a helicopter rotor. McCall pulled Granny into the bushes. They did not have long to wait. The helicopter appeared over the Chateau, angling down to the roof of the building. It powered down and the rotor blades slowly came to a stop. Ji-Yeon stepped out onto the flat roof. McCall knew that hand signals were not going to cut it. He gripped Granny's elbow.

"Not your fight anymore," McCall said, softly. "We came to get Deva and Daniel Blake. At least we know we are in the right place. We go into together. I will take care of Ji-Yeon. Are we clear on that?"

It took a moment for Granny to respond as he gazed up to where Ji-Yeon was talking to three members of his entourage who had also stepped away from the helicopter. Then he nodded. He and McCall ran from the grassy verge to the patio area at the back of the Chateau. French doors opened into the house. McCall and Granny accessed the back entrance which was not locked. They found themselves in shadowy darkness. A corridor led down to a front reception area. Moonlight streamed through the picture windows where a marble staircase led up to the upper floors. A computer sat on the reception desk. Granny quickly accessed it and brought up a schematic diagram of the Chateau. The rooms and corridors were all displayed. McCall leaned in, tapping the relevant data. He indicated the big staircase that led down to the floor below. Granny nodded and held up five fingers. *Give me five minutes to find out if the basement rooms are locked or not.* McCall nodded. He made sure they both had their walkie-talkies to communicate. Granny killed the image on the computer screen. He moved quickly to the staircase and descended it. McCall climbed the staircase toward the second floor.

They did not have much time.

Granny reached the basement area in the Chateau which was in shadow. He listened for a moment, but there was no sound of a guard stationed down there. The lower floors had several rooms including a music room, an office, which was deserted and a well-stocked wet bar with mirrored walls. All of them were in shadow. From the schematic diagram he had brought up onto the computer screen, Granny knew there was a room at the back of the house which had access to the lake. It was locked with a padlock. Granny took his walkie and spoke softly into it.

"Got a locked door in the basement area. Going to open it."

McCall's voice echoed from his walkie. "Copy that."

Granny put away the walkie and knelt at the heavy wooden door. He listened, but there was no sound at all. He realized that the room within was probably soundproof. He set down the Heckler & Kock submachinegun on the polished parquet floor and took out some skeletal keys from a leather pouch in his pocket. He knelt at the door and went to work on the lock.

McCall reached the top of the marble staircase on the second floor. Moonlight streamed through the big windows, although the corridor outside the rooms was shrouded in shadow. A man was walking down the corridor carrying a modified AK-12 Russian assault rifle chambered with 39mm cartridges. McCall recognized him as one of the last of Samantha Gregson's mercenaries, Aleksanteri Karjala. Before the terrorist could even react, McCall tackled him, knocking the assault rifle out of his hands. Karjala lunged for McCall who avoided his blows and slammed the mercenary into a wall. He brought the man down to his knees and came around him. He wrenched the terrorist's head to one side and heard his neck snap in the stillness. There had been no time for him to use any finesse. He wrapped his arms around the man's legs and carried him into one of the libraries on the second floor. McCall dumped him behind a couch and closed the door.

Four minutes and counting.

It took Granny thirty seconds to jimmy the lock on the basement door. He put away his skeletal tools and opened it. The room was sparsely furnished with heavy drapes sealing the light from outside. There were two people in the room, tightly bound, one lying on the carpeted floor, the second lying stretched out on a leather couch. The man on the floor did not stir. The woman was Deva Montgomery. Her dark hair was splayed out across her forehead. Granny recognized the prison garb she was still wearing, as if they were stylish pajamas. She looked up in the darkness with the heavy drapes closed, not recognizing him at first. He was just another tormentor who had beaten her, maybe several times.

Granny moved through the stillness of the room until Deva Montgomery could see his face properly in the dim light. Even then, he was not sure she recognized him. She stirred, at first cowering away from him. Her prison tunic was lying open across her chest. Granny saw that her breasts had many discolored bruises on them. There were large welts across her stomach. Her right eye had been almost closed and there were contusions on her face and her arms.

Granny set down the Heckler and Koch submachine-gun on the parquet floor and knelt beside her. "I don't know if you will recognize me, Deva, because Ji-Yeon had already isolated you in the prison camp. But I am going to get you out of here."

She was staring up at him, disoriented, as if she did not understand.

"Keep still."

Granny took out a stiletto knife from his belt. She flinched involuntarily and he reached out to calm her. "I am going to cut away these restrains from your wrists. Okay?'

She finally nodded, looking at his face. "You were in the prison camp," she said, her voice hoarse and guttural. "You were there with my sister Liz. She said you had a funny name."

"It's Granny," he said. "Keep very still. I don't want this knife to touch your skin."

She nodded again. The knife was razor sharp and cut away the bonds. Deva brought her wrists together and gently massaged them. She sat up a little straighter on the couch, then was seized by a coughing fit. Granny held onto her.

"You're all right?"

"Asthma. It comes and goes. Usually when I am stressed." Granny steadied her, but she waved him away. "You're here alone?"

"I'm here with a man named Robert McCall. He destroyed the North Korean prison camp."

Deva's voice rose a notch in alarm. "It was destroyed?"

"Wiped off the face of the earth. The prisoners escaped and that included your sister Liz and the other western prisoners being incarcerated there. Long story, but we came back here to find you."

An edge of panic touched her voice. "But there are only two of you?"

"There is a third man of the team waiting for us in a helicopter in the trees beyond the Chateau. It is a lot for you to take in. Take a deep breath. You are going to be okay now."

"There are guards in the house and on the grounds," she said.

"Yeah, we've run into a couple of them. Just stay with me. Can you stand?"

Her voice was getting stronger. "Yes."

"Okay, I'll help you up."

Shakily Deva got to her feet. Somewhat self-consciously she pulled her prison uniform down across her breasts with a shaking hand. Gingerly Granny helped her button the buttons on the tunic. She looked over at Daniel Blake who lay on his side in the dimness of the room.

"Daniel was beaten repeatedly," Deva whispered. "I don't know if he is conscious. They were very cruel to him. Like animals."

"I'll check him out," Granny said. "Stay right here on the couch. Don't move until I can put an arm around you."

"I can stand," Deva insisted.

"All right."

"Where is your friend Mr. McCall?"

"He'll meet us directly."

Granny grabbed his 9mm submachinegun and moved to where Daniel Blake lay in the darkness of the room. He looked at the Omega chronometer on his wrist.

Four minutes and counting.

▶ 29 ◀

MCCALL MOVED THROUGH the darkened library to where French doors stood with heavy drapes. He unlocked them and stepped through onto an ornate balcony. There were three balconies at the front of the Chateau. The grounds were deserted but McCall saw the figure of a guard standing now at the other end other suspension bridge. He was too far away to see where McCall was from his position. McCall climbed the railing onto the second balcony, crouched low, ran down it to the third balcony. He looked over to where some French doors opened into a study. He gripped the Heckler and Koch submachine-gun tighter.

He climbed over onto the third balcony.

Granny cut through the ropes binding Daniel Blake's wrists. He rolled him over and was gratified to see that Daniel was conscious. His eyes fluttered open. Granny could see that he had also been badly beaten. Deva knelt beside them, taking Daniel's hand in her own. Her eyes mirrored her anguish for him. He smiled up at her seeing that she was freed from her bonds.

"You're doing okay?"

"I'm doing fine, Dan."

"I've got him," Granny said, tossing the ropes away. "Can you get up? I am getting you both out of here right now."

Daniel was weak and Granny could see he did not have the strength to talk more. He put his arms around him and lifted him up onto his feet. The journalist swayed there but managed to keep his balance. Deva got to her feet, still holding Daniel's hand.

"We're going to meet up with Robert McCall," Granny said. "You're going to have to climb a staircase and that will put us in the reception area of the Chateau."

"I can do it," Daniel said.

"There are always guards outside this door," Deva said.

"I'll deal with them," Granny said. "We have to hurry."

Granny helped Daniel on one side and Deva on the other. They approached the door of the room and Granny opened it. They moved out into the corridor outside which was deserted. Granny consulted his Omega diver's chronometer.

Three minutes.

Cutting it close.

McCall moved to the French doors that off closed the study. There was no movement in the darkened room beyond. They opened at his touch. He entered and closed the French doors behind him. The room had a large desk, two deep armchairs, a state-of-the-art Bose Lifestyle Entertainment System and a glass cabinet that housed fluted glassware including Heracles kneeling at the *Gates of Hades* with the two-headed hound Kerberos. It held a yellow dragon jar, Italian pottery ceramic mugs, handcrafted Antique Candle Holders and a collection of rare coins: Julius Caesar Gold Aureus, Athens Silver Owl Tetrad, an Alexander Gol Stater from the Macedonian Empire and an image of Kotos, a sea monster from Ancient Lore, all of them priceless pieces of antiquity. On the other side of the antique desk was an antique 1918 wooden Dentistry handcrafted chest, an Antique filing cabinet and an early 19th Century Mahogany cane rocking chair. There were several delicate antique Chinese Rosewood screens sectioning the room with the motif of a blossoming cheery tree on them.

Ji-Yeon came at McCall from out of the darkness wielding an ornate *Geom Jingeom* double-edged dragon sword. There were several antiques in his collection including an antique Japanese Katana Samurai Sword, a Shinto WW11 Japanese Samurai Sword and a Ten Ryu Samurai Sword with a silk-wrapped handle. Ji-Yeon's face was contorted in rage that a stranger could have violated his inner sanctum.

McCall parried Ji-Yeon's wild swings. The sharp blade of the sword came down with vicious force, smashing an antique English Oak and Brass Chiming Clock. Ji-Yeon struck again, but his attacks were uncoordinated, as if a wild rage had seized him. McCall sidestepped his lunges and kicked out with his leg. The kick shattered Ji-Yeon's left knee, but he barely acknowledged the attack. He swung again at McCall's face. McCall hit the terrorist with a right brachial Stun that had numbed the terrorist's arm. McCall transferred his weight from one foot to the other, keeping his hands up to deflect blows to his body. Ji-Yeon stumbled as his right leg gave out on him, but it was a feint. McCall's right hand grabbed for Ji-Yeon's collar, but the Korean was waiting for that. He sidestepped and executed what was called a *Buffalo Punch* in martial arts where an opponent could theoretically take down a stampeding buffalo. McCall ducked under the punch which would have taken the top of his head off. He trapped the man's hands at the hilt of the Samurai sword and twisted it violently. The blade flew out of Ji-Yeon's hands. The Korean lashed out at McCall with vicious palm strikes. They rocked McCall, sending him crashing into the ornate desk. Ji-Yeon followed them up with brutal knife hand strikes at McCall's head. McCall came under the blows and delivered a series of elbow strikes to the Korean's body. McCall threw him back into the ornate free-standing glass cabinet. It smashed apart, raining ceramic mugs, Grecian vases and the rare coin collection cascading to the floor.

Ji-Yeon staggered out of the shattered glass cabinet with obscene daggers clinging to his face and arms. McCall used hammer fists to the terrorist's body. That weakened him further. He came around Ji-Yeon's body using a reverse neck choke hold known as a *sleeper* hold to cut off Ji-Yeon's oxygen. The terrorist retaliated, executing a twisting neck break, hurling McCall bodily over his shoulder. McCall hit the ground hard, rolled over, avoiding another hammer strike to his body. He smashed a palm strike to Ji-Yeon's temple which sent him reeling back into the shattered glass cabinet. He knee was useless to him now. Blood flowed from the daggers sticking out of his face. Snarling, he threw the glass cabinet at McCall, who sidestepped it. It crashed to the floor. The Korean had one more move left. He held a glass dagger in his hand which he stabbed down at McCall's face. He executed his own version of a Buffalo Punch which trapped the man's hands around the Samurai sword and twisted it violently. The Korean terrorist struck the floor. McCall put his arm around Ji-Yeon's throat in what was called an *anaconda choke*. Then McCall arched his back to apply the choke hold.

Ji-Yeon struggled as the air was constricted in his lungs. McCall twisted the man's head around and his neck snapped. McCall let him fall to the floor. He staggered to his feet, fighting to get air back into his lungs. He looked down at his opponent lying motionless in a shroud of broken glass. He glanced down at the chronometer on his wrist.

Seconds before the five minutes deadline was up.

The study door slammed open and another of the Soviet guards entered. He was wearing the same camouflage uniform with the distinctive Scorpion patch on one shoulder and the Special Forces Battalion patch of the snarling lion on the other. He brought up his AK-47 rifle, but McCall pulled out the stiletto knife from his wrist and threw it. It struck the guard in the throat. He collapsed to the floor. McCall stepped over him into the corridor outside. An alarm was now ringing stridently through the Chateau.

McCall ran to the big sweeping staircase and descended it. His timing was immaculate. Granny came up the stairs from the basement floor at the same moment with Deva and Daniel Blake. He looked at McCall and the evidence of the fight.

"Ji-Yeon?"

"Dead."

It took a moment for Granny to process that, then he just nodded.

Deva Montgomery extricated herself from his embrace and took McCall's hand. "Is that monster really dead?"

"Yes."

"You're sure?"

"I'm sure."

A shudder went through Deva's entire body. "Thank God." McCall continued to hold her hand. "You're all right?"

"Yes. You are Robert McCall, right? My sister mentioned your name."

"I'm getting you out of here."

"I'm so grateful."

"Daniel is in a bad way," Granny said. "He needs medical attention or he's not going to make it."

Four uniformed Soviet Army Officers ran down the hallway from the back of the Chateau armed with AK-47 rifles. Two more of them came down the sweeping staircase. McCall brought up his submachinegun and fired two short bursts, sending two of the Officers crashing to the floor. Granny decimated the two other Soviet Officers who sprawled down the marble stairs. Granny gathered Deva back into his arms.

"With me!" McCall said. "Right out the front entrance!"

He and Granny walked backwards, shielding Deva and Daniel with their bodies. Two more of the Soviet armed guards came from the back of the building. McCall fired another burst from the submachinegun, forcing the Officers to take refuge behind the reception desk. By that time Granny, Deva and Blake had reached the main doors.

Outside the Chateau McCall and Granny came under heavy fire from more of the Soviet troops. They sheltered behind one of the ornate marble fountains and returned the fire, sending the solders scrambling into the bushes and patio furniture bordering the Chateau. Deva knelt beside Daniel Blake.

McCall accessed the number of Ji-Yeon's security force at about twenty. But that number could go higher if more troops were summoned to the Chateau. The militia had them pinned down. Bullets sang off the fountain and ricocheted off the flagstones.

McCall could not see way out for them.

Beside him Granny fired a burst at the enemy from the protection of the marble fountain. "This is going to get old real fast," he said. "Sooner or later Ji-Yeon's security forces will rush our position."

"They could also emerge from the Chateau as soon as their numbers have increased," McCall said.

"That's the Dunkirk spirit," Granny said wryly. "This would be a good time for Hayden Vallance to come storming in here with guns blazing."

"Too far away," McCall said.

"Ya think?"

McCall looked behind them. More Soviet troops would be pouring out of the Chateau at any moment. McCall and Granny were seriously outnumbered. They had no way of reaching the suspension bridge which was their lifeline back to where Hayden Vallance was waiting for them in the helicopter. That was assuming that he had not been overrun himself by Ji-Yeon's taskforce.

Not good.

Granny returned another barrage of gunfire. "We need to get out of here!"

"I'm open to any suggestions," McCall said.

"I'll give you cover fire. You take Deva and Daniel and try reach the suspension bridge."

"Not viable."

"It's better than being blasted apart where we are."

Granny raised his submachinegun and took out two more of the Soviet troops. McCall took out two more. Bullets exploded around them. Deva cowered from them, at the same tine trying to tend to Daniel, who had lapsed back into consciousness. McCall reached for his walkie and tried to call Vallance. The interference was like white static. He shook his head.

"Our communications are being jammed."

Two of the Soviet Officers rounded the side of the Chateau, blasting the marble fountains with gunfire. McCall took them out. Granny fired at two more who had broken cover, dropping them to the flagstone path.

"Time's on their side," Granny said. "They can wait us out."

Deva cowered down beside her rescuers, frightened and distraught. "What can we do?"

At that moment McCall looked up. A Sikorsky CH-53K King Stallion helicopter angled down out of the sky. It was followed by two more Sikorsky choppers that angled over the Chateau at about 100 feet. Almost immediately Black Ops United States Army commandos started repelling from them in camouflage uniforms, helmets and eye protection. They wore heavy leather gloves with double-leather palms fingers that slid over the rope with a rope safety belt, a high-end tether and a L4 nylon type four rope with a rappel seat. They repelled about eight feet per second. Halfway down to the grounds of the Chateau they released the tension on the rope and moved their brake hands out to a 45-degre angle to regulate the rate of descent. They had caps with the letters *Strike Force* on them with an uncoiled green cobra snake. Their faces were covered for the most part with black scarves. They fired AK-47 rifles as they repelled down toward the flagstone paths that crisscrossed the grounds. The Soviet troops fired back, but the Black Ops troops had the upper hand because surprise was in their side.

"Black Ops," Granny said and let out a war whoop. "God love them!"

"What's happening?" Deva asked.

"The cavalry has arrived," McCall said.

He took hold of Deva's arm. Granny leaned back down and scooped Daniel Blake up into his arms. The descending paratroopers fired short bursts on their weapons even as they continued to descend. The Soviet soldiers returned fire, but they were outgunned. The paratroopers landed on the grounds on the Chateau. They quickly spread out, communicating with hand signals, taking out more than a dozen of the armed Security personnel. The commandos had virtually decimated most of the Soviet troops.

"You got Daniel?" McCall asked.

"I got him!" Granny said.

"Let's do this."

McCall and Granny moved from the shelter of the fountain, in formation, Granny taking the lead, McCall turned around, aiming his Heckler and Koch submachinegun in front of him. They ran toward the suspension bridge. McCall dropped two more of the enemy force when they broke for cover. More of the US commandos landed on the grounds, releasing the ropes through the rappel rings. They quickly spread out, taking out more than a dozen of the armed Security personnel.

The firefight was fierce.

McCall, Granny, Deva and Daniel reached the suspension bridge. There were no other hostiles waiting for them. McCall saw one of the figures of the commandos pull down the black scarf from his face. Even at this distance, McCall recognized him immediately. Granny pulled up, protecting Deva and Daniel with his body.

"Who brought the cavalry?"

"Control," McCall said.

Granny turned around. "You can't be serious?"

"He came through for us." McCall said. "I wonder when the last time he jumped out of a helicopter in full Black Ops camouflage gear."

"This has to be a first," Granny said.

McCall steadied Danial who was conscious again.

"Stay with us, Daniel!"

"I am all right."

"Not far for you to go. Maybe a half mile."

"I can do it," Daniel said again, his voice barely audible.

McCall turned and saw that the commandos had the situation in hand. Ji-Yeon's private Security Force threw down their weapons, raising their hands in the air. One of the commandoes raised his hand as if acknowledging McCall. He knew it had to be Control. He gave his old boss a wave, then he took hold of Daniel's shoulders and Granny grabbed Deva's hand. They ran down the suspension bridge and plunged into the heavy foliage that surrounded the Chateau.

Hayden Vallance was waiting at his Global 6000 Vista Jet when they emerged from the woods. He had heard the fighting around the Chateau. "One more minute and I was coming to get you," he said. "You cut it a little close."

"We were trapped by Soviet troops on the grounds," McCall said, "but Control arrived with a platoon of Black Ops commandos. I left them mopping up the aftermath."

"Wonders will never cease," Vallance said. "Get in!" Granny helped Deva into the helicopter with Vallance's help. Daniel Blake moved out of McCall's arms, standing straighter.

"I can climb in myself," he said.

McCall nodded. He let the journalist walk under his own steam to the waiting helicopter. He had almost made it there when—

A gunshot echoed from the dense undergrowth—

McCall whirled. Granny jumped back down from the chopper and caught Daniel as he slumped to the ground. McCall saw a lone figure in the trees some distance from the Chateau lowering a high-powered telescopic rifle. Depending the weight and muzzle velocity of the 9mm bullet, it had to have been fired at least 170 yards from where the shooter had been standing.

It was a marksman shot.

McCall saw the figure of Samantha Gregson standing in a copse of beech trees. She gave McCall an ironic wave. McCall had no way of reaching her from this distance. Samantha broke down the high-powered rifle and disappeared into the foliage. McCall knelt beside Daniel Blake.

The bullet had taken out the top of his forehead.

McCall felt a kind of rage he had never felt before. Granny started to run from the helicopter toward where Samantha Gregson's had been standing, but McCall put a restraining hand on his arm. There was no way either of them could have reached her. McCall lifted Daniel's body up into his arms. Hayden Vallance jumped out of the helicopter to McCall's side.

"There may be more Soviet troops descending on the Chateau, McCall," he said, urgently. "We have to move!"

Without a word McCall lifted Daniel Blake's lifeless body onto his shoulder. Granny climbed back into the chopper with Deva Montgomery. McCall gently laid down Daniel's body. Vallance climbed in and fired up the helicopter.

A moment later he took off into the darkened night sky.

► 30 ◄

DEVA SAT IN the co-pilot's set, her hands folded on her lap, processing the tragedy she had just witnessed. Granny sat down beside McCall. He looked down at the Chateau grounds where the Black Ops forces had overrun the building, taking control of the facility. There was not a flicker of emotion on McCall's face.

"There was nothing you could have done," Granny told him over the rush of the wind. "You didn't even know Samantha Gregson was *there* at the Chateau. She was biding her time. Waiting for the right moment."

"She knew what she was doing," McCall said, savagely. "That bullet was meant to kill Daniel. She knew that would cause me the most pain."

"You can't save them all, McCall," Granny said, softly. "Samantha was counting on that. We'll find her again."

McCall did not respond.

The helicopter soared into the cloud cover leaving a serenity in the silence behind them.

Hayden Vallance landed back at Murmansk Airport where he switched back to his Global Vista Jet 9H-VJJ and took off again before any ground troops could hail him. He was going to land in the town of Gavle in Sweden

349

where he knew there was a first-class hospital, but Deva wanted to go on.

McCall had no trouble with that.

Hayden flew them back to New York City with a brief stopover in London for refueling. Granny took Deva to the New York Weill Cornell Medical Center at 525 E. 68th Street. He had her admitted and took her to a private room in the hospital. McCall waited until the doctors had checked her out. Deva had been through an ordeal, but she did not have any life-threatening issues.

McCall left the hospital.

He had an appointment with his own doctor.

It had been a small microchip RFID tracker.

Samantha Gregson had inserted it under the skin on McCall's wrist about the size of a grain of rice. He had it removed in the surgery of Dr. Ellyn Graham whose offices were on Madison Avenue on 57th Street in New York City. She was a doctor who had come to see McCall when her daughter had gone missing for three days. McCall had found her in the company of some questionable friends. He had taken care of them and handed her daughter back to her folks. She had sworn she would never scare them again like that. Since that time Dr. Ellyn Graham had become McCall's friend and her daughter was now in college, having left her wayward ways behind her.

It had taken just seconds for the RFID tracker to be removed from McCall's skin. Dr. Graham had been concerned. How had this microchip been inserted beneath McCall's skin without his knowledge? She knew that teenagers had been experimenting with microchip trackers that were imbedded under the skin to allow them to attend rave parties. A dangerous fetish that was growing in popularity. Mc-

Call had told her that the reason for the tracking device had a more sinister purpose, but he had left it at that. As soon as the small tracking device had been removed from his skin, between the shoulder and the elbow, the device had immediately malfunctioned. It was dead. Samantha Gregson had tracked him right up to the time she had fired a high-powered rifle at Daniel Blake's head and ended his life. Dr. Ellyn Graham wanted to know about what happened to McCall, but he had told her it was best that she did not know. He had been targeted by a killer who would try again. The doctor sighed and took McCall's hand. He had promised her dinner one night.

"Do you think that be can be accomplished before some psycho tries to kill you?"

McCall smiled. "I'm sure that could be arranged."

But he did not tell his doctor when that time frame would be.

Granny called Lisa Montgomery from the Cornell Medical Center who had returned from London to New York City. She had rushed down to the hospital for a tearful reunion with her sister. Granny waited at Deva's bedside.

"I thought I had lost you," Liz said through her tears.

"You would have if it hadn't been for Robert McCall," Deva said.

"Remember I was the one who planted the tracking device on Ji-Yeon," Granny murmured. "Just saying…"

Liz Montgomery laughed through her tears, taking Granny's hand. "You guys make a good team."

"There are times. Most of the time I just live in McCall's shadow."

"That's not true," Deva objected. "But I could tell from the plane ride home that he was very troubled."

"He'll get over it," Granny said. "But you never know with McCall. Still waters run deep."

"I have my beautiful sister Deva back," Liz said. "That is all I care about now."

She hugged Deva again. When they broke, Deva looked at her sister and Granny. "You guys have something else to tell me?"

"We had great sex," Liz said. "Does that count?"

For the first time, Granny looked somewhat embarrassed. Liz squeezed his hand. "Don't sweat it, Granny. We could not have kept it a secret from my sister. She knows all of my secrets." Liz looked around the room. "Will Mr. Mc-Call be back?"

"I don't know the answer to that," Granny said. "You never know what McCall is thinking about anything. He has some issues he had to deal with."

"But I wanted to thank him," Deva said. "I wouldn't be here in this hospital hugging my big sister if it were for him. He saved my life in that Chateau."

"McCall isn't good about saying goodbyes," Granny said. "Let's leave it at that."

Liz Montgomery took hold of Deva's hand and then Granny's.

"You're the two most important people in my universe," she said, softly. "I'm just so thankful that I have you back in my life. Both of you."

Granny smiled his lopsided smile and took her hand in his.

McCall found Hayden Vallance waiting for him outside the hospital on 68th Street. They walked together toward 1st Avenue.

"Where did you disappear to?" Vallance asked.

"I had an appointment with my doctor. It was something of an emergency. I took care of it. How are Deva Montgomery and her sister doing?"

"They're fine. Happy to be together at long last."

"What are *you* going to do now?" McCall asked him.

Vallance shrugged. "There's a war raging in Nagorno-Karabakh conflict in Armenia and Azerbaijan. Civilians are being murdered and displaced due to the Government instability and human rights violations. Cooperation in Europe, the OSCE, acts like a mediator in trying to resolve the crisis, but Azerbaijan does not recognize the constitutional and legal framework of the negotiations."

"And you're from Armenia."

Vallance smiled. "Not many people know that. I'm going to take a trip out there to see for myself, but in the meantime I will be spending some quality time with a blonde named Brittney who writes children's books and who thinks I am one of the good guys." Vallance stopped on 1st Avenue, looking at McCall. "I'm sorry about Daniel Blake. Take care of yourself. I won't always be around to haul your ass out of the fire."

It was McCall's turn to smile. "I'll keep that in mind."

Vallance left him and found a pub on the corner. He did not ask McCall to join him. McCall looked after him for a long moment, then walked away.

A week later McCall met up with Alexa Kokinas in Tribeca in Columbus Park. She had recovered from her injuries at the hands of the *Elite*. There was evidence on her face from the beating she had sustained by the rogue cops, but it was artfully covered with makeup. She wore flared jeans and a pale orange shirt and a Levi Strauss

& Co Gold Label original jacket. A single gold bracelet graced her wrist. McCall and Alexa strolled down the leafy boughs on either side of them. Her voice was stronger. McCall had asked her how she was feeling now that she had been released from the hospital. She had told him that she was fine. A silence extended between them that McCall did not interrupt.

After another long moment, she said in her halting delivery: "Not doing well."

McCall knew the answer to his question, but he needed hear it for himself.

"Why is that?"

"I'm a cop," she said. "Frank Macamber, Pete Hightower, Martin Rabinski. Those rogue cops took that away from me. Without that I have no purpose to my life."

"Maybe I help with that."

Alexa shook her head ruefully. "Deafness I can deal with. Kind gestures will finish me."

"I understand that," McCall said, "Are you up for going for a ride with me?"

Alexa stopped, looking at him. "To where?"

"There is someone I want you to meet."

"I cannot meet new people. Too tough for me."

"This will only take a few minutes."

Alexa regarded him a moment more, then shrugged, "Sure, why not?"

McCall took Alexa in his Jaguar and parked it in front of the 7th Precinct. They got out, moved into the brownstone building and up the flight of stairs to the bull pen. As soon as they walked in, the detectives at the 7th Precinct broken into applause. Steve Lansing rose from his desk and shook McCall's hand. Then he smiled at a bewildered Alexa.

"Welcome to the 7th Precinct, Miss Kokinas," he said. "I'm Detective Steve Lansing. I will introduce you around to the squad, but there is one face here you should recognize with no trouble."

Officer Tony Palmer stepped forward and grasped Alex's hand, which McCall could see was shaking. "Good to see you, Alexa. You look terrific."

"What are you doing here?" she asked him.

Before Palmer had a chance to answer that, the door **to** the glass-fronted office opened and a burly, no-nonsense Police Captain stepped out. He had a brusque manner which disguised a compassionate and caring cop. Steve Lansing introduced him.

"Alexa is Captain Ben Keaton, our boss here at the 7th Precinct."

"I've heard a lot about you, Officer Kokinas," Keaton said. "Good work ethic and somewhat fearless. I like that. You are going to be joining the squad. Detective Steve Lansing will get you squared away. That corner desk will be your new home. I run a tight ship here at the 7th, but you will find that out for yourself. I know you have been through quite an ordeal, but that is over now. Let us kick the elephant-in-the-room down the stairs. You are hearing impaired. Is that right?"

"Yes," Alexa said.

"So what? Detective Lansing has brought me up to speed about you. You will be a 2nd-grade Detective here on the squad, no favors, no special privileges, you will have to earn that. Do not prove me wrong. Are we clear so far?"

"Yes, sir," Alexa said, overwhelmed.

"Good. We are not too formal around here, as you will also find out. Officer Palmer just transferred here to the 7th Precinct. I understand he was your partner at your old precinct. He told me that said you have a sweet tooth, so we're bending the rules today."

A couple of the detectives brought out a chocolate cake from the Captain's office. Captain Keaton handed Alexa a knife. Alexa just stood nonplussed, looking at the faces of the various detectives. She turned back to Robert McCall, who had stayed at the back of the room. He just nodded to her. She turned back, tears filling her eyes.

"I won't let you down, Captain," she said in her halting fashion.

"I have no doubt of that," Keaton said. "Now cut the cake so we can all get back to work."

Palmer moved to Alexa's side. More of the cops on the 7th Precinct crowded around her. There was round of applause as she cut the cake. One of the detectives handed the first piece to Alexa, then started to hand out pieces of the chocolate cake to the other detectives. Steve Lansing took McCall off to one side and lowered his voice.

"I met with Assistant District Attorney Cassie Blake this morning. I believe she is your ex-wife."

"There was a time," McCall murmured.

"She's going to drop all of the charges against Jerry Kilpatrick. He did not participate in Alexa's rape, although he admits to being there in that warehouse on the Lower East Side. He will turn State's evidence against Frank Macamber in a plea-bargain deal. Maybe jail time, maybe not. That is up to the Assistant District Attorney. That will not sit well with the other cops in this city, but Macamber's reputation as a scumbag was well known. Jerry Kilpatrick will be out of law enforcement, but he will not be facing a lynch mob of fellow cops. He did the right thing. He will testify before the Grand Jury."

"That is good to hear," McCall said.

"I know that Jerry Kilpatrick comes from a family of cops," Lansing said. "He'll pay the emotional price for that."

McCall looked over at Alexa Kokinas. She was talking to the other detectives and to Captain Keaton, animated and relaxed. Her voice level had gotten stronger. She turned suddenly to look at McCall and her broad smile told him everything he needed to know. He raised a hand to acknowledge her.

"She'll need some time to get used to the idea," McCall said, "that she has a family now. Even if they *are* cops. Take under your wing, Steve. She'll be safe there."

Lansing nodded. "I'll do that. You did a good thing, McCall. We'll take it from here."

McCall shook Steve Lansing's hand, then moved through the squad room and went down the stairs into the street.

McCall invited the old Korean couple Kyung-Jae and his wife He-Ran to the convenience store off Broome Street in Greenwich Village. It had been completely renovated. Workman were still working on the place, but McCall was told that would be finished very soon. He had wanted Kyung-Jae and He-Ran to see their new home.

"You should be back in business next week," McCall said.

The old Korean couple stared at the new counters and fixtures in a state of shock. Then Kyung-Jae turned to McCall and shook his head.

"How much did this cost you, Mr. McCall?"

"It's on the house," McCall said.

Tears flooded He-Ran's eyes. Kyung-Jae said: "We cannot accept such a gift,"

"Those men came for me, the ones who attacked you and your wife," McCall said. "This the least I could do for you."

Kyung-Jae nodded, still overwhelmed. His wife held out her hand and McCall grasped it.

"You will come to visit us?" she asked.

"This is my old neighborhood," he said, gently. "I would miss you."

Kyung-Jae just nodded and smiled.

McCall met Kostmayer in the Dead Rabbit Irish pub on Water Street. He was sitting at the bar on the ground-floor under the *King Henry's Road W. 12* sign. The place was jammed to the rafters. Kostmayer slid into the bar-stool beside McCall and ordered a Guinness. The noisy ambiance in the place was infectious.

"I caught up with Samantha Gregson in Prague," Kostmayer said, "but I missed her by ten minutes. She was accompanied by a terrorist named Khalid Rehman Mohammad. He was the last one on our list of the *Memento Mori* mercenaries. As Hayden Vallance would say, a very nasty piece of work." Kostmayer's Guinness arrived and he took a swallow. "Pretty much a wasted trip."

"Not wasted," McCall told him. "Control is also looking for Samantha. When he has some intel on her he will pass it along. But she *is* a dangerous psychopath. He has made it a priority to find her."

"That's good to hear." Kostmayer looked him. "I hear you're leaving New York."

McCall smiled. "For an old spymaster, Sam Kinney is terrible at keeping secrets. I'll be moving out of the Liberty Belle Hotel in a couple of days."

"What prompted this aberrant behavior?"

"It was time."

"That's not an answer."

"Best one I can give you."

"I heard what happened outside that Chateau in Russia," Kostmayer said. "Daniel Blake was a causality of war. There was nothing you could have done to prevent that."

"I could have stopped it from happening," McCall said, quietly.

"You rescued Deva Montgomery against all odds. She is safe in New York because you would not leave her behind. That's has to count for something."

"It did," McCall said. "Just not enough."

Suddenly McCall sensed a disturbance in the force, as he remarked ironically to Kostmayer. Candy Annie came careering through the people jammed at the bar. She was dressed for work at Langan's Irish pub and restaurant just off 7th Avenue and Times Square. It had been closed for awhile, but it had just recently re-opened and the management had offered Candy Annie her old job back. She clutched McCall's hand while Kostmayer ordered her a glass of champagne.

"Mickey tells me you're leaving the city," Candy Annie said, as if distraught. "You can't do that! You are the reason I ventured outside into the New York City streets! I was very happy in my little niche down in the subway tunnels. Well, not happy, but contented. Then you introduced me to another world, to an *up-world*, where I could be free." Kostmayer handed Candy Annie her glass of champagne. "Thanks, Mickey." She looked back at McCall. "Tell me this isn't true."

"I've tried to talk him out of it," Kostmayer said. "That is like trying to roll a beachball up a hill."

McCall found Candy Annie' hand and trapped it in both of his. "Slow down, Annie. Take some deep breaths. I won't be gone forever."

Candy Annie took a swallow of her champagne to calm her nerves. "So, you'll be back, right?"

"I will. When the time is right."

Candy Annie shook her head. "This is just awful," she said, and took another gulp of her champagne. "What will I do without you in my life?"

McCall glanced over at Kostmayer. "I'd say you're on your way to finding that out."

She clutched Mickey Kostmayer's hand without quite crushing it. "We're an item," she confessed.

McCall smiled. "I guessed that."

"He's the best thing that has happened in my life since... well, since *you!*"

"Now if I could get Candy Annie to unbutton her shirt once in awhile," Kostmayer added, "and rescue her bra from the washing machine, I'd be ahead of the game."

Candy Annie gave his arm a fond pat, not quite knocking him to the floor. McCall had to admit that her shirt *was* unbuttoned almost down to her navel. She turned her attention back to him. "Will you promise to hurry back to us!"

From anyone else but Candy Annie, McCall would have thought she was pouring on the saccharine a little sweet, but there was no guile to her.

He nodded. "I'll do that."

"Can I give you a hug?"

"Bring it on."

McCall had to avert his eyes from her curvaceous figure, which did not leave much to the imagination, while Candy Anne kissed him on the lips. McCall wondered if he needed a shot of adrenaline to get his heart beating again. When Candy Annie came up for air, McCall thought it was time for him to leave. He slid off the barstool. Kostmayer held out his hand and McCall took it.

"An occasional postcard might be nice," Kostmayer commented. "Even an email if you think of it."

"I'll see what I can do." McCall glanced at Candy Annie. "Take care of her, Mickey. You've got a special girl there."

"I know that," Kostmayer said

McCall finished his Glenfiddich and pushed through the boisterous crowd. Candy Annie was still distraught. She took Kostmayer's hand. "Why don't I think that I will ever see him again?"

"You will."

"Bad people are always trying to kill Mr. McCall."

"He is tough to kill," Kostmayer said. "Or reason with. Or understand. I've seen this coming for a very long time."

"But he'll be all right?"

Kostmayer was ironic. "It's the bad guys who get in his way who should be worried," he murmured and took another swallow of his Guinness.

The memorial service was held for Daniel Blake at the Congressional Cemetery in Washington D.C. Rain sleeted through the beautiful cemetery. McCall stood apart from the mourners at the graveyard in the shelter of some oaks and maple trees. Granny stood with Liz Montgomery at the gravesite holding her hand. Beside them were her sister Deva, some officials from the State Department and several freelance journalists. Control stood on one side of them. He looked for McCall and found him but made no move toward him. He knew McCall too well to intrude on his private grief. Daniel Blake had become a symbol to him of his own mortality. There had been nothing McCall could have done to stop Samantha Gregson from taking Daniel's life, but Control knew it had taken its toll on him. He had not seen McCall since his return from the Chateau in Pylos in Russia. McCall had resigned from the *Company*. His life would be taking a new turn, although Control had no idea what that would be. Mc-Call had once said that the two of them were like two old warhorses. Control had taken that description to heart. He did not profess to understand what motivated Robert McCall except he had an inherent sense of justice. He knew that McCall would always to the right thing for the people he helped. But would that be enough?

Where did the *Equalizer* go when there was no one there to equalize *his* odds?

The memorial service for Daniel Blake began. Control glanced around at the souls that McCall had touched: Liz Montgomery, her sister Deva, Mickey Kostmayer, Brahms, Sam Kinney, Candy Annie, Jackson T. Foozelman, even Granny. They all owed him their lives in some way or another. Control looked back at the trees and saw with some regret that McCall's figure had disappeared.

▶ 31 ◀

MCCALL HAD INTENDED to pack up his suite at the Liberty Belle Hotel, but Sam Kinney had other ideas. He wanted the suite to be left just the way it was for Mc-Call. No one would be renting the rooms. As far as Sam was concerned, the suite belonged to McCall anytime he wanted to use it. No charge. McCall wondered what the owner of the hotel thought of that, but Sam just shrugged. The owner of the hotel was rich as a motherfucker and sailed most of the year on a yacht in Monaco. But that was okay, Sam said, because he never liked sailing anyway. The old spymaster brought a bottle of Remy Martin cognac Louis VIII which McCall thought must have set him back about $4000 a bottle. He produced two Waterford Lismore handcrafted crystal glasses and poured himself and McCall two shots of brandy.

"I've been waiting for a special occasion to toast you," Sam said. "This cognac has a special woody flavor. Figs, dates, prunes, dried apricot and vanilla. If I cannot talk you out of leaving, we might as well have the good stuff. You will come back. I know that. And don't pick up any emotional strays along the way."

McCall smiled. "Sound like good advice."

"You won't pay attention to an old spymaster like me, but I'm saying this for your own good. You care too much. Take some long walks in the countryside and if some damsel-in-distress desperately needs your help, tell her to take a hike."

"How did you get so wise?"

"I was born an old man," Sam said. "When the doctor spanked me my teeth fell out."

McCall laughed. He and Sam Kinney drank their cognac. "I was going to wish you good luck, McCall," he said, "but I don't believe you'll need it."

"Prepare for the worst, hope for the best."

"That's right."

McCall nodded. Sam offered McCall his hand. "Good luck, McCall."

McCall shook his hand. "I will drink to that."

They finished their Remy Martin cognac together, then McCall picked up a small suitcase, opened the door to the suite and closed it behind him.

McCall grabbed a cab outside the Liberty Belle Hotel heading for JFK.

Sam Kinney let a tear fall unbidden from his old eyes.

McCall took a flight from New York City to Vancouver, Canada and disembarked at the Pacific Central station. He had no destination, but he took a Gastown walking tour and travelled up to Whistler to stay at the Nika Lake Lodge. He did no skiing but strolled through the picturesque town. From there he took a cab to the Capilano Suspension Bridge which was 140 metres long and 70 metres high that hung above the Capilano river. He strolled across the bridge above the massive fir trees of North Vancouver. It was somewhat of a daunting experience that he had always promised himself he would make. After that he caught the Polar Bear Express from Cochrane to Moosonee through the Boreal Forests and the Artic Watershed. He boarded the Simoe historic train with its restored 1920's couches that travelled to Island Falls, Fraserdale, Otter Rapids and Onakawana. He travelled on to Jasper, Lake Louis, Quesnel, Kalooops, and onto Toronto and Halifax. He had turned off his cell phone once he got to Vancouver. No one could reach him. The Via Rail train had bi-level glass-dome luxury coach cars, a gorgeous dining room and an outdoor viewing platform. The scenery and the breathtaking landscapes resonated with McCall as the train thundered it way across Canada. He knew it would not last. The pain he had felt at Daniel Blake's death was ephemeral at best. He had to absorb it and let it go.

On the way to Banff in the Canadian Rockies a young woman in her late twenties joined the train. Her name was Rebecca Sinclair and she was beautiful and feisty. She had immediately struck up a conversation with McCall that he thought was enchanting and captivating. She had dark hair, an hourglass figure and possessed a wicked sense of humor. At Banff they disembarked because Rebecca had wanted to visit the Calgary Rodeo. But during the afternoon her attitude had changed. She was moody and distracted. McCall thought she had seen something at the rodeo that had disturbed her. They stopped at Bill Peyto's Smokehouse with its western motif. Rebecca had a cheeseburger and a Mule Kick, the local Park Jim Beam Vodka with spicy ginger beer and lime. McCall had Burnt Ends, a brisket made with Kansas City-style BBQ sauce with horseradish aioli. Finally, McCall leaned forward.

"Mind telling me what has upset you?"

She shook her head. "There's nothing to tell."

"I think there is. I am good at listening. You are frightened by something."

Rebecca looked at him in surprise. "You can tell that by just looking at someone, can you?"

"Sometimes."

She looked around the restaurant, then a few tears spiralled down her beautiful face. She said softly: "The son of a bitch is going to kill me."

McCall sighed and nodded. *Damn!* Sam Kinney would be proud of him. He had lasted one whole train trip before getting involved with someone else's problems. But he did not like the idea that this vivacious, effervescent young woman had been threatened.

At which point the floodgates opened.

Rebecca had met her ex-husband Roger Forrester in college. It had been a whirlwind romance. They were married two months later. At first the relationship was great. They did not want children for at least five years. Rebecca was working at an art college. Her husband had just earned his degree as an engineer and was working on developing video games. The sex was great, but her husband had become more and more moody. He had a sadistic streak that had come as a shock to Rebecca. He would fly into rages, then he would be contrite and melancholy and beg her forgiveness. McCall thought it was a familiar pattern. Roger drank heavily and had slapped her around when the mood took him. Rebecca had filed for divorce, when was uncontested, and both went their separate ways. But Roger had started coming over at all hours of the night, uninvited and abusive, until Rebecca had to take out a restraining order against him. After that, she had not seen him for two years, but then the email messages and the harassing had started again. Roger's mood swings got worse. Rebecca was in fear of her life. She had taken this trip to Vancouver, a place she had visited many times as an art student, to get away from her ex-husband and his predatory friends.

Rebecca had finally run out of words and emotion. "I don't know where to turn."

McCall shook his head. "I'm sorry but I can't help you."

Rebecca reached into her Gucci bag and removed a folded piece of paper. She smoothed it on the table and pushed it over to him. It was an ad she had cut out of the newspaper. It said: "*Gotta a problem? Odds against you? Call the Equalizer.*"

"I have carried this around with me for months," Rebecca said. "I never called you. Never got the nerve to try. But when I met you here on the train, I knew who you were. So, is there no truth to this 'Equalizer' thing?" Before McCall could respond, she shook her head. "It was just a crazy idea. I don't know what I was thinking of."

Rebecca's voice echoed in his head. His own sense of justice was a part of him. Kostmayer had known that, and so had Granny and Control. Theoretically, Daniel Blake had meant nothing to McCall, and yet, somehow, he had meant *everything* to him. It was the loss of a vital human being that had disturbed him. There would be a reckoning for that injustice that would have to be dealt with. The account with Samantha Gregson would be settled. McCall's quest to help people who had nowhere else to turn was a need in him that he recognized. Sometimes it was not as clear as it should be. But it was the only course of action he could endorse. He leaned over to her.

"You're right. It's what I do."

"You'll resolve this situation for me?"

"I will."

"You're not just stringing me along because you feel sorry for me?"

"No."

She smiled at him through her tears. "Far out."

"Do you have a picture of your ex-husband?"

Rebecca accessed her cell phone and turned it over so McCall could see it. Roger Forrester was a good-looking man with a ready smile and startling blue eyes.

"Don't let the matinee idol look fool you," she said. "He's a predator."

"Did he follow you to Vancouver?"

Rebecca was startled. "I don't know. That thought never occurred to me. Could he have been here in Calgary at the Rodeo?"

"He might have," McCall said. "But you didn't see him?"

"No. But that would explain the sick feeling I've been having in the pit of my stomach for days."

They finished their lunch and walked back to the train which was waiting on the tracks. McCall searched the train but found no sign of Rebecca's estranged husband. The Rocky Mountaineer train pulled out of the station and they were on their way to their next destination. At each of the train stops McCall made a sweep of the carriages and came up empty. Finally, Rebecca relaxed in his company, her spirits rising with new hope. The train thundered through the night. Rebecca had asked McCall to visit her in her sleeper car. Just for a nightcap. McCall ultimately had demurred, but there was a strong attraction between them. When the train pulled into Montreal six days later, McCall did not think he could stall Rebecca's amorous inclinations much longer. Not that he had really wanted to. There was something very special about her.

Rebecca had wanted to look around Montreal and they agreed to meet back at the train station at 6:00 PM.

McCall thought it was about time to plug back in his cell phone. He had eight messages, all of them from Mickey Kostmayer. McCall knew he would not be calling him without a good reason. He connected to Kostmayer who answered on the first ring.

"I've been calling you for three days," he said. "I left you a bunch of emails."

"I put my cell phone away," McCall said. "What's up?"

"Candy Annie is missing."

A cold shiver ran through McCall. "What do you mean she's missing?"

"I came home to the apartment three days ago and she was gone," Kostmayer said. "Her clothes were gone. It was her birthday a few days ago and I gave her a couple of small gifts. She left them in the bedroom on the dresser. I did not have a fight with her. Everything between us has been great. I haven't heard a word from her since."

"Maybe she went back under the streets of New York to that niche where she used to live," McCall said.

"I thought of that," Kostmayer said, "I went down there. I found that old guy, what is his name again?"

"Fooz."

"Yeah, Jackson T. Foozelman. He took me to the subway tunnel where Candy Annie had lived. She had moved out weeks ago. The new tenants in the subway system had never heard of her. I went to the restaurant where she worked, Langan's Brasserie on 7th Avenue, but she had quit her job."

"But there's nowhere for her to go here in New York City," McCall said.

"No, there's not," Kostmayer agreed. "I went to St. Luke's church on 8th Avenue to see if she had gone there to see my brother, Father David Kostmayer, but he hasn't seen her. She would not have just left without a word to anyone. Candy Annie does not deal well with the real world around us."

"No, she doesn't," McCall agreed. "I am in Montreal right now at the train station. I can fly to you by midnight. I have someone with me. A young woman named Rebecca Sinclair. She's being stalked by her abusive ex-husband."

"Something things never change," Kostmayer murmured. "Get here to the apartment as soon as you can."

"I'll be there," McCall promised and severed the connection.

He was worried. Candy Annie's ebullient personality could be easily exploited by a stranger. He found that deeply disturbing. He got a cab back to the train station.

And two things happened simultaneously.

McCall saw Rebecca picking up a Montreal Globe newspaper on the concourse. She was being following by her ex-husband Roger Forester, whom McCall recognized from the photograph that Rebecca had shown him. McCall shouted a warning to her, but she did not hear him. She climbed onboard the Rocky Mountaineer train. Roger Forrester climbed onto the train after her.

At the same time, McCall saw Samantha Gregson, looking chic in a tailored suit, boarding the train in the company of Khalid Rehman Mohammad, the last of the *Memento Mori* mercenaries.

McCall sprinted down the platform and climbed onboard the train as it pulled out of Montreal station.

●

Made in the USA
Monee, IL
03 January 2023

24355221R00207